An Extraordinary Year

Theresa Konwinski

DEDICATION

This book is lovingly dedicated to Frank, Aaron, Amy,
and all kids of a certain age...

CONTENTS

Acknowledgments   i

January

1   Epiphany   1

2   Snowed In   Pg 11

February

3   The Valentine Box   Pg 22

4   The Gravel Pit   Pg 34

March

5   Mom's Big Secret   Pg 42

6   Birthday   Pg 53

April

7   The Honor System   Pg 66

8   Smorgasbord   Pg 74

May

9   Mr. Henderson   Pg 86

10   Peaches   Pg 93

11   Summer Comes At Last   Pg 100

June

12   Shiloh Stevens   Pg 108

13   Button   Pg 117

July

14 Summer Storm   Pg 126

15 Three-Mile Square   Pg 131

16 Vacation   Pg 144

August

17 Grandpa Falls   Pg 162

18 Camp   Pg 169

19 Miss Ruth   Pg 179

September

20 Goodbye to Freedom   Pg 188

21 The Baby Sister and the Big Change   Pg 201

October

22 The Worst Thing I Ever Saw   Pg 210

23 Halloween   Pg 220

November

24 Cortege   Pg 232

December

25 Christmas Fruitcake   Pg 243

26 Plain Days   Pg 253

ACKNOWLEDGMENTS

This book could not have been written without the family relationships I have enjoyed over my entire life. Not only are my mom and dad key players, but my three brothers, Robert, Mark, and Michael figure prominently within these pages. I lovingly acknowledge them all and thank them for an upbringing and family life that created many precious memories. My story is their story, and their story is my story.

Also, no book reaches publication without the help of many trusted people. I want to gratefully recognize Susan Anderson, Debra Ball, Dorothy Konwinski, and Ruth McCloud-Wolff for their encouragement, advice, editing skill, support and friendship. I want to especially thank Ruth for permission to use her beautiful painting, "Fireflies" for the cover of this book.

Some of what you are about to read is true; some of it is fiction. I will leave it to you to figure out which is which....

1 EPIPHANY

My mom took down the Christmas tree every year on New Year's Day, but in 1963, she saved the tree out in the back yard for a reason I didn't know right away. The tree stood against the side of the garage, pieces of tinsel still attached, flittering in the wind. After having had so many decorations and lights all over it, the tree looked forlorn and lonesome out there where the ground was white and the sky was gray. This was the dead of winter in Ohio, and the Christmas tree now matched the season.

January 6 was the celebration of Epiphany. Along with all the other people who went to Calvary Evangelical United Brethren church, we were going to the gravel pit to burn our Christmas trees. Mom told my little brother Jim and I about this on January 5. I think she sprung it on us at the last minute because she knew we would protest. Anyway, she said that this was being done in remembrance of the Three Wise Men first visiting baby Jesus and bringing him some pretty fancy presents. I thought it was kind of weird that we would have a fire to remember that the Three Wise Men came to see Jesus because when I thought of fire and religion, I thought about a place I didn't want to go when I died. Plus, I thought we had already heard all the Wise Men stuff we needed to at Christmas when we sang "We Three Kings of Orient Are." That was actually one of my favorite Christmas songs.

"Will we at least roast some yummy marshmallows?" Jim asked hopefully.

"Not likely, son, but we'll say some prayers and probably go back over to the church and have some hot chocolate," Mom told him.

This was sounding like a dud of a party to me. I guess it wasn't supposed to be a party exactly, but anytime you have a bonfire, it just seems to make sense that you would be having some kind of party around it.

"Mom, do we really have to go? Haven't we gone to church enough for a while? Geeminy, we were up there all the time getting ready for the Christmas play and decorating. Then we had to be there for the actual play and all the different Christmas services. Can't we just go burn up the trees and come home?" I was pleading my case, afraid I was going to have to dress up one more time. I was getting kind of sick of wearing a tie and my good shoes. Our church really celebrated Christmas a lot, having a play, a big choir production, Christmas Eve midnight service and all the regular church stuff. We did it at Easter, too. Church, church, church. I didn't mind church, but I didn't want to overdo it. I just wanted to go to enough church that I could avoid the fiery place.

"John, we won't be up there long for this service. On top of that, you'll be wearing warm clothes and boots – not your dress up clothes. I can read your mind, you know." How did moms do this? Read your mind, I mean. My mom was an expert at it, and I couldn't figure out how she knew exactly what I was thinking, exactly when I was thinking it. She did that all the time.

Jim had already left this conversation and moved on to playing with the Rock 'em Sock 'em robots that he had gotten for Christmas. He was sitting in the middle of the living room floor trying to play by himself, which was goofy, of course.

"Here, I'll play you," I said to him. I got down on the floor with him and took the red robot.

Bash! "Here's a knock-out punch for sure!" I announced, but the blue robot kept his head on.

Pow! The blue robot hit my robot back. I thought Jim almost had me with that punch, but somehow the red robot stayed intact.

Bang! Bop! We kept at each other until finally, the blue robot crumpled under my superior boxing ability.

2

"You win again." Jim looked dejected.

"What do you think about this Epiphany thing?" I asked Jim. He was my younger brother, but sometimes he had a few things to say that were worth listening to. It didn't happen all that often, but I was interested in what he thought about another church event.

"I don't know. All I know is we're going whether we like it or not," he shrugged. There was something in his voice that was so resigned to the idea that I knew he was right and that I may as well give up any hope of skipping out on this particular event. We packed up the robots and went to our respective rooms.

I was in a gloomy mood. Christmas had been so great! I knew Christmas was more than just presents and parties, but school would be starting back up soon and I was savoring every minute of freedom I could. I didn't really want any more church obligations, or truthfully, any other kind of obligation. I wanted to just watch TV or read my new Hardy Boys mystery. I had gotten "The Clue of the Screeching Owl" for Christmas and I hadn't even started it. Or I'd rather go sledding at the gravel pit than burn trees in it. But there was no going against Mom on these things. You just had to accept it and get through it.

Our poor Christmas tree still sat out in the backyard, branches getting brownish with needles lying on the snow underneath where it stood against the garage. I'm not too mushy of a guy, but that tree had looked beautiful just a week or so before. It seemed strange to see it outside now, and our living room seemed kind of empty without it.

That gave me a thought. If we didn't have the old Christmas tree anymore, we couldn't really take it up to the gravel pit for the Epiphany meeting. We could just stay home. School started back up the very next day anyway. We would need a good night's sleep, not that I had ever cared about that before. A plan was starting to hatch in my nine year old brain. Gosh, if I could think this clearly now when my tenth birthday wasn't till March, just think how much smarter I would be when I did finally turn ten.

I knew I would have to be especially careful with my plan. No one, especially Mom, must know I had anything to do with the disappearance of the tree, and I would have to act fast because January 6 was the next day. I spent the better part of the afternoon scheming up a plan to thwart the Epiphany.

After dinner, I told Mom I was tired and was going to go lay down.

"Are you feeling all right? Let me feel your forehead." Mom reached over and put the back of her hand against my forehead. "No fever. Let me see in your throat." I opened my mouth as wide as I could. "Well, it doesn't look red and I don't see any white patches," she pronounced.

"I feel fine, Mom, just tired." I didn't want to go through a Perry Mason questioning, especially since she was so darned good at reading my mind.

"Ok. Well, I'll check in on you after I finish the dishes."

I didn't really want that and I certainly didn't need that. I knew there was no chance of it not happening, though, so I went to my room, laid down on my bed and stared up at the ceiling, visualizing each step of my plan as I would be carrying it out. It was wickedly brilliant.

After a while, I heard Mom coming down the hall. I grabbed my Hardy Boys book and opened it up so she would think I was reading. The door opened and there was Mom, smiling at me with her sweet Mom smile. How could I be so evil as to try to deceive her? I was immediately flooded with guilt.

"How are you doing, John? Do you still feel ok?" she asked.

"Sure, Mom, sure. I really am fine. I just felt kind of tired and thought I would read for a while tonight." I was pretty sure she bought it.

"All right. Well, we're going to watch some TV and pop some popcorn later if you feel like joining us."

"Yeah, thanks. I'll probably just keep reading, so don't worry about me." I couldn't have seemed more innocent.

I did start reading my new mystery book that evening. I felt kind of bad about Mom and how sweet she was, and I thought if I did some reading, at least I wouldn't have been telling a real big lie – just a little one. But reading made me sleepy, and I had to really fight to stay awake. I knew Mom liked to watch the late movie sometimes on Saturday nights, and I was sure hoping this wouldn't be one of those nights.

Finally about ten o'clock, I heard Mom and Dad coming up the steps and heading for their room. My door opened and Mom put her head in, but I just pretended I was asleep. She came over and put her hand on my forehead again. I had to lie really still so she wouldn't know I wasn't sleeping. I also had my clothes on under the covers. I thought that might make me feel hot, but she must have thought I was ok because she didn't say or do anything. It was not an easy moment for my master plan.

Once it seemed like the house was settled, I quietly pushed back my covers and tiptoed over to the closet to get my coat. My closet door was kind of creaky and I had to open it very slowly to keep from making noise. I knew how to do this from watching "Espionage" on TV. I thought I could make a pretty good spy when I grew up.

All I had left to get was my boots. I wasn't planning to be outside long enough to need my hat or a scarf. I needed gloves, though, because the pine needles on the Christmas tree were all dried out and prickly. Pine needles really hurt when they are dried out like that.

I managed to avoid the squeaky steps down the staircase. I didn't turn on any lights, but felt my way through the house, slowly and carefully. Our boots were right by the back door where we had left them after playing outside that day. Once I got them on and buckled, I was feeling braver, certain that my mission would be accomplished. I opened the back door and made sure I unlocked it. That would have been the end of me for sure, forgetting to unlock the door so I could get back in the house.

It was really dark outside. Our small town had few street lights out where we lived, which was more on the edge of town, not right in the center. It was starting to snow, and it was so quiet and serene that I felt like I was in a wintery dreamland. It was kind of a nice feeling. But I had to focus! I didn't want to be out there too long. The longer you're doing a job like this, the bigger the chances you'll get caught. I knew that from "Espionage" too.

I got to the garage and found the tree, still leaning up against the side where Dad had put it to keep it out of the wind. I grabbed it by the trunk and started dragging it out to the back of our lot. I intended to throw it over the back fence into an open field that separated us from some other homes. The Petersons lived across that field. I was sure they were asleep and would not see my activity.

Getting the tree across the fence was a little more of an endeavor than I had anticipated because the snow was deep out there and hard to wade through. Plus the fence was at least as tall as I was, so I had to hoist the tree up over my head to get it across into the field. I didn't want to get pine needles all caught in my coat, so I attempted to hold the tree like a pole vaulter would hold his jumping pole and try to heave the tree over. After about three attempts, I finally managed to plunk that tree on the other side of the fence. I was breathless and tired, and I still had to slog back through the snow up to the house. The snow was falling pretty fast, it was really, *really* dark at the back of the lot, and I felt more anxiety now than I had when I started out.

I tried to run up to the back of the garage at least – make quicker time, was my thinking – but I fell flat on my face between the back of the lot and the garage, out by the plum tree. I got up, tried to brush myself off a little and started back on my way more cautiously. It seemed like an hour before I finally got to the back door of the house and made my way inside.

I was a snow-covered mess. I put my gloves in my pockets, peeled off my coat and hung it on the hooks dad had put on a board from an old rowboat Grandpa had owned when my Dad was a little kid. "Fisherman's Dream," the board said. Dad said it made sense to put coat hooks on it since it had fish hooks in it when he was young. My dad was always saying stuff like that.

I put my boots on the mat by the door where we put snowy or muddy boots. That way we didn't track up Mom's clean floors and get ourselves in a world of trouble. I retraced my route up the stairs, changed into my pajamas and crawled into bed, exhausted from my adventure.

The next day, January 6, I woke up late, no doubt from my escapade the night before. I wandered downstairs, where Mom was making waffles.

"Well, good morning, sleepy head. I thought I was going to have to come up there and roust you out before long." Mom had a big smile on her face, and I felt a little guilty about the lie I was getting ready to tell her.

"Well…you know I was really tired last night. I still feel kind of tired today." The second part of that was not a lie.

"Just take it easy today. I don't want you to get sick because we have to go away tonight and school starts back up tomorrow." Mom seemed a little too cheerful about the school part.

Dad came into the kitchen to refill his coffee cup. "Honey, I forgot to tell you that the back door was standing wide open this morning and it was cold as anything in here. I guess I forgot to lock it. The wind must have blown it open, and it was that way all night. Probably wasted a lot of fuel oil heating the outdoors, doggone it. Don't let me forget to check it before I go to bed tonight."

A wave of guilt washed over me. It was one thing to mess up Mom's Epiphany plan. It was another thing altogether to waste fuel oil heating the outdoors. Leaving the door open in the winter was a big deal with my parents. Dad always said, "We don't live in a barn!"

I didn't feel too hungry, but I ate my waffles with Log Cabin syrup and went to get dressed. I don't think anyone had noticed that the Christmas tree was long gone. I looked out the windows of the living room and saw that about three inches of snow had fallen overnight. No wonder I was having such a hard time getting back to the house.

We had to go to regular church that Sunday morning. I prayed a little bit about what I had done and asked God to forgive me for not wanting to go to the gravel pit that night. Then I spent most of the day reading "The Clue of the Screeching Owl" and watching TV. Jim wanted to play a board game he had gotten for Christmas – the Jetsons. I played it with him for a little while, but I couldn't really concentrate. I was wondering what was going to happen later when Mom and Dad realized there was no Christmas tree for the Epiphany party.

At about five o'clock, Mom called us in to supper. She had made her beef vegetable soup – "it'll help keep you warm later," she said – and homemade bread. I loved her homemade bread, too. When you bit into it, you knew you were chewing something, way different than Wonder bread, which we had most of the time, or Nickle's bread, which we had when the bread man came by our house.

When we got done eating, Mom asked us to help her pick up the table and then go get dressed for the Epiphany. She still didn't know.

"I'll go drag the tree around to the front of the house," Dad said. "Then we can just go out the front door and walk up to the gravel pit right from there." He didn't know either.

I picked up my dishes and Jim's, too. I wanted to be especially helpful since Mom was getting ready for a big disappointment.

"Thank you, John. I can take it from here. It won't take long to clean this up, so go get your warm clothes on."

"Mom, do we HAVE to go? It's so cold out, and it snowed a lot. Can't we just stay home?"

"No, son. We're going. This is a time to celebrate with all of our friends at church," she countered.

I turned and headed for the stairs with my head hanging. Just as I got to the bottom step, I heard Dad come in with an announcement. "Hey, honey, the tree is gone. It must have blown away last night during the snow storm. I thought I had it where it couldn't get picked up, but it's gone."

Victory! I sat down on the bottom step and waited for Mom's reply.

"Well, that's no bother," she said. "No one is going to care whether or not we actually bring a tree."

"Yup," Dad replied. "I don't think anyone will care."

Defeat! Complete and utter defeat! My exquisite plan, so meticulously carried out, had failed in the end. I got on my feet and trudged up the stairs. Jim was already on his way down.

"You better hurry up," he said. "Mom will not like it if we're late. You know how she is."

Grudgingly, I put on two pairs of jeans and two pairs of socks. I put on two tee shirts and a flannel shirt, too. Then I put on a sweater. Hopefully, it would be enough.

I headed back downstairs to get my coat, hat, gloves and boots. When I reached into my pocket to get my gloves, they were still a little bit wet. Wadded up in a ball in each pocket, they hadn't been able to dry out.

Yippee, I thought.

Out the front door we all traipsed, down the street, up the alley, across Main Street and over to the gravel pit. There were already a bunch of church people there, singing Christmas carols. I couldn't figure this thing out. Christmas was over. Just the same, we joined in the singing and kind of bounced around a little to keep warm. Finally, the singing part was done and Pastor Miller gave a little talk.

"Who were the Magi?" he asked. Jim raised his hand, but I don't think Pastor Miller really wanted an answer. "They were astrologers who knew enough about Hebrew scripture to understand that a Messiah had been promised, and they were looking for signs in the heavens. When they saw that sign – the star in the East – they made a long and no doubt arduous journey to find the Christ child. In Matthew 2, we read this: 'And when they were come into the house, they saw the young child with Mary his mother, and fell down, and worshipped him: and when they had opened their treasures, they presented unto him gifts; gold, and frankincense and myrrh.' Now we all know that Jesus was not in a house – he was in a manger in a cold, dirty stable. He was wrapped in swaddling clothes. He didn't come into this world with much, but what He left this world is a gift far beyond what we could ever repay. The Wise Men helped spread the revelation of Jesus Christ to the whole world. If not for that, we might not have this church community we enjoy today. Let's bow our heads and say a prayer of thanks for that gift."

Everyone prayed in silence for a couple of minutes. Finally, Pastor Miller said, "And all God's children said...."

"AMEN," answered the people. Everyone had big smiles on their faces, and they didn't even seem like they were cold or anything. They started shaking each other's hands and visiting like it was a day in the middle of the summer. It did, actually, warm up there at the gravel pit as everyone's very dry Christmas trees went up in a blaze. The flames shot high into the night sky, and most everyone watched in silence.

We all walked over to the church together and went down in the basement to where we always had our church dinners and so forth. A lot of the ladies had brought pies and cookies. I had been so preoccupied with my own activities that I hadn't even known that Mom had made a peach pie and brought it up to the church that morning when we had come to regular church. At least that's what Jim told me. I had a piece of peach pie and a cup of hot chocolate and listened to the grown-ups talk about weather and school starting back up tomorrow and work stuff. Mrs. Light asked me if I was ready to go back to school. Mr. Clymer rubbed my hair all around and gave me a little sock in the arm. It didn't hurt. Nancy Burner asked me what I got for Christmas. Mom was busily putting out more desserts on the tables and talking with the other ladies about recipes. Dad was talking with the men about Viet Nam and some other political stuff I didn't understand. All of a sudden it hit me. These people were like an extended family, the people who would help look out for me if my mom and dad weren't around. No kid would want to escape that kind of friendship. I watched the familiar faces with a different feeling than when I had come to the Epiphany party. Bright eyes, rosy cheeks from the cold, and everyone with smiles on their faces...they cared about each other, and that included me. That was my own revelation, right there in the church basement where earlier in the day, I had not wanted to be. At nine-almost-ten years old, my epiphany was that I was in the right place at the right time with the right people. 1963 was off to a good start. It was going to be an extraordinary year.

2 SNOWED IN

January is a cold month in Ohio. Cold and snowy. We had to wear boots to school pretty much every day in January, as well as scarves, mittens, hats, sweaters. We had to wear so many clothes under our coats that we could barely move. You could only fit two kids in each seat on the bus even if you were both skinny, just because of all those clothes and heavy coats. It was mostly always bitter outside with the wind and all. Your face would just about freeze up unless you had one of those ski masks where only your eyes, nose and mouth have little openings.

We had to walk up to the Calvary church to get on the bus. The bus did not go by our house like it did for some kids. I never really knew why that was for sure, but I guess we lived enough on the edge of town that it was easier for the bus driver to just pick up a whole bunch of kids in one location rather than drive out our way. It was a small town; you wouldn't think they'd have any trouble picking us up at our houses. It was ok, though, because on the walk up to the church or on the way home in the afternoon was where I learned a lot of things I didn't know, like different cuss words or who was a hood now – that kind of stuff. It sort of helped you know what or who to stay away from. Some of the older kids who had girlfriends and boyfriends would hold hands on the way home and junk like that. I also stayed away from them - too mushy for me.

The best part of January was when it would snow so much we would have a snow day from school. It didn't occur too often, but we prayed for it. We would listen to the radio in the morning after a big snow and keep our fingers crossed. Jim would stand by the radio in his PJs with his fingers crossed, his arms and legs crossed, and even his eyes crossed. He was only eight and he already wanted summer vacation. Just wait till he hit fourth grade, like I was in. Then you *really* need a vacation. Anyway, we would listen for Bob Oxley's familiar voice, reading off the list of schools that were closed for the day. Once we got to our place in the alphabet, there was either sadness and moaning or jubilation and yelling.

On January 13, 1963, it was only 16 degrees outside. The wind was whipping and blowing snow around so hard, you could hardly see out as far as the street. It was a Sunday, but we didn't go to church that day because the weather was so bad. Mom and Dad read the Bible to us, and we all had family prayer together. What Mom and Dad didn't know is that Jim and I had begun our prayers for a snow day the next day.

That next morning, we were actually up early. I looked outside after I rubbed a little of the frost off the inside of my bedroom window...it looked like Alaska. Jim and I bounded down the steps to the kitchen, just knowing that we were going to have a day of freedom. I was starving and ready for breakfast so I could get on with my day. About halfway through my oatmeal, Mom turned on the radio. "I guess we better listen in," she said. She sounded like she dreaded to hear the news, but I was ready – ready for a day of sledding at the gravel pit, ready to build a snow fort, ready for a snowball fight with the guys. It was going to be a good day.

"Good morning, listeners," I heard Bob Oxley say. "You're listening to WFIN – the Bob Oxley show. Have you got your coffee? Do you have the chains on your snow tires? Do you have extra scarves and mittens? You're going to need them."

Jim and I looked across the table at each other. We had stopped clinking spoons against our cereal bowls, just waiting to hear the rest of the vital information.

"It's only 12 degrees out, ladies and gentlemen. The winds are coming out of the northwest at 25 miles an hour with gusts up to 38 miles per hour. It's going to be brutal out there. If you don't have to go out on the roads, you shouldn't – they are not in good shape. Because of that, there are many school closings."

This was it. The moment we had prayed for.

"The following schools are closed today..." Bob Oxley said. Then he started down his list. It seemed like forever before he got to the W's.

"Apple Grove, Bentley, Carey, Fayettesville, Green City, Hanover, Indian Lake...."

On and on Bob Oxley droned until we finally heard it. "Washington." With that, there was a great whoop from my brother as we pushed away from the table and began jumping around the kitchen. We never heard another word Bob Oxley said.

"Settle down, you two, and finish your breakfast." I could clearly hear Mom's frustration. "Even if you two are home, I still have to go to work. What am I going to do with the both of you?"

As if on cue, Bob Oxley began another list – a list of businesses that would be closed. Now Mom listened more intently. She worked at the hospital, which never closed, of course, but maybe Dad could stay home.

"Day shift at Union Carbide..." came out of our radio in the voice of good old Bob Oxley. Dad would be home! That meant a game of Monopoly, too. This day was getting better and better.

Just about that time, Dad was wandering into the kitchen with his coffee cup in his hand. "You don't have to go to work today," Mom announced.

"Yeah, Dad. You can go sledding with us and we can play Monopoly," I said.

"Hmmm. Well, first we better find out about how Mom is getting to work." He turned to Mom. "Did they say anything about the roads?" he asked her.

"Bob Oxley said they are pretty bad," she replied. "You know I have to go in, though."

"Ok. The boys and I will drive you in and pick you up."

I don't mind telling you, I was excited about this idea. I wanted to see how much snow there was and just be out in it. With Dad, we would feel like we were on an adventure, but safe.

After we brushed our teeth and washed our faces, we got "bundled up" as Mom put it. Dad was warming the car up and getting the snow off the windshield so he could see where he was going. Once we were all set, we piled in the car. We pushed the front seat forward so we could get in, but Jim was having trouble with all those thick clothes on. He was partly in, partly out.

"C'mon, Jim. It's freezing out here!" Mom said, bouncing around to keep warm. I thought she actually looked kind of frozen. I hooked my arms under Jim's and shoved him in the car the rest of the way. He sort of tumbled across the back seat; then I got in. Mom put the back of the seat up and jumped in, too. She slammed the door shut as fast as she could against the wind, and Dad took off. The back tires started to spin on the driveway.

"Oh, brother," he said. "Here we go...keep your fingers crossed!"

We didn't drive fast. The wind was blowing snow across the road in waves, sort of like looking at the ocean and seeing the waves come in to the shore. The snow was very deep on either side of the road. You could tell a snow plow had been down Route 12, but it was still slippery in spots. I could see why Bob Oxley told us to stay off the roads. Jim fell back to sleep in the car, but I felt kind of nervous because I could see how bad it was. Dad held on to the wheel real tight...his hands looked white from gripping the steering wheel so hard.

It seemed like it took forever to get Mom to work, but we made it. Dad took Mom around to the back of the hospital where most of the workers went in. "I'll see you around 4:30," he said. Mom leaned across the seat, kissed him on the cheek and said, "You guys be careful going home. That was not a pleasant trip and the wind is not letting up." She tried to open her door, but she couldn't get it open because the wind was blowing against that side of the car. Dad had to get out and go around to help her.

"We'll wait till she's inside before we take off for home," Dad said. She turned and gave us a little wave as she opened the hospital door, and Dad slowly pulled away.

It took us as long to get home as it had taken to get to the hospital. We had to wake Jim up when we got there. I've never seen anybody who could sleep as much as Jim. Just about every time we got in the car, he fell asleep.

Once we were inside and had peeled off the multiple layers of clothing we had put on, Dad said to me, "I think we should use this day in some productive way. You boys don't have school and I don't have to work, but Mom has to work, and they are likely to be a little short-handed at the hospital today. What do you say we clean up a little around here and try to make a nice meal for when she gets home?"

That wasn't exactly what I had in mind for the day, but I understood why he was saying it. My mom worked really hard at her job and after the travel ordeal, it might be nice for her to not have to worry about fixing a meal when she got home.

"What should we make for dinner?" I asked.

Dad scratched his head. "I'm pretty sure Mom has a ham in the refrigerator that she was thinking of making. I know how to fix that. You just put it in the oven. There's not a lot of food I really know how to fix, but we can cook the ham and I know how to make mashed potatoes."

"I can get some green beans out of the freezer," I offered.

"That sounds good. Let's do that," Dad said. "That will all be easy and will be a nice hot meal after we get her home through all that snow again."

"What else can we do to help Mom?" Jim asked.

"How about if we dust and run the sweeper?" Dad said. "Can each of you dust your rooms and pick up? I can take care of the rest of the house if you two can just do that. Then we'll decide what to do with the rest of the day."

We went off to our respective corners of the house and began cleaning up. Mom would be so happy! I got done pretty quickly, but of course, Jim was kind of poking along. I went into his room and found him sitting on the floor with a pile of toys all around him.

"What are you doing?" I asked. "You're supposed to be cleaning."

"I found a bunch of my toys from a long time ago." Jim acted like he was in another world. He was picking up different toys, turning them in his hands and looking them over. He had an Etch-a-Sketch (which was really mine), a little bowling game, a Fred Flintstone car (also mine), and some baseball cards lying all around him. He even had Hershey's kisses leftover from his Christmas stocking. "This seems like stuff I had when I was a baby," he said.

"What the heck are you talking about? You just got that stuff last year!"

"That seems like a long time ago," Jim countered. "I already played it out."

I was thinking Jim needed to take another nap, but if he did, we wouldn't be done with our work in time to go sledding or play Monopoly. "Put that junk away and let's get going!" I had no patience for my little brother's musings on this day.

I ended up helping Jim get his work done. Dad was cleaning up the bathroom when we got downstairs.

"Are you boys done?" he asked. "Did you do a good job or just half a job?"

"No, Dad. I helped Jim a little bit and we did a good job. Mom will be pretty happy, I think," I answered.

"Ok. Well, I'm almost done here and then we can decide what's next."

I was hoping that meant sledding.

Jim and I went into the living room and turned on the TV. All that was on were some game shows and some "I Love Lucy" repeats. I didn't like any of that stuff, so we turned it back off. Jim had the Etch-a-Sketch, trying to draw a picture of an airplane, which was turning out pretty bad.

Dad came into the living room and said, "Boys, I know it's a snow day, but I don't think this is a good day to be outside that much. The wind is blowing way too hard and your Mom will kill me if you guys get sick from being out in the bitter cold. Plus, think about this. Every kid in school is going to be a little bit behind because of this snow day. What about if we do a couple of lessons – just practice reading and some arithmetic?"

I know that he could see my disappointment. "I bet none of the other kids are doing school work," I said. "I'll bet Dave and Scotty are down at the gravel pit."

"I have a feeling Dave and Scotty are NOT at the gravel pit," Dad said. "I have a feeling that their moms are making them stay out of this weather. Ok. I understand how you feel. We'll take a break and have some lunch, then everyone reads or does arithmetic for one half hour, then we play Monopoly."

At least there was some reprieve from school work eventually. I sighed and went into the kitchen to eat my peanut butter and jelly, a Dad staple lunch.

My reading book was called, "The New Tall Tales." It had some good stories in it, but some of it was kind of boring. Dad told me to read whatever the next tall tale was. I could tell he didn't really know what the tall tales in the book were about. It didn't matter. I just did my reading and looked at the questions at the end of the chapter. I figured Mrs. King would ask us some of those.

Jim was working on arithmetic with Dad. He wasn't too bad at adding and subtracting, and his work didn't take him too long. Dad went over his spelling words with him, too. He was pretty smart for a little brother. I wished I could remember my spelling words as well as he did.

Just about that time, the phone rang. It was our friends, the Cramer family. Mary Beth Cramer told Dad they didn't have any electricity because of the storm. Her husband, Dan, had been injured at work in the refinery and she was worried about their family not having any heat or electricity. I didn't know Dan had been hurt, but when Dad got off the phone, he told me about it. I guess Dan's pants had caught on fire and his legs got burned. It sounded pretty bad to me.

"Dan's got to have his bandages changed and some kind of soaks put on his legs," Dad explained. "We're going to get back in the car and go get them and bring them out here. They can stay with us till their power comes back on."

"Where will everybody sleep?" I asked.

"We'll figure it out later, son. Right now, let's get ourselves back in our warm clothes and get on the road. Their house is going to get cold pretty fast as cold as it is outside, and we've got to get Dan somewhere warm." My dad really liked Dan. They had been friends for a long time, longer than I was alive. "Let's get that ham in the oven," he continued. "It can be cooking while we're gone."

Jim and I got ready. Dad dealt with the ham, then went out and warmed the car up again so we could take off. The Cramer family didn't live too far from us, but they had a son and a daughter, Joe and Jackie, and I wasn't sure how all four of them were going to fit in the car with the three of us. The roads weren't in too much better shape than they had been when we took Mom to work. I was kind of worried about what would happen when it was time to pick her up, which wasn't that far away now. This day was turning into more of an adventure than I had even planned.

When we got to the Cramer's house, Mary Beth was in her coat on the front porch, getting snow off the steps. Their driveway was pretty much covered in snow, but Joe and Jackie were out trying their best to shovel some of it away. Dad pulled into the driveway just a little ways so he wouldn't get stuck. He left the car running and said, "You boys stay right here. Just stay in the car."

The wind was still blowing hard; so hard that the snow that Joe and Jackie were shoveling would blow right back in their faces. Their cheeks and noses were real red, like my Uncle Sal after he had a couple of shots at the family Christmas dinner. My mom used to get so disgusted about that! Anyway, Jim and I stayed in the back seat and waited. Mary Beth took Dad in the house, and before too long, they were coming out with Dan, Mary Beth on one side and Dad on the other. They were trying to help him walk across the snow to get in our car. I could see that it was none too easy, and Dan looked like he was in pain.

I jumped over the seat to the front of the car so I could open the door for them. It took a while for them to get across the lawn because Dan was having a hard time, but they finally got to the car and they helped Dan get in the front seat. By that time, Joe and Jackie had put away their shovels and they got in the back seat with Jim and me. Mary Beth had ducked back into the house, and she came back out with a little suitcase, locking the door behind her. Because it was hard for Dan to move around much, Mary Beth got in on Dad's side of the car and slid across to the middle of the front seat.

"I'll bet you kids weren't expecting to spend your snow day like this, were you?" Mary Beth asked us all.

"No, but it's ok," I said. Joe and Jackie were a little bit older than me, so they just sat back in the seat and looked out the window. I think they were kind of worried about everything, especially their dad. Dan was quiet on the ride home, but Mary Beth talked up a storm.

"We had power till about 9:30 this morning," she said. "When it went off, we thought we'd just wait for a little bit and see if it came back on, but it never did. The house was starting to get cold, and I just know that Dan needs to be someplace where it's warmer. His legs won't heal up right, I don't think, unless we have him somewhere where it's warm. I can't tell you how much we appreciate you coming to get us, especially when the roads are so horrible."

"Yeah, and we still have to go get Mom," Jim spouted up.

"Oh my lands!" Mary Beth exclaimed. "Now I feel terrible! I never even thought about her being at work in all this."

"Don't worry," Dad said. "We got her there this morning without any problem, and we'll get her home, too, even if I have to hire a dogsled team."

"Good golly, I hope so," Mary Beth said, kind of under her breath.

It was a long trip home. Joe and Jackie just stared out the window mostly, Jim fell asleep again, and I listened as Mary Beth explained to Dad what the doctor had said about Dan's legs. Dan had kind of fallen asleep, too, but he would wake up a little bit now and then to tell Dad about what his boss did when his pants caught on fire, which was to spray his legs with a fire extinguisher. I had seen fire extinguishers at our school, but I didn't know how to use one. I asked Dan about it, but he had drifted back off.

We finally got home and had to go through all the difficulty of getting Dan moved again. I could tell he was in a lot of pain because of the look on his face. He didn't complain, but you could tell it really hurt. Dad helped him get on the couch, and we put his legs up on a couple of extra pillows we had in the hall closet.

Right about that time, we smelled it…THE HAM! Dad opened the oven and pulled it out. It was in a pan wrapped up in tin foil, and when Dad peeled back that tin foil, it looked like the ham was awfully brown…browner than Mom made them. Dad looked at it for a couple of minutes, then turned to me and said, "Well-done. I like meat well-done." He smiled, wrapped the ham back up and put it back in the oven. "I'll just turn it down to 'warm' so it's not really cooking anymore," he said. He changed the temperature on the oven. Mary Beth came in right then and said, "I can help get dinner ready." She and Dad were talking about potatoes when the phone rang. Jim ran to get it, like he always did. He always wanted to be the one to answer the phone.

"Da-a-a-d, it's Mom," Jim yelled. Jim must have thought Dad was deaf or something – even Dan stirred on the couch at the volume of Jim's yelling.

Dad went into the living room where the phone was located. He sat down on the telephone bench and picked up the receiver.

"Hi, honey. Yes, uh-huh. Oh, ok. That's probably smart. We'll just see you tomorrow, then. You have everything you need? Yeah, there will probably be a lot of that. Ok. Hey, we have the Cramer gang here at the house. Their power went out this morning. Yeah, that's what Mary Beth was worried about, too. We cooked a ham for supper, so we're in good shape. Don't you know, the boys and I even cleaned the house this morning, so we're really in good shape. Uh-huh. Yes, they did a good job. You would be proud. Ok. Well, I love you too. Tell Pauline I said hi and thanks for taking care of my beautiful bride. See you tomorrow." Dad hung up.

"Well," Dad reported, "Mom is going to stay in Hanover tonight with Pauline Elder. She said she'll just borrow one of Pauline's nightgowns and wash out her unmentionables and just wear the same things to work tomorrow." He chuckled. "I told her there would probably be a lot of people wearing the same stuff to work tomorrow."

Mary Beth laughed along with Dad. "She's quite a trooper. You know, it's probably better that you don't have to go out in this again. Maybe the roads will be better tomorrow."

"Oh, I'm sure they will. Once the wind dies down, which it's supposed to, the snow plows will be able to keep them clear," Dad said.

Jim had reappeared in the living room with the Monopoly game. "Can we play Monopoly now?" he whined.

"Sure, let's play," Dad said. We got Joe and Jackie and me, Jim and Dad and sat down at the kitchen table. I wanted to be the race car, but Joe wanted to be the race car, too, so I let him have it. I figured with his Dad being laid up and all, he could use a little boost.

"I'll finish getting dinner ready," Mary Beth said, and she went to work pulling out pots and pans and finding the potatoes and such. Mary Beth was a good cook, so I knew she'd produce something great. It wouldn't matter if it took a lot of time to cook – Monopoly was a game we played for hours, usually till Jim got mad because he didn't have any money left.

That night after a delicious-if-slightly-overdone ham dinner, we watched the news about the storm and also about the Viet Nam war. We got to watch "The Outer Limits" that night. Usually Mom didn't like us to watch that, but Joe and Jackie wanted to watch it. Since they were older, their parents thought it was ok, so we all watched it together. Dad and Mary Beth figured out all the sleeping arrangements. Dad took the couch, he and Mary Beth helped Dan into my mom and dad's bedroom where they would sleep. Joe slept in the recliner, Jim and I slept together, and Jackie took Jim's room. It all worked out fine. There was a lot more activity in the bathroom than usual, and everyone just had to wait their turn. We only had one bathroom in our house…some of my friends had more than one in their houses, but we only had the four people usually and we never needed another one, though it would have been handy right now. It was all right – we all got along fine, really.

We took the Cramer family home the next day right before it was time to pick Mom up. The power was back on – Dad made sure before we left them there – and we went on in to Hanover to get Mom. She was really happy to see us and about hugged us all to death. We were glad to see her, too, but gees, did she get all mushy over it!

The rest of January was about like every other January…cold and snowy, but not like January 14th. We got in plenty of sledding and snowball fights, thankfully. We didn't have to take Mom to work anymore because the roads never got that bad again – she could drive herself. Dad's work never let him stay home anymore that winter, either. That's just Ohio for you. Snow up to your neck one day, no snow at all the next. It might be cold outside, but it's warm on the inside when your family and friends are around, and I think that makes it all pretty good.

3 THE VALENTINE BOX

February was a particularly exciting month for the girls in my fourth grade class, but not for me or any of the other guys I hung around with. February brought that most dreaded of holidays, Valentine's Day. All the guys hated Valentine's Day with a passion, which is kind of funny when you think about it since 'passion' is what Valentine's Day is all about.

On the first Monday of the month, our teacher, Mrs. King, was just a little too happy to make the announcement all of us guys dreaded.

"Children, it's only a couple of weeks until Valentine's Day, and it's time for us to think about getting our valentine boxes made!" She sure seemed awful cheerful about all this. Our class was about half boys and half girls – there might have been a few more girls – and with that many boys dreading Valentine's Day, you'd think she'd be a little discouraged. Not so.

"I have some lovely construction paper, lace doilies, ribbon and glitter. You'll be able to make a valentine box that is a reflection of you as a person," Mrs. King continued. As a person? What in the heck else did she think we were? Gorillas? Well, she might have thought that about Alan Bell, now that I think of it. He was kind of a beast in class sometimes and was regularly sent to the principal's office.

22

"You'll need to bring in your shoeboxes or whatever kind of box you are going to use tomorrow so that we have plenty of time to get them decorated. When we're done, we'll put them on the windowsill and you may begin bringing in your valentines to drop in your friends' boxes. Then on the 14th, we'll have a little party and you can open all your valentines." Mrs. King had clearly thought this all out, and there was no chance we were going to be able to skip this activity, as much as we might want to.

That evening when I got home from school, I had a snack of popcorn and an apple and while I munched my popcorn piece by piece, I mulled over the idea of this valentine box. I couldn't use lacy stuff and glitter to be a reflection of me. I didn't think the other guys in my class were going to go for that either. I had to think of something else to make my valentine box manly.

"Mom, how could I decorate a valentine box to make it kind of manly?" I asked as I stuffed a couple of pieces of popcorn in my mouth. "Mrs. King has a bunch of girl stuff that she wants us to use, but I don't want to put pink construction paper and lacy junk on my valentine box. I don't even want to have one, but we have to, so I just have to come up with a better plan than glitter and ribbons."

Mom cocked her head to one side and seemed to be thinking about this for a minute or two. Finally she said, "John, Valentine's Day is supposed to be a celebration of love, so you want to have a valentine box that seems kind of sweet. I have to think about it a little bit, but I bet we can come up with something that is nice and is about love – at least something *you* love - but is not too girly. Let me think a little tonight. When do you have to work on them?"

"Tomorrow. I have to take a box in there tomorrow and start working on it," I moaned.

"Ok, well don't fret. Just pick out a box to take to school, and if you have to start decorating them tomorrow and we haven't come up with a good idea, you can just cover it in white paper and put your name on the lid. At least that's a start, right? And it will buy us a little time to come up with a really great idea. It's going to be fine. We'll come up with a spectacular idea!" Mom's creative juices were going. I could just about see the wheels turning in her head.

I went to my room and started fishing around in the closet for some kind of box to take to class. I didn't want to take anything that was too big. I wasn't really figuring on getting a lot of valentines. Mom always made me take one for every kid, and of course, Mrs. King had provided us with a list of everyone in class so that our moms and dads could see to it that we didn't leave anyone out. I guess that was a good idea, really, so no kid would go home feeling bad that they didn't get a lot of valentines. I thought I probably better look for a box big enough to hold a valentine from each of the other kids. That's just how it was in our school.

I finally found a shoebox that would work. It had a pair of my old Sunday school shoes in it, and I put those aside. Maybe Jim could wear them. He got a lot of my hand-me-downs. I put the shoebox with my school books and sat on the edge of the bed. I looked around my room for a few minutes. What is a reflection of me as a person? What exactly did that mean?

I had a poster of John Wayne on one wall. It was pretty big and would be way too much for a shoebox. I did like cowboy movies and I watched them with Dad pretty regularly. I thought about what other cowboy stuff I had that I could use, but I couldn't come up with anything. I didn't really own a lot of cowboy stuff at the time, despite my enjoyment of cowboy stories and movies.

I looked at my rock collection. I had a pretty good assortment of rocks that I had picked up down by the creek and down by the railroad tracks, both places we weren't really supposed to go by ourselves. But how could I attach the rocks to the valentine box? I guess I could use Elmer's glue, but I figured they would never stick or maybe even one of the guys would swipe one. They were really cool rocks...some gray and very smooth and round, some pink and speckled with glittery-looking pieces, some black and white striped like a zebra. They would look good on the outside of a valentine box, but I couldn't take the risk.

I liked dogs. I thought for a little bit about how I could make a dog valentine box. I could cut some pictures of dogs out of magazines and paste them on the box. I could try to glue some Milk Bone dog treats on the top. They were making them in different flavors now, so maybe using different colored treats would make the valentine box look cool. I could glue a treat by a picture of a dog's mouth so it would look like he was eating the treat. And frankly, I wouldn't care if someone stole the dog treats. They weren't as precious as the cool rocks I had gathered in my wanderings around town.

I went down to the living room and looked in the magazine rack to see if I could find some old magazines that might have pictures of dogs. The only dogs I could find in Mom's lady magazines were in advertisements, of course, but those pictures would work.

I went to talk to Mom since the last thing I wanted to do was have her hot under the collar because I started cutting up her magazines without asking.

"Mom, I have an idea for the valentine box. What about if I put pictures of dogs on it? I love dogs and that might be an ok idea. I would have to cut some pictures out of your magazines, though..." I trailed off.

"John, I actually think that's a good idea, but I have another idea for you. Tell you what, let's get supper out of the way and then we'll talk about it, ok? I've got to get supper on the table before your dad starves." My mom had kind of a set time that we had supper, and I think it was mostly because Dad came home from work ravenous every day.

Once dinner was over we got the dishes done. Jim weaseled out of drying, which was his job, so I had to do it. He said he had to do his spelling words. Well, I had stuff to do, too! It didn't matter. I dried the dishes for Mom and then we sat down at the table.

"John, I think I have a brilliant idea for your valentine box that will make it the hit of the class. What is one of the things that you love the very most in this world?"

Golly. There were a lot of things that I loved. My family. The gravel pit. Christmas, but that wouldn't work since it was Valentine's Day. Ice cream cones from the Twisty Freeze. Going down to the creek, but I wasn't about to say anything at all about that. Fishing. Baseball. Baseball! That was my favorite sport.

"Baseball!" I exclaimed.

"You got it," Mom said. "What about if you covered your whole valentine box in baseball cards? Pick out some of your favorite players and glue them on the box with their faces out, but then you could put some of their statistics by the side of each player. That would be a really unique valentine box. I'll bet no one else would have one like that – definitely manly."

I thought I probably had the smartest mom ever. I told her I liked the idea and immediately went to my room to start picking out my favorite players. I had a lot of good cards, so this would be easy. Hank Aaron, Roberto Clemente, Don Drysdale. Those guys would go on the valentine box for sure. Willie Mays, Al Kaline, Joe Pepitone. I couldn't leave them off. Let's see, that would be three for each side of the box. I needed a couple more to go on top. Mickey Mantle and Sandy Koufax. Those guys were kings in my mind. They would definitely go on top.

I was actually starting to get excited about the valentine box. I knew I would have the coolest valentine box of all. No lace and goofy stuff like that for me. It was going to be a man's box all the way.

I put my baseball cards into an envelope and put the envelope in the shoebox I had picked out. Then I thought I better go show Mom what I had planned.

Mom and Dad were in the living room. Dad was reading the paper and Mom had just turned on the evening news. I sat down on the couch beside her and opened the box so I could show her my baseball cards.

"I found this box with some old Sunday shoes in it. Jim can have those because they're too little for me. Then I went through all my baseball cards and picked out these guys." Mom started looking at the cards, asking me about each player – who they were, what I liked about them.

Dad looked over his paper. "What are you two talking about? Since when did you develop such an interest in baseball, honey?" he asked my mom.

"John has to make a valentine box and he didn't want it to be too girly, so I suggested he cover it in baseball cards," she answered.

"You did WHAT?" Dad jumped up out of his chair, newspaper now scrunched up in his hand. "You can't use baseball cards for that!"

"Why in the world not?" Mom asked. "I thought it was a good idea. The valentine box is supposed to kind of suit the personality of the person who makes it, and John loves baseball, so why wouldn't we use the baseball cards?"

"Because they might be worth money some day!" Dad was pretty excited now, but not good excited. He was upset excited.

"How do you know that?" Mom asked.

"Because, honey, I pay attention to these things. I hear people talk. Just last week Don Machinski told me he had heard that a Honus Wagner card went for about $2,000. You can't just stick baseball cards on a box for Valentine's Day."

"Well, I must say I think that's entirely ludicrous." Mom was insulted; I could tell from her tone. "Baseball cards are just pictures on cardboard. I can't imagine anyone in his right mind paying $2,000 for such a thing. And besides, can't you always get more baseball cards?"

"Yes, of course you can," Dad said. "But they are newer and they are not worth as much because they aren't as old. Let me see those cards, John."

I handed the cards over to Dad. He looked at each one carefully, inspecting the front, the back, even the edges of the card.

"These are in pretty good shape son. Where have you been keeping them?"

"In the drawer with my socks," I answered. "These are some of my favorite players, so I keep them in my drawer. Jim keeps his baseball cards in his toy box."

"In the toy box!" Dad was really animated now. "In the toy box!" His face was getting kind of red.

"Oh for Pete sake," Mom said. "You'd think you were protecting a gold mine under the house."

"My dearest darling wife," Dad said. "You do not recognize the value of these things. John, please don't glue these cards on your valentine box. Let's try to come up with a different plan."

I took the cards and the shoe box back to my room, dejected. I didn't know what I was going to do now. I thought I better work on my homework and just figure it out tomorrow at school. Like mom said, I could just wrap the box in white paper for now.

The next morning, I went down to breakfast, still thinking about Mrs. King's not-so-exciting valentine project. With my dad's heart attack about gluing the baseball cards on my valentine box, my little ship of hope had been dashed on the rocks of gloom. I ate my cereal, but it tasted like cardboard. What was I going to do?

The only comfort I had was that the rest of the guys were kind of in the same situation. We all had to come up with an idea for a valentine box, and not one other guy was any happier about it than I was. I was going to school with a heavy heart.

All morning long, we just worked on regular stuff – reading, arithmetic, and spelling. When we went to lunch, I sat with my best friends – Dave Hansen, Scotty Wilson, and Rusty Barnes. It was a sullen group, all of us thinking about the stupid stuff we had to do that afternoon.

"I hate this girl crap," Dave started the conversation.

"Me, too," Rusty answered. "My dad said just go along and don't get into trouble. He said the pain won't last long…it's only till Valentine's Day."

"Yeah, my mom and dad kind of said the same thing," Scotty added. "We just have to get through Valentine's Day and then it's all over for another year. I don't think they make you do this stuff in fifth grade, do they?"

"I doubt it," I said. "No fifth grader in their right mind would want to make a valentine box." I looked over at the table of fifth graders. "You won't catch Buzz Dillon making a valentine box."

Everyone turned to look. Buzz Dillon was one of the most unpleasant kids in fifth grade. He was wolfing down a bologna sandwich. It was creepy to watch him eat. He just stuffed food in his mouth. He ate like he never saw food before, my dad would have said.

"Well, we have to just do what Mrs. King says," Scotty piped up as we turned back to our own food. No one felt too hungry after watching Buzz smashing bologna into his mouth, so we put our own food back into brown paper bags we all carried, got up and tossed them in the trash, and headed for the gym. We were allowed to go to the gym for a little bit after lunch if we ate fast enough. We liked to shoot baskets, so we spent the rest of our lunch period working out our valentine box frustrations.

The bell rang, and it was time to head back to class. We still had to do social studies, so we got through that and then it was time to start the dreadful chore of valentine boxes. My shoe box had gotten a little crunched up on the bus that morning, but I straightened it out as best I could. A bunch of girls had gone up to Mrs. King's desk and were grabbing the ribbons, doilies, and bottles of glue and glitter. Most of the guys were hanging around their desks, looking like the weight of the world was on their shoulders. The only guy who was up at Mrs. King's desk was Mike Green. Mike was an ok guy, but he was about the smartest kid in the class so he was kind of Mrs. King's pet. We kidded him about it sometimes, but I don't think he even cared if we thought he was the teacher's pet. He seemed kind of proud of it.

After the girls and Mike got all their fancy supplies, a few of us guys wandered up to the desk to see what was left. I was happy to see that there was some plain white paper and some scotch tape. I took that. Scotty ended up with red paper, Dave got some pink paper (he would never live that down), and Rusty got some silvery-looking paper that kind of had glitter built right into it.

We all started covering our boxes. The girls were well on their way, cutting out hearts and gluing them on their boxes, outlining them with glitter and so forth. Some of the girls wrapped ribbons around their boxes. Mike Green was like a mad artist at work. No doubt his valentine box would be fancier than the girls' boxes. That was just how he was; everything done the absolute best.

Rusty was up at Mrs. King's desk as I was working on the lid to my box. He came back with some red ribbon and some black construction paper. He had a gleam in his eye, like he had a wicked idea. I watched him cut out four circles and glue them on each side of his box near the corners. What in the heck was he doing? Then he took some red ribbon and put a stripe across the top of his box the long way, extending down over both ends. After that, he took a red colored pencil and wrote the number "98" on either side of the ribbon on top of his valentine box.

"What are you making?" I asked him. This was very interesting.

"It's a race car," Rusty said. "It's the race car of Parnelli Jones."

"Wow! That was a great idea!" Dave had walked over to Rusty's desk and was looking wistfully at Rusty's race car box. It really was a good idea.

"Does anyone have a pink car?" Dave asked Rusty.

"Aw, heck no! And besides that, you can't steal my idea," Rusty insisted.

"Aw, heck! What am I going to do with pink paper?" Dave muttered to himself as he returned to his seat.

I turned back to my plain white box. I had to come up with something if Dad wasn't going to let me use my baseball cards. Maybe I would just leave it plain and put my name on it. I didn't really care if I even got any valentines.

That evening after supper, I asked my dad again about the baseball card idea.

"John, you don't understand this yet, but famous baseball player's cards are worth a lot of money in some circles. I want you to protect your cards, not put glue all over the back of them. In fact, we should get some kind of protective case to put them in. Trust me on this. Someday you'll be glad you didn't ruin them," he told me.

That was it. There was no use asking anymore. I went off to finish my reading for school the next day, resigned to the idea that I would have a plain old valentine box.

I was sitting on my bed, doing my reading when Mom came into my room and sat down on the chair next to my desk.

"John, I know you would like to use your baseball cards on your valentine box. I wish we could convince Dad, but he really does know a lot more about this stuff than I do, and I think we have to trust him on this."

"Yeah, that's what he said. It will be ok. I'm just going to leave my valentine box plain. It will be fine. No one really cares," I told her.

She rubbed my head and said, "Don't worry. This is probably the last year you'll have to do this anyway."

"That's what I'm counting on," I answered.

The next day at school, all the valentine boxes were in the windowsill. Most everybody had theirs decorated. Rusty's was the best of my real good friends. Dave, Scotty and I still had plain boxes.

Scotty came in to homeroom with some of those green soldiers that have flat bottoms on them. He had some Elmer's glue, and he went right over to his valentine box and started gluing soldiers on the top of the box. He put some of the soldiers standing up, but some of them were lying down on their sides.

"What's that supposed to be?" I asked him.

"The soldiers are in a war and the some of them got killed and the red is their blood going all over the place," he answered.

"Do you think Mrs. King is gonna go for that?" I honestly didn't think she'd approve.

"I don't know. I'm just going to tell her I'm making a valentine box for the soldiers in Viet Nam."

I told him I thought that *might* sell it, but I was skeptical. Rusty had a little tiny American flag he glued on the top, too. "They're defending Pork Chop Hill," he said. The flag might make the bloody valentine box more palatable to Mrs. King.

We were supposed to work on our valentine boxes a little more that afternoon. I was still at a loss, but Dave stole Rusty's idea, even if Rusty didn't want him too. He added black wheels and some pink ribbon that was darker pink than the paper that covered the box and made a race car out of his valentine box, too.

"This will be a racecar for a girl," Dave said.

"There are no girl race car drivers!" Rusty announced.

"But there might be someday," Dave countered.

"Yeah, we'll see about that," Rusty harrumphed, though Dave became an instant hit with the girls that afternoon.

Once again, I was left with a white box, no decorations, not even my name yet. Everyone knew it was mine, though, just because I was the only kid who hadn't really done anything to speak of with their valentine box.

"John, don't you have any ideas yet?" Mrs. King inquired.

"No ma'am, I don't." Of course that was not exactly true, but I didn't know what else to say. I just sat there with the valentine box on my desk, looking around at everyone else putting the finishing touches on their own creations.

When I walked in the front door at our house, I could tell Dad was already home from work because I heard him whistling. I was working up the courage to ask him one more time about the baseball cards. Valentine's Day would be here and I would still have my plain old white box, uninteresting and unappealing.

I walked into the kitchen, and there at the table, Dad was sitting with Mom. They had my baseball cards laid out, and they were covering them in Saran Wrap. Dad was folding pieces of Saran Wrap over each card, and Mom was taping it on the back so it would stay put. I knew Dad wanted to protect the cards, but this seemed crazy to me.

"Hey, John! What do you think?" Dad said with a big grin on his face.

"Well, ok, I guess, but aren't there some things out there you can just put the cards in? You don't have to wrap them with Saran Wrap." I was still a little dumbfounded.

"Oh, this isn't to preserve your cards," Dad said. "This is just to protect them when you glue them on your valentine box."

It took me a minute to process what he had just said. I had been so prepared to present my case that he caught me off guard.

"You mean I can use them for my valentine box?"

Dad laughed. "Yeah, son. That's what I said."

I dropped my books on the kitchen counter and went up and gave him a big hug. Then I gave my mom a big hug. "Thanks you guys. I didn't know what the heck I was going to do. Mrs. King was bugging me about it today, even."

"Well, when I was un-wrapping my sandwich at lunch today, it just hit me that we could do the same thing with your cards. The Saran Wrap will keep the glue from getting on the back of your cards, but you can still use them to decorate your valentine box." Dad was a genius!

I was so happy I sat down and helped them with the rest of the cards, and then I helped Mom get supper around. It was a good evening, and I went to bed anticipating how cool my valentine box would now be.

The morning bus couldn't get to school soon enough. I went to my home room and got my valentine box right away.

"Did you get an idea, John?" Mrs. King asked.

"I sure did," I replied. "Can I borrow the glue?"

Mrs. King produced the Elmer's out of her locked supply cabinet and I went to work. Mickey Mantle and Sandy Koufax on top, just like I had planned.

When the guys got to school, I was putting the finishing touches on my valentine box.

"Wow, that's the coolest valentine box I ever saw," Dave told me. "I wish I would have thought of that. I have a million baseball cards."

Rusty stood there for a few minutes and just looked at my valentine box. "I have to say, that's the best valentine box in the whole class." That really meant something to me, coming from the guy who dreamed up a race car all on his own.

The valentines began to show up from different kids, a few every day between the day I finished my box and Valentine's Day. I never took mine in till about the day before the party. I hated addressing them – you know, having to sign every one of them and all that. With each valentine, I crossed another kid off the list.

On Valentine's Day, Mrs. King brought in heart-shaped cookies with pink icing and some Hawaiian punch. Then it was time to open our valentine boxes.

Everyone got a valentine from every other kid. No one got left out, so that was good. Everyone in the class told me how cool they thought my valentine box was, even the girls. One of the girls, Patty Smith, wrote me a real mushy valentine. I think she kind of liked me in February.

I was sure glad my dad and my mom had been able to compromise about me using my baseball cards. It helped me know that whenever there was a conflict about things like who was going to get to swing first at recess, or which team was going to get the ball first when we played basketball at lunch time, we could work it out like Mom and Dad had…no fighting. Just talking.

4 THE GRAVEL PIT

If you wanted a thrill in the cold month of February, the gravel pit was the place to be. The gravel pit was exactly what it sounds like – a big pit in the earth that men used to dig gravel out of. I don't know what they did with all the gravel. I didn't really care to tell you the truth. I mean, I never even asked my dad about it. I knew that pit existed for us kids, primarily. That was all that mattered.

The gravel pit resembled drawings of a moon crater we had in our science books. It was deep, wide, and had lots of hills within it. Why would this be such a fun place? Sledding.

In the winter time, my favorite sport was sledding. A lot of kids liked ice skating, which we did down at the creek and sometimes on a pond at the Lieb family farm. I never got very good at skating, and my dad said it was because I had weak ankles, whatever that really means. I could walk ok, so how could my ankles be weak? Anyway, I couldn't skate worth a darn. We weren't wealthy enough to go skiing…that always seemed like a rich person's sport because of having to go to ski resorts, get those fancy ski clothes and all that. I did think that ski lifts looked like fun, but nope…sledding was it for me.

I loved watching the bobsled competitions on "Wide World of Sports." I loved hearing Jim McKay announce all the thrills of victory and the agonies of defeat - he was the best. Anyway, at the gravel pit I would pretend that I was on a bobsled team and that we were at the Olympics and that Jim McKay was calling the run. I would try to maneuver my sled to the scariest parts of the gravel pit and keep from wrecking. It was not always easy.

There was a part of the gravel pit we all called Dead Man's Curve. Only the bravest guys would go on Dead Man's Curve because it truly was dangerous. I knew more than one kid who broke bones on Dead Man's Curve. My mom really didn't want us to go sledding on that part of the gravel pit, but how could we not? That was the big challenge. I figured what she didn't know in this case wouldn't hurt her, and I was on Dead Man's Curve every winter as many times as I could get there. How could you ever hope to become a champion bobsledder if you couldn't maneuver Dead Man's Curve? I had to swear Jim to secrecy. He was such a little fink sometimes, especially when he was in trouble himself. He would rat you out in a heartbeat to take the heat off of him. That's little brothers for you.

In 1963, Jim was eight and I was going to soon be ten. I had been going to the gravel pit for as long as I could remember – at least since I was seven - and Jim had always tagged along with me since *he* was seven. Now that he was eight, he was interested in trying Dead Man's Curve. I was a little skeptical that he could handle it, but he kept bugging me and bugging me. I knew that if I didn't help him learn how to handle Dead Man's Curve, he'd tell on me to Mom and we would both have lost our sledding privileges.

"C'mon, John. I'm eight now. I'm not a baby anymore," Jim pleaded with me one day as we were on our way to the pit.

"Jim, you don't really know what you're getting into. I just want to warn you, Dead Man's Curve is serious business. You can't go into it scared, or you will wreck for sure. You have to have confidence, hang on for dear life, and go for it," I explained to him. As the big brother, I felt I had an obligation to let him know just how tough this was.

"I'm not scared. I've seen you do it a million times, and I've seen a bunch of kids do it a million times. I know how to go around Dead Man's Curve. I bet I could do it today with no help from you or anyone!" Jim got kind of bullheaded sometimes.

"Well, if you're sure you want to. I guess I started going on the curve when I was about eight, so you may as well start trying it," I answered. I wasn't about to lose my sledding privileges because

Jim got mad at me about Dead Man's Curve. I just figured I'd have to watch out for him.

When we got to the gravel pit, Dave, Rusty, and Scotty were already there. So was Debbie Carruthers. Yuck. I just stayed away from her as much as I could. Rhonda Borden was there and she was ok. She liked to play stuff like "king of the hill" and she played touch football with us in the fall. She wasn't a big whiner like Debbie. There were some other little kids there, but they were sledding on the little hills that were right near the pit. In fact, a couple of Jim's good buddies from school were over there, and that's where Jim went when we arrived. He started sledding with his little buddies.

I joined up with Dave, Rusty and Scotty. Rhonda and Debbie came over to talk to us, too.

"What do you guys want to do today?" Dave posed. A dumber question had never been asked.

"Well what do you think? Sled!" I declared. "There's nothing else to do up here anyway."

Debbie started whining right away. "It's so cold out! I'm glad I wore my ski outfit." I think she said that to sort of brag because her parents were rich and their family did go skiing.

"If your ski clothes aren't warm enough for sledding, how do they keep you warm for skiing?" Rusty asked her. I don't think she knew exactly what to say to that because she kind of tossed her head and went over to where the little kids were.

"Good call, Rusty. Way to get rid of her," Scotty said.

"You guys, she's not so bad. She's just a little on the prissy side," Rhonda said. "You just have to ignore some of the stuff she says; then she's all right."

"I'm glad *someone* thinks so," Rusty said and we all started laughing except for Rhonda. Rhonda was really nice and probably would never say anything mean about anyone.

I picked up my Flexible Flyer. "I'm first on the curve today!" I took off for the approach of Dead Man's Curve and threw my sled on the slope. "See you later!"

I lay down on my sled and shoved off with my foot. The snow had just fallen the night before, so it was a little slow getting started. Once I hit the first hill, things went a little smoother, but it still wasn't as fast a run as I'd like. Dead Man's Curve felt like nothing because it was such a slow run. This would probably be a good day for Jim to learn the curve. None of the guys or Rhonda were even clapping or yelling, which we usually all did for each other. It was just a slow run.

I finally got to the bottom of the pit, grabbed hold of my sled and started trudging back up on the one side of the pit that wasn't quite so steep. I made my way around the brim to where my buddies and Rhonda were waiting.

"What the heck happened, man?" asked Scotty.

"I don't know – new snow, maybe? It's too loose. It's not packed down enough and there's no ice under it. We may have to work it down," I answered my puzzled friends.

"Well, let's go!" said Dave. "If we all just keep sledding down it a bunch of times, it'll get better."

We lined up and each took a turn. We would wait till the guy in front of us had safely made it to the bottom before the next guy would go. I hollered over to Jim.

"Jim, bring your sled over and get on the curve!"

I think he had almost forgotten about Dead Man's Curve when he met up with his friends. He looked kind of surprised for a minute, but then he grabbed his sled and ran over to where I was standing, waiting for my next turn.

"Jim, it's kind of slow going today, so this is a good day for your first time on the curve. We're all trying to go down a whole bunch of times to get the snow packed down a little, so why don't you go right before me. Then I can watch how you do and give you some pointers and stuff."

Jim looked at me for a full minute. Then he put his sled down on the ground and said, "See ya later." Off he went, heading down the hill on his stomach. He was doing really well as he came into Dead Man's Curve, and we had packed the snow down enough that it seemed like we were all going faster. Jim held on, made it through the curve and all the way down to the bottom of the pit. When his sled came to a stop, he stood up, raised his arms in victory, and began jumping up and down.

Rusty looked down at Jim and yelled, "Hey get out of there so the next guy can go!" Then he turned to me and said, "First time, huh?"

"Yup," I said. "First time." Honestly, I had to admit I was proud of him.

We had each made several runs, including Jim, who was doing just great. He wasn't the least bit scared, and I think he got the hang of Dead Man's Curve faster than I did when I first started sledding on it. One thing was for sure. He would never rat me out now because he was devoted to that curve. Sledding would never be the same for Jim after this.

Debbie Carruthers must have gotten tired of playing with the little kids and she must have figured out that what we were doing was infinitely more fun because she came over to where we were continuing our runs.

"I got a Flying Saucer for Christmas this year," she said. "Want to ride it down the hill?"

I was used to my Flexible Flyer and wasn't too sure about taking a saucer around the curve. "Where is it?" I asked her. "I didn't see you with any saucer."

"I've got it at home, but it won't take me long to go get it," she said. She turned and took off running - at least as good as she could run in the snow. I could never figure her out. Why in the heck would you come to the gravel pit on a snowy day without your sled or in her case, her saucer? She was so weird.

By this time, the little kids had gotten kind of bored, I guess, with their baby hills. They were starting to come over to where we were. I knew they weren't ready for Dead Man's Curve, so I tried to get them to go back over to the little kid area. They were about as stubborn as Jim.

"We don't want to go over there," one little kid said. "We want to stay over here with you guys,"

"Ok," I said, "but you can't go down this hill. It's too steep, and the track is too fast. You could get hurt."

"We just wanna watch you," said the littlest kid of all.

"Ok, ok. Just stay off the hill," I said. Who let all these six and seven year olds up here anyway, I thought to myself.

Rusty, Dave, Scotty and Rhonda had completed several runs. "I'm getting hungry for some lunch," Dave said. "I think I'm going to go home."

"Wait," I said. "Debbie went home to get her saucer. She'll be back in a minute, probably."

"Of course she would have a saucer," Rusty said sarcastically. "Those things are for little kids to sit down on and spin down the hill."

"Well, all I know is she said it's fun," I said. "I wouldn't mind trying it myself."

Just about that time, we could see Debbie in the distance, carrying a shiny metal disc that was curved up kind of like a shallow bowl. The sun glinted off the metal, and it made me realize that thing might be really fast. There was just something super-cool about it...that shiny metal...you could probably fly on that thing. I liked that thought.

Debbie was out of breath by the time she got to where we were waiting and watching. "Here it is, guys! The Flying Saucer. Who wants to go first?" Debbie asked.

"Why don't you go first? It's your saucer," Rhonda spoke up.

"Well, I'm not used to Dead Man's Curve," Debbie said. "Maybe one of you guys should do it first so I can see how it should be done."

"I'll go," I said. I grabbed the saucer out of Debbie's hand and put it on the ground. "Time to fly!"

I sat cross-legged on the saucer and shoved off with my hands. There were little handles on either side of the saucer that you could hold on with. I was flying right away. You kind of bounced up with every bump you hit, but it was really fun. I didn't have any trouble with Dead Man's Curve, and I didn't think the other guys would, either.

At the bottom, I stood up and waved my approval up to the gang. They all yelled and waved back. I picked up the saucer and made the trek up the hill one more time.

The other guys and Rhonda all took a turn on the saucer, and each one pronounced it highly suitable for sledding. Even Jim took a couple of turns. The littler kids wanted nothing to do with the saucer, but Jim had already passed the Dead Man's Curve test, so he was fearless now. He would be viewed as a god by the rest of those little kids for a long time after that.

"Debbie, don't you want to try it out now?" asked Rhonda.

Debbie hesitated for a minute. "Well, I've been watching you guys. Do you really think I can do it?"

"Sure! Of course!" was the chorus from all of us, but I really kind of doubted she was ready for it. I didn't want to discourage her, though, because usually she was such a wimp.

"Ok. Here I go!" Debbie sat down on her saucer. She kind of slid it back and forth a couple of times, like she was hesitating. Rusty was standing directly behind her, and I think he could see she might be chickening out because all of a sudden, he put both of his gloved hands on her back and shoved as hard as he could.

Debbie took off flying. The snow was really packed down by this time, and there was enough ice built up that the track was much faster now. Debbie was screaming and the saucer was picking up speed. She was going very fast when she came into Dead Man's Curve.

Right before you get to the curve, there's a little hill that you have to bump up over. It usually kind of throws you into the curve, but of course, Debbie Carruthers knew none of that. She hit that hill and suddenly, the gravel pit was silent, including Debbie...she was flying on her Flying Saucer. I don't know how long she was air-born, but every one of us stood there with our mouths open watching her head for outer space. Except that gravity exists.

I don't know how far Debbie flew before she came back to earth in a tumble. The Flying Saucer was still flying, but Debbie Carruthers was rolling end-over-end down to the lowest part of the gravel pit. The saucer landed before Debbie came to a stop at the very bottom.

For a minute, Debbie Carruthers laid there on the ground, not moving, maybe not even breathing. We weren't sure. We stood around the brim of the gravel pit in complete shock.

"We gotta help her!" Rhonda, being the kind one, was the first to start down the hill. All of us guys followed. It wasn't easy because like I said, it had gotten pretty icy now.

We were about halfway down the hill when suddenly, Debbie jumped up and to our surprise, started laughing hysterically.

"That was the most fun I ever had!" she said. She was laughing so hard she could barely even talk. She was kind of stumbling around and she finally fell back on the ground, still laughing. By that time, we had gotten to the bottom. Rhonda helped her stand back up.

"You guys, that was the most fun I ever had," she repeated. "Let's go again!"

"Uh, that might have been enough for you for one day," Rusty said.

"No, no, I'm fine," Debbie said. "Wow! What a ride!"

We all kind of just looked at her, and she said, "What's wrong? Why are you staring at me?"

"Are you sure you didn't hit your head?" Rusty spoke up again. "You're acting kind of nutty."

"No, I didn't hit my head," Debbie said, clearly disgusted at the suggestion. "You guys think you're the only ones who are tough enough for this hill. Well, surprise, surprise, because I am, too." Then she smiled, and everyone kind of just shook their heads and smiled, too.

"Well, the least you could do is to help me back up the hill," Debbie said. She had returned to her old self.

We helped Debbie Carruthers back up to the top of the hill. We all were starving at that point and wanted to go home for lunch, so we went our separate ways till the next time we would ride the snow. I still didn't really like Debbie Carruthers that much, but I did gain some respect for her that day, and for Jim, too. He was growing up and I was starting to think he might possibly turn out to be not too bad of a brother after all.

5 MOM'S BIG SECRET

One thing I've noticed is that life can change in a second. Heck, it can change in a millionth of a second. You never know what's coming next. That can make life a little scary, but it can also make it exciting. I kind of go back and forth between the two.

In March, my mom was getting tired easy and also throwing up a lot in the mornings. At first, we thought she had the flu, though it seemed kind of weird that she would be sick for that many days, and it wasn't every day. She would seem ill for a couple of days, then be ok for a couple of days. I didn't want Mom to be sick, and this was scary. There are all kinds of creepy diseases out there. I didn't want her to have any of them.

Mom was getting up extra early in the morning so she had time to throw up and such before she got ready for work. I noticed that she started keeping saltines by her bed. I thought that was kind of weird, too, since she never wanted us to eat food in our bedrooms. She thought the crumbs would attract critters; at least that's what she told us. "Crumbs attract critters," she would say. Mom definitely did not like critters in the house.

I didn't have the nerve to ask Mom what was going on because she didn't seem particularly upset about it and in a way, I didn't want to know. I just wanted it to go away mostly. I didn't want her to be sick, and I started praying for her at night so maybe this sickness would end.

One morning, Mom was throwing up like crazy. I could hear her clear up in my bedroom. Enough is enough, I thought to myself. I went downstairs and parked outside the bathroom door till she came out. She looked terrible. She was pale and had big dark circles under her eyes. She looked like she hadn't slept in a week. I knew that look from watching doctor shows on television. Cancer. That had to be it. I threw my arms around her.

"Well, good morning, son," Mom said. "To what do I owe this display of affection first thing in the morning?"

I was trying to be brave. "Mom, we have to talk about something serious. I know you're very sick, and I'm worried about you, so you have to tell me why you are sick. You just have to. I know you probably don't want to worry us, but I am more worried if I don't know, you have to tell me."

Mom smiled and said, "John, this early morning is not the time to talk about it, but I promise that tonight your dad and I will sit down with you and Jim and let you know what is going on. I promise you, it's nothing bad. Can you trust me on that till tonight? We've all got to get ready for school and work, so it has to wait. Can you hang on till tonight?"

What choice did I have? "Ok," I muttered as I headed back to my room to get dressed for school. If she said it wasn't bad, I had to just believe her, right?

I still thought about Mom at school a lot that day. It was hard to concentrate on science or English when you knew your mom was sick. How could being sick not be bad? Did she just say that to try to set my mind at ease while I was at school? Was she going to have to have surgery? I kept thinking about all the scary-looking situations I had seen on Dr. Kildare and shows like that. It was just hard to be at school that day.

Our school bus picked us up and dropped us off at Calvary church. That's where we went to church on Sundays, too. On this day, when the bus dropped us off, I decided to go in the church.

"What are you doing?" Jim asked me.

"I'm just going to stop in and see Pastor Miller," I answered.

"I'm not going to church when it's not Sunday," Jim said.

"I don't care. Go on home. I'll be there in a little bit," I told him. He stuck his tongue out at me, turned heel and headed for home.

Our church was a nice place to go when you needed to be quiet. There was red carpet up the main aisle, and on either side were pews made out of wood. That wood could get pretty hard to sit on if you had been there too long, but it was nice to look at - a warm golden brown color, the same as the altar and the pulpit. At the front of the church, high up on the wall, there were three stained glass windows. In the middle, there was a giant Jesus with the words "John 3:16" on a banner under his feet. On either side of him in the smaller stained glass windows were lambs lying down. There was a lot of bright blue and red in the stained glass around Jesus and the lambs. I loved those windows, and a lot of times in church, I was really looking at them and not listening too much to what Pastor Miller had to say. Right at that moment, the memory made me feel kind of bad since I was coming to see him about my worries.

I walked up the main aisle and turned left at the altar. Pastor Miller's office was over that way in a corner of the sanctuary. I hesitated for a second or two because now that I was here, I wasn't sure how I was going to start this conversation. I just felt like he could help me not feel so worried, so I took a deep breath and knocked on the door to his office.

"Come in," I heard from the other side of the door.

I opened the door slowly and peeked in. I wanted to make sure no one else was in there with him.

"Hi John!" Pastor Miller jumped up from his desk like he was real happy to see me. He strode right over and offered me a handshake. He pumped my arm up and down and said, "I'm surprised to see you here. How are you?"

"Oh, I'm fine Pastor, but I'm worried about my mom." There it was, just as plain as anything. "If I talk to you about stuff, you're not allowed to tell anyone, right?"

He got a concerned look on his face. "Golly, yes, our conversation will be completely private. Come right over here and sit down. Let's talk about this worry. First we should pray, though."

Pastor Miller prayed quite a bit; that was one thing I had learned about him.

"Heavenly Father, thank you for John and for him being a loving boy, loving enough to care about his parents and his brother. Help us to sort through any worries John has and for him to know your peace. Amen."

I wasn't all that concerned about my brother, but about my parents...Pastor Miller had that right. I started telling him about what my mom had been going through and how worried I was. "She's going to talk to us tonight. She said this morning that she and Dad would sit down with Jim and me tonight and tell us what's wrong with her. I've been worried all day. What if she's got cancer or something?"

Pastor Miller had a little bit of a smile on his face. That surprised me because he was a pretty nice guy and I never thought he would think that someone being sick was something to smile about. "John, do you know how much God loves you right now? He is looking down on you and likely feeling very proud of a young man who cares so much about other people. Based on what you have told me, I have a feeling that you have nothing to be worried about and that, in fact, tonight your mom and dad are actually going to have exciting news for you. I'm glad you came to see me, and if you want to come back after you hear your mom and dad's news, I want you to feel free to do so, but I really think you haven't got one thing to worry about. You'll have to let me know, though, what you find out. Ok?"

That was it. There was no more from Pastor Miller. I promised I'd let him know, but I didn't feel reassured in the least. I had expected some kind of comforting, but walked away without the sense of peace he had prayed for. I thanked him for his time and headed back out into the church sanctuary. I sat on the front pew for a minute and said my own little prayer that my mom would be ok. That was all I cared about at that moment.

After dinner that evening, Mom and Dad kept their promise. They called Jim and I to the living room and we turned off the TV. Mom settled on the couch and took hold of Dad's hand. She took a deep breath and started the conversation.

"I know you guys have seen me getting sick to my stomach in the mornings. I know you, John, have been particularly worried. You guys see too much scary stuff on TV. You probably watch way too much TV in general now that I think about it. Well, anyway, I'm not sick like what you see on those doctor shows. In fact, I'm very well. It's just that I'm pregnant – you guys are going to be big brothers. Dad and I are pretty excited about it, and we hope you will be, too."

You could not have told me news that shocked or dismayed me any more than this. Pregnant? Big brother? I was already a big brother. I wasn't sure I wanted to do that again, but Jim was jumping up and down like a nut.

"Big brother, big brother, I'm going to be a big brother," Jim was kind of singing. Mom and Dad were smiling and holding hands and Jim bounced into them, trying to hug them.

"Hold on, partner", Dad said. "You can't be jumping on Mom like that now, ok?"

"Sorry, sorry, sorry," Jim said. "I'm going to be the big brother now!" Mom and Dad just laughed at him. That's all he could focus on – being the big brother. He had no idea of what was in store for him. I had gotten pretty expert at big brothering after eight years of practice on him, but he knew nothing about what was to come.

"How come you throw up all the time if having another baby is all that's wrong?" I asked. I was still feeling a little suspicious.

"It just kind of goes with the territory," Mom answered. "I don't really know exactly why it happens, and it will ease up pretty soon. For right now, I just take it easy on my stomach first thing in the morning, and sometimes I have to eat a few crackers before I even get out of bed. That seems to help. That and Coca Cola...."

"Are you sure you don't have cancer?" I interrupted.

Dad started laughing. "Yes, that's it, and she'll have a very big tumor in her stomach pretty soon. It will be so huge it will stick out to about here." He put his hands way out in front of his stomach to show us how big the tumor would be.

"Bob, don't tell them that nonsense!" Mom said. "You guys, don't pay a bit of attention to your dad. I don't have cancer. I'm completely fine. I'm just going to have a baby."

"Will it be a boy or a girl?" Jim asked.

"You big dummy, how can she know that?" I said, disgusted with the whole thing.

"Well I just wondered," Jim said. "I really don't even care because whatever it is, I'll be its big brother."

"Yes, you most certainly will," Dad said. "You'll have to learn how to help Mom like John helped her when you were a baby, Jimmy boy."

I didn't really remember ever helping Mom with Jim except maybe to go get her a clean diaper for him or stuff like that. Jim could have all of that he wanted. I wanted nothing to do with another baby, personally. All they do is cry and pee their pants and eat. That's about it. They're not good for much, and even with a few years on him, Jim still wasn't good for much.

"John, are you ok?" Mom asked. "You don't look too happy."

I didn't want to hurt her feelings. "I'm fine, Mom. I just was worried about you, that's all."

"Well there's not a thing in the world to worry about. We're going to have a baby!" I could tell she was pretty happy about it. "I hope it's a girl this time," she continued. "It would be nice to have another girl in the house with me."

Geeminy Christmas! It was bad enough trying to figure out where we were going to put another kid let alone have it be a girl. I couldn't even think about that possibility. What if she turned out like Debbie Carruthers? Criminy!

I had a weird dream that night. Mom was dressing me and Jim up in these pink dresses and trying to put ribbons in our hair. We kept trying to get away from her, but her arms would stretch out real long like Plastic Man and she would catch us and pull us back close to her and keep fussing around with these pink ribbons. It was a nightmare.

At school the next day, I told the guys about the baby over lunch. They were all pretty much as disgusted as I was except for Dave, of course.

"Hey, maybe it won't be so bad. Well, that is if you get another boy, at least. A girl wouldn't be so bad, either, if they like sports and stuff. You just have to train them right," Dave opined.

"Cripe, our house isn't that big," I said. "I'm not even sure where we're gonna put this kid."

"Oh, your parents will figure it out, you can bet on that," Rusty said. "Parents always figure out how to fit another kid in."

Scotty had remained quiet through much of the conversation, but he finally spoke. "My mom got pregnant last year, but then she lost the baby. She cried for weeks. It was terrible. They didn't know what happened or why the baby died, but it did, and that's a heck of a lot worse than if the baby actually makes it all the way here."

I had never even thought about anything like that. In fact, I had never heard of a baby dying before it was born. Something like that would break my mom's heart and I immediately hoped it wouldn't happen to her.

"Gosh, Scotty, that's terrible," I said. "Is your mom ok now?"

"Yeah, but sometimes we go out to the baby's grave and put flowers on it, and then she usually cries a little bit. I think she still feels pretty sad about it," he answered.

Right then and there, I decided I was going to try to help Mom, help keep her well. We had to get that throwing up issue over with and her not be sick. I knew that if her baby ever died, she would just about die, too. Now I had a whole *new* thing to worry about.

As Jim and I walked home from the bus stop, I decided to not tell him about Scotty's mom, but to try to convince him that we had to do everything we could to help Mom.

"Mom is going to need us to help out more around the house," I started. "That means both of us, ok?"

"Sure. I always help her around the house," Jim said.

Yikes. Jim's idea of helping was not exactly what *I* would call helping, so I was a little concerned about his commitment.

"No, I mean, really help her," I said. "Keep our rooms picked up, help fold the laundry, all that kind of stuff."

"Ok. I get it. I know how to do all that." Jim's words sounded good, but I knew the reality. He was always trying to weasel out of chores. I was determined to not let Mom down, though, so I would just have to keep Jim focused.

That evening after dinner, we heard a knock on the front door. Dad answered and found Pastor Miller standing on the porch.

"Good evening, Bob. How are you?" Pastor Miller cheerfully asked.

"We're just great. Come on in," Dad said as he opened the screen door and ushered the pastor into the living room. "Can I get you some coffee?"

"No, I can't stay long. I was just passing by and thought I'd stop in to say hello, see how you all were doing."

"Well, we're doing really well," Mom said. "We're just starting to let people know that I'm going to have a baby. It's very early, but I've been sick so much that I went to the doctor right away...I just had a feeling...."

"Well, that's very good news, indeed!" Pastor Miller looked right over at me when he said that, and he winked as if to say 'told you not to worry.'

"I think the baby will be here in later September if our calculations are right," Mom continued. "Then we will have a March baby, a June baby, and a September baby."

"All you need then is a December baby and you can have one every quarter," Pastor Miller said. I didn't really get what he meant by that, but he, Mom, and Dad all started laughing. I didn't think it sounded too funny. We sure didn't need four kids in the family.

"Is there anything your church family can do for you at this point?" Pastor Miller asked.

"No, not at all. We're doing just fine – just the usual early pregnancy tiredness and so forth," Mom answered.

"Well, we're here for you, and we'll definitely put you on the prayer list, that all will go without a hitch," Pastor Miller said, and he stood up to leave. "Hey, John, would you mind stopping by my office on your way home from school tomorrow? I have some new rocks in my rock collection I wanted to show you."

I didn't know anything about the pastor's rock collection, but I figured he was just covering his tracks so he could talk to me about Mom's baby.

That next day after school, I sent Jim on home. He was oblivious to this whole situation with Mom anyway. All he could think about was being someone's big brother. I don't remember ever being that excited about becoming his big brother.

I walked up the steps to church and pulled open the heavy, carved wooden door. Pastor Miller was right in the vestibule and he gave me a big smile.

"Hi, John! I'm glad you could stop by. Come on into the office. I really do have something to show you."

We walked through the sanctuary to his office. The door was open and he motioned for me to sit at a little table that was there by a window. There was an empty glass on the table.

Pastor Miller pulled a box out of his desk drawer. "I wasn't kidding about the rock collection," he said. "I really do have one, and I have some new, interesting rocks I thought I'd show you."

Inside the box were some of the coolest rocks I ever saw. Pink, purplish, black with stripes – just all kinds of rocks. One had glittery stuff in it. "Is that gold?" I asked.

"No, it's fool's gold – also known as pyrite," he answered. Then he started dropping all the rocks in the glass that was sitting there. I didn't know what in the heck he was doing, but he said, "Look at how much room in the glass those rocks take up." Anybody could have figured that out. I didn't know where he was going with this when he picked up a little box that said "Myrtle Beach, S.C." on the top and started pouring sand from that box into the glass with the rocks. When the glass was nearly full up to the top, he stopped and said, "Doesn't look like there's much room for anything else, does it?"

"No," I answered. "There isn't any more room."

"Well, just watch this," he said, and he got a glass of water off his desk and started dumping it in the glass with the rocks and sand. He got every last drop of water in there with the rocks and just looked at me.

"What do you think about that?" he asked.

I sat silently and looked at the glass. I still didn't know what this had to do with anything. I was confused as all get out. Then Pastor Miller smiled and spoke quietly. "John, sometimes when a family is going to have a new baby, the older kids kind of feel like they're being pushed out of the way. It can be kind of scary, thinking about sharing your parents with another child, and you already have one brother, so it's maybe even more of a concern to you. Am I on the right track with this? Are you worried about your mom and dad maybe not having enough time for you and Jim with another baby on the way?"

"Well, really, I was worried about Mom at first. I really thought she had a bad disease or something. But then when she told us about the baby, I just wondered how this is all going to work. So yes, I'm worried about things being like they are now. How will Mom and Dad be able to love another kid and take care of it? We don't even have enough bedrooms in our house for another person. Stuff like that.... "

"Ok," Pastor Miller continued. "Think about this glass being like your mom's heart or your dad's heart. The rocks represent God – that's the first thing they made room for in their hearts, in their lives. Then the sand is them - they made room for each other. Sometimes married people don't think they have any more room for anything but the rocks and the sand, and then surprise! Along comes the water – that's you, Jim, and the new baby. Do you get it? Your mom and dad's hearts have a lot of room for God, for each other, and for all of you kids. Your mom and dad have big hearts, and there's room for an awful lot in them."

I had to just sit for a minute and think about all this. I knew Pastor Miller was right about my mom and dad having big hearts. They didn't just take care of me and Jim. They helped my grandparents, they helped their friends, they helped with things in our town like big town get-togethers and so forth. They helped other people in our church. They helped with school. They had really big hearts. I never had a thing to worry about.

"I get it, Pastor Miller. I get it." I stood up to leave.

"Never forget, John – love actually grows by giving it to others. The more we give away, the more we get back. The same is true for your parents, for you, for Jim, and for everybody. Love grows when we give it away. As our circle of loved ones gets bigger, our hearts also grow with the love we get in return. That's what love really is all about, I think. Giving it away and letting it grow."

"Thanks, Pastor," I said as I extended my hand to him. He gave me a hearty handshake and said, "Now, why don't you get on home and do something that is helpful to your mom. She'll need you a lot in the upcoming months. This is a good way to start growing your love." He smiled, and I left the office. He was a pretty good guy, Pastor Miller.

When I got home, Mom was in the kitchen, home from work. She was busy washing the dirt off some fresh carrots, and boy, she sure looked tired. "Mom, what can I do to help you with dinner?" I asked.

Mom turned to look at me, a little shocked by my question. "Well, gosh, son, we're keeping it pretty simple tonight, but if you really want to help, would you mind setting the table?"

"No problem. Oh Mom, I just want you to know that I love you and since you're going to have a baby, I will try to be a good helper so you feel better and not so tired and sick."

Mom dried her hands off with a towel and walked over to where I was pulling knives, forks and spoons from a drawer. She wrapped her arms around me and said, "I love you, John. You have such a big heart."

Gosh, I guess what Pastor Miller said was working already.

6 BIRTHDAY

My birthday is in March...March the 13th to be exact. I was born on a Friday, so my dad used to kid me about being "...the biggest jinx ever born." He was only teasing me, though. I overheard him tell Mom one time that instead of the biggest jinx, I was the best thing that ever happened on a Friday the 13th. I always knew he meant it.

Since I was born in 1953, this was my 10th birthday. Ten years old. That sounded pretty old to me and I felt like I had an edge on some of my buddies whose birthdays were later in the year. They would be nine for several months before they would catch up with me.

I never really wanted a lot of stuff for my birthday. I was happy I was born and all, but I just never had a million things in my head that I wanted. This year was an exception. I wanted a new bike.

There are few things more important than a good bike, I've figured out. The bike I had was one we had bought second-hand from a man in Findlay whose kids were grown up and had new bikes. It was a Huffy and it was fine...it got me around and so forth, but at age ten, I thought it was time to pursue excellence. I wanted a Schwinn Corvette.

The new Corvettes were just coming out. I wanted a three-speed with a headlight, a front carrier for when I went up to Connally's grocery for Mom, stainless steel rims and whitewall tires. The only acceptable color was radiant red because Ohio State Buckeye fans couldn't have blue or green. I knew exactly what I wanted. I also knew how much they cost...$76.95. That's a lot of money. My mom and dad often told us that money didn't grow on trees. In fact, they told us that so often that one time I took a one dollar bill that I got for running errands for Mr. Conaway and tied it to the plum tree out back. Then I coaxed Mom and Dad into coming out to see it just for a joke. I think they thought it was funny in a way and not funny in a way.

I had seen the new Corvettes at Sears and Roebuck. I had also seen the price tag. I knew that this was probably not going to happen for my birthday. It was just too much. I tried to start thinking of a way I could get that bike. Maybe if I contributed some money of my own....

I was a pretty good saver. I didn't like to buy things just for the sake of buying them. My mom called me Silas Marner because I kept all my Christmas money from Grandma and Grandpa, any money I earned doing chores for Mom and Dad or other people in town, any change I found under the football bleachers up at the high school, any change I found down by the railroad tracks...just any money I got. I hardly ever bought anything. Sometimes I would think I was saving up for something in particular, like a new racecar or a new game. Then when I would get to the store, I would look at the toy, think about it, and decide to wait. Because I did that, I had about $18 saved up. That was a long way from $76 and probably not enough to be helpful to Mom and Dad when they were deciding about a new bike for me. How could I get that bike?

I decided to just be straightforward about it with Mom and Dad, but I knew I better carefully choose my timing. One evening after we had eaten a delicious spaghetti dinner (my mom's spaghetti was the best!), with Dad leaning back in his chair, rubbing his full stomach and Mom getting ready to jump up and do the dishes, I came out with it.

"Can I talk to you guys about something?" I asked.

"Well, sure son. What is it?" Dad set his chair back upright and Mom sat back down, looking concerned like moms do when their kid says they want to talk to them about something.

"My birthday is coming before too long, and I know exactly what I want this year. It's a big present and I know it's a lot of money, but I think I have a plan to get this particular thing without you guys having to spend all your money," I started. I think I was talking pretty fast because I wanted to get this out in the open and I was a little nervous about the whole discussion.

"Well, out with it, boy! What's the mystery present?" Dad was smiling, so that was a relief.

"I want a radiant red Schwinn Corvette bike with three speeds and a headlight. There's some other details too, but that's the basics," I spit out.

"I kind of thought you might be interested in those bikes. I saw you looking at them the last time we were at Sears – you remember, when I had to get a new crescent wrench and I was over in the Craftsman tools?" Dad said. "I saw you looking that bike over pretty good."

"They're the best bikes ever!" I said. I had a feeling Dad would understand because he had seen the bike, at least. He knew what I was talking about. Sure, another guy would know how important a good bike was.

"Well, Schwinn is a good quality bike, but are you sure you're big enough to handle that bike?" Dad asked. Mom had remained quiet all through the conversation so far, but she was clearly interested in the subject of my ability to handle the Corvette. I could see one of her eyebrows go up and that was not a good sign. If she had reservations, she could put the kibosh on any new birthday bike.

"Exactly how much are they, John?" Dad continued.

"$76.95." There was dead silence for a minute.

"Well, that *is* a pretty big birthday present," Dad finally said.

"That's why I wanted to talk to you," I quickly replied. "I would be willing to put in as much money as I have if you guys could help provide the rest of the money. I don't mind putting in my money for my own present because I know it's really a lot of money. What do you think about that idea?"

"How much money do you have, John?" Mom asked me.

"I have $18, but I could try to earn some more."

Mom and Dad looked at each other for a second, and you could almost see that some kind of message was passing between them, just through their eyes.

"Son, we'll have to talk about this a little bit. I know you'd like to have a new bike. You actually *need* a new bike. And what's more, you're a good son and we'd love to give you a new bike this year. Let us think about this a little bit, ok? We promise not to keep you waiting too long, but we do need to figure this out. Since Mom's going to have another baby, we have to just think ahead about finances and such. Not to blame our finances on the baby, but we just have to make sure we're paying attention to such things. Do you understand what I mean by all that, John?" Dad said in a quiet voice.

"Yes, I really do," I replied. "That's why I wanted to offer to help with the money part. I understand about money not really growing on trees." I smiled at them and they kind of chuckled. They knew I was hinting back to my plum tree money leaf trick.

"Ok, let us have a day or so. All right?" Mom smiled.

That was the best I was going to do for that day. At least it was all out in the open. I started thinking about some ways I could maybe earn some more money before D-day – March 13.

There weren't a lot of opportunities for odd jobs yet in my town. Winter was just coming to an end. There wasn't enough snow to shovel. No one was out picking up sticks or doing spring cleanup yet. In the winter time, no one asked you to run errands for them. I was at a little bit of a loss. Then I had an idea....

People in our town were always having garage sales. You could find some cool stuff in peoples' garage sales and usually get it at a bargain price. I got a basketball for twenty-five cents once. I also got an electric motor for my old bike for fifty cents from Mrs. Monroe's garage sale, but it didn't last too long. Sometimes people asked too much money for their junk, and I passed on all of that. Like I said, I didn't like to spend my money that much. I just tried to buy things I really wanted. But the whole garage sale concept gave me an idea of how I could earn some more money.

I had baseball cards galore. I had some good ones, too. I also had some old toys that would probably just get passed down to Jim unless I sold them at my own sale. It wouldn't really be a garage sale, but I thought I could figure out a way to sell stuff on lunch hour at school or something...maybe go over to different friends' houses and make a sale.

The very next day, I talked to the guys over lunch.

"Hey, I want to get rid of some stuff. I've got too much in my room and a bunch of toys I don't want anymore. Are any of you guys interested in any of my stuff? You know what all I have, right?"

"Just exactly what 'stuff' are you talking about?" Rusty asked. "Are you talking baseball cards or dolls?" Everyone started laughing at the thought of me having dolls. They knew I didn't have any dolls, for criminy sake. I gave him a look to let him know I didn't think he was too funny.

"Yes, you nerd - some of my baseball cards, some of my old toys that I don't use anymore. Maybe if one of your brothers or sisters would want some of that stuff..." I trailed off, waiting to see if I could stir up any interest.

"I'd definitely take a look at your baseball cards," Dave piped up.

"I'd look at your race cars, too," Rusty said. "It sort of depends on how much you're going to ask for these things, too, you know."

"I'd never rip you guys off," I told him. "I'm just getting rid of old things and trying to make a little money on it."

"What for?" Scotty asked.

"A new bike," I answered. "A Schwinn Corvette."

Scotty gave out a low whistle. "Wow. Those cost a lot. How are you going to get that much money?"

"I'm working out a deal with my mom and dad. I hope they will give some of the money as part of my birthday present. I told them I'd help put money in for a new bike because I know they cost a lot."

"So you're selling your stuff?" Rusty asked. "Gees, that's not even like a birthday present at all."

"What do you mean? Maybe your family has a lot of money, but mine doesn't," I said. "My mom and dad work hard and we're still not exactly rich. I don't feel bad about putting money in. I just know I can't get $76.95 together."

"My mom and dad don't have a lot of money either. I didn't mean anything by it," Rusty said. "It just kind of stinks that you have to try to give money for your own present."

"I don't care as long as I can get that bike," I answered. "It's a beauty – red, with white sidewalls and stainless steel rims. It has a headlight and a front carrier. That would be a good place to put my transistor when we go for bike rides."

All the guys nodded in agreement. Then Rusty spoke up again. "I think I could help you with this project," he said.

"How so?" I asked.

"I'm a good salesman. I have made the most money for our Scout troop three years in a row doing slave days. You know, where you do work for people – sell your services – become their slave for a day? I could help you get everything set up in your room, then we could get people to come to your house and buy the stuff."

"Uh, you're not exactly that good at organization," Scotty said. "Why don't you let ME help him get his room set up, and you go out and bring in the customers."

"Whatever works. John, you might be able to get enough money to buy the bike yourself," Rusty said.

"I doubt that. I don't have *that* much to sell, but what I do have is good, so at least maybe I can get some more money than I have."

"How much do you have saved up?" Dave asked.

"$18," I answered.

"Oh, brother. You have a LONG way to go," Rusty said. "A mighty long way. Don't worry, though. We've got a plan!"

Rusty was famous for making plans, but sometimes his plans kind of ran away from him. Like the time he planned to sneak into the girls' bathroom and steal all the toilet paper. His master plan kind of blew up in his face when he went in there and ran into Mrs. Miller. Yup, that one landed him in the principal's office.

That night at dinner, Mom and Dad gave me the news about the bike.

"Son, we had a chance to talk about it, and we can put together $40 for your new bike. That's still a long way from $76.95. Are you sure you wouldn't look at a less expensive model for this year?" Dad started.

I know they must have seen the disappointment in my eyes, but they had to understand how determined I was. "No, Dad. I appreciate the $40 because that's still a lot of money, but I really want that Corvette. I've never wanted anything so bad in my life."

"And that's something, coming from Silas Marner," my mom said to no one in particular.

I continued. "I've had a hand-me-down bike for a long time. I want a good bike now. I want a bike that will last me a long time. I don't think they'll ever make a bike that's better than the Corvette," I pleaded. "I just have to figure out how to earn the rest of the money."

"How much did you say you have?" Mom asked.

"$18, but I'll figure out a way to get the rest."

"John, think about it. How are you going to get another...?" Mom was figuring it up in her head. "Another $20, give or take?"

"I'm not sure yet, but I'm going to start working on it right away. Just promise me you won't go buy me a Huffy or something. It's not that Huffy bikes are bad...I just really want a Schwinn. And the amount I will need is exactly $18.95." I was more determined than ever.

I retreated to my room and began going through the toy box there. I had a million of those little green soldiers, so I put those in a pile together. I found a couple of old yo-yos that still worked. I put those to one side. I still had some old stuffed animals that some girls might like. I had them ever since I was a baby and sure didn't need those anymore! I had an Etch-a-Sketch and a Fred Flintstone car I didn't play with anymore. Who cared if Jim still played with them? They were mine to sell and I needed the money. I wondered how much I could get for all this...would it be enough? I couldn't charge too much for anything. My friends didn't have a lot of money either, so I had to get the right price on everything in order to sell it. I had seen people at garage sales dicker back and forth about prices and knew that would happen with the kids, too. I kept digging around and found my King Zor and Mr. Mercury. Out they came from the depths of the toy box. I also found my Satellite jumping shoes. They never worked that great. You were supposed to feel like you could jump over the moon or something, but that was all just to get you to buy them. My mom tried to tell me that you can't believe everything you see on television commercials, and after I got those jumping shoes, I knew what she meant.

Well, I had a good start on my sale, anyway. I went to bed that evening thinking about how much money I might be able to make on my stuff.

After school the next day, I started going through baseball cards. This was a little trickier. After my experience with the valentine box, I knew I better not sell any of my good cards, but I had plenty of cards that were less-famous players and I thought I still might be able to make a little money off of those. I pulled out about twenty cards of major league players who were okay guys but who weren't really the stars of the game...I crossed my fingers they would sell. Scotty came over right before dinner and helped me get things set up in my room. We organized anything that was for sale on my bookshelf and on the little table next to my bed. We also set some toys up on top of the toy box.

Rusty was waiting for me up at the bus stop the next morning. He looked pretty excited.

"Well, I've already got seven kids who want to come over to see what you've got for sale. Can we get them there tonight?"

"Tonight! Holy smokes, I have to check with my mom about that."

"What if we did it right after school? She doesn't get home right away, does she? You could probably have a lot of stuff gone by the time she even gets home from work. Heck, it could all be over before she even knows it!" You would have thought he was getting a cut.

"Well..." I hesitated, "We're not really supposed to have anyone over before Mom and Dad get home from work. We're supposed to be working on homework and junk like that."

"Crud all Tuesday!" Rusty exclaimed. "Do you want that bike or not?"

"Sure I do. I just don't want to get in trouble and maybe make my parents say I can't have it even if I do have the money." I knew my parents pretty well when it came to how they thought up punishments.

"I guarantee you. We'll have this thing wrapped up and all the kids back out of there before your mom and dad ever know a thing about it." Rusty seemed awfully confident, but my birthday was only a week or so away. There really was no time to waste. I knew he was right.

"Ok. You get them rounded up, but they *have* to be there by four o'clock and they have to all be gone by that next half hour. My mom can show up about any time after that, so that's got to be the cut-off. One half hour."

"No problem. I'll keep everything rolling. All you'll have to do is count your money." Rusty was nodding his head and you could see the wheels turning in his brain. Rusty was a schemer. I could see him becoming a big-time business genius when he grew up.

When I got off the bus from school, I ran home. I had to get the house open and get myself settled in for the big sale. At about quarter till four, the doorbell rang. On the front step was Rusty, followed by a line of kids. There were way more than seven. I started to feel a little panicked.

"Hey, let us in. We've got customers waiting," Rusty commanded.

I stepped back from the doorway and let him in. He turned in the doorway and announced, "Only five kids at a time. The rest of you will have to wait till those five come out. Each group will have ten minutes to shop and make a decision. If you don't find anything you want in that ten minutes, you leave empty handed. You won't want to do that because there's some great stuff in here." Rusty was in charge.

With that, the first five kids in line stepped into the house and I showed them to the bedroom. My bedroom wasn't too big, so it was pretty crowded in there, but the potential buyers could mill around a little and look things over. It really didn't take too long, to be honest. Everyone in the first group found something they wanted. I had tried to be fair in putting prices on stuff, and no one argued with me about paying. I made $7.50 with the first group. Only $11.45 to go.

The next group came in. There were some little kids and some older kids in the second group. The little kids bought all the green soldiers and the older kids bought some baseball cards. I'm sure glad my dad wasn't there to see it because he still probably would have had a cow over me selling baseball cards. Anyway, the second group brought in another $5.75. Now I was down to only $5.70 that I needed to make.

The third group came in and the Etch-a-Sketch got sold, the Fred Flintstone car got sold, and Mr. Mercury got sold. I really didn't have that much left, and I made $3.75. I was short by $1.95.

"Are there any other kids out there?" I asked Rusty.

"I don't think so. I think that was it. How did you do?" Rusty responded.

"I didn't make it." I looked down at the money I had in my little money box. I couldn't believe I was going to be short by only

$1.95. I just didn't feel like I could ask my mom and dad for one more cent. I had told them I'd get the rest of the money.

Just then we heard a knock at the door. It was an insistent knock, like an impatient person. I opened the front door and there stood Debbie Carruthers.

"Do you still have anything for sale?" she asked. No matter what she said, Debbie Carruthers always sounded like she was looking down on you.

"Well, there's not much you'd be interested in, I don't think," I told her but she kind of pushed past me.

"I'd like to decide that for myself," and she flounced into my room.

"You've only got a couple of minutes...." I trailed after her. Rusty and I watched as she surveyed the now greatly minimized contents of my room. She picked up this and that, turned things over in her hand and carefully scrutinized all the toys that were left. Then something on my bookshelf caught her eye. On the third shelf sat my Yogi Bear and Booboo stuffed animals. Not that! Mom had given those to me to remind me of how Dad sometimes called me BooBoo because of being born on Friday the 13th. After she bought them, Dad had started talking like Yogi Bear sometimes. He could do a pretty good imitation of Yogi saying, "Here's to you, too, BooBoo." Mom would definitely miss those if they were gone.

I quickly picked up a teddy bear that was lying there. It only had one eye, and my mom had called it "Pirate" and made an eye patch for it when I was a couple of years younger. "What about this?" I said to Debbie.

She glanced over but didn't even really look too long. She was focused on Yogi and BooBoo.

"How much for these?" she asked.

"Those aren't really for sale," I answered.

Rusty elbowed me in the ribs. I could tell by the look on his face he thought I was an idiot.

"Well, that's the only thing I'm really interested in," Debbie said. "I would pay you top dollar for them."

"What's 'top dollar' mean?" I asked.

"That means you just tell me how much and I'll pay it to you," Debbie said.

"They're $2," Rusty barged in.

"Sold!" Debbie said, pulling out exactly two crisp one dollar bills. She practically threw them at me, yanked Yogi and BooBoo off the shelf and flounced back out of my room exactly the way she had flounced in.

"We did it!" Rusty shouted.

"Yeah, we did it," I answered, but I didn't feel too good about Yogi and BooBoo. I knew Mom would be hurt that they had been sold like someone's old junk.

Rusty went home, and five minutes hadn't passed before my mom got home from work. I stayed in my room, hoping she wouldn't come talk to me for a little bit. I needed time to process what had just happened. I had sold a lot of my childhood, but I had gotten enough money to get my new bike.

It didn't make any difference what I was hoping about Mom because she was there in no time flat.

"Don't tell me you're cleaning your room, John!" She seemed surprised, so I guess she hadn't seen any of the kids carrying their loot home while she was driving through town.

"Yeah, I had a lot of old stuff to get rid of. My room looks a lot better, don't you think?"

"It surely does. This is about the least cluttered I've seen it in some time. She looked all around the room, her eyes settling on the book shelf. She didn't say anything, but she paused for a minute and I knew by the look on her face that she was mulling something over.

Dad got home from work and while we were at the dinner table he asked me, "John, how are you doing on raising the rest of the money for your bike?"

"Well, actually, I've got it."

Mom and Dad both looked up, surprised. Dad even dropped his fork on his plate with a loud clink. "What do you mean you've already got it?" he asked.

"Yeah, I've actually got it."

Mom and Dad looked at each other and back at me. "How exactly did you get the money?" Dad asked.

"By selling some of my old toys to some of the kids from school. I don't need as many toys now as I used to think I needed, so I decided to get rid of some stuff."

"Like what?" Dad said.

"Well, you know, little green soldiers, my Etch-a-Sketch...."

"Golly," Mom said. "Jim could have used some of that stuff."

"Well, honey, they were John's belongings, though, and if he wanted to use it to make money for his bike, well, that's his decision, really." Dad was supporting me. He was probably glad he didn't have to get rid of all that junk at some point.

"You made enough to pay for the rest of the bike?" Dad asked.

"Yes sir. With my $18 and your $40, that's $58. I needed to get $18.95 and I ended up with $18.95. I got exactly what I needed."

"Did you remember taxes?" asked Dad.

I hadn't even thought about taxes because I didn't really know what that meant. I just sat there wondering how much more money I needed to take care of this tax business.

Dad must have noticed that I was a little unnerved about the taxes. "Never you mind, John. I'll take care of the taxes," he said. "You've worked hard and given up your own toys to get this money...I'll take care of the taxes."

"Thanks Dad," I said. Gees, what in the heck else could I need to round up before I could get my hands on that beautiful new bike? I raised my glass of milk like I was giving him a toast and said, "Here's to you, Dad."

"Here's to you too, BooBoo," he answered. My mom immediately shot me a glance.

"Say...." She didn't get to finish before my dad butted in, but she had a look on her face that let me know she had figured it all out.

"What do you say we run over to Sears and pick up that bike right now? You can have it early, just in case there are some nice days coming up this spring."

I wanted to get out of there before Mom could start drilling me over the missing stuffed animals. "Sure!" I said. "This will be the best birthday ever!" I hoped my enthusiasm would keep her from asking the question I knew she wanted to ask.

The bike was everything I knew it would be. I was happier than I could ever remember being. Even Dad said it was a great bike. "I can understand why you'd want this, John," he said.

Mom looked at my new bike when we got home. She smiled and said it was nice, but she didn't say too much more. I knew what was on her mind.

She came into my room right at bedtime and sat on the edge of my bed.

"John, where's Yogi and BooBoo? Did you sell them?" she asked.

"Yes, Mom. I did." I didn't know what else to say right at that point.

"Did you have to sell them?" She sounded sad.

"Mom, those toys were the final toys I sold. That sale put me at $18.95. I needed to sell them for the final couple of dollars."

Mom sat on the bed beside me for a minute before she spoke.

"Son, I wish Dad and I had enough money to have bought the bike outright for you, but you understand why we couldn't do that, right?" I shook my head and she continued.

"Thank you for being such an understanding son about that. Jim's kind of little to understand about money yet, but you are very smart and you're observant and wise beyond your years in some things." I didn't know what all she meant by that, but it sounded like a compliment.

"John, your childhood is flying by. You didn't need Yogi and BooBoo anymore, did you? Sometimes I want you to still be little like Jim, and you're not. You're growing up too fast for me, but I promise not to try to keep you little forever." She smiled. "I'm glad about your bike, I really am, and I'm proud of you for having the ingenuity to earn that money. You're a good boy, John, and I love you very much. I feel lucky to be your mom."

Mom felt lucky to be my mom? That was amazing to me. "Mom, I'm the one who's lucky," I said.

She gave me a little hug and kissed me on the forehead. "Get some sleep. I'm sure after school tomorrow you're going to want to ride that bike, even if it's cold." She laughed and stood up. "Say your prayers, ok?" She left the room.

I was glad Mom understood about the bike, and I was glad she thought she was lucky she was my mom. I knew that her feelings weren't hurt and that she would still think of me as her little BooBoo. Moms are just like that.

7 THE HONOR SYSTEM

Richard Rader was a friend of my dad and he went to the same church as us...the Evangelical United Brethren church. He was a farmer and had a very big farm outside of town. I liked going to his farm. I always thought the equipment farmers used was interesting. I wanted to drive a tractor in the worst way, but I knew my mom would have a cow if I ever did.

We always called Richard Rader "Mr. Rader." That's how we were supposed to address adults unless they told us it was ok to call them by their first name. Mr. Rader never really said anything about calling him "Richard" so I figured I better stick with what my mom and dad told us to do. Anyway, Mr. Rader had chickens on his farm, and those chickens could lay the eggs! Holy smokes! I never saw so many eggs in my life as when I went to Mr. Rader's farm.

Chickens are kind of goofy birds. I didn't really know too much about them because we never had any chickens at our house. I learned a lot about chickens from Mr. Rader in 1963. I also learned a lot about how people can be even goofier than chickens.

Mr. Rader had a little playhouse in the yard that his daughter had used when she was a kid. After she got older, she didn't want to play in there anymore, so Mr. Rader turned it into an egg house. Here's how it worked...the egg house was a place where people could just go in, put some money in a lockbox, and then take eggs out of a refrigerator he had put in there. You could get fresh eggs on the honor system. Mr. Rader was never in that playhouse to collect the money. He just left the door open and people could go in, all on their own, and take home fresh eggs for their family. My mom used to do that all the time. I kind of liked going in that little playhouse with her for some reason. We never did anything but pick up eggs. Drop fifty cents in the box, take a dozen eggs, and head for home. That was the whole trip in a nutshell.

One day when we were picking up some eggs, Mr. Rader came over to talk to Mom. We had just gotten out of the car when he came out of his house.

"Well good afternoon! How are you folks doing on this fine day?" Mr. Rader greeted us the same way every time he saw us.

"We're good, Richard," my mom said. She was allowed to call him Richard, of course. "I needed to stop by because I've got to bake a cake for a family reunion this weekend and I'm completely out of eggs." Now I have to tell you, I was very excited to hear that my mom was baking a cake because no one, and I mean no one, could bake a cake like my mom – light, tender, moist and tasty. Cake baking was good news.

"Well, if it's eggs you need, I've got plenty." Mr. Rader opened the door to the playhouse and ushered us in, even though it was so small and the refrigerator took up so much room that all three of us could hardly fit in there. When my mom opened the refrigerator door, I had to back out of there and stand on the step to the playhouse, it was that small. I don't know how any kids ever played house in there.

Inside the refrigerator there were about a hundred boxes of eggs. That's when I learned how many eggs chickens could lay.

"Mr. Rader, how many chickens do you have here?" I asked him.

He took off his hat and scratched his head for a second, looking up at the ceiling like he might see the answer up there. "I've got about one hundred hens and eight roosters or so I believe..."

"Can I go see them?" I wanted to know more about these birds...where did they live? What did they eat? How in the heck did he get all those eggs picked up?

"Son, we've got to get home and I'm sure Mr. Rader has plenty to do today, too," my mom said. She had that look in her eyes that told me not to beg or make a fuss about it.

"Well, suppose you come back on a day when you don't have so much to do and I have my work caught up a little bit?" Mr. Rader suggested. "Then I can show you all around the farm, teach you about the chickens, and maybe take you on a tractor ride. Would you like that?"

"Heck yes!" I must have nearly shouted. I was a little worried about him mentioning the tractor ride because I figured Mom would be in a tizzy about that. In fact, she didn't say anything about it on the way home, so I knew she was already stewing over it. She had been raised on a farm, so she already knew how fun tractors were. I was hoping she wouldn't forbid me from getting on Mr. Rader's tractor.

A couple of Sundays later, Mr. Rader was shaking Dad's hand after church, so I decided to ask if I could come over to his farm pretty soon.

"Mr. Rader, are you caught up on your farm work?" I asked.

He laughed really loud when I said that, and my dad smiled at me. "Son, farm work is never really caught up."

Mr. Rader spoke up though, and he said, "I know you've been wanting to come over and see a little more of the chickens. What about maybe coming over next Saturday? We'll make a day of it. You can help me gather eggs if you want to."

"Gees that would be great!" I said. Of course, I had no idea what gathering eggs would be like, but I thought it would be fun to spend a day at Mr. Rader's farm.

The very next Saturday, I was awake at dawn. I was so excited about working on the farm that I couldn't sleep anymore. My dad was up early, too, but he always got up early. It wasn't because he was excited or anything. It was just his way.

"Are you ready to be a farmhand today?" Dad asked.

"You bet! This is almost as good as Christmas. I'm going to get to take a ride on Mr. Rader's tractor, too."

"Uh, you might not want to mention that to your mother this morning," Dad warned. "She saw a pretty bad accident on a neighbor's farm when she was a teenager, and she's been kind of scared about farm equipment ever since then."

"What kind of accident?" I wanted to know more about this revelation.

"Well, one of her neighbor's kids was riding on the tractor with his dad, but he lost his balance somehow and fell off the tractor. He got his arm run over by the tiller, and his arm was pretty cut up, left with a lot of scars, but he was kind of lucky that his arm didn't have to be amputated."

I knew what amputation was because I had seen war movies on television that showed guys having amputations after getting hit by a grenade. The Army guys would be yelling, "Don't let them take my leg, Sarge, don't let them take my leg!" Amputations were scary to think about but I really didn't think I would lose my balance, and if I did, I just knew Mr. Rader would not run over me.

"I'm sure I'll be fine, Dad, but I won't say anything, and I promise not to do anything dumb on the tractor."

"I trust you to behave yourself," Dad said with a smile.

We had a little breakfast, I got washed up and dressed, and Dad took me over to Mr. Rader's place. Mr. Rader was already outside doing some work, and we met him at the door to his barn.

"Well sir, are you ready for some hard work on this fine day?" Mr. Rader said. He always, *always* called it a 'fine day' no matter what.

"I guess I am. I don't really know much about farms, but I'll try to be a good helper if you just tell me what to do."

Dad and Mr. Rader made an agreement about what time I was to be picked up, and Dad took off. It was up to me to listen, learn, and show what a good worker I could be. I was determined.

The first thing we did was just walk to the back yard and look at the apple trees growing there.

"I have to keep an eye on these trees to make sure the bugs aren't eating them up. Otherwise, we'd have no apples in the fall. Sometimes I have to spray the trees to keep the bugs away from my apples. I also have to prune these trees sometimes so that they produce more apples. It might sound funny, but pruning off old branches and so forth can help the tree produce more fruit." He told me he'd show me what he used to prune the trees with when we got to the barn. For now, the only thing I saw in the apple trees were a few small flowers barely hanging on and a couple of robins.

Next, we walked out into the wheat field. Mr. Rader had field full of winter wheat, but the plants were not ready to be harvested quite yet.

"You have to plant about a million seeds per acre of land to get this kind of crop," Mr. Rader told me, "and you can't plant it too deep."

A million seeds. I couldn't even imagine what that would look like. I was learning all kinds of stuff about farming.

We walked along the back fence row at the end of the wheat field. That fence was supposed to help keep out unwanted little animals, but I don't know if it really did the trick.

"Sometimes I have to make some repairs to the fence because the wind knocks it around a little, or sometimes a deer will wander through here and mess it up." I was really wishing we'd see a deer, but Mr. Rader said the only time he saw them out in the field was around sundown.

Finally, we got to the chicken coops. We were a little behind in gathering eggs, but Mr. Rader got me my own bucket and he showed me what to do and we got right to it. It wasn't really as much fun as I had imagined, and of course, you had to be really careful so you didn't break any eggs. With 100 chickens running around, I thought they might get mad and try to attack you when you took their eggs away, but the chickens didn't seem to care that much. They just walked around, scratching at the ground and making those little clucking sounds that chickens make. That is, except for the roosters. They sort of strutted around like they were kings. A couple of times I heard them do their "cockadoodle doo" sound, but mostly they just seemed to be watching the hens.

We had to clean the eggs up and put them in egg boxes, then we carted them in a wagon up to the playhouse refrigerator. "More eggs for more customers," Mr. Rader said.

We took a little break for a snack. We sat down at a picnic table under a big maple tree, and Mrs. Rader brought out some cookies she had just made along with milk for our snack. Mr. Rader said it was getting too warm for coffee, so he drank milk, too.

"How are you boys doing?" Mrs. Rader asked.

"I am having a lot of fun," I answered. "I never knew so much about being a farmer."

"Well, there's plenty more to go," Mr. Rader said with his crooked smile. "We better get back to work pretty soon – drink up, John."

We walked out to the barn. First Mr. Rader had to sharpen some tools that he used for cutting down tall weeds and stuff like that. He told me that one time he had gotten into some poison ivy while he was cutting down weeds and that he had an itchy rash for over a week. That definitely did not sound like a fun part of farming.

"Shovels, hoes, and scythes must be sharp or you'll wear yourself out just trying to use them. Farming is hard enough work as it is, but if you have dull tools it's ten times harder. There's a lot of equipment maintenance that farmers have to do."

After working on his tools, Mr. Rader started the tractor up. "Farm equipment like my tractor must be maintained on a regular basis or it doesn't work right either." He let the tractor run for a little bit and talked to me about how tractors had changed farming, making it easier for farmers to have larger farms and grow more crops. I could tell he really knew a lot about his work, and I was learning a lot about it too. Then he said, "Let's go." I got up on the tractor with his help and we took off. We went out of the barn onto the driveway to his house and just rode around a couple of times. It wasn't long, but it was long enough for me to understand how loud tractors are when you're sitting on top of them. It was fun, but I knew I'd never be a farmer when I grew up. It was just an awful lot of work.

By the time we got done with the tractor ride, Dad was pulling into the driveway. I ran out to meet him and Mr. Rader followed.

"What did you learn, son?" Dad asked.

"I can't even tell you everything I learned! I learned about apple trees and winter wheat. I learned about taking care of fences and tools. And I got to ride the tractor. Oh, and we also had some cookies."

Dad laughed and said, "I suppose it's time to get you out of Richard's hair." He shook hands with Mr. Rader and said, "Thanks, Richard. I'm sure he had a remarkable morning."

Mr. Rader smiled and said, "He's welcome here anytime. I can always use a good worker to help out with gathering eggs."

"I promise I'll come back and help you again when I don't have school, which is only on Saturdays and Sundays...that is, unless Mom would let me skip."

Mr. Rader laughed pretty hard. "I don't think you want to be doing any of that, now. You just come over when you want to. I'll always be glad to see you."

We went home, and I don't mind telling you, I was kind of tired. I know I went to bed early that night, much to my mom and dad's surprise.

I went back to Mr. Rader's farm several times over the next couple of months to help him with the eggs and get some of Mrs. Rader's cookies, but one Saturday, when dad pulled into the driveway, we saw Mr. Rader out by the playhouse with a hose. He was spraying down the playhouse. I wondered why he was washing the playhouse till I got out of the car. Dad got out with me and walked over to see that there were dried eggs splattered all over the outside of the playhouse.

"What in the world, Richard..." my dad started.

Mr. Rader looked up and said, "Well, we might be done with the honor system."

Dad and I just looked at him, so he continued.

"Apparently last night someone came in and decided to have a little egg-throwing party. Take a look for yourself."

I went into the playhouse. Dad just stayed on the step and looked in after me. There were broken eggs all over the place in there. They were pretty well dried-up, and it was a mess, a total mess. The refrigerator door was closed, but when I opened it up, there were only a few broken eggs lying in the bottom, and egg boxes just thrown back in there. I was crunching egg shells with every step I took, so I went back outside.

"John, I won't really be able to have you over today, I don't suppose. I'm going to have to get this mess cleaned up before it gets so hardened it's like cement. Then I'm going to have to get all my regular work done."

I looked up at Dad, and he looked back at me. I think he knew what I was thinking.

"We can help you get this cleaned up, Mr. Rader, so then you can do all your regular work."

Dad spoke up, too. "You bet, Richard. We can't leave you with this mess on your hands."

Mr. Rader turned off the hose for a minute and shook his head. "I can't ask you two to do that...."

We didn't listen. We just rolled up our sleeves and Dad said, "If it's ok, I'll run in the house and just call my wife and let her know I'm going to be here for a little while."

Mr. Rader nodded, and I ran out to the barn where the buckets and brooms were and brought back some stuff to help clean up with. I've never seen such a mess in my life. We couldn't leave him there with all that...hundreds and hundreds of broken eggs. When you're working away cleaning up that kind of mess, you think a lot about why someone would do that and you also think about who....

I had a feeling I knew who did it, but I didn't say anything. There was a teenager in our town, Big Jake Parker. He was mean as anything. He was even mean to little kids, clunking them on the head with his class ring or taking their lunch boxes to steal any treats he could find in them. He was a senior in high school, but I don't think he did too well, grade-wise. He was always getting kicked off the bus for being mean and starting trouble. It had to be him.

It was a full day's work getting all the egg mess cleaned up. I know Mr. Rader appreciated the help. Mrs. Rader brought out some cookies again, but I noticed her eyes were red, like she had been crying.

I learned a lot from working with Mr. Rader, but one of the most important things I learned about is that sometimes farm animals are smarter than humans. You didn't see farm animals trying to hurt or be mean to each other.

Dad and I were pretty tired when we got home that day. Dad told Mom and Jim about the egg mess while we were having dinner.

"Big Jake Parker," Jim leaned over and whispered to me.

"My money's on him," I whispered back.

The next day, at church, people were crowding all around Mr. and Mrs. Rader. I didn't get to talk to him, but when he saw me, Mr. Rader winked, and I gave him a wave. He was such a hard worker. I felt bad for him.

After that, the egg house was closed. There was no more honor system for egg customers because Mr. Rader started taking his eggs somewhere else to sell them. I guess you just have to realize it's pretty hard to have an honor system if there's no honor.

8 SMORGASBORD

TAKE ALL YOU CAN EAT,
BUT EAT ALL YOU TAKE!

The words were stenciled with black magic marker on banners and hung on the wall right behind the serving tables. If you had a big appetite, you could do some damage, but the sign was my mom's way of reminding everyone that there were starving children in Africa.

I had never heard of a smorgasbord until my dad got involved with the town council. He was an elected councilman, and I was proud of him for that. What I didn't know about him being a councilman was how much our family would be involved in raising money so that our town could buy land for a park. That's where the smorgasbord came in....

One night my dad came home from a council meeting. I was watching "My Favorite Martian" on TV, and I wasn't paying a lot of attention to what he and Mom were talking about at first, but Mom's voice got a little louder, so I sort of *had* to pay more attention because she was drowning out the TV.

"You know that most of the work to be done for this will be done by the women of this town! I already work full time and have all the kids' activities as well as being pregnant and having this household to deal with. How am I supposed to add on this project?" I could hear mom questioning.

"Honey, I know you want this park for the kids as badly as I do. Yes, it's definitely a lot of work, but I'll help you anyway I can. I know all the men will be doing their best to help with this project. We know it can't all be heaped on our wives. The men can help cook the meat for this thing – we're all pretty good at the grill."

"Well, it's too bad there are no women on the town council or you would likely have realized that it is a huge burden for every female in the community."

Back and forth they went like that. I didn't think Mom or Dad were mad, but I could tell there was some tension between them over whatever this issue was. The discussion continued at a quieter volume, and I went back to Uncle Martin and Tim O'Hara and the crazy situation they had gotten into. "My Favorite Martian" was one of the best shows on TV.

The next evening at supper time, Mom and Dad started talking about "the project" again, but Jim and me were sitting right there with them, so we got to hear what it was all about.

"John, you kids need a nice park to play ball in and so forth. The town would like to buy the land around the gravel pit from Harold Benson, but we don't have enough money."

"Can't you just write a check?" Jim asked.

My dad laughed pretty hard about that. "Sonny Jim, you can't write a check until there's money in the bank unless you want to spend time in the pokey," Dad said. Jim frowned and started shaking his head "no" to that one.

"We need a park!" I said. "We have to play tap football in the church back yard, and we don't have any good space at all to play baseball," I contributed. "Do you think we could have a swimming pool like they have in Mt. Cory?" The thought of a pool was very appealing to me. Our town was always hot as heck in the summer time.

"I doubt we'll ever have a pool," Dad said. "There's a lot of expense in having a pool. Our town is too little to support that."

I didn't know exactly what he meant by that, but I figured it meant we would still be going to Mt. Cory to swim. Mt. Cory already had a nice park, and we went there many times for baseball games, especially tournaments, and their pool was tops. They had diving boards – both low and high – and they had a slide. We had so much fun over there, but it always depended on whether some parent had time to take us the eight mile drive. I was sure wishing we could have a pool within walking distance.

"So how are we going to get the money for our own park?" I asked.

"We're *all* going to be working very hard," Mom said, "and I want to emphasize the ALL. The town council in its infinite wisdom has decided that a smorgasbord will raise enough money to buy Harold Benson's land."

"Now honey…" my dad started.

"No, they need to know what we're getting into," Mom said. "Boys, your dad and I want you to understand something. We are willing to work very hard to help get this land for the park, but I have decided that it's going to be a family affair. If Dad and I are willing to work hard in order for you kids to have a nice place to play, you have to be willing to work hard, too."

"I'm willing, Mom," I said. "I can do a lot of stuff, but what is a smorgasbord? I never heard of that word."

"A smorgasbord is a huge feast where people pay a certain amount of money and then they eat till they are full. For instance, we might charge a man five dollars to come in to the smorgasbord. He might be pretty hungry and he can fill up his plate with food as many times as he wants to."

"So it's sort of like a restaurant?" I asked.

"Not exactly, John," Dad answered. "People in the community will have to provide the food – they'll donate the food as well as their time – and we'll have to hope and pray people show up to buy that food. That's how we'll make the money we need for the park."

I still didn't exactly understand this thing, but I knew that I wanted to help my mom and dad with it because it meant we would have a good place to play finally.

For a few weeks, we didn't hear any more about the smorgasbord. I was beginning to think everyone had forgotten about it until Mom called a family meeting.

"Ok boys…the ladies in town have a got a plan together for the smorgasbord, and I want to talk to you about it because you both will be involved on the evening we actually do this thing. All of us ladies will be making different dishes to bring to the high school – that's where we're going to have it – in the gym. Dad and some of the other councilmen have been asking businesses to donate things like Styrofoam plates, napkins, plastic silverware, and meat. The men will cook the meat, the ladies will help serve the other food, everyone will have to help with clean-up, and that's where you kids come in. When people eat their food and leave, you will be responsible for picking up any trash left behind and cleaning off the tables. Do you understand me? Do you think you can do that?"

Jim and I said "yes" at exactly the same time. Jim wanted swings and a slide at the park while I was thinking about baseball diamonds and also still dreaming of a pool. Both of us would do anything to have a nice park to play in.

"Good! I'm very proud of you boys. I think all the children who are old enough to help are going to be working alongside you, so you won't be alone. You know, many hands make light work."

Jim looked a little puzzled so I explained to him, "If a lot of people are doing the work, that means that it gets done easier." Jim just nodded his head. I guess he figured it made sense.

The smorgasbord was going to be on a Saturday evening. My mom and dad both were making a lot of phone calls to get people to bring different kinds of food up to the school. My mom said to me that she was sure tired of sitting on the phone in the evenings. I could understand that. It seemed like she may as well just glue the receiver to her ear.

As Smorgasbord Saturday got close, my mom started making cookies, cakes, and pies. Dessert was her specialty, and she had all kinds of good recipes. For the cookies she made chocolate chip, oatmeal raisin, molasses, snickerdoodles, frosted sugar, and ranger cookies. For the pies she made apple, peach (which was my favorite), black raspberry, cherry, coconut cream, sugar cream, pecan, and butterscotch. For the cakes she made chocolate, yellow, spice, German chocolate, red velvet, and orange. Our house smelled good for three days straight. She also made some salad dressing for the salads. I had never seen her make salad dressing before; she always bought that, but she said it would be less expensive for the committee to make it, so she wanted to help with that, too. My mom worked so hard. She told me she took a few vacation days from working at the hospital so she could help with the smorgasbord. It didn't seem like very much of a vacation to me.

On Smorgasbord Saturday, as Jim and I had taken to calling it, we slept in a little bit. Mom didn't wake us up until later than usual, "Because," she said, "You'll need a lot of energy for tonight."

Jim and I were eating some Cheerios when a horrible thought hit me.

"Mom, what about guys like Mr. Sorensen, who can eat a whole lot of food? Did you guys think about that? He can eat two or three plates full of food! I've seen him do it at Scout banquet. He could wipe out the smorgasbord."

Mom laughed and said, "Yes, John, we've thought about that. We have to just take our chances. Some people will come and take advantage of the price and the homemade food, but most people really will just take a normal amount. They understand that we're trying to raise money, so they won't be piggy about it."

I wasn't totally convinced. I had seen Mr. Sorensen in action.

Dad took Jim and I up to the high school kind of early. We had to help Dad get a few things ready. Dad and the other men from town were getting the grills set up and all the utensils and so forth that they would need. They had these forks with real long handles on them so they wouldn't get burned while they were grilling. I had never seen big grills like the ones they had for this smorgasbord. About five guys could probably stand at one grill and not be crowded. Dad asked Jim and I to help make sure there were a certain number of chairs at each long table in the gym and to make sure that there were enough trash cans around. By the time we got done, Mom was coming in the big glass gymnasium doors with a couple of pies. I ran out to help her because I knew she had way more than that to bring in, and I wanted to do everything I could to help her because of the baby and all. I had seen how hard she had worked the last few days. When we got all the pies, cakes, cookies and salad dressing carted in, Mom went out to the grill area to talk to Dad.

"I'm going to take the boys home to clean up," she said to Dad. "I'll feed them before we come back. You should stop back home and have a little lunch, too, honey."

"I'll be there in a little bit," he answered. Then he stopped, looked at Mom real hard, grabbed her by the shoulders and kissed her right on her lips. "You've worked so hard, darling. I'm proud of you," he said.

Mom just smiled and winked at him. "You'll pay me back by taking me out to dinner," she said. "I don't think I want to do any cooking for a couple of days."

"Deal!" Dad replied. "We'll go to The Dark Horse and get a steak."

Personally, I would rather have gone to Wilson's and gotten a hamburger and a frosted.

After we had lunch, Jim and I fell asleep for a little bit. It had been a busy morning. I don't know exactly what time it was when Mom came and woke us up.

"Boys, it's time to wake up and get cleaned up a little bit because it won't be too long before it's time to go."

I washed my face and brushed my teeth. I put on a clean shirt after I combed my hair. Jim did the same. We wanted to look good for our jobs. We were hoping that if people saw how good we looked and how hard we were working, they would know they were supporting a good cause. Maybe they would restrain themselves on the food. Especially Mr. Sorensen.

The school parking lot was still pretty empty when we got there. At first when I saw how empty it was I was afraid that meant no one was coming, and after all the work my Mom had done.... No customers would have been terrible. But I had nothing to worry about because when the smorgasbord started, I found out just how full the parking lot could get. I also found out how tired your legs can get, but that came later of course.

The men were already grilling meat. It was mostly chicken, but I did see some hamburgers, hotdogs, and other meat, too – I guess it was steak, but I didn't know for sure. Mom, Jim and I went into the school, and it was like a beehive in the cafeteria kitchen where people were making huge pots of green beans and corn and mashed potatoes. The oven was going, too, and the kitchen was really hot. Someone said they were making some ham and beef roasts in the oven.

Mom asked me if I thought I could set up a chair and card table by the door so that as people came in, the person taking their money would have a place to sit. I made Jim come with me. I knew he would be my responsibility because before too long, my mom would be busy as all get-out.

When Jim and I went out into the gym, we saw food covering all the long tables up front. End to end, those tables were completely covered in food. Each dish had a spoon sticking out of it. There were a few ladies behind the tables talking. They had aprons on and they were pointing at different dishes on the table talking about who had made what and what was still in the kitchen to bring out and so on. I had never seen so much food in my entire life, and I wanted to be the first person through the line, but I knew I had work to do. Jim and I set up the card table. It was kind of hard to do because it was old and the legs were kind of stiff, but we got it done. There was one folding chair for the table, and I got that set up. The smorgasbord was ready to begin.

At 5:20, I noticed some people outside the glass gymnasium doors. They were standing in a line, smiling and talking to each other, shaking hands and such. The men who were outside grilling started bringing in big pans full of meat, and more ladies came out in aprons and stood behind the tables, ready to serve the delicious-looking food that was in all those dishes. At 5:25, I was horrified to see food's nemesis, Mr. Sorensen. He walked right up to the front of the line and stood next to the brown-haired lady who was first in line. They kissed, and I figured it must be *Mrs*. Sorensen. If she could eat as much as he could, we were in trouble. She was pretty small compared to him, so I was hoping we were safe with her.

One of the adults, Mrs. Donnell, was going to be the money taker. At 5:30, she looked around the gym and called out, "Ok everyone, HERE WE GO!" in a real loud voice. Then she walked over and unlocked the gym door. She barely made it back to her seat before the Sorensen's were at the table.

"That will be $3 each, please," Mrs. Donnell said.

"Here's a ten – keep the change," Mr. Sorensen said.

"Thank you so much!" Mrs. Donnell exclaimed. She clearly didn't have any idea what was about to happen at the food tables. The line of people kept pressing up to the money table, and I backed away to a spot behind the basketball bleachers, which were folded up to make room for all the tables.

I didn't have any work to do right then because no one had been eating yet, so I stayed out of sight and tried to keep an eye on Mr. Sorensen. Jim was standing by me, and we both watched in amazement as Mr. Sorensen got spoonful after spoonful of food. He had ham, mashed potatoes, baked beans, corn, applesauce, three-bean salad, regular salad, potato salad and homemade bread. I thought his Styrofoam plate would break. But even more amazing, Mrs. Sorensen had all the same things! They walked to a table, sat down and started eating. By this time, a lot of other people were moving along the food table, filling up their plates. At this rate, we'd never be able to feed all the people that were in line. But miraculously, as one food dish emptied, another appeared from the depths of the cafeteria kitchen. Ladies would take one dish off the serving table and replace it with another dish of some piping hot food. Steam was drifting up from the new dishes. The gymnasium was getting noisy as people sat down with friends and started talking with each other. There was laughter from the corner where Mr. and Mrs. Sorensen sat. Little kids were being led, prodded, and practically drug through the food line. You could hear them saying "I don't like that!" or "I want a hotdog!" After a little while, a few people started getting up, and I went out to clean up where they had been sitting.

I approached the far corner of the gym with Jim in tow. As I got closer, I could see that Mr. Sorensen was just about finished with his plate. Several other people in that area were done, so I started cleaning up where they had been sitting. Mr. Sorensen, head down shoveling in some potato salad, peeked at me out of the corner of his eye. "Leave their forks, son. They just went for seconds," he said.

My prediction was coming true. The people were going to polish off all the food; people were still waiting in line and these early birds were going to eat every bit of the food.

I threw away the plates and plastic silverware I had accumulated and took Jim by the hand. "We have to find Mom." We scrambled back to the kitchen where Mom was putting the finishing touches on some carrots. They looked good.

"Mom, just what I thought. Mr. Sorensen is eating a *lot* and all the other people are too! The smorgasbord will go broke!" I cried.

She smiled at me and finished up the carrots. "Take these out to the table, John, ok? Can you carry it all right?"

"Mom, did you hear what I said? The smorgasbord is going broke!"

Mom wiped her forehead, sighed and said, "John, do you see all this food in here? Look around you, son. The smorgasbord will not 'go broke.' We have plenty for everyone. Now take the carrots out, ok? Thank you." She was flushed and looked like she was about to pass out.

"Are you ok?" I asked her.

"Yes, John. I'm fine, but I'm busy."

I took the carrots out and noticed Mr. Sorensen back in line. Plate number two. I didn't think Mom recognized the gravity of this situation, but a few more people were leaving, so I got to work on the clean-up detail.

The line of people for the smorgasbord seemed endless. I have never seen so many people standing in a line like that before, but the line kept moving. Dishes on the food table disappeared empty and reappeared, full and steaming hot. My brother wasn't really a lot of help with the clean-up work, but he did help me a little bit by carrying around a garbage bag for me to throw junk in. Some of our friends were helping, too, but it was mostly me, Dave Hansen, Scotty Wilson, Rusty Barnes, Debbie Carruthers, and Jim, for what he was worth. We kept those tables clean and ready for the next customer.

When I saw Mr. Sorensen filling his third plate, it was all dessert. That was a little bit of a relief because I figured it meant he was just about done. I walked up near to him to see what he was taking just in time to hear him say, "That's the best-looking piece of peach pie I think I've ever seen."

My mom's peach pie. It was all gone except for one piece, and Mr. Sorensen had his eye on it. I had been hoping that when all was said and done, there would be one piece of peach pie left for me. I could see my hopes were dashed.

Mr. Sorensen saw me looking at him. "Isn't that the best-looking piece of peach pie you ever saw?" he asked me.

"Yes sir. I know it will be good because my mom made it," I answered him.

He reached for the pie, put it on a small plate and said, "Why don't you have a break and a piece of pie? I'll take over your job for a little while."

You could have knocked me over with a feather. I took the pie and mumbled "thank you, sir" to him. He took my cleaning cloth and my garbage bag and started picking up trash that had been left behind on some tables nearby. I sat down in stunned silence and took a bite of my mom's peach pie. It was delicious. Mr. Sorensen was laughing and talking to people and working like the rest of us had been. I think he was enjoying himself.

I finished up my pie and thought I actually felt like I had some more energy again. I guess that's why taking a break is good – you get your energy back. I went over to Mr. Sorensen.

"Thank you for the pie," I said. "I can take that cloth from you now and get back to work."

"Well, son, you're welcome. I'm glad you got to have some of your mom's pie. You only owe me fifty cents." I had a moment of panic. I didn't have fifty cents. He must have seen the shocked look on my face because he laughed and said, "Boy, you don't owe me fifty cents! I was teasing you. I just saw how hard you've been working and thought you could use a little break and a piece of pie." He laughed again. Man was I ever relieved. I was envisioning myself asking my mom or dad for fifty cents because I ate Mr. Sorensen's pie, and after me complaining about how much he might eat!

Mr. Sorensen reached out to shake my hand. His big hand pretty much covered mine. He gave me a strong handshake - he shook like he meant it.

"Great meal!" he said. "Thank you very much and good luck with your park." He turned and started to walk away.

"Thanks for the peach pie!" I called after him.

He didn't turn around, but just put his arm up as if to say "you're welcome" and kept walking towards the door. There was still a line of people and they parted to let him through, just like Moses parted the Red Sea in that movie about the Ten Commandments.

Jim and the other kids and I worked hard that night. So did our parents. By the time the smorgasbord was over, everyone was beat. There was some food left, just like Mom had said, and all the workers got a plate and ate, but we were almost too tired to bother. I wasn't that hungry, having had peach pie.

We still had clean-up work to do, so as different people finished up their own meal, they would get up and start taking dishes out to the kitchen to be washed, pick up garbage, or other jobs. The men were busy trying to get all the grills cleaned up...they had stopped grilling meat about an hour before the smorgasbord was over, but some of the coals were still red when you stirred them around. I always liked looking at charcoal glowing like that. It would have been perfect marshmallow-roasting time if anyone had been hungry. No one was.

We all slept like the dead that night. That's what Mom called it – sleeping like the dead. About 8:30 in the morning, bright sunshine in our windows woke Jim and I. We wandered out to the kitchen where Mom and Dad were having coffee.

"Good morning boys. How are you guys doing this morning?" Mom got up to get us some orange juice out of the refrigerator.

"Fine. Do you know how much money we made last night?" I asked.

"Not yet, but there will be a full report at the council meeting Monday night," Dad said.

"I hope it comes to a million dollars," Jim yawned.

"Me, too," I added. I was still focused on a swimming pool.

"I doubt it will be that much," Dad said, "but I think we're going to be in good shape to buy Harold's land."

The town *was* able to buy Mr. Benson's land. Mr. Benson even let the town borrow one of his tractors to dig around and make a baseball diamond. Some of the fathers who were good at construction got together and made a community building. They also made benches for the baseball teams as well as some small bleachers for the parents to sit on, though a lot of parents still brought lawn chairs all summer. There was enough money to buy a swing set and a slide and to also make a big sandbox. That sandbox could hold a lot of little kids.

The pool did not materialize. It was just too expensive, I guess, just like Dad had told me. My dream was shattered, but I did get over to Mt. Cory to swim several times during the summer, and I guess it all worked out all right because me and my buddies had a lot of fun over there. In the end, we figured out it was kind of a treat to go somewhere else once in a while, get out of our own little town.

I saw Mr. Sorensen at a bunch of our baseball games. Sometimes he brought Mrs. Sorensen with him too. He sat up on the top bleacher, usually, and he would yell the loudest for our team of anyone else in the bleachers. One time after a game, he walked up beside me and said, "Had any peach pie lately?" Then he laughed a big belly laugh and walked on ahead.

Our park was a real great part of our town. I was proud I had helped get it. My mom and dad had always said that the best thing about getting stuff was working hard so you could appreciate it. I finally knew what they meant in the summer of 1963.

9 MR. HENDERSON

Every morning starting in May, an old man from our town could be seen heading toward the creek, bamboo pole over his shoulder. Every day he wore the same clothes: a straw hat, a flannel shirt, dungarees and boots. The shape of the hat was the only thing about the old man that ever seemed to change...it looked like someone sat on it every so often. The material of his shirt was growing thin at the collar, the elbows, and the cuffs. His pants were baggy, olive green denim work pants. They must have been too long, because the legs were always rolled up around the bottom. His leather boots were scuffed and cracked, but they looked like they were probably the newest article of clothing he owned. He carried a sort of knapsack with him, and tied onto that knapsack was his fishing bobber. That red and white bobber was the biggest one I had ever seen, and no one could tell if he had his lunch in that knapsack, or his bait.

His name was Henderson. Most of us never knew his first name; he was just Old Man Henderson all our lives.

Anyway, like I was saying, every morning Old Man Henderson would head for the creek. We usually saw him when he passed our house. He never spoke to anyone. He always looked down at the ground, though he never looked to me like he really *saw* the ground. He walked slowly – maybe he had the rheumatism like my grandpa. When he walked, one hand held the bamboo pole over his bent shoulder; the other hand held onto the strap of that raggedy knapsack with the bobber tied on it.

In the evening when he came back home, he never had any fish. I never saw him carrying one fish home with him unless he was keeping them in his knapsack. He always looked so tired – so very old – on his way home at dusk. It's long days out there fishing.

Now, it is well-known that children can sometimes be cruel. Even in our little town, we could be pretty mean. Some of the kids started calling the old man "The Fisherman" just as their way of poking fun at him. In the evenings, some of the older boys would holler at him.

"Hey, Fisherman, let's see your trophy!"

"Hey, Fisherman! What did you catch? What time's the fish supper?"

But Old Man Henderson never looked up or acknowledged that he heard them at all. He always looked down at the ground and just kept trudging towards home. He lived in a very small house on the west end of town. It was a pretty run-down place from the outside, but no one saw the inside. The most we ever saw of the inside for many years was a dim glow through the windows at night when we were out running around town.

One day I saw Mr. Henderson walking in front of our house, probably heading to the creek. He was looking down at the sidewalk, kind of bending over like he was looking at something very small, and he was sort of kicking at it with his foot. I decided it was time to be brave and go talk to him. I really didn't like that my buddies made fun of him, and my mom and dad always told us we should be polite to older people. "Respect your elders," they said. So, I just walked out to where he was standing and said, "Good morning, Mr. Henderson." He gave me a glance and went back to his sidewalk inspection.

I finally saw what he was doing. A big beetle was on its back, slowly waving its legs in the air. It was helpless to turn over, and that's what Mr. Henderson was trying to do...he was trying to push that beetle over on its right side so it could walk away.

"That bug'll die if it don't get turnt over," Mr. Henderson said. He had a soft, pleasant voice, which surprised me. His voice didn't go with that leathery face.

I reached down and just turned the beetle right side up with my hand...that was easier than trying to do it with big old clunky boots on your feet like the ones Mr. Henderson wore. The beetle toddled off.

"Thanks, boy," he said before moving on. I felt proud that I had talked to him even when I was kind of scared to do that.

One Saturday in May 1963, Jim and I went down to the creek to do some exploring. We weren't really supposed to be down at the creek without an adult, but we were feeling ornery and bull-headed that day I suppose, so we went without parental guidance or blessing.

Jim and I were crawling around in the wild growth of weeds and bushes that flourished along most of the creek, looking for nothing-in-particular, when we heard a little splash, like maybe someone was trying to skip a stone across the creek. It had to be Old Man Henderson; nobody else was ever down there at that time of the day.

We stood up and saw an area where the bushes weren't so thick. There were lots of trees by the creek - mostly cottonwoods, their leaves turning against the wind and making a sound that Jim and I always thought might be how ocean waves sound as they roll in. None of those cottonwoods were as big as the one Old Man Henderson was sitting under.

His bamboo pole was lying on the ground beside him, the line extended out into the water. He didn't have the bobber on the line, and I remember wondering how he knew when he had a bite. Old Man Henderson was leaning up against the tree; he looked like he was half asleep. The knapsack was lying on the ground, too; it was open, and there was a stack of papers on top of it by the bobber.

I wanted to go over and talk to the old man, but Jim was scared. I was still a little bit scared, too, but I had to act brave, being as how I was the older of us. Finally convinced that it would be ok, Jim followed behind me over to where Old Man Henderson rested.

As we approached him, I tried to make sure I crunched some sticks and weeds under my feet so the old man would know we were coming and wouldn't be startled. This went completely against how my dad had taught me to walk most quietly in the woods; each step toes first, heel second. Old Man Henderson, if he heard us, never even looked up.

When we were standing almost on top of that old knapsack, I said, "Hi, Mr. Henderson."

Only then did he look up, slowly, and only long enough to see who we were. He nodded his greeting.

"Are you catching anything today?" I was trying to start a conversation with him.

"Ain't no fish in this creek worth catching anymore," he chuckled. I had never heard him laugh. He didn't seem like a person who ever laughed.

I sat down on the ground and looked at the knapsack. The stack of papers was really a bunch of letters all tied up with twine. They were pretty old letters, judging by the way the envelopes were all raggedy along the creases, just like that knapsack.

"Your folks know you're here?" He wasn't accusing.

Somehow, I couldn't fib. He had looked straight at me. His eyes were amazingly blue - like the blue summer sky, actually - and I felt like he could see clear through to my heart. He already knew what my answer would be, but I mumbled, "No sir," anyway.

He turned away and looked out over the creek. It was the wide part of the creek. Here and there you could see circles inside circles inside circles where some of the water life had surfaced for a second.

"You out of school now?" he asked me.

"Not quite – we have a couple of weeks to go," I answered.

"You know how to read good?"

"I always get an A on reading," I told him proudly, straightening my shoulders a little.

He sat for a minute, looking at the creek. His mouth was sort of fidgety and twisted up, like he was giving some pretty serious consideration to something.

Slowly, then, he turned and picked up the pile of letters from the knapsack. He untied the string, took a letter out of the top envelope, and looked at the yellowed paper a moment before handing it to me.

"My eyes ain't so good anymore. Will you read it to me?"

I thought his eyes looked like they were very good, but I decided to read it anyway. The letter was dated October 7, 1906. Right away, I could tell it was a lady's handwriting, all curly and frilly-looking.

"Dear Jonas," I read. His first name was Jonas.

"Dear Jonas,

How are you doing by now? I was glad to hear that you got your house built. I'm sure it must have been a very happy day for you when you drove in the last nail. Knowing you, I'm also sure that it's a lovely place. I'd give a lot to see it.

That's the reason I'm writing you, Jonas. I won't be coming to join you in your new house.

I know I promised to wait until you could send for me, but you've been gone such a long time, and you didn't write very often. I began to feel like maybe you were changing your mind about us getting married. After a year had passed and I had only heard from you a few times, I had to face up to the fact that you no longer seemed to love me or want me to be your wife.

Eventually Arlen Walker and I started courting. Arlen asked me to marry him, and I said yes. We are getting married in the spring.

Jonas, I am so sorry if I have hurt you. I really gave up hope that you were coming back for me or I would have waited – truly I would have.

I'm sure you will find another woman to be a good wife to you. Maybe someday, if you ever come back here, we can get together and brag about all the children we'll surely have by then.

Take care of yourself, Jonas. I hope you will not think too unkindly of me, and I hope you will be happy.

My best to you,

Amelia"

I just sat there for a minute. I was pretty embarrassed by the letter. Old Man Henderson just sat there, too. He didn't say a word; he kept on looking out over the creek. It wasn't until he turned to take the letter from me that I saw that his eyes were all watery. I couldn't believe it.

He must have seen my surprise because he said, "Durned sun hurts my eyes. They're awful bad these days."

I mumbled something about Jim and I getting ourselves home. Jim had fallen asleep and I had to wake him up. I never told Jim about the letter.

That evening, Rusty Barnes and David Hansen sat with us on our front porch after a particularly hard-fought baseball game. We were cooling off with some orange popsicles when Jonas Henderson passed by on his way home. Dave and Rusty started hollering all the usual taunts at him.

"Hey there Fisherman, let's see your catch!"

"Lay off him, you guys," I said, but they laughed and laughed. I just sat there watching the old man. He never looked up. He kept going like always, except there was something different – almost like a missing puzzle piece.

Holy cats, wouldn't you know a couple of days later Jonas Henderson was found dead in the house he had built for Amelia. I wasn't really surprised, somehow. It just seemed like he was so tired.

After his body was at the undertaker's, the constable went through Jonas Henderson's house. A few of the townspeople hung around outside, curious as to what the constable would discover, but they didn't find much there. Then again, no one expected to.

I walked down to the creek that afternoon without Jim. I needed to think about things. I went to the tree where I had watched Jonas Henderson break down, and I saw what had been missing the night before.

The knapsack was lying right where I had seen it last. The letters were still lying on top of it, including the one I had read to him. The edges of the letter turned up and fluttered in the breeze. Jonas' big red and white bobber was still tied to the flap of the knapsack.

I picked up the letters and noticed that they were from Cincinnati, Ohio. I put them back inside the knapsack and tied it tightly shut. I even made a special knot on it that my dad had shown me a long time ago. I pulled off the bobber and threw it into some weeds.

Jonas Henderson would have been embarrassed if anyone found those letters. They contained all his heartbreak and loneliness. I knew what I had to do.

I loosened up my shoulder, just like we did for baseball warm-ups. Then I threw that knapsack as hard as I could, out into the middle of the creek.

That day, I took the long way home.

10 PEACHES

Sometimes you learn things about people that you would never realize unless you just take the time to get to know them. That's how it was with Peaches.

Her real name was Mary, and she was the tallest girl in our class. Her mom and dad were real tall, and her dad was a huge man. I always thought of mountains when I saw him. Just one of his hands was as practically as big as Jim's whole head.

Peaches was a nice girl. Her family was kind of poor, and her clothes were usually not exactly the best. I think her mom maybe made some of her clothes. She was kind of plain, but pretty smart, and never got in any trouble at school. She was not popular with any particular crowd. I sat with her on the bus once in a while, but I was careful about it because the guys would kid me about having a girlfriend if I did it too often. A lot of the time, Peaches was just by herself. Because she was big, she sometimes got made fun of by the guys, and she didn't seem to fit in with the smaller girls. She looked older than everyone. I guess it was because she was so much taller and bigger than us.

She was the girl the teachers always called on when they needed someone to run down to the principal's office or when they needed someone to help make copies of stuff on the mimeograph machine. Peaches always seemed willing to do any extra stuff the teachers wanted her to, and she always had a smile on her face, even when people were not being so nice to her.

One day when classes were changing, I was walking down the hall with Dave Hansen. It gets really loud in those halls with everybody getting stuff out of their lockers and hollering back and forth, but on this day, it seemed louder than ever with a lot of yelling and laughing, and that's when I saw some of the other guys picking on Peaches while she was getting books out of her locker. They weren't pushing her around or anything like that...Mrs. Crow, the principal, would have been all over them if anything like that was going on. They were just teasing her about being tall and that kind of junk.

"How's the weather up there?" Danny James kidded, and Carl Davis asked Peaches, "Do you get nosebleeds being up that high?" Peaches just smiled and laughed like she didn't care. But one of the other guys, Lynn Giddens said, "Hey, when God made you, he made a B-I-I-G mistake!" At that comment, Peaches' smile disappeared and she turned back towards her locker. I heard her say, "I gotta get to class you guys...lay off, now." They all just laughed, shoved each other in the shoulder like they thought they were pretty cool, and walked away. I felt bad for her, but I walked on because I had to get to class, too, and our teachers weren't too forgiving if you showed up late. I didn't really know what to say or do anyway, but I thought about that incident off and on the whole rest of the day.

I had one class with Peaches. We had different homerooms, but I did have the one class – Social Studies. Peaches sat up front where she could be called upon easily by the teacher to go do some errand. Mrs. Miller was our teacher, and Mrs. Miller was not everyone's favorite. She tried to be – she thought she was pretty funny - but she sometimes said mean things in the attempt.

I'll never understand this any more than I'll ever forget it, but on this day, as the students were filing in and taking their seats, Mrs. Miller looked at right at Peaches, who was smiling and proud to be up front as always, and said, "Mary, could I borrow one of your loafers? I'd like to go out on the river this afternoon and my rowboat has a hole in it." Mrs. Miller laughed, and the other kids who heard it started laughing, too, but Peaches looked shocked, like someone had just told her that her dog died or something. She never said another word for that whole class. I'll never get over it…why would a teacher make fun of someone because they had big feet?

Adults think kids will forget stuff like that. They don't know how much they can hurt kids' feelings. And guess what? The very next day, Peaches sat right in the front of Mrs. Miller's class again, just in case Mrs. Miller would need her for anything. If it was me, I would've been in the very last row of the classroom, probably in the corner, drawing airplanes or thinking of ways I could seek my revenge. But not Peaches. She was smiling and answering questions just like every other old day.

In the afternoon I made an effort to catch up to Peaches in line waiting for the bus so I could sit next to her. I didn't care if the guys made fun of me this day. I just had to try to understand how Peaches put up with people treating her so bad sometimes. She never did anything to deserve it, that's for sure. I didn't think I would have the courage to stand up to people with a smile on my face like Peaches did. I think I would have been more likely to slug someone if they said those mean things to me. Peaches put up with a lot.

As we sat down on the bus, I tried to figure out how to approach the subject. I didn't want her to feel worse. I could not seem to find the words, but we talked a little bit about how hard arithmetic was and how crummy the school food was. I was kind of hoping that she felt a little better just having a normal conversation with someone, but I felt bad that I couldn't bring myself to tell her how lousy I thought she had been treated.

I never did like it when someone made fun of another person for things they couldn't help. I also didn't like the feeling that I hadn't helped things to be better for that person in some way. We learned at church to treat others like you would want to be treated and help others when they need a hand. I saw my mom and dad doing that for neighbors, the shut-ins from church, and our grandparents. After all that teaching, I had failed at helping someone, and that was bugging me, so after dinner, I asked mom if I could go for a little bike ride. "Sure, as long as your homework is done, and make sure you're back in this door before the street lights come on. You've got school tomorrow," were Mom's words as I headed out to get my bike.

Peaches lived several blocks away from us, but I knew exactly what route to take because of us riding the same bus. It didn't take me long to get there, and when I did, Peaches was sitting on the front porch swing, pushing it back and forth just slightly with her feet, wearing the loafers that Mrs. Miller thought could become a rowboat. She was reading a Screenplay magazine with Doris Day on the front. I put my bike by the fence and walked up the sidewalk to the porch steps.

Peaches looked up, surprised to see me, I think. "Hi, John," she said. "What are you doing here?"

"Oh, I was just out for a bike ride and thought I'd stop by." I stood on the porch steps feeling kind of uncomfortable now that I was here, but I couldn't back out. "I kind of wanted to talk to you about something."

"Well, sure." She moved over to one end of the swing and I sat down at the other end.

There was no good way to do this but to just start talking. "Peaches, how do you put up with some of the hateful things people say to you? And *why* do you put up with it? Doesn't it make you mad?"

Peaches looked down at Doris Day and was quiet for a minute or two. It seemed like forever, and I could hear the crickets chirping. I thought to myself that I probably shouldn't have started in on this mess. But when she had been quiet for a little bit, she looked back up at me and said, "Well, it's been going on all my life, I guess, and I have just tried to learn how to work with it."

"What the heck does THAT mean?" I said. "Don't you want to just slug someone?" I realized I was practically shouting.

She sighed. "Yes, sometimes I really do wish I could slug someone," she admitted, "but you can't do that without getting into more trouble with that person or with the adults. Slugging someone doesn't really help, so why bring more trouble? They're just going to get mad and maybe make your life more miserable, so I just try to smile and keep it friendly. I keep thinking that if I do that, eventually people will lay off. That's what my mom says: 'Just ignore them and they'll quit picking on you eventually.' So I don't let people know that they hurt my feelings. Sometimes when people are laughing at me, I try to make them laugh even harder so they think I'm in on the joke. It doesn't always help, really, but it just seems like the best way to handle it. I've had to do it for a long time, so I guess now it's just part of me."

"What about what Mrs. Miller said to you the other day, and she's a TEACHER, for criminy sake!"

Peaches got quiet again for a second. "Yeah, that was a little bit harder – I wasn't expecting it from a teacher. But after I thought about it, I thought maybe she was just having a bad day or something. Maybe some kid in the class before had been acting like a jerk to her. You know Buzz Dillon is in that class, and he's a punk. I think he's a hood," she said in a soft, conspiratorial voice. "I saw him smoking a cigarette one time."

I had to kind of shake my head because I wasn't sure I was hearing her right. I had never heard another kid talk like Peaches was talking to me.

"You know," she continued, "even my own brothers have teased me ever since I was born. When I turned about 8 or so, they started calling me 'Moose.' Dad told them they couldn't call me that, and really, it did hurt my feelings pretty bad. I cried a couple of times over that name. But my brothers said, 'Well what can we call her then?' and dad said, 'What about Peaches? She has a peaches and cream complexion.' To be truthful, I hated Peaches, too, but it was better than Moose, I guess."

I decided right then and there I'd never call her Peaches again.

"But how do you not just punch some of these jerks in the nose? Why do you keep helping Mrs. Miller? Why don't you just tell her to shove off?" I asked.

"Well, like I said, I just don't think it will help. I've tried making some smart remarks back sometimes, but it's like a game I'll never win. I know I'm not pretty, and I know I'm not the most popular girl in school; I know I'm a giant, so I just try to think about what I am good at and try to keep getting better and better at that stuff, like being smart or being funny. Someday, I know someone will see that I am a good person to be around and will want to be my best friend or invite me to a party or all that kind of stuff. You know, the world is a pretty big place and we haven't met everyone yet. Heck, I haven't even ever been out of this town, really. There's a lot to see and do out there in the world, and somewhere, maybe when I go to college, I won't get made fun of anymore. I just know it."

I don't know how long I sat there without answering Mary. She looked older than most of us, and she sure sounded older, too. I felt like I was talking to a teenager or something. Or maybe even to my mom.

"Do you want to go for a bike ride with me and maybe go over to the Twisty Freeze to get an ice cream cone?" I finally asked.

"Sure! Just let me check with my mom, ok?" She disappeared into the house and soon returned with her little purse strapped over her shoulder. I grabbed my bike and waited for her to get hers from their garage.

"You know, I think it's pretty swell that you came over to my house tonight. You're one of the only people who ever is really nice to me, and I appreciate it," she said as we got settled on our bikes.

"Oh, it's nothing," I said. And compared to how Mary thought about the world, it really *was* nothing.

At the Twisty Freeze, we both got the dime cones dipped in that chocolate that gets hard on the outside. We sat on the picnic bench that was in the grass next to the parking lot and we talked about what subjects we liked in school and what television shows were our favorites. I found out that Mary wanted to be a music teacher when she grew up and that she was taking piano lessons. She said that her dad would get laid off from work sometimes, and that they couldn't afford piano lessons all the time, so she just kept repeating the lessons she already had taken and using the same books to practice and get good. Once in a while, her piano teacher would slip her a new book and tell her to just try working on the songs in it. Mary said she was starting to get a lot better because of that. I was glad to hear that someone else was thinking Mary needed more kindness in her life. I told her about wanting to play football in high school but that I didn't know if I was big enough. She joked, "You should have had *my* mom and dad if you wanted to be big." Even I laughed at that one.

We eventually got on our bikes and headed for home. I don't know how long we were sitting at the Twisty Freeze, but after that evening, I never felt bad about Mary again because I made sure I talked to her or sat with her on the bus a little more often. Not because I felt like I had to, but because I wanted to. She was a nice girl, and she was smart...way smarter than me.

After the end of that school year, Mary's dad got a good job and they had to move away. She finally got out of our little Ohio town to see what else was out there in the world. I thought about her many times, wondering where she was and if she had found friends in her new town. I learned a lot about human beings from Mary and how hope can get you through a lot of rough times. Even when it's all a big unknown, you have to keep hoping that things will work out. It might just be the only way to get through.

11 SUMMER COMES AT LAST

May 25 – a wonderful day! A fabulous day! The greatest day of the year! Summer vacation from school!

The last day of the school year is always highly anticipated, but this year seemed particularly important. I was ten, and my summer was likely to be filled with more adventures than ever before. I'd be allowed to ride my bike farther by myself. I'd probably get more playing time in baseball because I could run faster, catch better, and throw farther now. Since I was ten, that meant Jim was eight and had developed his own circle of friends, so he wouldn't be trying to hang around with me and the guys as much. That in itself was a huge relief. All around, I expected it to be a great summer.

We couldn't get to summer till we got through that one last day of school, though. The last day of school was always kind of irritating because you just wanted to be free so bad. I knew Mrs. King would have all kinds of chores for us to do in order to get the classroom cleaned up and ready for the next poor slobs that came to fourth grade in the fall.

Sure enough, when we got to school and got settled, had taken attendance and said the Pledge of Allegiance, Mrs. King started in with the list of the day's activities.

"This morning, we'll be going through all the textbooks and making sure to remove any papers you may have left in them, erase any pencil marks you may have made in them and make sure the back bindings are still in good shape. If the back of your book is broken, we'll do some repair work with this tape I have right here." Mrs. King held up a big roll of bright red tape. "This tape will hold just about anything together, so your books will still be good for the next class who uses them."

Why anyone would want to use these books again was a mystery to me because they were generally so boring. Our science book wasn't too bad, and our social studies book was kind of interesting when they talked about how America was discovered and what the first settlers went through and stuff like that. Our social studies book was probably my favorite, and when I watched cowboy movies on TV, I remembered what I learned at school and decided whether or not the events were properly portrayed in the movie. I thought I had become pretty expert at sniffing out inaccuracies. My mom said I ruined most of the movies for her because I was always saying whether something was true or not true. She was just teasing me when she said that. At least I think she was.

Well, anyway, Mrs. King continued on. "After we've finished going through our textbooks, we'll start cleaning out cupboards. I'll need some volunteers to clean the erasers and wash the blackboards. I know that no one really likes those jobs, so I appreciate any help from volunteers on that. If I don't get volunteers, I'll just have to make assignments."

Cleaning the blackboard wasn't really that bad, but cleaning the erasers was another story. You had to take them outside and beat them together to get all the chalk dust out of them. The only good thing about the job was that you got to go outside and you could kind of take as long as you needed to get the job done. Sometimes I milked it, I have to confess. I'd just knock the erasers together real slow so it took a longer time to get all the dust out. Fast or slow, chalk dust would fly everywhere; get in your hair, on your clothes – everywhere. My mom could always tell when I had been assigned to eraser duty. She would have a holy fit when she saw my dust-covered jeans. I raised my hand immediately and offered to do the chalkboards, hoping to avoid the erasers.

"Mrs. King, I'd be happy to wash the blackboards for you today," I spoke up.

"Why thank you, John. Thank you for volunteering. I appreciate that very much." Mrs. King then looked around the room. "We have a willing volunteer for the blackboards. How about someone for the erasers?"

Dead silence. Not one person spoke up or raised their hand.

"John, since you've been kind enough to volunteer for the blackboards, I guess I'll ask you to kind of finish out that job by doing the erasers also. Would that be all right?" Mrs. King was smiling her sweetest smile.

Would that be all right? Gosh darn it, NO. That would *not* be all right. Criminy. I was already doing the blackboards. There had to be some other kid who could be assigned. Mrs. King's sweet smile started to look more sinister to me. Kind of like someone in the mafia. In the movies, mobsters smile at you while they're getting ready to pull the trigger. That's how Mrs. King looked right at that moment. All I could do was mutter, "Sure."

"Thank you so much! That will be a huge help to me," she said.

Dave, Rusty, and Scotty were all snickering at me. I could hear Rusty muttering "teacher's pet" under his breath. I shot them all a look to let them know to lay off.

Mrs. King spoke again. "After we've had lunch, we'll make sure you have each gathered up all your own belongings, and then we'll have some fun before we break for the summer, ok? However, you must know that all the fun can't take place if we don't get our work done. Is everyone clear on that?"

All the kids shook their heads "yes" in silence. As for me, I thought the best fun of all would have been if she let us out early, but that didn't seem likely.

All morning long, we worked diligently at the jobs Mrs. King had listed. It actually was amazing to me to find all these papers I had stuffed in textbooks without thinking about it. I didn't have to take anything home to show Mom and Dad anymore, so I threw them all away. I also found some pictures of airplanes and tanks I had drawn when I was bored. I kept those, saving them in my satchel. I figured I could hang them on the walls in my room.

Cleaning out the cupboards was interesting, to say the very least. That's where all the art supplies were kept, extra textbooks (more textbooks to check!), extra tablets, rulers, and crayons were kept, as well as extra boxes of tissues in case any kids had a cold.

There were about fifty boxes of Kleenex in there. The kids next year would be all set, even if they got the plague.

Finally, it was lunch time. I thought it would never arrive. I sat with the guys, even though I was kind of annoyed with them.

"Why the heck didn't any of you guys volunteer to help with the erasers or the chalkboards?" I asked. "We could have done this stuff together and gotten it done in no time anyway."

"Why would we volunteer when sweet little Johnny spoke up?" Rusty teased.

"Yeah, you're such a good, good little boy," Scotty chimed in. Scotty and Rusty were laughing. Dave kind of stayed out of it. Dave never liked trouble, really.

"You guys think you're real funny. You think you're real cute." I could not think of a good retort to save my life. I was mad, though, and I wanted them to know it.

"Oh, cool down, hothead. You'll have the job done in no time and she'll probably give a good report on you to your mom and dad and to next year's teacher," Rusty said. There might be some truth in that, but it didn't make me feel any better right then.

"Yeah, well, maybe she'll tell YOUR parents how lazy and useless you are." I probably shouldn't have said that.

"Lazy? Useless? Just because we didn't volunteer to do erasers? John, you're making way too much of this job. You'll have it done super easy and fast. I might have ended up helping you, but I sure won't now." Rusty was mad, too.

"I think I'll finish my lunch over with Bill Sterling," Scotty said. "He put together a new model airplane from World War II I'd like to see." Scotty left the table.

"I think I'll join them." Rusty left too.

Dave and I sat there together for a few minutes. I felt pretty low.

"Don't worry, John. You guys are all too hot-headed sometimes. They'll come around," Dave consoled.

"I know. We have these little arguments sometimes, but we're all friends and it will end up ok. I know it." I might have been trying to convince myself a little bit, too.

I looked over and saw Rusty, Scotty, and Bill in animated conversation. Bill didn't really hang around with just one group of kids. He was friends with everyone and no one at the same time. He just didn't have a *tribe*, I guess you could say.

When lunch was over, we went back to our classroom. We started gathering up all the stuff that was ours so we could take it home for the summer. I had already kind of started taking a few things home and was down to just minimal supplies in my desk. That made my job easier, so I was done pretty fast. Every once in a while I saw Rusty or Scotty looking over at me or talking quietly together. I knew by the end of the day, we would all make up for our fight.

When everyone was done (Debbie Carruthers was last, which was no surprise since she carted in the most junk of anyone), Mrs. King announced that we were going to be heading outdoors. We were supposed to head for the playground farthest out from the school where the sixth graders usually played. We left the building by the front main door, walking two by two as we had been instructed. Nobody wanted to violate any rules on this, the very last day of the year.

When we turned the corner around to the back of the school, we got the shock of our lives. There was a big picnic table covered with a red-checked table cloth and there was a big container of some red-colored drink. There were paper plates and cupcakes and potato chips. There were some jump ropes, some Frisbees, and best of all, squirt guns! We definitely were having a party to end the school year, and when we saw all that stuff, we basically took off running like a stampede. Mrs. King was calling after us, "Slow down, slow down," but it was too late. The steers were out of the barn.

I grabbed a squirt gun right away. It was already filled with water! This was going to be a blast. I noticed that my buddies also grabbed squirt guns.

"Duel at twenty paces," Rusty said to me.

"I accept your challenge, sir" I replied in my best Southern gentleman imitation, bowing low.

With that, the fight was over, but the squirt gun fight was on.

Mrs. King was right. We had so much fun that afternoon. It made me almost wish school could go on for another day or so, but then I knew that there wouldn't be any squirt gun fights if it did go on, so better to take a vacation in the end.

Once we had plenty of play time, Mrs. King called us all over to have our snacks. She had made the cupcakes herself, and they were really good. The red drink was cherry Kool-Aid, my favorite kind next to lemon-lime. Before we knew it, it was time to go in and get ready to get on the bus.

It suddenly hit me. I hadn't done the chalkboards or the erasers! I went right up to Mrs. King's desk. I was kind of hoping she'd let me off the hook, to be truthful.

"Mrs. King, I didn't get the erasers or chalkboard done yet," I said, "and it's almost time to get on the bus."

"Not to worry, John. I can run you home." I should have known she'd have a backup plan.

"Are you sure it wouldn't be too far out of your way?" I thought I might be able to discourage her a little.

"Oh, not at all. In fact, I was planning to visit my mother for a few minutes after school today, so it will be no problem at all. She just lives right down the road from you."

Right at that minute, the final bell rang. While every other kid shouted and laughed and practically ran out of the building for the last time that year, I was plopping my satchel on top of my desk and retrieving the bucket and sponge to wash the boards.

Mrs. King was working at her desk. I guess she still had work to do to end the year. She said she had to "get grades in." I think that meant that she had to record all of our final grades for our report cards. As I was washing the board, she told me no one flunked, so that was good, I guess.

When it was time to clean the erasers, I put them in my now-empty bucket and went outside. I hadn't been planning very well I soon discovered...I was hot and sweaty from running around playing squirt gun fight, and I was kind of wet from washing the blackboard. As I began beating erasers together, chalk dust was flying as usual and sticking to me like crazy. By the time I was done with the erasers, which seemed to have an extra abundance of dust on them because nobody had cleaned them for a while, I was caked in yellow chalk dust clay. My mom would have a conniption.

As I returned to my classroom, Mrs. King was just getting her purse out of her desk drawer and turned to see me enter the room. She actually gasped. It must have been worse than I imagined. She was probably thinking about how having me in her car would make her car a disaster area.

"My goodness! Those erasers must have been worse than I thought!" she exclaimed.

I put the erasers back where they belonged in the tray that is connected to the blackboard. So this is how my school year ends, I thought. No friends, only dust and clay.

"Come on, John. Grab your things and I'll get you home. I'm sure you're going to want to get a bath." Mrs. King smiled at me, and patted me on the back. She really wasn't such a bad teacher.

I grabbed my stuff and we went out and got in her car. I know Mrs. King had to be thinking about what a mess I was going to be leaving behind.

When we got to my house, Mrs. King stopped the car by the curb. "John, I can't thank you enough for helping me. You really saved me a lot of time today, and I'd like to give you this." She reached into her purse and pulled a five dollar bill out of her wallet.

"Oh, no," I said. "You don't need to pay me. My mom and dad always tell us that you don't do everything just because you think you'll get a reward."

"Believe me, John. It was worth $5 to me to have that work done so I could work on everyone's grades. I want you to take this and I won't leave till you do. I was thinking you could use it for something new for your bike or even just to get ice cream at the Twisty Freeze. If you don't take it, I'm giving it to your Mom to spend on you." Mrs. King seemed pretty firm about all this, so I took the money and put it in my pocket. Sheesh. If she gave it to Mom, I'd wind up with new shoes or something.

"Well, thanks. I guess I could use it at the Twisty Freeze for sure," I said. "I'll tell my mom what you said so she doesn't think I coaxed you into paying me. She doesn't like us to ask anyone for stuff, like even at my grandma's house. Mom always tells us when we're on the way over there, 'don't you kids go in and right away start asking for cookies'."

Mrs. King laughed pretty hard at that. I don't know if I ever remember her laughing that way. "Well, John, don't you worry. I'm going to send your mom and dad a note with your final grade card, letting them know what a good student you've been and how helpful you were over this school year."

"Gosh, thanks," I said. I knew my mom would be bragging about me to everyone in the family when she got that note.

I got out of the car. "Thanks again, Mrs. King."

"Thank you, too, John. It's been a fun year. You have a good summer, now." Then she sped off to her own mom's house.

I walked into the house thinking about how I would spend my five dollars. Treats at the Twisty Freeze were getting a little more expensive, and the money would come in handy on a really hot summer day when a slush might be needed. Good deeds don't always pay off right away, but this good deed would have great consequences all summer long. Yup. Summer was finally here at last.

12 SHILOH STEVENS

Shiloh Stevens was the coolest kid I ever knew. It kind of made sense that a guy like him would also have the coolest name I ever heard.

In 1963, Shiloh Stevens was 13. That was three years older than me or any of the guys I hung around with. But he wasn't like a lot of the 13 year old guys who thought we were all still little kids. Shiloh Stevens was friendly to us and really, to everybody. He always had a smile on his face like he was the happiest guy in the world.

All the girls loved Shiloh Stevens. I didn't see it, but all the girls swore he looked like Frankie Avalon. I guess Frankie Avalon was considered a good-looking guy. He was famous and all because he starred in a movie about surfing and hanging around on the beach. Anyway, the girls were always trying to get near Shiloh Stevens, doing goofy stuff like pretending they needed his help or just acting weird. Even the high school girls loved Shiloh Stevens. On the bus, if the seat next to him was empty they would sit by him and not act like it was a pain.

Shiloh Stevens had the whitest teeth of anyone I knew, and he had black eyes...not brown, but black. He had real dark hair that was kind of wavy, and he always had it combed. He was different from most of the guys because we almost all had flat tops and pineapple haircuts from the barber. Shiloh Stevens looked like he should be on the front of a magazine or something. I think that's why the girls liked him. But you know, all the guys liked him because he was nice and funny and friendly to everyone. Even big Jake Parker liked Shiloh Stevens. I think he helped Big Jake with his homework sometimes – I saw them talking about arithmetic on the bus one time and as soon as Big Jake saw me looking at them, he shot me the evil eye. I turned my head back to the seat in front of me in about one second. Big Jake was mean to a lot of the kids and I didn't want him to set his sights on me. Anyway, I'm pretty sure Big Jake had a homework buddy in Shiloh Stevens.

I don't really remember the exact details of how I got to know him, but I think it might have been one time when I ran to Connally's grocery store uptown. My mom needed a loaf of bread and I always volunteered to run up to Connally's when she needed something. I had gotten my new Schwinn Corvette in 1963 – the best birthday present I ever got – and I liked to ride it all over town and around the three-mile square whenever I got the chance. Shiloh Stevens was coming out of Connally's with a Snickers bar just as I got there and parked my bike.

"Wow, that's a nice bike," he had said.

"I got it for my birthday," I replied. "You wanna ride it while I get some bread for my mom?"

"Sure," he smiled, and he jumped on like he was hopping into a real Corvette...he was just that cool.

Connally's was a little general store, so it didn't take me long to get the Wonder bread for mom. When I came back out, Shiloh Stevens was standing there with my bike, gleaming his white teeth at me. He could have been in a toothpaste commercial.

"This is a swell bike. You can fly on this thing!" he said.

I felt so proud at that moment. I had a cool bike and even the very cool Shiloh Stevens thought so. I felt like I had just won a million dollars or something.

That's the first real conversation I remember having with him – a guy who seemed like part god. For the rest of the day, it didn't even seem real. After that, whenever I saw Shiloh Stevens or he saw me, it was like old friends. We talked about baseball or my bike or all kinds of interesting things. Sometimes we would go up to the Twisty Freeze and get a slush. His favorite flavor was lime and mine was grape.

One day, Shiloh Stevens rode his bike by my house. I don't think he actually knew we lived there, but I was outside on my hands and knees helping my mom pull weeds out of the flower beds and he saw me.

"Hey, John!" he called.

My mom and I both looked up. My mom momentarily stopped working and looked at him. "He looks just like Frankie Avalon," she kind of whispered to me.

"Are you allowed to go for a bike ride? I was going to go around the three-mile square and then stop for a slush."

"Mom, can I go? I promise I'll help finish up when I get back," I pleaded. I felt kind of bad because of her being pregnant and all, but I really wanted to go.

She rubbed her growing stomach, thought about it for a minute and said, "I think I can finish up here, but maybe later you can collect the trash from all the different rooms in the house and get it bagged up for me."

"Deal!" I smiled.

I pulled my bike out of the garage and met Shiloh Stevens at the end of the driveway. "Let's go!" I was happy for a break from weeding, that's for sure, but I was also happy to go for a bike ride with my friend, the guy who seemed to be everybody's friend. I felt so lucky to know him.

We had to go past the Hankins farm as part of our ride. It was near Whistler's Grove. A creek ran parallel to the Hankins' driveway. We stopped for a minute and stood on a small bridge over the creek, watching some snakes that slithered through the murky water. Shiloh Stevens was fiddling around with a silver dollar he kept in his pocket all the time. "Just in case I need it," he told me once. He was turning it over and over – heads, then tails, then heads, then tails. He was looking at the Hankins farm the whole time.

"Do you know Jenny Hankins?" he asked me.

"Well, I know her a little bit just because she rides on our bus, but she's two years older than me, so I don't really know her very well. She says 'hi' to me sometimes."

"She's the girl I'm going to marry someday," Shiloh Stevens told me. I was so shocked I took a step or two backwards and almost fell in the creek.

"Gosh, how in the heck do you know that?" I asked. I had never heard any guy talk about getting married. This was almost too much for my brain to handle. I mostly tried to avoid girls.

"I just know. She's sweet, and she's smart, and she's pretty. She wants to be a doctor. Have you ever heard of that? A girl doctor? I think she's the most amazing girl I ever knew. Any girl who wants to be a doctor…" he trailed off.

"There aren't any girl doctors! I've never even heard of such a thing!" I was so shocked at the talk of marriage that I thought for a minute he had gone goofy, and to think of a girl doctor…impossible. I shook my head.

"Well, you might not have heard of them now, but one thing I know…if Jenny says she's going to be a doctor, she's going to be a doctor. You can see it in her eyes. She's got something going on in that brain." Shiloh Stevens stopped, turned, and looked at me. "You have to have a girl with a brain. You have to have a girl who can think about stuff with you."

I was ten years old. This conversation was making little sense to me and I was beginning to wish I'd just stayed with mom doing the weeding.

We got back on our bikes and pedaled slowly around the three-mile square. All the time, Shiloh Stevens was talking about Jenny Hankins being a doctor and being so cute. I listened to him, though I was having a hard time understanding where this was all coming from. Shiloh Stevens, the coolest guy I had ever known, was in love. The only girl I really loved was my mom. Girls were generally trouble so I just kind of stuck with my mom in the love department.

When I got home, Mom was in the kitchen peeling potatoes for supper. She gave me a big smile, and I started noticing her face. She was kind of pretty, and I wondered if I'd ever be in love like Shiloh Stevens. She glanced over as I walked towards her.

"John, you have a bewildered look on your face," she said with a smile.

"Mom, how do people fall in love?" I asked her.

She threw back her head, put her hands on the counter and laughed right out loud.

"Good grief! Where is that coming from?" she asked me.

"I was just wondering about it. We were talking about it on our bike ride because Shiloh Stevens is in love with Jenny Hankins. He says he's gonna marry her someday."

Mom laughed again. "John, romantic love is too hard to explain, and the chances are very good that you will fall in and out of love many times before you finally decide on that one special girl you want to marry." She went back to peeling her potatoes, still chuckling and muttering under her breath a little bit about "these kids, where do they get this stuff from," and other mom-type comments like that.

That was the beginning of June, right after we got out of school. I didn't know that the subject of love would get even more weird as the month went by and even more confusing, too.

Towards the end of June, I was out riding my Corvette one day. I had gone down by the old railroad tracks that few trains ever went on anymore. Sometimes you could see some woodchucks down there, and I had even seen raccoons toddling across the tracks. I also saw a skunk family once, but I made sure to steer clear of them. My mom would have had a fit if I'd gotten sprayed by skunks.

I parked my bike and started walking down the tracks. I was looking for any coins or anything that might have gotten dropped down there. You could never tell what you might find if you looked. I was looking pretty hard when I thought I heard a noise like someone crying. I know my head shot up because it kind of hurt my neck. I was rubbing my neck and being kind of mad at myself over it, walking in the direction of the sound when I saw a leg with a Red Ball Jet shoe on it. Almost every kid I knew wore Red Ball Jets or PF Flyers, so I didn't know just who it was, but I knew it was a kid. The leg moved, so I knew the kid was alive, and I went over. There in the tall grass was the coolest guy I ever knew.

I started to say, "Shiloh, why are you crying?" but I had never called him just Shiloh before. I always called him Shiloh Stevens, so to only call him Shiloh now didn't sound right.

"Hey…" I said softly.

He looked up at me with his hand over his eyes. I wasn't sure if he was just trying to guard them against the sun or if he was trying to keep me from seeing that he was crying. I sat down a couple of feet away from him and just stayed quiet. When he put his hand down, his eyes were red. He had been crying for a while, that's for sure. I didn't know what to say or even to think.

"Hey," he replied. He looked away for a couple of minutes so I just stayed there and kept my mouth shut.

When he finally looked back, he said, "Please don't tell anyone."

"Of course not!" I replied. "I would never do that."

"I know." Shiloh Stevens looked down at his hands. "You're a good pal, really, for only being ten and all."

That made me feel good. Shiloh Stevens called me his pal, and I knew I had to try to help him with whatever was making him so unhappy that it caused him to actually cry.

"What happened?" I asked. "Did your grandpa or grandma die or something?"

"No, they're already dead and I'm all cried out over that a long time ago when I was little. It's worse."

I couldn't think of anything worse except maybe if your parents died. I didn't think I could spit that question out of my mouth because it had suddenly gone very dry. I tried licking my lips and swallowing a couple of times, but it didn't help.

"John, have you ever heard of a divorce?"

"Yeah, I'm pretty sure I've heard of some people getting a divorce. I think I heard my mom telling my dad about some Hollywood movie stars getting a divorce or something."

"Well, my mom just told me that she's getting a divorce from dad."

I didn't even know what to say. That sounded horrible.

"She told me she hasn't been happy for a while and that her and dad were going to see a judge to get a divorce. She told me she decided she was moving away to Chicago."

"Chicago! What in the heck...are you going with her?" I'm pretty sure I shouted.

"No. She wants to live by herself and she said it wouldn't be good for a boy to live with his mom, that I'm getting to the age where I should be with my dad. My dad's a great guy and all, but how can we live without my mom? We don't know how to cook or do laundry or any of that."

"Why does your mom want to live by herself?" I butted in. I had never heard of such a thing.

"She says she's tired of not having a nice enough house and doing all the work and not having freedom to do what she wants."

"What in the heck does she want to do?" I asked my good friend.

"I don't know. I really don't know," Shiloh Stevens shook his head. "She thinks dad doesn't do enough stuff around the house and she says he'll never change and she's unhappy and she just has to get out. She really didn't tell me any more than that, and I just can't understand it. I've never felt so low."

My friend, Shiloh Stevens sat on the ground looking like a little broken bird. I never thought I would see him like that in all my life. A little broken bird that fell out of the nest.

We just sat there for a while. I don't even know how long. Once in a while he would cry a little bit, but then he'd stop and just stare off into space. He looked like he was sick, really – pale under his June tan. Then all of a sudden he jumped up and started pacing around like a crazy man.

"She doesn't deserve my dad! She doesn't even think about how hard he works all day! He's out earning money to bring home so she can buy curtains or whatever stuff she wants and she's mad because it isn't enough? She doesn't deserve my dad."

Right then, I was glad I was not Shiloh Stevens' mom. He hated her; you could tell it. But then he stopped and looked at me. He had kind of a creepy look on his face, a look I had for sure never seen on Frankie Avalon. There was no smile, and his black eyes looked like glass. He looked like he could kill someone with those eyes. His jaw was set hard. He was clenching his white teeth behind pinched lips, and I thought it would be best not to say anything for a minute or two. In a couple of minutes, the look on his face relaxed a little, but he was not the Shiloh Stevens I knew anymore. He looked determined, but I wasn't sure about what.

"You know, I'll never marry Jenny Hankins. Nope. I'm not getting into marriage. What if I didn't make enough money to suit her? Doctors make a lot of money. I'll probably never make that much money. She'd probably divorce me. Nope, I'm never marrying Jenny Hankins. Maybe I'm not marrying anybody, ever."

I stayed still in the grass and just listened. Then I said, "My mom says we'll probably fall in and out of love a lot before we get married."

Shiloh Stevens looked at me and gave a smile, but it was not a nice smile. It was an evil smile, the likes of which I had never seen on his face before.

"I think the trick might be to never fall in love in the first place," he said. He walked over and picked up his bike out of the long grass. "I gotta go. I'll see you around."

He jumped on his bike and took off towards town. I went to get my bike and noticed I had a flat...there was a small piece of glass in the back tire that I must have missed out there by the railroad track. My dad wouldn't be too thrilled about that, but in a way, it was good to just walk home. It wasn't easy, having to push a bike with a flat tire, but it was just better to walk and take some time to think about what my friend had told me. I hoped my mom and dad would never get a divorce.

Dad was home by the time I got there, and I caught him laughing in the laundry room with Mom, his arms around her waist and looking over her shoulder while she ironed a shirt for him. Who will iron shirts for Shiloh Stevens' dad, I wondered.

For a few weeks Shiloh Stevens and I went for bike rides, but we never spoke of the divorce again except one time when he said, "You know, my mom is being a jerk but I don't want to feel like that about her. She's my mom." That was the last time we ever talked about it at all.

It wasn't really too much longer after that conversation before Shiloh Stevens told me that he and his dad were packing up to move out of town. I rode my bike over to his house to see him before he left.

"We're going to Columbus," he told me. "Dad says he can't stay around here. Everybody looks at him like he's pathetic or something because his wife deserted him, and he can't take it."

"Does he have a job in Columbus?" I asked. I was thinking about how Mrs. Stevens had thought they didn't have enough money.

"Oh, sure. He got a good job, actually. He's going to work for Ohio State University, so I'll get to go to college there, too. I might decide to become a doctor and look up Jenny Hankins after all."

He smiled, and it was the first time I had seen those white teeth since he told me about the divorce. I was sure glad to see that smile come back to his face, even if it was all about a girl again.

"I don't know what I want to be yet," I said, "but maybe I'll go to Ohio State, too."

"Ok," he replied. "I'll look for you when you get there."

That was the final conversation I ever had with the coolest guy I ever knew. The day they left, I went by their house on my bike and saw them finishing packing up the station wagon. Shiloh Stevens looked up and saw me. He grinned and waved, but he kept helping his dad. I went over to Mrs. Downing's house and parked my bike behind her hedges. I sort of tried to stay out of sight because I didn't want Shiloh Stevens to think I was weird or anything, but I knew it was the last time I would see him. I watched as he and his dad put the last load in the car. Then they got in and slowly pulled out of the driveway. I watched as the car got littler and littler and finally went around a corner where I couldn't see it anymore at all. I got my bike and rode over to their driveway and looked at the FOR SALE sign for a minute. I couldn't believe he was really gone. I think I just wanted to see if some part of his spirit was still there and if I could soak it in. Where the sidewalk bumped up against the driveway, I saw something shiny. I got off my bike to go examine it.

Shiloh Stevens had left his silver dollar on the end of the sidewalk. I wanted to call out to him somehow, let him know that he had lost his lucky silver dollar, but of course, he was long gone. Then I had a thought...I wonder if he had left if there for me to find.

I looked at the silver dollar and turned it over in my hand; first heads, then tails, then heads. I put it in my pocket. You know, just in case I ever needed it.

13 BUTTON

We had three different dogs while we were growing up, but not one of them stole our hearts like Button.

When we first got Button, I was surprised. He was not like any other dog we had ever owned. Our dogs were always mutts - not too beautiful – just regular dogs. Button was fluffy and white with curly hair and brown eyes. He looked like a girl's dog. Mom wanted to name him Button, because as she put it, "He's cute as a button! We should name him Button!" I thought to myself, "What the heck kind of name is Button for a boy dog?" Jim spoke right up and said it was a dumb name, but Dad sided with Mom and she won that battle.

I figured this dog was a house dog, destined to sit on someone's lap half the time. I never thought a white, fluffy dog would ever want to go out in the back yard and roll around in the grass with us. Jeepers, was I ever wrong about that! This dog was smart! He loved to go out and run all over creation with us. You could throw him a ball a thousand times and he would fetch it for you and bring it back so you could throw it again. If he got tired, which wasn't very often, he would just lay down in the grass with that ball right in front of him. He wouldn't take his eyes off you for one second for fear you'd get that ball away from him before he was ready to be done playing.

He learned to do quite a few tricks early on; he was just that smart. He could not only fetch, but he could sit, stand on his hind legs, and roll over on command. Mostly he would do that stuff for treats, but sometimes he did it even if you didn't have the goods.

We got him an old stuffed animal to play with. It was some ratty old teddy bear Jim still had around from when he was a baby, but Button loved that toy. He took it in his bed with him at night and was very protective of it. Funny thing was, he'd take it in his mouth with a good hard grip and throw it in the air sometimes. Then he'd try to roll on it. He couldn't, of course, because it was a stuffed teddy bear and it was too full of stuffing for him to roll over, but that didn't keep him from trying.

Button thought he was a guard dog. He would sit on the arm of dad's chair and stare out the window as if he were on duty at Fort Knox. I don't know what was going through that dog brain of his, but he acted like he was so brave he would go up against the meanest guy in the world if he had to. Dave Hansen and Scotty Wilson rode by on their bikes one day and Button really let them have it more than usual. Of course, they knew Button was not mean, so they just laughed. He was such a goofy dog. He barked at everybody – he barked at the mailman, he barked at the Nickels bread man, he barked at the ice cream man. Personally, I think he barked at the ice cream man because he wanted to let us know the ice cream man was coming down the street. If we got a popsicle, Button got a popsicle, usually for free. I tell you, that was one smart dog.

Button thought he was the bravest, fiercest dog around, but anyone who saw that curly white hair would know this was not a fierce dog. Nevertheless, he reserved his loudest, fiercest barks for the door-to-door salesmen who came through our village once in a while. He made sure mom knew there was a stranger at the door who she probably wouldn't really want to talk to and shouldn't have anything to do with. I have a feeling this got started when the Electrolux salesman came by one day and talked my mom into a vacuum cleaner demonstration. After that, Button assumed anyone carrying a demonstration case had some loud, scary device inside and he made sure those guys didn't stick around too long. Button saved his family from all manner of unwanted company.

Button also liked to chase other animals. He would chase birds flying by where he could see them. He would chase squirrels, cats, and just about any other animal he spied. Once I saw him chase a rabbit around the back yard. That rabbit didn't know where the heck to go. He kept hopping as fast as he could, and Button kept running as hard as he could, around the lilac bushes, behind the tool shed, over around the grape arbor. I thought that rabbit was going to collapse, and he *did* stop dead in his tracks at one point. I knew it would be all over for that rabbit, but dad stepped in and kept Button from getting too close. The rabbit must have caught its breath because after a second, it made its escape.

Button thought he was king of the world. He had a special bed, all his toys, and a family who adored him. What more could a dog need?

A blue ribbon.

Our village had a kind of homecoming celebration every summer. It wasn't big…there weren't rides or anything like over in Fayettesville, but everybody came. There was always a lot of good food around, including homemade ice cream, so the homecoming was a big hit with everyone in town. Even though it was just a small celebration, it did start off with a parade. The high school marching band always got things going, and the cheerleaders were always at the end. Just about anybody could be in the parade, so in between the band and the cheerleaders there were all kinds of sights. The firemen and constable drove their trucks and paddy wagons in the parade. Sometimes someone would dress up like a criminal in a black and white striped suit, and the constable would pretend to capture him and put him in handcuffs. The 4-H kids made floats and some of the farmers would pull them with a tractor or a truck. Some kids decorated their bikes and rode them. Politicians running for mayor and junk like that would just walk in the parade, shaking hands with people along the sidewalks, handing out pencils with their names on them. Jim and I thought the best part was when the Shriners would drive their tiny cars all over the road like they had been sneaking a little of grandpa's homemade grape wine. They would honk their horns, and those horns always had some kind of goofy sound like, "Ah-OOO-ga!" Jim would just about fall on the ground laughing. The parade always ended up at the park where all the food was, and everyone would dig in and just hang around. The older people would sit and talk while us kids ran around and played freeze tag or red rover.

In the summer of 1963, the people who planned the homecoming decided what we needed was a "best dog" contest. Well, at my house, we knew Button would be the hands-down winner of any "best dog" contest. He was "cute as a button," of course, and he was so smart. There wasn't a dog in town that could beat Button in a contest like that.

We gave Button a bath, which he did not like at all. He fought us tooth and nail while we were getting him into an old washtub, but once he was in there he stood as stiff as a statue, glaring at us with those brown eyes. I had a feeling he would never forgive us for giving him baths. And after all the salesmen he had saved us from!

On the day of the parade, Button couldn't have looked better. He was clean, brushed, and mom put a little ribbon on his head.

"Why in the heck does a boy dog have a ribbon on his head, Mom?" I protested.

"Because it's adorable. He's sure to win."

I was pretty sure he would win without him having to endure such indignation, but mom insisted. I got a leash that had belonged to our last dog, Ralph (mom never liked that name), and hooked it onto Button's collar. I noticed that the clasp didn't hook quite as well as when Ralph used it, but Ralph was a lot bigger dog, and I didn't think Button could pull free. That's another thing I would be wrong about.

All the kids who had a dog in the contest also had to walk them along in the parade. I was being extra careful with Button because he loved to run so much. He was pretty good on a leash, though, and we got through the parade without any problems. I remember seeing Mom, Dad, and Jim along the sidewalk, clapping and waving to us. I was pretty proud because, of course, I knew Button was the best dog of all.

When we got to the park, we had to get through the pie-eating contest and a contest with men seeing who could lift their wives and some other boring stuff like that. Grown-ups are so nutty sometimes. Finally, it was time for the best dog judging.

Everyone who had a dog in the contest had to take their dog up on the stage, which was really just an old flatbed trailer that someone had decorated up with crepe paper. I had secretly planned to have Button do some little tricks while he was up there on the stage, and I had a few treats in my pocket just to make sure he performed as usual.

We all lined up on the flatbed, facing the crowd. I could see Mom, Dad, and Jim near the front. A few of the village councilmen, the constable, and one of the firemen were the contest judges. Debbie Carruthers' dog, Beatrice, was the only other dog with a ribbon in their hair. I always thought Debbie was kind of mushy and weird, and she had a dopey-looking little dog with real long hair hanging over its eyes. The rest of the dogs just looked like regular dogs. They kind of tried to walk around and sniff each other, but Button sat very still right by my feet. He certainly was on his best behavior. I have a feeling he smelled the treats in my pocket and knew a reward was coming.

As the judges walked by us, I decided the time was right to show what Button was capable of. I told him to roll over, and he did. Treat. I told him to "sit pretty," which meant stand on his back legs, and he did. Treat. I told him to play dead, and he flopped on the trailer bed like he had been shot. The constable laughed and laughed about it. Button got two treats for that one.

It probably didn't take long for the decision to be made, but when you have to stand up in front of a whole bunch of people like that, you think you're up there forever.

After a while, the head judge made an announcement.

"My friends, there are many fine dogs among us tonight, but we must pick only one dog to be named Best Dog of 1963. After extremely careful consideration, and recognizing that every dog here is special and unique, we are awarding the Grand Prize to Button!"

My mom started bouncing up and down a little bit, and my dad wrapped his big arm around her shoulders. Jim actually turned a cartwheel but he banged his feet into someone standing next to him and my dad had to kind of get him straightened up. I know I was grinning hard because my face kind of hurt. The head judge came over and tied a blue ribbon around Button's neck. It had a big round medal with "#1 Dog" printed on it. I thought Button would try to get it off and start rolling on it, but he was intent on something else.

Over near some bushes about twenty feet from the stage was a rabbit. Of course, Button saw it before I did, and he took off before

I knew what the heck was happening. That dumb leash clasp had opened right up, and he was running full tilt. I ran after him, dad ran after him, Jim ran after him, and Mom just froze with her hands by her cheeks.

"Don't chase him! He'll just run harder!" someone shouted at me as I raced by.

I couldn't even see where Button had gone. I had seen some movement in those bushes, but I had missed the exit from the bushes and didn't know which direction the rabbit and Button had run towards. I just ran blindly, calling his name and not even really considering that I might be going in the completely wrong direction.

The rest of the homecoming went on, but Dad, Jim, and I all kept looking for Button. Mom decided to go home and see if maybe he would turn up there. You heard about that sometimes – a dog getting lost and somehow finding their way back home. I knew Button wasn't that kind of dog...he would keep running till he was in Nebraska.

When the streetlights came on, Dad said, "Boys, we better call it quits for tonight. We don't have flashlights with us and I have to work tomorrow." I was so upset I didn't know what to do. I knew I wouldn't be able to sleep. Jim was just dragging along. He was little and got tired easier. He would be able to sleep.

It was a restless night, and as soon as I heard Dad's car start up for work, I was wide awake. I skipped steps trying to get to the kitchen, where mom was sitting, the steam from her coffee curling up and disappearing into the air. She didn't say anything, but the look on her face told me Button was not home.

That day, and every day for one solid week, the sun blazed on our shoulders as Jim and I and all of our pals searched for Button. I'm quite sure the different neighborhoods in our village got tired of hearing kids call out, "Button! Button! Here, boy!" every couple of minutes. I was starting to feel like we had no hope of ever finding our dog again, but I always carried a few treats in my pocket, just in case.

On Sunday, we went to church with Mom and Dad, even though I begged them to let me skip and just go looking for Button. They told me we might better think about praying for Button, that he was ok and that he would come home or that we would find him. So pray, I did. I never prayed so hard in my whole life for a boy's dog that looked like a girl's dog.

Church didn't really make me feel any better, and I couldn't just hang around the house acting like things were normal. That afternoon, I went for a walk down to the creek where Jim and I weren't supposed to go by ourselves and sat under the tree where I had first learned about Jonas Henderson and Amelia. I hate to admit it, but I cried a little bit, and it wasn't because the sun hurt my eyes. The sun did make me doze off, though. I dreamed I was running, running, calling out something, but in the dream, I couldn't understand my own words.

A little sound woke me up. It was just a small, little sound, kind of like a baby whining. I had to get myself more awake; then I stood and started looking around. I looked in some bushes not too far from the tree, but nothing. There was some long grass closer to the creek, but I couldn't find anything there, either. I stood and listened for a minute. The sound was a little bit farther away, and I tried to listen carefully so I could walk in the direction it came from.

Around a little curve in the creek, some kind of big pipe jutted out into the water. It almost sounded like the noise was coming from that pipe. There was an old burn barrel on the path, and I had to figure out whether to walk between the barrel and the creek, or the barrel and the tall grass on the other side of the path. Because of the slope of the ground, either way was tricky. I chose to go between the barrel and the creek.

Once I had picked my way around the burn barrel, I could get a better look in that pipe. I got down on the ground on my hands and knees and carefully crawled along the bank of the creek to get as close as I could without going in the drink. The noise wasn't getting louder, and I wondered what I was getting myself into.

I had to lay on top of the pipe and bend my neck down over the end of it in order to get a good look, and that's when I saw Button, inside the pipe, shivering. He was a mess. I wasn't sure how I was going to get him out of there because there was some kind of big bolt sticking through the center of the pipe. I tried to reach in, but I could just barely touch Button's head.

"Hold on, boy. I'm gonna get you." I tried to give him one of the treats out of my pocket, but he didn't even seem interested.

At the time, I didn't know how deep that creek was. I only knew that mom and dad didn't want us down there without them because we weren't good swimmers yet. But I knew how to dog paddle, and I knew I had to find a way to get my dog, even if it meant getting in the creek, and that's what I decided to do.

I took off my shoes and socks and dropped myself down off the end of that pipe into the cool water of the creek. I held on to the pipe with one hand to keep from going under and reached my other hand into the pipe. I could touch Button's head, and I could feel something around his neck. I could put my fingers under that thing, whatever it was – maybe his collar – and I tried to pull him towards me. He yelped - something was hurting him – but now that I had found him, I was desperate to get him out of there. I didn't know what that pipe was for. Maybe water would be flowing in or out of it and drown Button. Maybe a water snake would show up. I had to act.

I took hold of whatever was around Button's neck and began pulling slowly. I was afraid he'd get cut on that metal thing inside the pipe, and sure enough, he did whimper a little and yelp a couple of times. It made me stop pulling for a minute, but something inside me just said, "You have to get him out of there." I took a deep breath and gave it one good try – I pulled him out by his blue ribbon.

I knew as soon as I got him out of there that he was hurt. He had gotten all tangled up in some kind of old net or fishing line that someone had thrown away. His hair was filthy and all matted. He had the net around one of his front legs and one of his back legs, and it was clear that he never would have gotten himself free. I couldn't even get the stuff off of him. His back leg was bent out kind of weird, and I thought it might be broken. His hair was full of brambles, too, probably from chasing that dumb rabbit. He looked pretty skinny, but he was alive. I took off my shirt and just left my tee shirt on so I could wrap Button up in something soft to carry him in. I put on my socks and shoes and started out for home.

My clothes were all wet and sticking to me, and I'm sure I was a strange sight to any neighbors who saw me, but I hadn't gotten too far back into the village before Scotty saw me and ran to meet me – he knew what I had wrapped up in my shirt. Before long, a couple more of my friends had joined up with us. No one could believe Button was still alive.

When I got to our sidewalk, Mom, Dad, and Jim came out of the front door. They had seen me at the gate and assumed that inside my shirt was a dead little dog. But Button made fools of us all again because he was the bravest dog in the village, the best dog in the village, the Number One dog in the village.

The vet told us that Button's hip was out of the socket. The vet had to put it back in, and that was no fun for Button. He never did walk or run quite the same again, but once he got a little of his weight back on and recovered from his ordeal, he still liked to sit on the arm of dad's chair and look out the window, making sure no unwanted salesmen or wily squirrel could disturb our peace.

Just so you know, Button made it through all that but only lived a few more months. In that time, he had all the treats he wanted. Eventually, you could see that his hip was causing him a lot of pain. He slowed way down and he never jumped or stood on his back legs anymore. One morning when I went down to breakfast, I noticed him just lying on his bed. He didn't lift his head to greet me like he usually did, so I went over to check on him and pet him a little. He didn't respond. He wasn't moving, and he wasn't breathing. I was old enough at age ten to understand that even dogs have to die, but it was still hard. I went to find Mom, and then we told Jim. Dad was already at work, so he didn't know about Button till he came home.

At my mom and dad's house, out back by one of the silver maples where the squirrels used to tease Button, there is a little fenced area where Button rests. Mom always puts some flowers around his area – she usually plants petunias. Girl flowers for a boy dog who was the best dog a boy could have ever had.

14 SUMMER STORM

When the temperature hit ninety-seven and the wind stopped, we only thought it was miserable-hot. When the sky turned yellowish and there was an eerie quiet over our world, we started taking canisters of water to the basement and trying to remember which windows to leave open. Was it east or north?

Jim and I didn't want to stay down in the basement. Mother and Dad weren't camped out there yet, so we came back upstairs and sat on the front porch glider.

No quiet is like the quiet that precedes a tornado. There is no movement in the trees or the grass, not the faintest hint of a breeze, no sound of any kind. It's almost like the world is on hold for a little while. It wouldn't be so spooky if it didn't sneak up on you. Everything is completely normal, and then, all of a sudden, earth seems to stop turning.

Jim started the glider in motion. The squeak of the springs was comforting somehow. Neither of us said anything – there was nothing to say, nothing to do but wait. We just sat and listened to the squeaky springs of the glider. We couldn't tell how much time we would have to be outside, so we let the sound lull us each into our own private thoughts. We waited. Squeak. Squeak. Squeak.

Just as suddenly as the quiet had settled, the wind started up. At first, it was a cooling breeze that dried the sweat on your brow. Within minutes, it was a hard wind that bent and almost snapped off the branches of the big oak in the front yard. The rain fell, at first a steady downpour, then in sheets.

The hair on the back of my neck tickled. I stopped the glider with my foot.

"It's time to go in, Jim."

We were both reluctant to move. Out there on the porch, it was like watching a movie about our own town. Everything was familiar: the houses, the sidewalks, Mrs. Reynolds' rose garden. Only we were detached from it - detached, so we wouldn't feel so sad if it wasn't all the same when we emerged from the basement, our temporary tomb.

I kept remembering the only tornado I had ever seen, two summers ago.

I had been playing baseball with David Hansen and some of the other guys at the sandlot. Jim was too little to play ball then, so he was climbing around in a small tree. It was hot as the blazes that day, and I was not the only one sweating to death. I was wishing our town had a swimming pool, but the closest swimming pool was over in Mt. Cory, and we didn't go there very often. Of course, there was the creek, but we would have gotten tanned by our mom or dad if we jumped in the creek. The only thing that was saving us that day was a slight breeze that blew the sweat off of our faces once in a while. If it wasn't for that breeze, we'd have had to just go sit in the shade or go over to the Twisty Freeze and get a slush.

I was out in center field when all of a sudden, the wind stopped blowing and a quiet settled down over us. The sky turned a weird yellow color. It was spooky. It was actually Dave's mom who had come running across the sandlot yelling at us that day.

"You kids get home right now! C'mon! Get moving! Get home right now!"

We didn't even ask why. Something in her voice made me start running. I ran like the time we were playing baseball against the Little Giants when Dave had hit a good, solid grounder and I took off from second base to try to get a run in. The Giants had good fielding though, and the shortstop got the ball from the left fielder when I was halfway between third and home. Now I was running just like I was between third base and home.

Home.

I hollered for Jim, and he scrambled down from his perch in the tree. We ran across the lot, down Park Street to Dogwood, on to Birch, where many of the trees would soon not look the same. We turned left on Oak to 456 and raced up the stairs through the screen door, which slammed behind us. Mother was just coming up the basement steps.

"I'm glad you boys are home. Get some candles out of the buffet. Get some matches, and get into the basement under the steps."

Again, we didn't ask. I got the candles, the matches, and headed downstairs. I knew what this meant. We had all kinds of drills in school, including fire drills, atomic bomb drills, and tornado drills. This was like a tornado drill, only at my house.

The stairs to the basement were pretty steep, and I remember that Jim was still a little short-legged. He was ahead of me, trying to go as fast as he could, but he was having a hard time. I had stuff in my hands so I couldn't really help him. I saw him pitch forward and land on his shoulder on the cement of the basement floor. I got down there as fast as I could, put down the candles and such, and helped him get up. We got under the steps, Jim clutching at his arm and crying quietly.

Then Mom was there in a flash, almost appearing out of nowhere, it seemed. She held Jim gingerly, smoothing his hair. She didn't cry, but her face looked tense and white. It scared me to look at her face, so I looked up and out the basement window from my roost.

The wind blew harder and harder. The sky had turned dark; it looked like night sky. I remember thinking about dad and wondering where he and the men he worked with were holed up. I know that's what Mom was thinking about, even though she was sort of cooing in Jim's ear.

Jim was still crying, but at some point I couldn't really hear him anymore. My head was filled up with the sound of the wind. It roared all around us; I felt like a train was running through our house. Everything was going to fall down around us, and I couldn't move. The house seemed to shake and make a weird, high-pitched wheezing noise like when Jim had the croup. I could hear something thrown up against the house, and I thought I heard glass breaking somewhere.

"Put your arms up to cover your head like you would do at school," Mom called out. She had to shout because the wind was so loud. I remembered what we had learned in tornado drills at school and followed her suggestion. I also remembered that you should stay away from windows, so I crouched back under the stairs a little closer to Mom.

It seemed like a long time under those stairs during that storm, but finally, it was over. We had a lot of broken limbs in our yard, and the glass had blown out of the shed...that must have been what I heard while I was under the steps. Our town had suffered some damage, but nothing like over in Bentley, less than 10 miles away, where we heard a lot of houses had been completely destroyed and someone had actually been killed. Dad was fine and arrived home just in time to go with Mom, Jim and me to the doctor. As it turned out, Jim had broken his collar bone, so he acquired a new gray sling which he proudly wore for a week after his collar bone was pronounced "healed."

Now, in the basement again for this season's tornado, we waited for it to be over. It soon was. Tornados are the weirdest things...one minute they're there; the next minute, they're gone. We were all pretty relieved when we came out and saw that just like before, the damage to our town was minor. There were a few broken limbs laying in our yard. Our neighbors pretty much had the same kind of mess to clean up. People were out looking for damage and raking up leaves and other debris that had blown into their yards. I jumped on my bike and rode around the neighborhood just to see if everything was still intact, and it was for the most part. I guess out on the east side of town there was a little damage to some peoples' sheds and even some shingles off the roof of their houses, but all in all, things were in pretty good shape. Back at our house, Mother started cooking; dad sat down in his favorite chair with the evening newspaper; everything was going to be ok and our little part of the world was peaceful.

After supper, I saw Jim out by the oak tree in the front yard. He was crouched down beside a bunch of small branches that had been broken off by the wind. Jim was always finding some weird new bug or other creature to try to keep for a pet and I figured that's what he was up to now. I walked out to see what was so interesting. He didn't hear me come up behind him.

Jim was picking up pieces of bright blue egg shells and putting them in that old gray sling he had saved from two years ago. There were little tiny dead baby birds in the sling along with the shells, and Jim was crying. He wiped his eyes with the back of his hand, stood up and glared at me.

"It's not fair," he said defiantly.

I didn't know what to say to him. I got the shovel, and we buried the birds out behind the garden, wrapped up in Jim's gray sling.

15 THREE-MILE SQUARE

In July of 1963, for the first time ever, we ran into a stranger walking on the three-mile square....

The best bike rides were around the three-mile square. The three-mile square is just what it sounds like – a three mile ride that takes you around what would probably amount to quite a few big city blocks. Not being from a big city, I never really knew for sure what the comparable distance might be. One time we asked our science teacher, Mr. Osborne, and he told us that he thought that one mile might equal about ten city blocks. So the three-mile square would be about thirty blocks, if Mr. Osborne was right, and he usually was. He told us it was a little different for each city, so he wasn't sure either, but he was one smart guy and we trusted him. He was pretty much everyone's favorite teacher, too.

Anyway, the three-mile square was not a bike ride for little kids unless they had some older kids with them. My mom would never let me ride around the three-mile square by myself until I was ten, and even then, she preferred that we would travel in a group. Jim could never go without me being right with him, so sometimes he tagged along with me and Dave or whoever decided to go for a ride that day. Mom always told me that we had to watch out for strangers who might be walking around the three-mile square, but I never saw any until my tenth year of being in the world.

One sunny afternoon, I was bored out of my skull, so I asked Mom if I could go for a ride.

"Who's going with you?" That was usually her first question, just as it was that day.

"I don't know yet. I'll ask Jim if he wants to go, but I'll call the other guys and see if they want to go, too," I reassured her.

Jim was happy to tag along, as usual, and when I started making calls, only Dave and Rusty could go. Rusty lived the farthest away from me, and he was the last one to arrive at the house. We grabbed my transistor radio and hooked it in the basket of my bike with an old belt of mine. That way it wouldn't tip over and everyone would be able to hear it. It was always so fun riding around listening to the Beach Boys or Jan and Dean on CKLW, my favorite radio station.

Our house was on one of the roads that made up the three-mile square. We were on the east side of it. We started heading south, out where the houses got farther apart, down past the Hankins farm, past McClure's farm, eventually turning onto the south side of the square. We were listening to "Up on the Roof" by the Drifters and were about halfway down the south road when we saw someone walking towards us. We were pretty sure it was a man.

"I have never seen anybody walking down this road," Dave said. "Do you think we ought to turn around?"

"Don't be such a chicken," Rusty said. "It's probably just Mr. McClure or someone out checking their crops."

I can't say I was as confident as Rusty, but I thought it might be because my mom was always so skittish about "strangers" being around town. She probably worried a little too much about such things, being a mom and all.

"Let's keep going," I said. "I'm sure Rusty is probably right."

As we got closer, we could see it definitely was not Mr. McClure. The man was much taller and he was skinnier than Mr. McClure. It had been a while since he shaved – black stubble covered his chin and neck. He had kind of a beat up jacket on, even though it was hot as heck, and he carried one of those things like hobos carry – a stick with a handkerchief on it, probably carrying whatever possessions he had. He definitely was a stranger.

"Guys, I don't know…" Dave trailed off.

"Yeah, Rusty, I'm not so sure, either." I had hesitated to say anything, but I felt the hairs on the back of my neck starting to tickle.

"Gol, are you guys babies or what?" Rusty, who had been riding ahead of us, stopped his bike and turned to chastise us. "You don't even know a thing about this guy and you're ready to turn and run."

"That's the whole problem, wise guy. We don't know a thing about him," Dave retorted.

"What's that thing Mrs. King always said…don't judge a book by its cover." Rusty turned back to pedal south, but I noticed that even Rusty was going a little slower.

Closer, closer, closer we came to the stranger, who we could now clearly see was unshaven, kind of dirty-looking, and pretty skinny. He didn't look very old, really, and I wondered when was the last time he had anything to eat. He was looking right at us like he wasn't concerned about anything at all, like he was curious about this group of boys. Jim seemed to be sticking closer to me as we finally got within speaking distance of the man.

"Good afternoon, boys," the stranger spoke up. "Can you young men tell me if there's a place in town where I could grab a bite to eat?"

Rusty was first to stop his bike. "Sure, there's Janie's right down by the post office. "

"So where's the post office?" the stranger asked. "I walked through part of town and never saw it."

"You would have had to have been close to it. To get to this road, you would have had to turn right by the gas station," Rusty continued.

"That's exactly where I did turn," the man said. "Did I turn too soon?"

"Yup. You turned only about one block away from Janie's." Now Dave had spoken up. Jim was still close by my side, kind of hiding behind me. Every once in a while I could see him crane his neck around to gaze at this grizzly-looking man.

"Well, I guess I'll turn and go back the way I came. I've been walking all morning and I'm getting pretty darn hungry," the stranger said. Even from a distance I had thought he looked like a guy who hadn't eaten in a while and I was right.

"We don't have extra seat space on our bikes, or we could take you," Rusty volunteered. My mom would have had a heart attack if she heard that.

"That's all right. I'll make it just fine," the stranger said.

"We'll ride on ahead and wait for you up at the gas station," Rusty offered. "Then we can watch for you and make sure you get to the right place."

"Well, I'm much obliged," answered the stranger, and he pretended to tip his hat to Rusty.

We rode the rest of the south side of the square and turned onto the west side, which would take us back into town.

As we rode through the first few houses at the edge of town, we saw Scotty Wilson's mom hanging out laundry to dry. Scotty and his family must have made a lot of laundry because the clotheslines were full. She was bent over a laundry basket, grabbing the next item and when she stood up, she saw us and flagged us down.

"Where's Scotty?" I asked. "I tried to call him to come with us."

"Oh, he's at his grandma's house today, helping her with yard work. Boys, did you see a strange man down the road?"

"Yes," we all answered at one time.

"Did you speak with him or him with you?" She seemed a little nervous.

"Well, yes. He asked us where he could get something to eat, so we told him about Janie's. In fact, he's going to be coming back this way," Rusty said.

"Oh my!" Mrs. Wilson exclaimed. "You boys better get home. I'm going to let the town constable know there's a stranger coming back into town." She hurriedly hung up a familiar shirt I had seen Scotty wear and headed back into her house.

"C'mon guys. Let's get moving. Sheesh! She'll have the FBI in here to snag the poor guy before we get to the gas station," Rusty said. "People in this hick town get too dorky about this stuff." Rusty thought he was much more "city" than just about everyone in town though he was never mean about it. He had moved to our town from Elyria, so he did have more city background than the rest of us.

We waited patiently at the corner by the gas station. Jim wanted an Orange Crush, but I hadn't brought any money and neither had he. We just sat on the bench by the gas station in the hot July sun, bright and unrelenting. The glare was starting to give me a headache when we saw the man heading up the road, just getting past the first few houses at the edge of town.

"Let's go meet him," Rusty said. We hopped back on our bikes and rode towards him.

"You fellows didn't have to wait for me," the man said.

"Aw, we wanted to make sure you found Janie's all right," Rusty said. "It's not hard, but if you don't know your way around, you could still get kind of lost." This seemed ridiculous to me – our town was so little there was no way you could get lost. You might wander around a little while, but you couldn't get lost.

"Well, thanks." We had arrived back at the gas station. "So, which way do I go now?" the strange man asked us.

"C'mon, we'll show you," Dave said as he took off towards Janie's Diner.

Janie's really was only about a block north, and though we beat the man to the diner, he wasn't far behind us. Maybe knowing he was going to get some food made him have more pep in his step, as my dad would say.

Jim opened the door and held it, never taking his eyes off the man while he went in. Jim was checking him out, head to toe. He had not said a single word to the man.

We found an empty table right away, which was easy because no one was in there. Not one soul. Of course, it was the middle of the afternoon, but you would think someone would be in there getting a Coke or something. No one. Janie's was deserted. In fact, we didn't even see Janie.

"I'll go find her," I said. I walked to the back of the diner where the grill and kitchen were located. I figured Janie would be back there getting ready for the supper customers.

Janie had her head bent over, peeling potatoes like crazy. She was not as old as my mom, but she was out of high school, maybe in her twenties. She was not married, though I knew a lot of guys hung around the diner trying to get her to go out on a date. She usually just joked around with them. She worked at the diner all day every day, from sun up till it was time to go home at night. As I approached her, I wondered if she ever did anything for fun.

"Hey Janie…" I didn't want to startle her when she had a knife in her hands.

She turned to look at me and a big smile crossed her face. "Hey, Johnny boy! How are you? You look hot as the dickens. What have you been up to? Do you need a Coke?"

"Well, actually, I could use something to drink, but mostly I wanted to tell you that you have a customer out front."

Janie put down her knife, wiped off her hands on her apron and said, "Well thanks for letting me know. I didn't even hear anyone come in. Who is it?" she asked.

"I don't actually know," I answered. "He's a stranger, and be prepared because he looks kind of like a grub."

She looked at me for a second and then went to where she could peek around one of the columns between the dining area and the kitchen. She took a look and turned back to me. "Where did you find him?" she asked, giving me a puzzled look.

"He was walking around the three-mile square, and Dave, Rusty, Jim and I ran across him," I explained. "He asked us where he could get something to eat, so we told him about your place."

"Ok," she said. "Let's go see what he wants." As we approached the dining area, Janie suddenly stopped in her tracks and looked hard at the man. "Oh, my…" she said under her breath. Then she put the smile back on her face and continued out to the dining area. "Welcome to Janie's," she called out cheerfully.

The stranger looked up to see Janie and for the first time, he smiled. No one could resist Janie's smile – you just had to smile back at her.

"Thank you. It's good to sit down," the stranger said.

Me and the guys had sort of found ourselves a seat at other tables and were watching to see how things would proceed. Jim seemed to have gotten over his anxiety and was looking at the gumball machine by the dining counter where the stools were. I knew before it was all over, he'd be up on one of those stools spinning around till he got dizzy.

Janie gave the man a menu, pulled out her order tablet, and said, "Where all have you been?"

"Oh, here, there and a little of everywhere," he answered.

"Are you from Ohio?" she asked, then she immediately said, "I'm sorry – take a look at the menu, then I'll bother you with questions."

The stranger smiled again and turned his attention to the menu. "What do you have for about two dollars?" he asked.

Janie looked at him for a minute and then said, "We have the best two dollar steak in town. It's served with mashed potatoes, a salad, and pie for dessert. All the coffee you can drink comes with it, or since it's hot, maybe iced tea would be preferable?"

The stranger looked up at her and said, "That seems like an awful lot for two dollars. Are you sure about that?"

"You bet I am. I've run this place for nearly five years now, and that's the two dollar steak meal. Prices haven't changed since I took ownership." Janie's smile was like a hug.

"I guess I'll have the steak supper, then," answered the stranger. "That sounds right up my alley."

Janie disappeared into the kitchen and returned, balancing a tray that held glasses of ice. She poured ice tea for each of us, including the strange man we had brought to her diner.

"Janie, me and the guys didn't bring any money," I said. "We just wanted mister...well, this man right here to be able to find your restaurant."

"That's ok guys. It's a hot one out there." Janie returned to where she worked her magic on different foods. She was a good cook.

"Thanks, boys, for getting me here," said the man. "Seems like I'm going to get my fill, and you don't have to hang around if you don't want to. I can find my way back out of town."

"That's ok," Rusty said. "We should have been more polite by now and told you our names and we didn't ask your name, either. I'm Rusty." We each took turns telling the man our names except for Jim, who was horsing around with one of the plants Janie had in the window of the diner.

"I'm Jack Michaels," said the man. "I'm from Lansing, Michigan, and I'm walking my way back home."

"Gees, don't you have a car?" Dave asked.

"Don't be so rude, Dave!" Rusty scolded. "Gees, where's your manners?"

"I didn't mean anything by it," Dave retorted. "I just think that's a heck of a long way to walk."

"It is," said Jack Michaels. "It sure is. But I don't have a car. And that's ok. This gives me a chance to see the country a little bit."

It was right about then that I noticed a little star on the collar of the man's jacket. I knew it was some kind of military thing, but I didn't really know what it meant. Just as I was pondering this, Janie returned from the kitchen with a big plate of food, still steaming from the kitchen. She set it down in front of Jack and retreated to the kitchen, returning with a salad in a bowl.

Jack pulled out his two dollars and Janie said, "Keep it, sir. It's my honor to serve an American soldier. When did you get home?"

He looked at Janie for a few seconds before he replied. "Just a few days ago. I got into Camp Lejeune on Tuesday, hitched a ride as far as Cincinnati with a big rig, got another ride into Lima, and now I'm here. I walked from Lima to your town. I think I have to go through here to get to Findlay; then I hope I can beg another ride off of someone up to Michigan at least."

"You were in Nam?" she asked.

"Yes, and a God-forsaken hell hole it is," he said. I got the impression he didn't really want to talk about it too much. He turned his attention to his food.

Just as Jack was making short work of his meal, the door opened and there stood Constable Roger Thomas, looking authoritative with his badge and his gray constable shirt on. He was really a pretty nice man, but when he had to do a constable thing, he kind of put on a tough face.

"Well, well, good afternoon, ladies and gentlemen," he said, looking around the diner at all of us. "It looks like we have a little party going on this afternoon." His eyes settled on Jack.

"Hi Rog," Janie greeted him. "Cup of coffee?"

"No thanks. Too hot for that. How about some of that tea I see?" He smiled, and I thought to myself, only Janie would call Constable Thomas by his first name when he was on official duty.

Constable Thomas took off his police hat, pulled up a chair and sat down just a little ways from Jack. "How are you today, sir?" he asked our new friend.

"I'm doing fine, sir, now that I've had one of Janie's delicious meals. I was pretty hungry when I walked into town, but I'll walk out of town with plenty of fuel in the tank." Jack smiled at the constable as if to reassure him.

"Where are you headed from here?" the constable asked him.

"I'm going home to Lansing. I have a bit of a walk as you now know. I'll probably try to hitch a ride with someone. Sir, just because I know you'd like to ask, my intentions are not to cause any trouble in this village. I only happened upon these boys and asked them if they knew where I could get something to eat. They kindly referred me to Janie, here, and Janie has been kind enough to provide me with a meal."

Janie reappeared in the dining room with a whole pitcher of tea and poured a glass for Constable Thomas.

"Jack here just got home from Nam," she said, looking intently at the constable. Her eyes were trying to give him a message, like "don't mess around with this guy."

At that point, Constable Thomas leaned back in his chair and looked hard at Jack. I think he must have seen the little bronze star that was on his jacket. His face relaxed.

"Son, I'm glad to meet you," the constable said. "How can we help you get to your home? Do your folks know you're back?"

"My folks died before I ever left. All I have now is my sister in Lansing. She and her husband know I'm home but they have kids and I didn't want them trying to come pick me up. I was going to take a bus, but I was short on cash because I've been sending some to her each month. I just kind of got myself in a little money trouble and decided, well, what better way to see part of the country? So I hitched a ride here and there and have been walking a lot." Jack looked tired now that he had finished his meal. Janie poured him some more tea.

"Thanks. This dinner was delicious. I know it cost more than any two dollars. I wish you'd take this money." Jack started to pull out his little bit of money again.

"Don't you dare!" Janie cried out. "I wouldn't take your money if it was the last dollar I earned. You've paid for this steak many times over with your service to our country."

"I sure wish everyone I met felt like you all do. Not many people think too much of us guys who have been over in Viet Nam. It's not a popular war. It's not a good place to be, over there, and I was really looking forward to coming home where people are friendly and willing to lend a hand to each other – just like you all have been. That's not exactly how it's been though." Jack sounded sad and exhausted. I wondered what kind of stuff he'd seen over in Viet Nam. Did he see guys getting shot? Did he see guys getting blown up? I didn't really want to think about it too much.

"Son, this isn't much, but could you use a good night's rest? I think we could put you up at the jail overnight. You could at least sleep on the one cot we have – it hasn't been slept on in years. You could get a shower in the morning and then get on the road again." Constable Thomas was sincerely trying to help. "Oh, and no charge. Get it?" Constable Thomas continued, laughing. "No charge." It took Jack a minute, but then he started laughing too.

"Roger, you are a hoot," said Janie.

"Well, actually, if you're sure it's no trouble, I would be much obliged," Jack said. "I'm about worn out, to be truthful, and it sure would feel good to get a hot shower."

"Don't forget to come in tomorrow morning and have some eggs and bacon before you set out," Janie told him.

"I'll be sure to do that." Jack stood up to leave with Constable Thomas.

Jim and I headed for home after thanking Janie for the tea. I figured Mom would be ready to tan our hides for being gone so long, but when I told her everything that happened, she was intrigued.

"I think I'll go get one of Dad's old shirts and take it up to him. You say he's pretty tall and skinny? I know Dad's got some shirts that don't quite fit him around the middle anymore."

"What did I just hear you say?" Dad was laughing as he entered the kitchen, home from work.

We repeated the whole story for Dad. You could tell he was thinking about how he could help, too.

"You know, I'll bet if we let some other people in town know about this, we could at least collect enough money to get this young man a bus ticket from Findlay to Lansing. I'm not sure how much they cost. Honey, will you call Greyhound and see, and I'll start talking to some of our neighbors." Now Dad was on a mission, and when Dad got on a mission, stay out of his way, that's all I can tell you.

Mom called Greyhound and found out that tickets were about $20. Dad had already hit up the close neighbors and raised about $5 of that. We figured we'd go out again after we had supper.

Dad and I walked all over town and collected enough money for the bus ticket. Fifty cents from this family, a buck from that family...everyone we talked to contributed. It was one of the best feelings! Dad called Constable Thomas and told him what we had done. Constable Thomas said that in the morning, we could meet up with Jack and that he, himself, would take Jack to Findlay so he didn't have to walk anymore.

The next day, a whole bunch of people from the village went up to Janie's for breakfast. Dad had taken a flag to hang up above Janie's counter, and we had the money in an envelope, ready to give Jack. Janie was really busy with all the customers. I had lots of practice cleaning up tables from working at the smorgasbord, so I helped Janie with that so she could concentrate on cooking.

Then, the door opened and there was Constable Thomas and Jack, looking like a much younger and more rested man. Everyone in the place started clapping like crazy, and people stood up and walked over to shake his hand and thank him for his service. You could tell he was about in a state of shock. Constable Thomas led him over to the only open table in the place. Janie came out right away and poured coffee for the constable and for Jack, too.

"What'll it be this morning, soldier?" Janie asked him.

"I guess I could do with some eggs and bacon and toast," Jack replied.

"What about you, Constable?" Janie inquired.

"I already ate at home, but I'll take a cup of coffee," he said.

While Janie cooked, people who had already eaten gathered around Jack and asked him questions and told him all kinds of stuff about their own war experiences. Some of the men had been in Korea, but a couple had been in World War II, and they really tried to make Jack feel welcome. It was like he had met up with his brothers or something.

After Jack had finished eating and all the people seemed like they had gotten their fill of talking about the Army and Marines and Navy, my dad came up to the front of the diner near the counter and clinked a spoon on a glass to get everyone's attention.

"If I could have your attention for just a minute, everyone...everyone, just a second...."

The diner quieted down, and Dad began to talk. "Jack, we all want to thank you for spending part of your life in Viet Nam to help the Vietnamese people. We know that young men and women coming back from that war are not always viewed very kindly. We've seen it on TV and we've heard it from our friends who have kids who served. We want you to know that in this town, we support our soldiers, even when we wonder about why we're sending them off to fight. We want you to know that we're glad you stopped by our town. We're glad you're home safe, and we want to make sure you get to your sister's house without any trouble. Therefore, it's my pleasure to present you with this money we collected for a Greyhound ticket to Lansing, a gift from the people of this town."

Jack looked like you could have knocked him over with a feather. He just sat there with his mouth open, looking at my dad, and then all around the diner.

"What...how did...what?" he said, glancing back and forth at all the friendly faces.

Constable Thomas spoke right up. "We're saying thank you, boy, and here's a little something to help you on your way." He took the envelope from my dad and handed it to Jack.

"When you're ready, I'll take you up to the bus station. It's not far – only about eight miles. You can get to Lansing in more comfort. What's more, we can call your sister before you go so she knows when to meet you."

Jack looked around the room some more. Finally, he spoke. "I can't remember when I've met such a kind group of people. I can never repay you...."

"You already paid us with your service," Al Fox spoke up.

"I'm eternally grateful, and I'm humbled by your kindness," Jack kind of croaked out.

"Well-earned and well-deserved." Dad shook Jack's hand. You know, with very few exceptions, that's just how people were in our town.

People started leaving the diner. Jack had another cup of coffee, then he and Constable Thomas stood to leave. Rusty, Dave, Jim, and I were about the only people left besides Janie. She gave Jack a little hug.

"Be safe and don't take any wooden nickels." Janie smiled real big and started clearing tables as Jack and the constable headed for the door.

"Thanks to all of you," Jack said quietly, turning to look at us one more time. "I'll never forget you."

And then he was gone. He walked into our village and just like that, he rode out.

We hadn't asked for permission from our moms, but all of us guys got on our bikes and took one quick ride around the three-mile square that morning. We were on the look-out…you never did know who you might meet out there.

16 VACATION

For my family, vacation each year meant one thing – traveling to North Carolina, the hottest, most humid place on the face of the planet. That's where my mom's mom and dad (who we called Mammy and Pappy) lived on a farm outside a little town called Rose Hill. I loved to go see them, but it was a miserable trip, usually, and it took about twelve hours in the car with Jim. Jim was not a good traveler.

We started out for North Carolina in the very early morning. My dad was one of those guys who wanted to always get an early start just in case there was any trouble with the car along the way. He didn't like to arrive too late in the evening, so we took off before sunrise. He drove as fast as the speed limit would allow, and sometimes faster. "Bob," my mom would say, "you better slow down! You've got a carload of people on the Pennsylvania Turnpike. You know how their state patrol is!" What she meant by that is that the state patrol in Pennsylvania liked to arrest people from Ohio for speeding. My dad always told her he was keeping an eye out for the cops. I don't know if he really was or not, but I sure did.

We stopped briefly in Breezewood, Pennsylvania, as we always did. That was the break point from turnpike driving to the other roads my dad had to take to get to my grandparents' house. We usually found someplace we could have a picnic, and my mom would bring out the cold fried chicken she had prepared for our trip. That chicken tasted so good by the time we got to

Breezewood. Cold fried chicken and Wonder bread…a meal fit for kings. On the trip, Mom always brought a thermos full of coffee, too, with cream and sugar in it because that's how my dad liked it. I liked it that way myself, and Mom would let me have a little bit while we traveled. She called it "kid coffee" because she liked hers black. Then Dad would gas up the car, we'd make a run for the bathroom, and before you could barely dry your hands, we were flying down the highway again. Dad hardly ever stopped…just for gas and for us to go to the bathroom. You better go to the bathroom when he was stopped for gas, or you could find yourself in a world of hurt.

When we got to Virginia, we started seeing sights that were more familiar to my mom than they were to me or Jim. There were lots of roadside stands where people would sell fresh fruit and vegetables. There were all kinds of stores along the way, too. My favorite place was Stuckey's. They had good food and lots of stuff to look at. They had Confederate flags and Union soldier hats. I always wanted one of those. They also had pecan log rolls. That was a particular favorite of everyone in the family. We didn't usually spend too much money on these trips because we just didn't have it, but one thing we got was a pecan log roll.

Once we crossed over into North Carolina, Mom started seeing signs for the Mount Olive pickle company. That was her favorite kind of pickle and you couldn't get them in Ohio. With her being pregnant and all, she wanted pickles in the worst way, but she only wanted Mount Olive pickles. Despite Dad's protests, we had to stop at a Piggly Wiggly to get some. She opened a jar right in the car, she was so hungry for them. I tried one, and I had to admit they were really good. Then Jim decided he wanted one, and he liked them, too. That's where the trouble began.

Mom handed the pickles to me in the back seat. "John, please put these in the picnic basket with the chicken," she said. I did as I was told, but it wasn't long before Jim pulled the jar of pickles out and took off the lid. He pulled out two of the pickles before closing the jar up and putting it back in the picnic basket. Mom must have smelled the pickles because she turned to look at what was going on in the back seat.

"Jimmy, don't eat too many of those. You'll get sick," Mom said. Jim looked at her and kept munching.

Jim's pickles were gone in a matter of minutes, and he got two more out as quietly as he could. You can't get around my mom, though, and she looked back again. "Jim, I wasn't kidding. Don't eat any more of those. Too much pickle brine will make you sick."

Jim kept right on eating. He looked like he had found heaven. If Mom hadn't got after him, he probably would have eaten the whole jar. After that last two, he fell asleep with his head leaned up against the window, which was only partially rolled down.

I watched all the scenery flying by us. I would have liked to ask Dad about some of the signs alongside the road that told stuff about the Civil War, but he was driving so fast I thought I better just let him concentrate on driving. Jim was asleep, and so was Mom. It was quiet in the car, all except for the wind blowing in our windows.

All of a sudden, Jim woke up. "Dad, I have to throw up!" he said. He looked kind of pale and I knew he wasn't fooling.

"Oh brother," Dad muttered. "Jim, I'm not anywhere that I can pull over. Do you have a bag or anything back there you can throw up in?"

Jim was holding his stomach and looking pretty wretched. "Dad, we don't have anything back here and Jim really looks sick," I said.

"Ok. Hang on. There's a roadside rest about twelve miles up here. I'll get there as fast as I can," Dad said. He gripped the wheel and sped up. I felt like I was in a space ship, he was going so fast. It was too late though, and I could tell it. Jim would never make it twelve miles.

"Uh-oh," Jim said, and that was it. Jim started throwing up and was it ever gross! There were chunks of pickle in the throw up and it smelled awful. It woke my mom up.

"Good Lord, what is going on?" she said before she turned around and saw Jim. "Oh for pity's sake," she said and then SHE started gagging. I guess pregnant women throw up kind of easy.

"Now don't you start!" Dad said, but it was too late for Mom, too. She started barfing, but at least she had a little garbage bag to throw up in. I could feel Dad push the accelerator on the car. It just wasn't his day, because before you could say "throw up," a North Carolina state patrol car was behind us with their red lights flashing. I could hear the siren loud as anything. "Good grief," Dad said as he tried to find a wide place along the road to pull over.

The state patrolman sat in his own car for a second before he approached Dad's window.

"Sir, do you know how fast you were...." The patrolman suddenly stopped talking and a weird look came over his face. He looked at my mom, who was holding her bag of vomit, and then he looked in the back seat and saw Jim's throw up all over the place. I guess he felt bad for my dad because he said, "Sir, I can see you have your hands full. Just take it easy on the speed. There's a roadside rest about ten miles up where your family can get a break and get cleaned up. Good luck." And with that, he headed back for his patrol car, smiling and shaking his head.

"Well, we caught a break on that one, I guess you could say. Of course, if everyone in the car wasn't barfing, I wouldn't have been speeding in the first place." Dad was pretty frustrated, I think.

"I'm not barfing, Dad," I said. "I don't even feel sick. I can help Jim get cleaned up a little back here. I have some tissues."

"Thanks, John. I'll get us up to that rest stop, but I'm not going to go fast, so hold your nose, I guess."

I was ok. I have smelled stuff worse than vomit before, like when I was at Mr. Rader's farm and we had to clean up the chicken coops. That was pretty bad. Vomit was nothing compared to that, though the pickles did give Jim's vomit a little acid-y kind of smell that wasn't too good.

We got to the roadside rest and got out of the car. Mom was doing better, but Jim still looked a little green. Dad went into the bathroom and got some paper towels with water on them. I got Jim cleaned up while Mom sat in the shade. Her stomach was getting pretty large now, and I tried to help her more because she was tired a lot. Dad started cleaning up the back seat.

"Geeminy Christmas, Jim. How many pickles did you eat?" he asked. I don't think he really expected an answer. He kept on cleaning as best as he could. When he was finally finished, he asked Jim, "Do you think you're done? Does your stomach feel any better?"

"Yes," answered Jim weakly. "I'm ok now." Dad opened the trunk and got Jim a clean shirt out of the suitcase.

I wasn't so sure Jim was done throwing up, but we loaded everyone back into the Oldsmobile and took off again. I sat in the front seat with Dad this time, and Mom sat in the back seat so she could keep an eye on Jim, who fell asleep back there, just like he did before. Our long trip had gotten even longer.

It was about the middle of the evening when we finally got to Rose Hill. I was sure happy to see the sign that said, "Welcome to Rose Hill, Home of the World's Biggest Frying Pan." I wondered how big that frying pan was...we had never seen it.

My grandparents lived in a small farmhouse that was on a road made out of sand: yes, sand, and their driveway was made out of sand, too. I thought that was the most interesting thing and never got tired of seeing that sand road. It was like the beach with no ocean. No one else I knew had a sand road.

Mammy and Pappy were sitting on their porch fanning themselves when we arrived. All around the porch, Mammy's hydrangeas were in bloom – the brightest blue – almost purple. The house and porch were raised up on stilts, so Mammy and Pappy had to go down the steps to come out and greet us. I noticed Pappy wasn't moving too fast.

"Oh lands, I'm so happy to see y'all." Mammy was crying, she was so happy. She did that every year. She cried when we got there, and she cried when we left. I know she loved us, and we loved her, too. She was the sweetest person ever. It always cheered me up to see her.

Pappy was not a man of many words, and he didn't hug us to death like Mammy did, but you could tell he was happy to see us by the way he put his hand out to shake ours. He was a very big man, and he worked really hard on the tobacco farm. He was tan from being out in the sun all the time. Mammy was tan, too, because she was always working out in her vegetable garden. My mom said they both had to work so hard because they didn't have very much money. I never cared about if they had a lot of money anyway, but I understood it meant they had to work really hard. When we came down on vacation, I always tried to help them with what I knew how to do. Pappy taught me about tobacco farming, and he also raised pigs. I was a little bit scared of the pigs because they were so huge, but he had an electric fence around them so they never tried to get out of the barnyard, and now that I was ten, I thought maybe I wouldn't be quite as scared.

"Come in, come in and get some iced tea," Mammy said. She made the best ice tea of anyone, and I was looking forward to it. I liked mine with lemon and that's how Mammy always made it for me.

Mom started telling Mammy about our trip, including the throw up episode. Mammy started laughing about that, and then Mom and Dad started laughing, too. I think Dad was so happy to be there after that long trip that he would have laughed at just about anything. He hadn't been laughing in the car too much, I can tell you that. Anyway, after Mom relayed the throw up story and everyone had a good laugh that was the end of it. We never talked about it again while we were down there. I think Jim was relieved about that.

We got a good night's sleep and when we got up in the morning, I could tell Mammy was already up because I could smell that she was frying country ham. That was one of my favorite things that Mammy made. The flavor was so good. She always made fresh biscuits, and if you put a piece of that ham inside a biscuit, well, you just couldn't ask for anything better, I don't think. We all loved Mammy's biscuits and ham. I was ravenous and ate two biscuits with ham. Jim only ate one. I think he was trying to make sure his stomach wasn't going to turn sour again.

After breakfast, Pappy asked me if I wanted to go out to the tobacco house with him. The tobacco house was where he dried out the leaves by hanging them upside down in big bundles. I loved that building and jumped at the chance to go out there. It had its own pungent smell, was warm but was dry. It was one of my favorite places on the farm.

"Come on, then, boy. Finish your breakfast and meet me out back by the pecan tree." Pappy would be ready to go, so I knew I had to speed it up a little.

When I walked out the back screen door, I started down the steps. I was looking over at the pecan tree for Pappy, and he was there with a shovel in his hand. "Wait, boy!" he called out to me. Something in his voice made me stop dead in my tracks.

"Look down at the bottom of the steps," Pappy said. I did, and I saw something I had never seen before in any of our trips south.

At the bottom of the steps was a very long black snake. My mom had talked about snakes in North Carolina, but I had never seen one. I was kind of scared of snakes because my mom told me about the poisonous ones that lived around there.

"Is it a water moccasin?" I called out to Pappy, frozen where I was on the steps. I had heard my mom talk about water moccasins, and they sounded like they could kill you with one bite.

"No, but there's no need to mess with him, that's for sure. I believe he's just a black rat snake. He won't bother you if you don't bother him," Pappy told me.

I stayed still as anything. I didn't want to attract the attention of any snake. I didn't care if he was poisonous or not. Finally, he slithered off under the house.

"Criminy, Pappy! Do they ever come in the house?" I shuddered at the thought, still a little scared to move.

"No son. They don't like humans any more than we like them. They just look for mice and such to eat. Come on, now. I've got work to do." I looked around a little bit to make sure the snake didn't decide to make another appearance. The coast was clear, so I scurried down the steps as fast as I could to catch up with Pappy. I felt safe around him. He knew exactly what to do about snakes.

When we got to the tobacco house and opened the door, it was just like I remembered. Big bunches of tobacco hanging upside down. The smell was wonderful – drying tobacco doesn't smell like cigarettes. I always thought cigarettes smelled bad, but drying tobacco smells kind of like dried hay, only a deeper odor than that. It's hard to explain, but I loved that smell. It's a warm smell. And it always felt warm inside the tobacco house. It's like the feeling of being warm got all mixed up with the warm smell of the tobacco. They kind of went together and you couldn't tell where one stopped and the other began.

Pappy walked around in the barn a little bit and felt the leaves of tobacco with his hands. "This is ready. We'll take this to the market today. Why don't you come over here and help me get this down?"

I was excited to help with this job and I was excited to go to the tobacco market with Pappy. This was men's work.

Pappy would take down the big bunches, and my job was to lay them on top of each other in a stack on a flatbed wagon he pulled with his tractor. The bundles were pretty heavy, but I kept up with Pappy. He was a strong man, and I wanted to show him I was getting stronger too, so I didn't complain about how heavy the bundles were.

When we got done, Pappy took me up on his tractor with him and let me ride back towards the house. I saw my mom standing on the back steps with her hand on her stomach, rubbing it like it hurt. I didn't know if she was ready to throw up again, if she was watching out for snakes, or if she was watching out for me on the tractor. I remembered what Dad said about her friend that got hurt on a tractor, so I knew she'd be fussing over me riding along with Pappy. I sat very still so she wouldn't feel so upset. She would see I was responsible enough to ride the tractor.

"Did you help your Pappy?" Mom asked when we got up to the house.

"He certainly did," Pappy interjected. "He did a good job. That boy knows how to work. I'm taking him to the tobacco market with me."

I smiled at Mom. I knew she would be proud of me for helping out. She smiled back and just said, "Behave yourself while you're there." She went back in the house, and my guess is that she was heading straight for the living room where she could put her feet up and sit in front of the fan. It was hot and humid as all get out, the air heavy, and it was still kind of early in the morning.

I helped Pappy transfer the bundles of tobacco from the wagon to the truck. He was sweating like crazy, and so was I. When we got done with the transfer, Pappy said, "I've got to run in the house. Go ahead and get in the truck and I'll be right out."

When he returned, Pappy handed me a red handkerchief that was wet with cold water. "Tie this around your neck, and it will help keep you cool," he said. I noticed he had done the same thing for himself. He was right – the wet handkerchief really did help.

We headed for Wallace – that's where the tobacco market was located. Pappy didn't drive as fast as Dad, but no one in North Carolina seemed to drive as fast as people in Ohio. It seemed to me that it was just a more relaxed place.

The market was really interesting. Lots and lots of tobacco farmers brought their crops there to sell. Guys who were inspectors would walk around the market, look at everybody's crops and then make them an offer on how much they would pay that guy for his tobacco. It was an auction, Pappy said. I had been to an auction once with my dad – there was a guy who was a really fast talker who got everyone to bid on different things they had for sale like old tools or glassware. This seemed a little bit different from that. Anyway, Pappy got a good bid on his tobacco – he was a very good tobacco farmer – and he sold every bit of it. We started out for home.

As we got to the edge of Wallace, Pappy asked me, "Could you eat a little ice cream cone?" I never turned down ice cream, so I said, "Yes." He pulled in at an ice cream stand called the Dairi-O. I knew Pappy wasn't rich and I didn't want to be selfish, so I asked for the smallest vanilla cone. He got the same thing. We sat at a little picnic table off to the side of the parking lot and enjoyed the cool vanilla frost in our throats.

"Boy, you worked hard today. This is your thank-you." Pappy was a man of few words, like I said.

"Thank you, Pappy. I appreciate the ice cream."

"You're welcome. Let's get on home," he said. We jumped back in the truck and made our way back down the highway to that familiar sand road. We could see Mammy and Pappy's house from the highway, and we could see that there was another car in the driveway. Pappy and I thought some of my cousins had arrived.

Sure enough, when we got to the house, Pappy said, "That's Em and her kids." We parked the truck in the grass so that it wouldn't be in the way when Em and her kids decided to leave, but little did we know that they wouldn't be leaving for a while....

When we got out of the truck and started making our way to the house, we heard screaming from the back yard and heard kids yelling. You could tell it wasn't *good* yelling like someone who's having fun, and I wondered if the snake had come back. Pappy and I made a beeline for the back yard.

My cousins David and Elizabeth were in the back yard, kind of running around and waving their arms. My aunt Emily was there with her daughter, Sherry, who was crying. Aunt Emily had Sherry's pants pulled down around her ankles and was looking at her behind. This was a strange sight, as you can imagine. I stopped where I was because I didn't want to see Sherry's behind, but Jim was standing right there, big as anything.

"What in tarnation is going on back here?" Pappy asked.

"Sherry sat on a pitchfork. Come see. She's got three holes in her butt cheek." Aunt Emily didn't really seem scared or upset, but just real matter-of-fact about the whole thing. Sherry, on the other hand, was screaming her head off.

"I'll go get the merthiolate," Pappy said.

"I'll get it, Pappy!" I called out to him. He gave me a little wave like he was saying 'ok,' so I ran in the house and called Mammy.

"Mammy, Sherry sat on a pitchfork and she's got holes in her butt and I need the merthiolate for Pappy," I called through the house.

Mammy came out of a bedroom with laundry in her hands. "You need what, John? Merthiolate? Sherry sat on a pitchfork?" She seemed stunned.

"Yup, that's what happened." Mammy immediately threw the laundry in on the bed it came from and went to the bathroom medicine cabinet. She grabbed some cotton balls, the merthiolate, and went with me out to where Sherry was still crying. At least she wasn't screaming anymore. Aunt Emily was kind of hugging her a little and Pappy was looking at Sherry's butt.

"How in the world did this happen?" Mammy asked when she handed Pappy the medicine.

"She was jumping out of the hay mow and she landed where she shouldn't have landed," Aunt Emily said.

"It hurts!" Sherry cried.

"You'll be fine," Pappy said. "It's not a deep puncture. Hold on now, this is going to sting." He swabbed on some merthiolate and set off a whole new round of screaming from Sherry. She broke free from Aunt Emily's hug and started dancing around, rubbing her behind.

"Stop it! I have to get a bandaid on there," Aunt Emily said.

Sherry stopped dancing around and my aunt put a bandaid on her butt. That's the first time I ever saw anything like that...a bandaid on someone's behind. I started laughing. I tried to hold it in, but I couldn't help it. I started laughing, then Jim started laughing, then Elizabeth and David started laughing, too. Jim fell down on the ground, he was laughing so hard. Even my aunt and Pappy smiled, but they didn't laugh out loud.

"Stop it! Stop laughing, you devils!" Sherry yelled at us, but we couldn't help it. We were all laughing so hard that tears were coming out of our eyes. Sherry took off around to the front of the house.

"Ok you kids, settle down," Aunt Emily said as she walked off to find Sherry, but she was still smiling.

We pulled ourselves together and followed Pappy in the house. Mammy was working on her laundry again, and Pappy filled her in on what happened at the tobacco auction. I asked where Mom was.

"She fell asleep, sugar. She's in the back bedroom sleeping," Mammy told me. She called us all 'sugar' or 'shoog' for short all the time. She called us that because she thought we were sweet, she said.

I went to the back bedroom door and opened it just a tiny bit. There was my mom, completely conked out on the bed. The trip really wore her out, but she was tired a lot because of being pregnant and all. I don't know how in the heck she slept through all the screaming and crying and laughing, but there she was, sound asleep.

The next day, the whole clan except Dad and Pappy went into Rose Hill to go to the Rexall drug store. Mammy needed to get a prescription for Pappy, and I wanted to buy some comic books because it was too hot to play outside all day long. Sherry wanted to get some Archie comics, but I wanted to get Superman or Batman. Jim tagged along with me, but he really didn't read comic books that much. He just picked up various things, looked at them, and then put them back on the shelf. He didn't know what in the heck he wanted.

"Jim, don't pick up every single thing you see," Mom said.

"I won't," he answered, but of course, he still did.

"Hey, let's get a vanilla coke!" Sherry said. "They're the best here!"

"Ok," I said. "I'll buy since you got your butt injury." This set off some snickers from Jim, but Sherry shot him a death ray stare, and he stopped chuckling pretty quick.

There was a soda fountain in the back of the Rexall, and we saw a guy behind the counter cleaning up. He smiled as we approached, and I noticed he was wearing an eye patch, but he had on glasses, too.

"What can I get you young'uns?" he asked.

"We'll take three vanilla cokes – small, please," I answered.

"Coming right up." The man turned to his work, first spooning out one teaspoon of vanilla in the bottom of each glass, then adding crushed ice, and then filling each glass with Coca Cola from a spigot. The concoction foamed up and nearly spilled over the edge of each glass. I had to help Jim up on one of the stools at the counter, but Sherry and I were both tall enough to get up there without any help. We each sipped on our vanilla cokes, enjoying the creaminess that the vanilla flavor added to the drink.

"Hey, Floyd, how are you?" My mom had caught up with us at the soda fountain counter.

"Hey, girl, I'm fine! It's been a while since I have seen you in here," Floyd answered with a smile. He seemed really happy to see my mom.

"Well, we only get down here about once a year," Mom said. "Daddy has been having some health problems, so we'll probably try to get here twice this year. I don't know for sure, though, because I'm going to have another baby."

"Well, I'll be durned," Floyd said, his smile widening. "Another baby. Myrtle tells me you have two boys right now."

"Yep, and they're both sitting right here at your counter," Mom told him.

"I thought them boys looked kind of familiar. Now I know why – they look just like you." I thought I looked like Dad, but I think Floyd was trying to give Mom a little compliment, so I kept my mouth shut.

"Well, they look more like their dad, but they have a little of me in them, too," Mom said. "Floyd, what in the world happened to your eye?" Only my mom would be forward enough to ask such a bold question. She never minced words, but I knew she must know Floyd pretty well to ask about his eye.

"Well, I had the cancer," Floyd said. When he said 'cancer,' it sounded more like 'can't sir.' People in North Carolina said stuff with a southern accent. Sometimes if they talked real fast, it was hard to understand, even.

"I sure am sorry to hear that," Mom said. "Are you doing ok now?"

"Why, I sure am. Never been better," Floyd replied. "My doctor says I am can't sir free. My fond hope is to remain that way."

"Well, thank the good Lord for that!" Mom said. "Kids, we're ready to go. Did you pick out your comic books?" When Mom was ready to go, you better be ready, too. We jumped down off our perches and started for the front, but we all called "Good-bye, Mr. Floyd." Mom gave him a little hug as we headed for the front of the store. We had already taken a look at the comics, so it was easy to grab the ones we wanted and get in line at the check-out. Mom caught up with us there.

"Comic books are getting kind of expensive," Mom said, looking at the prices on the front of the comics. "Do you kids have enough money?"

I had been saving some money from my chore allowance for this trip, so I knew I was in good shape. I wasn't so sure about Jim, but I told Mom I'd help pay for his if he needed me to. When it was all totaled up, we owed the store about fifty cents. That wasn't so bad for the great adventures we'd soon be enjoying.

On the way back to Mammy's house, Mom said, "Kids, guess what we're doing tomorrow?" Our ears perked up because we hadn't figured we'd be doing anything but working or reading or playing with our cousins.

"We're going to Wilmington. We rented a beach house for a couple of days, and you'll be able to play in the ocean!" Mom seemed as excited about this idea as us kids were. We started jumping up and down in the back seat of the car, at least as much as you can jump when you're sitting in the back of an Olds. We had never been to the ocean, not in all the years we had been making these trips to North Carolina. I had seen the ocean on television, and I was even more excited to see it in real life.

The next morning, we packed up just a few clothes – mostly shirts, shorts, and our bathing suits. Even Pappy was coming with us. Mammy said he needed a vacation, too. She and Mom got some food together to take along because we would still cook our own food at the beach house.

The trip to Wilmington didn't take long, and I could hardly wait to get down to the ocean. Our beach house was built on really tall stilts – way taller than Mammy and Pappy's house. You had to go up about a million steps outside just to get in the house. My dad said that was because of the ocean surge. I didn't really know what that was, but he told me it had something to do with hurricanes and such. The water could ruin your beach house if you didn't put it way up high.

As soon as we unpacked, Jim and I asked if we could go down on the beach. We all put on our bathing suits and grabbed towels. Mom and Dad came with us because they knew we didn't really know anything about the ocean. Mom said she felt funny in her bathing suit because her stomach was sticking out too much. Dad just laughed.

We had to walk over some sand dunes with real tall grass on them. Dad said it was beach grass. I didn't know there was such a thing till then. When we got over the dunes, we stopped dead in our tracks.

The ocean was huge. I had never seen so much water before. It was kind of loud, with the waves coming to shore. They were crashing around and making white foam on the top. It was amazing, and maybe a little scary. I kind of had a funny feeling in my stomach.

"Wow…" Jim said. I had to agree.

"Boys, when you go in this water, it's not like going to the lake. This water can pull you right down and under. You have to be careful. Let's hold hands," Dad said.

We all grabbed each other's hands and headed for the water's edge. The sand was kind of hot, and I thought that next time we came down there, I'd wear my flip-flops. The sand near the water was cool, though. It was wet and packed down. When you stepped on it, you sunk in just a little bit and left a foot print. Then the foot print would get washed away with the next wave.

We walked into the water a little farther out. I held on to Dad's hand really tightly, and Jim about squeezed my other hand to death. But it was ok. It was the first time we had ever been in the ocean. We only walked out to where it was about up to our belly buttons.

"That's far enough guys," Dad said, even though the water was only up to about the top of his legs. "That's deep enough for you to be able to jump the waves." He had to show us how to do that, and once we got the hang of it, it was so much fun! I wanted to just stay out there the rest of the day, but after a while, Mom said, "We better get back or you guys will be so sunburned you'll be sick."

"Aw, Mom, can't we stay a little longer?" we pleaded.

"No, not now, but you can come back later," she replied.

We reluctantly pulled ourselves back to shore and headed for the beach house. We had to shower the salt and sand off of ourselves in an outdoor shower, which I had also never seen before.

Aunt Emily and my cousins had arrived and were unpacking when we got to the top of the back steps at the beach house. Everyone had some lunch, though it was late afternoon and while we ate, I told my cousins about the ocean. They had seen it before, so they weren't too impressed with my description.

"I've been to the ocean a million times," Sherry said. "It's no big deal. We swim in there all the time." I thought to myself that I'd like to see her swim in those waves.

Finally, as sunset approached, Mom told us we could go back down to the water. "You kids stick together and be careful. We'll be watching from the shelter house."

We trudged through the sand – sand was hard to walk in – but it wasn't as hot as before. I didn't even need my flip-flops and they were getting sand in them, so I just took them off and walked bare-footed. I guess because the sun was going down, the sand got cooler. Anyway, we dropped our towels and sandals and so forth in a pile a little bit away from the water so all that stuff wouldn't get wet. We walked into the water and felt the coolness of it on our legs. This was a relief from the relentless North Carolina sun. Deeper and deeper we walked into the water until it was up to our thighs. I wanted to go farther out. It was starting to get a little deep for Jim – the waves pushed and pulled at us so that we knew we shouldn't go way far out. I walked on though, and so did Sherry. When the water got up to our waists, Sherry got a look of panic on her face and began to scream. It seemed like she was always screaming about something. She turned around and began to run back to shore, at least as much as you can run in the ocean.

From where I was, I saw our parents and Aunt Emily get up and start running towards us, having heard Sherry's eardrum-piercing screams. Just so you know, sand is hard to run in, too, and they were having their own share of difficulty getting to us. I started heading back in, not knowing what was wrong with Sherry.

Sherry got to the edge of the water and started peeling off her bathing suit bottom. What now? Had she got bitten on the butt by a sea creature of some kind?

I got to Sherry about the same time as my parents and Aunt Em. "Good grief, Sherry, what is wrong?" Aunt Em asked as she looked at Sherry's bare bottom.

"It stings, it stings, it stings!" Sherry cried.

"What stings?" Dad asked.

"My butt, where I got stabbed by the pitchfork," Sherry wailed.

"Salt water. The salt water…" Dad said.

"Oh, gees, for Pete's sake!" Aunt Emily said. "Sherry, the salt water is stinging your behind. Calm down. It will quit stinging in a minute. Pull your pants back up. We're out in public!" There weren't a lot of people on the beach right then, but they were looking in our direction to see what all the hubbub was about. Aunt Em said, "You'll get us arrested for indecent exposure and being a public nuisance."

Well, right then, my dad started laughing. He just let out a big guffaw that made the whole darn family start up again. Even Sherry started laughing once her behind stopped stinging so much, but she didn't laugh very long. A horrified look came across her face and she said, "Does this mean I won't be able to go in the ocean?"

"Well, you might better wait another day or so," Mom said. "Let a little more healing take place and then try again."

With this trauma, we all headed back for the beach house. Sherry was quiet on the way back. She got under the outside shower, and I noticed that she let it run on her behind for quite a while. "I'm trying to make sure the salt is washed out of there," she explained.

Sherry was able to go back in the water the next day and she got along all right. I was glad for her because our time at the beach house passed so quickly. I think Pappy was glad for the break from work, too, but a couple of days after we arrived, he announced, "Time to get back. I've got hogs to tend to."

We only stayed at Mammy and Pappy's a couple more days after that, but we had fun. Pappy helped me climb up in the pecan tree so I could check to see how the pecan crop looked for fall. It looked pretty good. My mom asked Dad to dig up a small Carolina pine tree to take home. She wanted to plant one in our yard because she loved those pine trees so much. I think she just wanted something that would remind her of North Carolina. Pappy had an old bucket that Dad could put the tree in with some dirt for the trip home. It was just a real little tree. Good thing, because there wasn't that much room in our trunk with our suitcases and so forth in there. Before we left, we went to the Rexall one more time, but this time, I got a grape Nehi. I also got a little surprise for my cousin Sherry.

On the day we left, my aunt and cousins came over early. Mammy made a huge breakfast with eggs, country ham, grits, and biscuits. I was stuffed. She and mom packed the picnic basket up with fried chicken again, too. Dad got all our stuff in the car. Pappy came in from chores and sat down by me on the couch.

"Boy, you sure are getting grown up now, and I appreciate you helping with the tobacco. You help your mother and daddy like that, too, all right?" Pappy had his arm around my shoulders. He probably could have picked me up with that one arm.

"I will, Pappy," I promised.

We all walked out to the car, and Mammy pulled a tissue out of the pocket of her apron. I knew she would cry. She just always did that. I gave her a big hug and told her I loved her.

"Be sweet, shoog," she said, as I headed for the Olds. The whole family was out by the sand driveway, giving each other hugs and saying a few final words to each other.

"Sherry, I have something for you," I said. I reached into the car and pulled out a bag from the Rexall store. I handed it to Sherry and said, "Be careful where you put it down."

Sherry looked at me, puzzled. She opened the bag and pulled out a plastic rake that had only three prongs. They weren't sharp prongs, but she knew what it meant. Jim took one look at it and started laughing all over again.

"You devil!" she said, but I knew she didn't mean it. She gave me a little hug.

We all got in the car and started backing down the driveway. I watched everyone waving to us for as long as I could. Mammy was waving her tissue, so I could see her the longest. Finally, when I could no longer see anything but specks, I turned around and settled in for the long trip home. It had been our best North Carolina trip ever. Even with the pickle incident.

17 GRANDPA FALLS

My grandpa was one of my favorite people. He was pretty old, but he did all kinds of stuff. He liked to hunt, fish, and take care of his coon hounds. He knew a lot about deer hunting and coon hunting. He also liked to hunt foxes, and my dad told me that he never saw a man who would actually run after foxes like Grandpa did. He was pretty slim and muscle-y from all that running. He could fix anything you could think of. If you had a broken toy, he could figure out how to fix it. If you had your fishing line goofed up on the reel, he could get it all straightened out. He could fix anything around the house for Grandma – anything. There was one thing I knew of that Grandpa could not fix all by himself though, and that was a broken bone.

Grandpa and Grandma lived in a small town not too far from us. Grandpa was a house painter and sheep shearer by trade. Those seemed like funny jobs to me. My own dad had to get up every day, and sometimes at night, to go work in a factory. He had to punch a time clock and be at work at a certain time and ask permission to take vacations and so forth, but Grandpa never had to do any of that. He just took jobs that people offered him, painting their houses or shearing their sheep. I should just say here that my Grandpa was a champion sheep shearer. He won many contests by shearing sheep really fast and getting a real long section of wool off the sheep all in one big piece. He was even on the front of a farming magazine in his county. It was a pretty big accomplishment because sheep are not all that easy to shear.

Sometimes they don't take too well to having their wool shaved off of them. It could be a little tricky.

Painting houses was a more peaceful kind of work, Grandpa always said. "When you're standing way up high on a ladder or up on a second floor deck, you can look around and see everything across the whole town. You get to watch the world at work. You can see kids playing, and men mowing their lawns. You can see mothers hanging clothes out on the line to dry. You can also see birds and squirrels up close-like, and see what a fine earth God gave us to live on." Grandpa loved his work. He must have been pretty good at painting houses, too, because he had people asking him to paint their houses all summer long.

In the summer of 1963, Grandpa told us he had more jobs than he could handle. "I'm not going to be around for Little League games and such this summer, John. I've got more houses to paint than Carter's got liver pills." I didn't know what in the heck liver pills were or why Carter had so many of them, but I could tell he meant he was going to be very busy. I never expected Grandpa to come to all of our baseball games, but I knew he really liked baseball a lot and he tried to come whenever he could. Unless, of course, the Cincinnati Reds were on the radio or television. He never missed a Reds game.

Grandpa worked steadily through that summer. Whenever we did see him on Sundays, he looked pretty tired. One time while we were at his house he even fell asleep and started snoring really loud, right while we were visiting! Jim started laughing at that, but I told him to be quiet because Grandpa was tired from working so hard. You should never make fun of a guy who is working that hard all the time. Jim felt pretty bad about laughing at him later on that week when we found out that Grandpa had broken his collar bone and his wrist. Here's what happened.

Grandpa had gone to this family's house – I think it was a family whose last name was Baer. The reason I remember that is because my dad went to school with a few of the kids from that family and he said he and some other kids used to call them "the little bare boys," which apparently made the Baer boys mad. My dad laughed every time he told that story. Anyway, Grandma called us and said that Grandpa was at the Baer family's house, painting away. He was just about done with the house when he somehow fell off the ladder. My mom was so upset. My dad was, too – Grandpa was his father – but he didn't start crying like my mom did. We packed up the whole household and headed for the hospital.

In the station wagon, Mom said to Dad, "Your father has no business climbing up on ladders like that anymore. He's getting too old to be doing this type of work." She sounded kind of mad, but I knew she was just upset because she loved Grandpa a lot.

Dad said, "Honey, you know how he is. If he had to just sit around all the time, it would drive him crazy. He's got to be doing something all the time."

"Well, does he have to be doing something that includes climbing around 20 feet in the air?" Mom asked.

"It's all he knows. That and sheep shearing. It's all he knows," Dad replied.

That kind of made me think that I would go to college someday so I would know some stuff that would help me have a job where I didn't have to climb on peoples' houses. I already knew I wanted to go to Ohio State, and that sealed the deal.

When we got to the hospital, the first thing I noticed was a weird smell. I think I had been in a hospital before, sometime when I was younger, but I didn't remember much about it. The smell kind of got to me. It was like an overly clean smell, but something under that smell that was weird. I couldn't figure it out, but I didn't like it much.

We had to go up in an elevator to see Grandpa, which made Jim happy because he liked to push the elevator buttons. That was some kind of big deal to him. He was so weird sometimes. Anyway, Grandpa was on the third floor of the hospital, which was the top floor. I guess that's where they put all the guys that had broken bones. I was kind of glad they had an elevator because it was getting hard for Mom to go up steps, she had such a big baby in her stomach.

Grandpa was in room 371. When we got in there, he was sitting up in bed, drinking some Hawaiian Punch. I kind of wished I had some, too. I thought maybe being in the hospital wouldn't be such a bad deal if they had Hawaiian Punch.

"Hey, John! Hey, Jim!" Grandpa greeted us. "Come on over here and let me see how much you've grown this summer! I have hardly gotten to see you two." I was kind of surprised to see Grandpa being so cheery with his broken bones and all, but it was a relief, honestly, and I could see that Mom and Dad were pretty happy about it.

"Dad, what in the world happened?" my dad asked Grandpa.

"Oh, I just got in too big of a hurry. I was getting ready to pack up all my equipment because I was done with the Baer place. I was down on the ground doing my final inspection, and I saw an area I missed up under the peak of the dormer, so I put the extension ladder back up and went up there to hit that spot. I was about done, when a dove flew by me and just about landed on my head. I kind of lost my balance. There was nothing to grab onto, and down I went. It hurt like a son of a gun, but here I am, alive to tell the tale!"

My dad laughed a little bit, but my mom shot him a look that said, "This is not funny!" and dad stopped laughing, or at least he tried to hide it.

Mom sat down in a chair next to Grandpa's bed and held the hand on his good arm. "Dad, won't you please consider giving up the painting business? You're seventy-three years old now. How long are you going to work? It's time for you to enjoy doing what you like to do, don't you think?"

"I *do* like to paint houses," Grandpa said. "Yes, it's a kind of work, and yes, it's hard some days, but when you're painting someone's house, you're giving them a reason to feel proud of their home, making it a nice place for them to come to after a long day at work. You're putting on some color and brightening up the whole neighborhood. You're giving strangers a beautiful homestead to look at when they're driving by. It's a kind of artwork to me. I'm Michelangelo!" He laughed at his own joke.

"Well, Dad, maybe you should just consider doing the lower parts of the house and having one of the local high school boys help you with the higher parts of the houses now," Dad offered. "You could still do what you love to do but not be taking as much risk, and think of it this way...you can be teaching the next generation all you know about painting houses – get these kids ready to either take care of their own homes or actually start a business like you have done."

Grandpa seemed to consider this idea for a couple of minutes. "You know, that might not be a bad idea...."

Jim jumped right in at that. "Grandpa, I could be your helper!"

Grandpa smiled. "You're too little now, but let's talk about that in a few more years."

I wanted to check out Grandpa's cast. It was white and hard as cement. Grandpa bent his elbow and raised his arm so I could see the cast all the way around his wrist. As I was examining the doctor's handiwork, I touched Grandpa's hand.

"Grandpa, your hands are so soft! How can your hands be that soft when you work so hard all the time?" I couldn't believe it. His hands were as soft as Grandma's.

"That's from sheep-shearing, John. There's something called lanolin in sheep's wool, and when you're shearing them, the lanolin gets on your hands. Lanolin makes your skin soft."

I had heard of lanolin on a commercial about women's hand lotion, so now I knew why mom had these bottles of stuff called "Angel Skin." I wondered why they named it that. How did they know what angel skin felt like? Maybe they should have just named it "Sheep's Wool." I guess they thought no one would buy it if it wasn't a fancy enough name.

Later that night when Mom and Dad thought we were asleep, I heard them talking about Grandpa and Grandma and how we were going to have to find ways to help them out a little more. It was odd to think about Grandpa and Grandma not being able to do as much as they used to. I knew this, though. I didn't want my grandpa to get up high on a ladder anymore either. I wanted him to be around to show me how to hunt and fish, and if he fell again, he could break a lot more than his collar bone and his wrist. Grandpa knew a lot about the world and he had a lot to tell me about. I thought maybe if Mom and Dad couldn't convince him, I could.

When Grandpa got to come home from the hospital, we went to see him. Dad wanted to know if there was anything he could do – mow the lawn, take care of the hounds, or anything like that. I knew Jim and I could take care of Grandpa's dogs.

"Sure, I appreciate it," Grandpa said. Dad went out to mow the lawn, Mom visited with Grandma, and Jim and I took care of Lucy and Lucky, the hounds. They were nice dogs, but man, could they bark!

When Jim and I came back in the house, I sat down by Grandpa and asked him if his wrist hurt.

"Oh sure, it's sore," he said, "but nothing I can't take." He was tough as nails, my grandpa.

I decided now was a good time to tell him how I felt about all this.

"Grandpa, my dad and mom want you to stop going up high on ladders. I do, too. I didn't like it when you fell. I was worried about you. And now, it just seems like it's work that's too hard for you. At least that's what I think. I know I'm just a kid and I don't do a lot of work like you do right now, but I don't want anything bad to happen to you." My words were pouring out of me because I knew I was just a kid and kids aren't necessarily supposed to tell grown-ups what they think.

Grandpa smiled at me and rubbed the top of my head, messing up my hair. "John, you're a good boy...always have been. Don't you worry about me. I know I have some limits now, and I have to face up to it. Your dad had a good idea for me and I'm going to follow that idea. You don't have to worry about me being on ladders anymore. But boy, you have to face up to something, too. Grandpas aren't meant to last forever."

I didn't like that comment at all. I knew it was true – people die all the time. But I wasn't ready to talk about that yet.

"Just be here as long as you can, ok?" I asked him.

"I promise you that I'll be here to go to your Little League games, watch the Reds with you, and take you fox hunting. I'll be here when you kiss your first girl and probably when you get married, too. But here's the most important thing to remember. Even when I'm gone, I'll still be with you. I'll be right inside here." He put his finger first in the middle of my forehead and then right in the middle of my chest, and I knew what he meant. Somehow, it made me feel better.

Grandpa had that cast on his wrist for about two months. He didn't have to wear his sling that long, and he didn't keep wearing it for attention like Jim did after he had broken *his* collar bone. Grandpa said that the sling was a "confound nuisance," so he took it off as soon as he could, and probably before his doctor told him too. That's just the way Grandpa was. He might have fallen off a ladder, and he might be getting older, but there sure was nothing wrong with his brain. People might have to change when they get older, and I guess no one can stop it, but one thing that doesn't have to change is how you think about life. Just go as hard as you can go right up to the end. I think that's what Grandpa tried to show us.

18 CAMP

Every summer, if we were lucky enough to have the money, I got to go to Camp St. Paul's. It was a church camp on Lake St. Paul, and even though you had to go to vespers and attend prayer services, it was a lot of fun.

The lake was clear and blue, but it had a big drop off about a hundred feet out from shore, and there were tales told around the campfire every year about young people who had ventured out too far and never were found. Those stories always gave me a little shiver up my spine. I couldn't swim well, so I always made sure I stayed close enough to shore that I could touch the sandy bottom and still have my head above water. Besides, not one kid was really swimming anyway…everyone was just splashing around, dunking each other and playing "chicken" and throwing beach balls back and forth when we were at the lake. I'm pretty sure everyone knew the stories about the drowned or missing kids, so everyone was just as happy to stay where they could participate in all the games the counselors had dreamed up for us. On some evenings, campfires would be held down at the lakeshore. That was when the spooky stories got told.

There were cabins for the boys and cabins for the girls. The girls' cabins were A, B, C and D. Ours were E, F, G and H. Each small, weathered, wood-shingled cabin held four kids. There were two bunk beds in each cabin, a table and chairs, and a little couch. There was a little private bed area for the counselor for that cabin. The counselor's bed area was right up at the front door of the cabin. I suppose that was just in case some homesick kid tried to take off in the middle of the night. Sometimes the counselors didn't come into the cabin for the night until a little later after we were asleep. They had counselor meetings they had to go to, but they always made sure that we were all down for the night first.

Breakfast was the best meal of the day at camp. First off, you would wake up early and catch the whiff of bacon being fried in the dining hall...it made you feel ravenous right away. I always woke up whoever my cabin mates were and got everybody rounded up so we could go to breakfast together because the next best thing about breakfast was that during breakfast, you planned your day. Of course there were activities that you had to attend, but you got a lot of free time, too, and this required careful planning if we were going to make the best use of it.

In the summer of 1963, my cabin mates were Larry Jamison, Joe Freed, and Frank Adams. All the girls liked Larry, so we called him "Little Larry Lover." He said he hated that, but he took it all right, and to tell you the truth, I think he actually kind of liked all the attention. Not that he was an attention-hog. He was an all-right guy. The girls thought he was cute, but we all thought he was a pretty funny guy, too. Everyone at camp liked Larry.

Joe was a farm boy. He came from an area where they grew a lot of cattle. He also had horses on his farm, so he was the guy who gave us tips when we went horseback riding with our counselors. Horses scared me a little just because they were so big, but at camp, they always had the tamest old horses that probably couldn't do more than trot, anyway. I tried not to show my nerves when we went out to the horse barn.

Frank was the shyest kid in our group, but he was really good at music. He brought his guitar to camp that year, and at the campfires, he would play songs like, "This Land is Your Land," and "If I Had a Hammer." Sometimes the counselors asked him to play a song like "Michael Rowed the Boat Ashore." I think it was because it had the word "hallelujah" in it. We had to have some religious stuff at campfires since it was church camp, after all, but I liked it best when he would try to play "Surfin' USA" by the Beach Boys or "Ruby Baby" by Dion. Those songs were a little harder, but Frank did a pretty good job on them. The time of day when Frank was the least shy was when he had that guitar in his hands.

There was a commissary where you could go buy little things you might have forgotten to pack like shampoo or toothpaste. They also had a big selection of candy, which I was happy about. I liked Sugar Daddies and usually got one every day. You couldn't really chew those things, so they lasted a long time.

On our next-to-last day of camp, Larry, Joe, Frank and me spent breakfast figuring out what to do with our free time as usual. We already knew we had to go horseback riding and do crafts that day. We also knew we had to go to Vesper Island that evening. Vesper Island was a little island in a man-made pond right in the middle of the campgrounds. It was where we went for what you might call church. There were benches made out of white stone and when you prayed, you prayed that the sermon wouldn't be too long because those benches were hard. There were willow trees all around the island, which made it look a little spooky at night. It was a good thing that Vesper Island was where we prayed and didn't tell ghost stories instead. You had to cross over a little bridge to get to the worship area, and the bridge was the best part of Vesper Island to me. You could look over the side and see fish swimming around in the pond - it was that clean.

Anyway, Larry had come to breakfast with a plan. "Let's dress up like ghosts and go scare the girls in Cabin B. Everyone thinks some kids drowned in the lake, so we could use our sheets and maybe some toilet paper for ghost outfits and get some sea weed and stuff like that to put on so we look all scary. We could get the sheets wet so they looked like we just came out of the lake...."

"Aw, you just want to flirt with those girls again before camp is over," Joe butted in. "I don't want to waste my time trying to scare girls. They'll figure it out anyway. No one really believes in ghosts."

I spoke up, too. "Are you sure we shouldn't be trying to get the whole gang to play some baseball or something? That seems like it would be a lot more fun. Maybe we could have a campfire and make s'mores after." I could never get enough s'mores.

Frank had been quiet as he usually was, but when he spoke up, I was surprised to find him siding with Larry. "C'mon you guys. I think Larry has a good idea."

Joe and I looked at Frank with our mouths hanging open. "Oh, for criminy sake, you can't be interested in this goofy idea!" Joe burst out. We noticed the outburst had captured the attention of Bob McCready, our cabin counselor, so Joe lowered his voice. "Frank, what in the heck has gotten into you? You're always playing baseball or tag or your guitar. You never even talk to any girls."

Frank leaned in and said, "Don't tell anyone, but I kind of like Sally Meadows. She's in Cabin B." The picture suddenly became clear. Larry wanted to *get* a little more girl attention, and Frank wanted to *give* a girl a little more attention.

Frank was a guy who had never made any demands on our time, and because he was such a quiet guy, I felt like I had to go along with him on this one. Besides, I kind of had a tiny little crush on Nancy Hardy, who was also in Cabin B. To me, she was the prettiest girl in camp, with brown eyes and brown hair that was real shiny and straight down her back. I wouldn't have minded having a chance to talk to her, even if it was by scaring her half to death.

We decided to take a vote, and the idea with the most votes would win. Larry started the voting. "All in favor of the ghost idea, raise your hand." Three of us raised our hands and Joe looked around the table.

"I can't believe you guys. I just can't believe it," Joe muttered, shaking his head. "Are you absolutely sure about this?" The other three of us shook our own heads in silent agreement. "Ok," Joe said reluctantly, "I guess I'm in."

Every spare minute of that next-to-last day was spent planning our escapade. We pulled the top sheets off our bunks. We didn't want to raise suspicion with Bob McCready by taking *all* the sheets. After horseback riding, we went down to the lake and looked around the edges of the shoreline to see if we could find some sea weed or other creepy-looking vegetation. We got a few handfuls of stuff and carried it back to our cabin in an old bucket Joe had found. While we were down at the lake, we went to the campfire area and got some burned up wood to use to make black marks on our faces or on our sheets or something. We weren't sure just how we would use it, but we took some back to the cabin with us. It wasn't easy sneaking all that stuff back to the cabin.

I could barely eat dinner. I don't know if I was excited about seeing Nancy Hardy later on or if I was worried about getting in trouble. Joe, Larry, and Frank didn't seem to have any trouble eating and they were making sure to act like everything was normal so no one would catch on to us and our genius plot. They were laughing and talking like it was a normal day.

Even vespers was tougher than usual to get through. For one thing, since it was the last night we would be in camp, the sermon was really long. I bet it was at least a half hour. Those benches made it feel like torture. Then they added on communion! We had to walk up and get a little teeny glass with grape juice in it and take a little white thing that looked like a piece of shiny paper. At our church, we had real bread for the host, but here, we had little pieces of shiny paper. I put it in my mouth, but I didn't know whether to chew it or suck on it. It got stuck in the roof of my mouth because my mouth was so dry. I had to put my finger in my mouth and dig it out of there. I knew that wasn't considered too holy, so I waited till I was back in my seat to do it, but criminy. I about choked to death on that thing.

After vespers, we had an ice cream bar over in the dining hall, and everyone started saying their goodbyes. Some people had books where they were getting peoples' autographs and the person might write some nice thing like, "Stay sweet!" or "See you next summer!" I didn't go in for that stuff, but I did walk up to Nancy Hardy and tell her she had a nice dress on. That was about all I could muster, but Nancy spoke to me – "Thank you," she said. She had the sweetest sounding voice I ever heard.

When we got back to our cabin, Bob McCready was there sitting on the couch, writing on some papers. "Hi, guys," he said. "I'm going to be going to the final counselor meeting tonight over in the mess hall, so once you guys get settled in, don't be surprised if you hear me leave. I think we're going to have a little party, so I might be kind of late."

Could fate really be that kind to us? Bob McCready would be late coming back to the cabin - it was perfect. We'd be able to pull off our mission and get back to the cabin before any of the counselors got wind of our deed. It was like an episode of "Espionage" on TV. Or Perry Mason, maybe. "The Case of the Camp Corpse Caper." That's what we could call it.

We spent a while talking to Bob and starting to get things packed up a little bit for the next day. Bob was a nice guy and a good counselor. He told us that we better start packing because it wouldn't make our moms and dads too happy if they had to wait for us to pack.

Finally, it was time for "lights out," the time of night when every cabin shut out all its lights and everyone was supposed to get to sleep. I had a leftover Sugar Daddy re-wrapped and saved under my pillow. I pulled it out and decided to eat part of it to maybe calm me down a little bit. I had to sneak it out because Bob was still up in his part of the cabin. I heard him puttering around for a little bit, and after peering into our area to see if we looked like we were asleep, he left the cabin for his counselor party.

"Sheesh. I thought he was never gonna leave," Larry hissed.

"Me, too," Joe chimed in.

We all got up and started working on our costumes. It wasn't very comfortable because the sheets were wet with lake water. We decided to put on our bathing suits under the sheets so we wouldn't get our pajamas all wet, and that was a very smart suggestion of Frank. He had clearly given this whole thing a lot of thought. Who would have ever thought that the shyest guy in the cabin would be so ready for a prank?

We didn't want to cut eye holes in the sheets because we knew that would be big time trouble, so we draped the sheets around us and over our heads, marking our faces all up with the burned wood from down at the lake. We made dark circles under our eyes. Frank had gotten some white powder from somewhere – I never asked him from where – and we put that on our faces so we would look pale and maybe like we were dead. We couldn't really turn the lights on because we didn't want anyone to see that someone in our cabin was awake, but we went in the bathroom and used Joe's flashlight to put on our scary makeup.

We had decided that we would start our scare routine by going to the cabin windows and just making some scary noises like you hear ghosts make in movies. "O-o-o-o-o-o-o-h," in a shaky voice seemed kind of dumb, but what other sounds do ghosts make? We didn't have any chains to rattle or anything like that, but we figured we could tap on the side of the cabin and just do other stuff to get the girls' attention.

It was pitch black outside. When you're out in the country like that, there are no street lights to guide your way, and of course, we didn't want to risk being seen anyway. Joe carried his flashlight, and he turned it on every once in a while just to see where we were going. He kind of shined it through his sheet so it wasn't too obvious and of course, it also wasn't too helpful. I tripped over a log like a big dummy, and fell down. I was tangled up in some tall weeds and that wet sheet.

"I've got dirt all over my sheet," I said. I had dropped my Sugar Daddy, too, which I had brought along to calm my nerves. I looked around but couldn't see it in the dark.

"No big deal," Larry said. "We want to look kind of dirty anyway, remember? Like we just came out of the lake." He had a lot of that sea weed stuff on his head and from what little I could see in the dark, he looked pretty scary to me.

We finally got to Cabin B. Joe and Frank took one side, and Larry and I took the other. We stood below one of the windows.

"O-o-o-o-o-o-h," I warbled.

"O-o-o-o-o-o-h," Larry warbled, too.

Nothing. Not a sound, not a rustle. Nothing. We walked around the cabin to find Joe and Frank.

"I think these guys are sound asleep," Joe said. "I told you this would be a big waste of time."

"Don't give up yet," Larry said in a hushed voice. "Let's go inside and really give them a scare."

We all tiptoed (as well as you can tiptoe in a sheet) around to the front of Cabin B. Larry peered in the front screen door to where a counselor would normally have been sleeping.

"The coast is clear. They're still at their counselor meeting."

Larry reached up and took hold of the screen door handle. He opened it slowly, which made it creak like a for-sure haunted house.

It was still awfully quiet in the cabin, and going up the one stair through the door was a trick because it was made out of wood and it definitely creaked loudly. I was thinking about where I lost my Sugar Daddy and what Nancy Hardy might think of me as I walked through the door.

Suddenly, the cabin lights were on and girls were screaming and we were chasing them, making all of our weird ghost sounds.

It never occurred to us that the girls were not the ones who had turned the lights on.

"Hold it right there, guys!"

We turned around to see not only Bob McCready, but the counselor for Cabin B glaring at us.

The girls retreated to their bunks and we stood stiff as statues in the spot we were when the lights first went on.

"You didn't really think you were going to get away with this little stunt, did you?" Bob asked us.

Not one of us had a good answer. Larry started to stutter something about it all being in fun, and Frank had kind of pulled his sheet around his face so only his eyes were showing.

Right about then, Bob and the counselor for Cabin B started laughing, and all the girls, including Nancy, started laughing, too. I didn't know what was so funny till I noticed they were all looking at me.

With long strides, Bob came to the back of the cabin where I was frozen. He reached for me, and I backed up, not sure if I was getting ready to get walloped or what.

"Hold on, Mr. Ghost," he said. "You must have been hungry."

At that point, Joe, Larry, and Frank started laughing, too. Bob touched the top of my head and said, "Hang on, this might pull a little bit." He grabbed something and pulled it off my head, taking a few of my hairs with it. He showed it to me…my Sugar Daddy. I rubbed the spot where he had pulled it off. My hair, or what was left of it, was sticky.

Criminy. I couldn't have felt more dumb.

Everyone was still laughing as Bob rounded us up and said, "Ok. Back to your own cabin, boys. There's going to have to be a little clean up before you can get into your beds, that's for sure."

We headed for the door with the girls' laughter still ringing in our ears, but as I got ready to leave, I turned to look for Nancy. She was standing by her bunk, looking right at me. I wasn't sure if it was my imagination, but I thought I saw her smile at me before she turned away to crawl between the sheets. It made the fiasco a little better.

The next day, we were tired because we had been up till about midnight the night before getting ourselves cleaned up and helping Bob get the sheets ready for the camp laundry. We got a pretty good lecture from Bob about responsibility and horseplay, but every once in a while he would just shake his head and start chuckling again. We never did ask him how he found out about our plan, but it seems like grownups have eyes in the backs of their heads. Anyway, when mom and dad came to get me, other than me being tired, I looked none the worse for wear, I guess. Mom about squeezed the life out of me with her hug, and dad went over to shake hands with Bob McCready. Dad, Bob and Jim walked out to the horse barn because Jim wanted to see the horses.

"Did you have fun?" Mom asked.

"Sure," I said. "It's fun every year."

"Did you make a lot of new friends?" Mom continued her inquiry.

"Sure, the guys in my cabin and a couple of other people."

"Is one of them that little girl in the blue shorts who is standing over under the maple tree looking at you?"

I turned like a shot and saw Nancy Hardy in blue shorts, standing under the maple tree. She was smiling at me and waved when I turned around.

"Why don't you go say goodbye to her?" Mom asked.

I shuffled towards the tree. How do mothers know about this kind of stuff? I never said a thing to her about any girls. How could she possibly know?

As I approached Nancy, she smiled even wider. "You look a little better this morning," she said. "You're cleaner, at least."

I pushed some dirt around with my toe and said, "Yeah. I guess that whole thing was dumb. We weren't trying to do any real harm, though."

I looked Nancy square in the eyes then, and I realized how dark brown they were. It was like looking into two bowls of chocolate.

"I thought you guys were funny. It's the most fun thing that happened this whole week," she said.

"Really? Didn't you go horseback riding or swimming or play baseball or do crafts? All that stuff was fun – way more fun than getting Sugar Daddy pulled out of your hair."

She laughed out loud and said, "Oh, I had fun all week, but you guys really made it all so much more fun. It's the best time I have ever had at camp."

Then she did something I never expected. She hugged me. I sort of stood there kind of stiff, but then I hugged her back a little bit.

"Goodbye, John. I hope I get to see you next summer."

"Bye, Nancy. I hope I get to see you, too."

I'll never forget how she looked as she walked back towards her cabin, her brown hair shining in the sun.

I walked back to the car, where Mom, Dad and Jim were now waiting for me. My suitcase was already by the trunk, and Bob McCready was standing by our car.

"Goodbye, Jo-o-o-o-h-n," he said in a ghost kind of voice. "See you next y-e-e-ar." He started laughing again as he walked back to the cabin.

"What in the Sam hill was that all about?" dad asked.

"Yes, and how did you get this little bald spot on your head?" I heard mom say as I climbed into the back seat.

I never answered her and she never pressed.

19 MISS RUTH

Everyone in our town loved Miss Ruth Anderson, and so did I. Jim even told me once that he wanted to marry her, but he was just a kid, of course. Miss Ruth was kind to everyone. She was always making people laugh because she had such a good sense of humor. Her sense of humor was not the hurtful kind where you make people laugh by saying something mean...she would never do that; she just was funny. She had a free and easy laugh that made you feel like laughing, too.

Miss Ruth was probably about 30 years old. I never really knew exactly how old she was, but she seemed too young for her husband to be already dead. He had been a lieutenant in the Marines in Viet Nam, and my dad said he got shot to death. It was terrible. He was the only soldier from our town who did not get to come back home alive. Pretty much the whole town went to his funeral, and they had an American flag over his coffin. Lieutenant William James Anderson, killed in action, they said. Miss Ruth kept a picture of him on top of the piano in her sitting room. It wasn't a picture of him in his Marine uniform...it was a picture she took of him playing the guitar and their dog, Wolfie, sitting by his side. The lieutenant had a cowboy hat on and he was smiling at the camera. It was a nice picture. Miss Ruth said it made her think about how much fun they had when they were dating and when they were married, and then she didn't think so much about the war and how she lost him.

Miss Ruth's house was not quite in the middle of town, but not quite on the edge of town, either. It was a really big house. My mom called it a Victorian house, whatever that is. Anyway, it had a stained glass window in the front, up on the top floor. I thought that stained glass window was amazing. She was the only person who had one of those. The rest of our houses were pretty plain – nice, but plain. Anyway, Miss Ruth's house had the stained glass window, wood floors that creaked when you walked on them, a big grandfather clock, and these glass doors that both opened up from the middle – she called them French doors - so you could walk out onto her back porch, which led down into her gardens. Miss Ruth sure loved gardening. She knew about all kinds of stuff when it came to gardens, animals, birds, and butterflies. That's just how she was.

Miss Ruth was also a painter. She painted pictures all the time. Big pictures with kids in them, old people, flowers, dogs, and trees. She was really good at painting, but she never sold her paintings. She gave them to people for presents. I'm telling you, that's just how she was. She was kind and generous.

Speaking of generous, Miss Ruth made popcorn balls for all the kids for trick or treat. My mom said once, "I don't know how in the world she can make so many popcorn balls every single year." We didn't know, either, but what we did know is that they were a particularly valued treat. Everyone made a beeline for her house on Halloween so we didn't miss out on them. They were delicious – sweet, but also salty and just the right crunchiness. There were always a million kids standing on Miss Ruth's porch on Halloween.

Miss Ruth had a giant doll house that was almost exactly like the house she lived in. It was full of teeny, tiny little house things like furniture and lights and dishes and so forth. At first, only the girls wanted to look at the doll house, but Miss Ruth started having scavenger hunts in the doll house. She had a list of things us kids had to find, and whoever found the most got an apple. It was fun and even the other guys thought so once they figured out what was going on.

I guess you could say that we all thought Miss Ruth was pretty much some kind of angel on earth. I haven't even mentioned that she was beautiful. She had curly blondish hair, kind of long, and a lot of times she wore long skirts and her husband's old shirts with the sleeves rolled up. When she was out in her garden, she always wore a straw hat with a big brim on it to keep the sun out of her eyes. She was just cool. I tell you, everyone I knew loved Miss Ruth.

One very hot day in August, I was riding my Schwinn by Miss Ruth's house, and I saw her digging around in some shrubs by her front porch, straw hat off her head and kind of hanging down on her back. I parked my bike and walked over to see what she was doing and if I could do anything to help her. I liked to be around her, even if I wasn't that keen on gardening.

"Hi, Miss Ruth! Whatcha doing?" I asked in greeting.

Miss Ruth looked up from her shrubs and said, "Well, hi, John. I'm getting some very stubborn weeds from around this boxwood. I have been a little neglectful of my landscaping lately, and now I've got some weeds with roots clear through to China."

"Maybe I can get them," I offered, though I thought to myself that if Miss Ruth couldn't get them, my chances were probably slim.

"It's ok – I think I've just about got it." She gave one giant tug and fell backwards on her behind, weeds in gloved hand.

"Victory!" she shouted, and we both laughed. "Come on, John. It's time for a break. Let's get some iced tea."

Miss Ruth took me around the back of her house where she had her gardening tools and a wheelbarrow that was pretty well full of weeds she had already pulled up. I thought she must love her gardens an awful lot to pull that many weeds. We walked up the steps to her back porch and she pointed me to a chair where I sat down. It was one of those wicker chairs with flowered cushions…the kind of cushions you sink down in and never want to get up from. Miss Ruth disappeared into those French doors of hers and then reappeared with two glasses of ice tea on a silver tray. The ice cubes clinked around in the glasses, and just the sound of that made me feel cooler. She offered me a glass first and sat down across from me at the little round glass table on her porch. She took a long draw on her tea, and I did too. It tasted so good out there in the hot sun.

"I think I'm about done for today," Miss Ruth said. "I've put in quite a few hours, but that's what I get for letting things go so long." She wiped some sweat from her forehead with the back of her hand. "I've been working on a painting most every day, and I just let the yard get out of hand, but it's in much better shape now."

"What are you painting, Miss Ruth?" I asked.

"It's a picture of my husband and Wolfie," she answered. "Would you like to see it after we finish our tea?"

"You bet I would." Miss Ruth's paintings were always something to see.

We finished our tea, and Miss Ruth took me in through the French doors. I carried our tea glasses in on the silver platter since she was nice enough to bring them out for us. I liked helping her.

We went into Miss Ruth's sun room, which is where all her art supplies were. She said she liked to paint in there because of the natural light that came in through the big windows. There wasn't too much in there except her art stuff, and she had a couple of stools that you could sit on. This was the only room in Miss Ruth's house I ever saw that was kind of messy.

When I walked around the easel to see Miss Ruth's picture, I recognized it right away. It was the same picture she had on top of her piano – the one of her husband in his cowboy hat playing the guitar. Wolfie was looking out in the painting, though – that was different because in the photograph, he was just looking at Lt. Anderson.

"Why are you painting a picture of something you have a photograph of?" I asked her. It seemed kind of odd to me.

"It's the same reason I wear his old shirts so much. It makes me feel close to him somehow…like I can bring him back to life, in a way. Painting him makes me study his face so I don't forget it. I have to look at each line on his face, how his eyes shined, how he smiled. That may sound odd, John. It's hard to explain, but somehow, it brings me peace." Miss Ruth's voice was kind of quiet, like she was thinking really hard about this.

"I think that if it brings you peace, that's a good thing," I said.

Miss Ruth looked at me and smiled. "Yes it is, John. It most certainly is a good thing. I try not to feel sad because Bill was doing something he felt strongly about when he was killed. It's no one's fault, but it has been very hard not having him here. We used to do everything together and we had so much fun. I doubt that I will ever know anyone that I could care more about."

"Don't tell my little brother Jim that," I said. "He wants to marry you."

Miss Ruth laughed really hard at that. "Oh, I adore Jim, but he's way, way too young for me."

"That's what I told him," I replied.

Miss Ruth was still laughing. "Come on out to the garden. I want to show you something."

We walked back out into the hot sun and down a little path of stepping stones to the very farthest garden. It was a rose garden. Miss Ruth had several separate gardens. She especially loved her roses, zinnias, peonies and cosmos. The peonies didn't have any flowers on them anymore, but the other plants had a million flowers all over them. It was beautiful. It was like something you'd see on television in a fairy tale or something.

We walked on past the main gardens to the very back of her property. There was almost a canopy of some kind of green plants with real big leaves. I had never seen such big leaves. Each leaf was bright green with eight spikes to it, almost like a hand with eight fingers. There were several plants, and those giant leaves overlapped. It was shady under the canopy, and Miss Ruth had put a little white wrought iron chair under the plants.

"Do you know what these are, John? These are castor beans. They are highly poisonous, so I never want you to touch them or have anything to do with them, but aren't they lovely? Isn't it interesting that something so beautiful can be so deadly?" Miss Ruth pointed out some red flowers that were opening up. "The leaves are so dark green, and the flowers are such a beautiful red. It's just hard to get over that these things can kill you."

"What do you mean, 'kill you'?" I asked her.

"Exactly what it sounds like, buddy. These plants can kill you. The seeds can kill you." Miss Ruth put her hands on her hips, looked up at the plants and continued. "There's a poison in them called ricin. It's very dangerous, indeed. But guess what, this is also the very same plant castor oil is made from. Have you ever had to drink castor oil?"

I almost gagged just thinking of it. "Yes," I answered. "One time, and one time only. It made me puke right after I took it, too." The very memory was disgusting to me.

"Yeah, I had to take it once when I was a kid, too," she said. "Disgusting, isn't it?"

"That's exactly what I was thinking," I said. "It's disgusting."

"So why are we talking about it?" Miss Ruth laughed. "Oh yeah, I was giving you a botany lesson."

"What's botany?" I asked.

"Oh, the study of plants," she said. "I'm not really a botanist – I just like to learn about different plants."

"Well, what are you going to do with your castor beans?"

"Just look at them," she said. "I just wanted to see if I could grow some in Ohio. I wanted to challenge myself."

"I wonder how one plant can grow something that helps you when you are sick, but it can also grow something that makes you die," I mused.

"I wonder the same darn thing. Great minds think alike, John."

We walked back through the flower gardens. Miss Ruth had a lot of different flowers, and her yard was full of colors and wonderful smells.

"Miss Ruth, do you plant so many flowers so you don't have to think about your husband so much?" I asked. I felt like I might have been too bold, but I couldn't help but wonder.

Miss Ruth took a minute to answer, and I could see her eyes focused on something distant – a memory, good or bad, was pulling at her.

"Well I have always loved flowers and other plants. I think it's good to work in the garden. It gives you a chance to separate yourself from the world for a while, think about life. And yes, honestly, it helps keep me busy so I don't think about Bill quite so much. You know, when you lose someone you love, you have to keep yourself busy or you could go crazy."

I wanted to tell her about Jonas Henderson right then, but I had promised myself I would never tell his story to anyone, so I kept my mouth shut. Plus, it was a different kind of situation altogether.

Miss Ruth could probably see that I was thinking because she cocked her head to the side and said, "You have some deep thoughts, young man. What could be going on inside your head?"

"Oh, I just feel bad for you losing your husband and for all the people who lose someone they love, I guess." I didn't have a better answer.

"Well, let's forget about all that for now. Tell me about how excited you are for school to start."

I groaned and immediately switched from thinking about death to that other nearly fatal misery – school. We talked for a while longer about what teachers I hoped to have and who I hoped would be in my homeroom. Finally I said, "Gees, I better get home. I told mom I was going for a bike ride and she'll have a cow if she doesn't hear from me pretty soon."

Miss Ruth smiled and said, "If I was your mom, I'd want to make sure about where you were, too. You get on home and come back any time. Maybe next time you're here, I can show you some of the tropical plants in the green house or we can do a little painting."

"Geeminy, you mean I could paint with paintbrushes on a canvas?" I asked.

Miss Ruth gave me that big smile that made you want to smile right back. "You bet, John. I'll show you a little bit about painting. Maybe we'll start with something like trees or flowers."

"I'd like that. Thanks for the tea and for teaching me about the castor beans and all," I said as I jumped on my bike.

"My pleasure," Miss Ruth answered, and I knew it was probably true. She did take pleasure in being around other people and talking to them about regular old everyday life.

As I rode home, I thought about how Miss Ruth liked other people so much that it must be even more lonely for her since her Bill wasn't alive anymore. She was probably about one of the best people I ever knew. I decided right then that I would stop in to see her a little more often, not to be a pest, but to be a friend.

The very next week, I stopped by her house. I knocked on the door, and she smiled when she saw me.

"Come in, John. Come in! You're just in time to see my masterpiece."

I walked into the sun room with her and saw that she had finished her painting of her husband. It was amazing. It looked exactly like the photograph she had taken. I didn't know how in the world she could get it to look so much like the real picture.

"It's great!" I said. "I don't think I could ever paint anything like that!"

185

"No one can at first," she said. "It takes a lot of lessons and work and practice to be able to do portraits. It's not easy, but you have to start somewhere, right?"

"I guess so," I answered. "I think I better stick with trees or something for a while."

"That's exactly what we'll do," she answered. "Come on. I have something to show you."

Miss Ruth took me over to a cupboard and opened the door. "I have some art supplies in here just for you, John. This is your cupboard now."

I was completely caught off guard by this act of thoughtfulness. I looked in there and saw all kinds of paints, paintbrushes, some practice canvasses, some drawing books, some rags to clean up mistakes...it was a real painter's treasure of art supplies.

"Gosh, Miss Ruth! This is about the nicest thing anyone ever did for me."

"I'm sure your parents have done a heck of a lot of nice things for you, but that being said, I'm glad to have you for a friend and I'm glad you're interested in art. We can start doing some lessons now and then if you'd like that."

"Sure I would. I'd love to learn how to do painting," I answered.

"Ok. I'll call your mom and see if it's okay if we get together for an hour or so each Tuesday. How does that sound?"

"Great!" I said. "I can't pay for lessons, though, Miss Ruth, and I don't think my mom and dad can, either."

"Oh, John. This isn't for pay. This is just for fun," Miss Ruth said. "I'll make sure to tell your mom that. Don't worry, okay? It will all just be for fun. I like having you around. You know, it doesn't look like I'll ever have any kids of my own, and I love kids, so it's fun for me to have you visit."

And that was that. Miss Ruth liked doing things for other people. That's why she made popcorn balls for all of us kids every Halloween. That's why she had tea parties with the girls and talked to all us guys about bugs and the things we liked. That's why she had the big dollhouse and did a scavenger hunt with all the kids. That's why she had those big flower gardens – she knew all the people in town loved them. Miss Ruth would have been a good mom, but she was an even better friend to everyone. It was pretty stinky that her husband got killed, but she took her sadness and made it into joy and love for other people. That's just how she was.

20 GOODBYE TO FREEDOM

September is a nice month in Ohio. It rains on some days but a lot of the days are warm and sunny, and the sky is a real, real bright blue. The only problem is that you have to go back to school.

The day after Labor Day was always the first day of school for us. The week immediately prior to that was the county fair, and without fail, we had so much fun at the fair that having to go back to school seemed doubly painful.

At the 1963 fair, I had been on every single ride, even the Scrambler. That ride was correctly named since your brains felt scrambled when you got off after your three minute spin. I had been on the roller coaster, though it was kind of a little one – not like the Wild Mouse up at Cedar Point, which kind of jerked you around a little bit and had some pretty high hills on it.

I had also been through every single barn at the fair: the cow barn, the horse barn, the sheep barn, the chicken and rabbit barns. I went through the 4-H barn and saw all the stuff kids in 4-H had made and the bigger projects their clubs had worked on. I went to the Grange building where all the ladies had their home-canned goods, and I had eaten probably the best grilled hamburger of my life at the Grange tent. Over the week of the fair, I had cotton candy and ice cream. I bought one of those candy apples where you have to bite through the hard cinnamon outer coating and it kind of burns your tongue till you get to the juicy apple underneath. I played ring toss and tried to knock over some milk bottles with a baseball, though I didn't do very well. Anyway, the fair was the best, and we tried not to think about school that whole week, though it was a dark cloud hanging over our heads.

It actually started the week before the fair. Mom had taken us school shopping. This was the worst possible shopping trip we could go on each year. New hard-sole shoes. New stiff blue jeans. New shirts. New tablets, pencils, scissors and pencil boxes. Jim got new crayons – I got new colored pencils to draw maps in Social Studies. I knew we didn't color pictures anymore in fifth grade – my friend Bill Schafer told me that. He was a year older than me and filled me in on fifth grade. I would have a new teacher and new rules to get used to. I didn't relish the thought and the fair brought a reprieve from thinking about school, even if it was only temporary. But now, the fair was over. Goodbye to freedom.

Mom woke us up extra early on the first morning of school. "I have to get you guys up and going before I have to go to work," she said. "C'mon, let's get moving. The bus will be at the church at eight and you'll still be in your PJs."

Jim was already in the bathroom brushing his teeth. I wandered on downstairs to get breakfast. I figured I could brush my teeth when I was done eating.

Mom poured me a bowl of Rice Krispies. In my state of early morning stupor, I listened to them '*snap, crackle and pop!*' for a minute before I dug in. I chewed slowly and tried to get myself awake.

"John, honey, you've got to get moving! I don't want you to wolf your food, but you've got to get going a little faster than this," Mom forewarned. "You'll never make the bus. I guess I should have gotten you guys up earlier."

Earlier! I started eating a little faster to appease her. I didn't want her waking me up even earlier the next day.

As I was finishing my cereal, Jim was walking into the kitchen. He was wide awake and actually seemed excited for the day. "Stop acting so happy," I muttered to him as we crossed paths.

"I think I will like school this year," Jim said. "I sure hope I'm in Mrs. Settlemaier's home room." He was a goofball sometimes.

I went upstairs, got washed up, brushed my teeth, and put on a pair of the new blue jeans Mom had bought. Gees, it was going to take some time to break them in – it was like trying to walk with

189

boards on my legs. I went back downstairs to find Jim rifling through all his new school supplies.

"I think I should have gotten scissors with points on them," he said. "These round scissors are for little kids."

"They'll be just fine," Mom said, exasperated by this time. "Come on you guys, get your things and get down to the church so you don't miss the bus. Oh, and don't forget your lunch."

We picked up our stuff and headed out for Calvary church, where the bus picked up most of the kids that lived out in our part of town. In the middle of town, the bus would stop at different kids' houses, but for the west and east ends of town, the kids had to all meet at churches that were on either end of town. The west end kids met at the Methodist church; we met at Calvary.

Jim and I really didn't mess around getting up to the church. We'd have been in big trouble if we missed the bus. Jim practically ran all the way to Calvary. I just walked fast. We were the last kids to arrive.

Scotty Wilson was waiting for me beside the steps of the church. "Gees, what took you so long? I thought you were gonna miss the bus."

"Naw, I just had a hard time getting awake," I told him. "I hate the first day of school, anyway."

"Me too. Criminy," Scotty said.

"Criminy," I said.

The school bus arrived – our same old bus, number 37 – but when the door opened, there was an unfamiliar face behind the steering wheel. It was a lady. She had bleached blonde hair and a scarf around her neck. She had on real sparkly earrings that hung down beside her neck. She wore a lot of makeup, and her lipstick smile was red as blood. We all just kind of stood there and looked at her.

"Hi kids! C'mon in or we'll be late," said the red lips.

"Where's Mr. Williamson?" Scotty piped up.

"Didn't you kids know? He retired last year. I'm Sharon Miles. C'mon in or we'll be late."

One by one we climbed the steps into the bus. I wanted to sit farther back on the bus this year, away from the real little first and second graders. But then again, not too far back where Buzz Dillon (who was following in Big Jake Parker's footsteps) might be waiting to give us a Dutch rub.

The first trip to school was pretty uneventful. I think everybody was in shock that it was time for school to start, so the ride was subdued. When we arrived at the familiar big red brick building, we all got off and trudged inside where Mr. Howard was waiting for us, giving directions to different kids about which homeroom they were in this year. Of course, all the first, second, and third graders just went to their rooms, but the fourth, fifth, and sixth graders had a homeroom because once you got to fourth grade, you started switching rooms for different classes a little more.

"John, Scotty – you guys are both in Mrs. Barker's homeroom," Mr. Howard directed us with a big smile.

At least one of my buddies would be in homeroom with me. That was good. We wondered where Dave and Rusty might end up this year.

Mrs. Barker had a good reputation as a nice lady and a fun teacher, so that brightened my outlook on this much-dreaded day. Scotty and I headed up the steps to the second floor where Mrs. Barker's homeroom was. As we entered the room, we saw kids just milling around…no one was in their seat yet.

"Hi boys," Mrs. Barker said. "Welcome to a new school year!" She was way too enthusiastic about this. "We're going to assign seats in just a couple of minutes – we're still waiting for about a half dozen children."

Scotty and I just stood by the blackboard and surveyed who all was in our homeroom for that year. Debbie Carruthers – yuck. She was such a stick in the mud, always trying to beat everybody else in their grades. Joellyn Mason. Sue Smith. They were all right. We also saw Pete Thompson, Brad Barnard, and Ron Hall. Those guys were decent guys. So far, so good. Before long, both Dave Hansen and Rusty Barnes showed up, too. All my best buddies were in my homeroom and it looked like we might end up with more guys than girls, which as far as I was concerned, was a good thing. At least, that is, until the most beautiful girl I ever saw walked into the room.

I had never paid much attention to girls except for my mom. Mostly, girls were a pain. But on this day, a new face was making me reconsider my position on females. She had long brown hair, and it was kind of curly, but not too curly. She had brown eyes and a smile that made the room feel suddenly warm. She had rosy cheeks, like she had just been outside running. I was mesmerized by this girl.

Rusty was talking to me about something and I was trying to pull myself back together as Mrs. Barker started assigning seats. I waited to put a name to this new girl's face. As one-by-one, we took our places, the new girl continued standing along the side of the room. She must be way back in the alphabet, I thought. Finally, I heard her name: Gina Vanelli.

Gina Vanelli. It sounded like a movie star name. Gina Vanelli. I knew I would have to get to know Gina Vanelli, the first time I ever remember being interested in getting to know any girl besides my mom. Oh, well, and Nancy Hardy from camp.

"You are in fifth grade, now, and your education really starts to change," Mrs. Barker called the class to attention. "Fifth grade is where you start putting together all the basics you learned in first through fourth grades, and your work gets a little more complex, but also more fun. You'll find yourselves changing as you learn, and as you grow, things that maybe didn't seem so fun before will now become more interesting to you." Boy, she was right on at least one count.

Mrs. Barker continued. "One of the things you all might be interested in is music. This year in music, you will learn more about different instruments, and you may decide that you'd like to be in band. Band is a lot of fun, and learning an instrument takes a lot of hard work. I am not a music teacher, so for music, you will have Miss Windom. She is new here and she's very excited to be working with students at our school. I guarantee music will be a lot of fun for you this year."

Dave raised his hand. "Will we still have to play our flutophones?" he asked disgustedly. Everyone started groaning because we all thought flutophones were dumb.

Mrs. Barker smiled. "No, I believe you have moved beyond that. That's what I mean…a lot of things change in fifth grade."

Our morning proceeded with the handing out of various texts and going over assignments for the next day. Mrs. Barker would be teaching us grammar, social studies, and literature. Miss Windom would teach music as we had already heard. Mr. Osborn would teach us science and Mrs. Jamison would teach math. Mr. Simmons would have us for gym. I knew Mr. Osborn and liked him. He was a good teacher. I didn't know Mr. Simmons or Miss Windom yet, so those two were questions in my mind. I was already fond of Mrs. Barker and I kind of knew Mrs. Jamison, so the year seemed to be starting about fifty-fifty overall as far as teachers went.

By 11:30, we were ready for lunch. We went down to the cafeteria. I had brought my own lunch, but paid the lunch ladies a quarter for a carton of chocolate milk. Dave, Scotty, Rusty and I sat down at one of the cafeteria tables and started discussing the events of the day so far.

"Are you going to learn how to play an instrument?" Dave asked around the table.

"I don't know," Scotty piped up. "I'm not that interested in music. I'm more interested in sports."

"Me too," added Rusty. "I like music and all, but I never saw myself playing any instruments."

"I'd like to learn how to play guitar like one of the kids I knew at camp this summer," I said. "I don't think they'll teach us guitar, though."

"Well, I'd like to play drums," Dave said. "I think it would be fun to be in a band."

We talked about teachers and how we thought the year would go, we talked about some of the kids in our class – who we liked and who were the nerds – and then we talked about new kids. There were a couple in the other homeroom, but in our homeroom there was only one – Gina.

I was sort of afraid to say anything because us guys were not all that interested in girls. Rusty was the first to speak up.

"Man, that Gina is cute! I never saw a girl as cute as her." I was horrified. Rusty liked her, too.

"She's ok," Dave said. "I'm too busy for any nutty girls, though."

"I think she's cute, too," Scotty said. Oh brother! Now there were *two* of my best friends interested in Gina. "What do you think, John?"

"I don't know," I mumbled, shoving some potato chips in my mouth. I figured if I had food in my mouth, they wouldn't ask me anymore questions.

The rest of lunch was spent wolfing down our food as fast as we could so we could go outside for a few minutes before music class. Outside on the playground, we didn't do much but walk around. Rusty beat a couple of guys from the other homeroom at tetherball, but mostly, we just walked around till it was time to go in.

Music class was on the first floor. No matter what kind of music it was, classes met in the band room. I was kind of interested to find out about Miss Windom and ask her about learning guitar.

Miss Windom was young. Mrs. Barker hadn't told us that. And she was kind of little. She wasn't much taller than me or Rusty. She looked like a kid herself.

"Hi, everyone! I'm so happy to meet all of you," she chirped. Her voice was high-pitched - childish almost - and she acted like she was pretty excited to see us. She kind of flitted around like a fairy...her size made her seem like Tinkerbell.

"Music is going to be so much fun this year. We will be meeting on Mondays, Wednesdays and Fridays during this period, and you will have gym on Tuesday, Thursday. You're going to be learning how to sing in different parts, learn about melody and harmony, and you're going to have an opportunity to join fifth grade band and learn an instrument. I'm going to pass out some flyers for you to take home to your parents so that they can come to the school on instrument night and help you decide what instrument you'd like to play if you are interested in band."

I raised my hand and Miss Windom acknowledged me. "Miss Windom, can we learn to play guitar?"

Miss Windom stopped and looked at me for a minute. "Would you tell me your name please?" she asked. Kids in the front row turned to look at me, including Gina.

"My name is John Reed," I said. "I'm in fifth grade."

Everyone started laughing at that. I never felt so dumb. Of course we were in fifth grade. Everyone already knew that. Gina was laughing, too. Man did I feel stupid.

"Oh, John, I'm glad we're all in this together. The first day of school is a little mind-boggling, isn't it?" Miss Windom was trying to let me off the hook for saying such a dumb thing.

"John, I'm glad you asked me about guitar. I know all of you kids may be seeing more and more people playing guitar, and it's a beautiful instrument. What makes you interested in the guitar?"

"I had a friend at camp who could play guitar, and I just really liked it," I answered.

"Well, guitar is not easy, and truthfully, we don't have guitar in fifth grade band, but we can talk to your mom and dad about getting a guitar. Yes, you absolutely can take guitar lessons, but I do not teach guitar, so you would have to take private lessons," Miss Windom informed me.

Private lessons. I knew what that meant. Money. I'd have to figure out a way to rationalize this with my mom and dad.

The kids in the first row all turned their attention back to Miss Windom except for Gina, who kept looking at me a little longer. She gave me a tiny smile and turned back to the front of the room. I was smitten by that smile and don't really remember much else of what Miss Windom told us that day, but I know it was all about band and instruments and singing songs and getting ready for some kind of Christmas show.

The rest of the day was science and math. It was hard to end the day with math because my brain was already tired. I sort of dozed off on the bus on the way home that first day, but woke up when the bus lurched to a stop at Calvary church.

"See you all tomorrow!" Sharon Miles cheerfully dismissed us.

Jim and I walked home. Jim didn't run this time. He was tired, too. When we got home, we let ourselves in the house and grabbed some chocolate chip cookies and milk. It was quiet for a little bit, then Jim started yakking about his first day of school. He got the homeroom he wanted, he got to sit by one of his buddies, he ate all his lunch, he had fun in gym and thought that would be his favorite class. On and on he went. About 4:30, mom got home.

"What's for supper?" Jim asked her before she even got to put her purse down on the counter.

Mom stood there for a minute with one hand on her purse, and the other hand on her hip. "Jim, looking at the cookie crumbs all over your mouth, I'm surprised you're even thinking about supper." She pushed her hair back from her forehead with her hand and continued. "I'm not sure, but I think we might just have your dad grill up some chicken tonight. How does that sound?"

"Cook-out!" Jim shouted and took off for his room.

Mom looked at me. "I guess he's ok with that." She smiled a tired smile. "How are you, John? How was your first day of school?"

I barely knew where to begin. "It was ok, I guess," was all I could eek out.

"Ok? I thought you'd be full of tales from your first day. Did you end up in homeroom with your friends?" she asked.

"Yup. We're all together. We have Mrs. Barker."

"Oh, that's great, son. She's an awfully nice teacher. I've worked with her on a couple of committees at PTA. Well, I'm going to go get some old clothes on and I'll start working on supper, I guess." Mom disappeared down the hall to change.

I had organized all my papers Mom was supposed to sign for me to return to school by the time she got back out to the kitchen.

"Son, can we take care of all that after we eat?"

I was fine with that idea. I wanted to ask about the guitar lessons and I didn't really know how to go about it. This gave me a little time to think.

After dinner, Dad sat down with the paper and Mom turned on the news. I waited till the news was over before I brought out my handful of parent notices and permissions for her to sign. In the pile of papers was the flyer about Instrument Night.

Mom went through each and every page dutifully and signed wherever she was supposed to. When she got to the music flyer, she asked me, "John, are you planning to be in band?"

This was the crucial interaction I had tried to plan for. "Well, I'd like to learn an instrument. I like music and think I could be good at it. I would practice really hard. I know it takes a lot of work." Dad had put down his paper and was paying attention to this conversation now.

"John, you're in a lot of sports. If you're in band, will you be able to stay in sports?" Dad loved sports much more than music.

"I think I could do some sports. You don't get in marching band till high school, and that's when it could mess up football. I'm not interested in doing that," I reassured him.

"Do you know what instrument you would like to play?" Mom asked me.

"Well, to be honest, I'd like to play guitar." There it was.

"Guitar? They don't have guitar in band," Mom said, and of course, she was right.

"I know, but that's really the musical instrument I'd like to play."

"Dad and I will have to talk about that, but I'll at least come to instrument night with you and we'll talk to your music teacher about options, ok?" It was clear that Mom didn't want to discuss it anymore right at that time, so I said, "Sure," and went over to the TV and turned on the "Andy Griffith Show."

The next day, at recess, I decided it was time to meet Gina. I saw her near the four-square court talking to some other girls. I walked over and the other girls scattered. I introduced myself. "Hi, Gina. I'm John Reed."

"Yes, and you're in fifth grade," she giggled.

I'm pretty sure my face turned red because she said, "Oh, I'm sorry – I was just teasing you. I'm glad to meet you John."

"Where did you go to school before?" I asked her.

"Our family just moved here from Pittsburgh," she said. "My grandparents live here, and my mom and dad missed them, so we decided to move here. My dad is a professor and he got a job at Findlay College."

"Well, gosh, it sure is nice to have you in our class," I said. "Do you like to go for bike rides or anything like that?" I didn't know where Gina lived, but I figured maybe we could explore town a little bit together. I could show her around, you know?

"I love riding bikes. Maybe on the weekend we could go for a bike ride together," she said.

"That's what I was thinking. I could show you around town a little bit and we could go get a slush or something at the Twisty Freeze. They won't be open after October, so we have to go before they close up for the rest of the year." I was so glad I had decided to come over and talk to her.

"That sounds like fun, John. I'd like that. When we go back to class, I'll write down our telephone number and give it to you. Then we can talk on the phone about going for a ride."

I felt like I wasn't even putting my feet on the ground as I walked back over to join the guys. It was time to go in, and everyone was focused on getting to the next class on time, so nobody really said anything to me about my talk with Gina.

That very night, Mom and Dad said they wanted to talk to me about guitar lessons.

"Son, it's not that we object to guitar lessons, but we wonder if you shouldn't start with a band instrument first, get some lessons at school, and then later on when you know a little more about music and if you're still interested, we can see about the guitar." Dad was making it more of a statement than a question, so I knew the decision was already made.

"Ok, I'll try that. I'm not sure what instrument I would want to play, though." I actually had been thinking about this, not feeling too confident that I had made my case for a guitar. "I sort of like the cornet, I think."

"That sounds like a good choice for a boy," Mom said. "Do you know how many famous trumpet players there are? I'll bet they started with cornet in school. On instrument night, I'll go with you and we'll see what they cost."

So there it was.

On our next music class day, we all filed in and sat in pretty much the same seats we had sat in before. Miss Windom reminded us that the very next week would be Instrument Night and to make sure we brought our parents. As we walked to our science classroom after music, I tried to walk up beside Gina.

"Hi, Gina. Do you know if you're going to be in band?" I asked her.

"Oh, yes! I have always wanted to be in band, especially when you get to high school. All the kids in band have so much fun going to football games together and stuff like that. Oh, yes. I am definitely going to play an instrument!" She seemed pretty excited about band.

"I'm going to, too. I don't know what instrument yet, though," I told her. I was feeling like Mom and Dad's decision might have benefits I hadn't thought about before. Gina was going to be in band, too, and that was definitely motivating.

The days passed and I got to talk to Gina off and on. I didn't want to seem overly interested because I didn't know what she thought about me, and I also didn't want the guys to get wise to my crush on her. They would have never let me live it down. Gina and I had not gone on our bike ride yet, but I hadn't forgotten about it, and I had saved her phone number in the cigar box where I kept my best baseball cards, the ones we wrapped in Saran wrap for the valentine box. That seemed like a long, long time ago now.

Instrument night came, and Mom and I went up to the school to see what the different instrument makers had to offer. I took Mom right over to the Conn-Selmer table because that's where I saw the cornets and trumpets. Then we walked around and looked at clarinets and saxophones and drums – that's where Dave was with his mom – and we saw flutes and French horns and trombones. After we had made the rounds once, I kind of felt more settled on the cornet, and we went back over there to get some information. There were a lot of music store owners there, too, and of course, they wanted you to rent or buy your instrument from them. I saw Gina and her mom talking to the man from Blechner's Music Store. Gina was holding a clarinet and seemed like she was trying to get a feel for it. She looked up, saw me looking at her, and smiled. She gave a little wave, so I took Mom over to meet her.

"Mom, this is Gina Vanelli," I said. "She's new to our school this year and we're in the same homeroom."

"Hi, Gina," Mom said. "I'm happy to meet you."

Gina smiled and said, "And this is my mom, Carla Vanelli."

Mrs. Vanelli had been talking to the man from Blechner's, but she turned and I could see why Gina was so pretty. Her mom looked like a grown-up Gina.

"Mom, this is John Reed. He's in the fifth grade." Gina winked at me when she said that.

"Hi, Mrs. Vanelli," I said. There it was again. I know darn well I was blushing.

"Hello, John. I've heard a little about you from Gina. She says you two are going to go on a grand tour of this town on your bikes." Mrs. Vanelli had a very nice voice. I thought she would probably be a nice person just from her voice.

"Yeah, we just have to figure out a day," I said.

I noticed that Mom was kind of looking back and forth at me, and then at Gina, and then back at me. I already knew she was putting two and two together. That's what moms do. They all have eyes in the backs of their heads, and are always figuring out the story behind the scenes.

"Well, we have to go," I said. "I've got to talk to someone about a cornet."

"I've decided for sure on clarinet," Gina said. "See you at school tomorrow!"

As we walked over to the Conn-Selmer table again, Mom said, "Gee, she sure seems like a nice girl, and she's awfully pretty."

I let it go. I didn't really want to talk to Mom about Gina just yet.

We rented a cornet and I went home thinking about how much fun it would be to be in band with Gina.

We weren't scheduled to have music until Wednesday, but for that class, Miss Windom taught us about how a band has a certain seating chart that they follow. All the instruments had specific areas to sit in. Then she told us where to sit, based on the instruments we were going to be playing. I was never more surprised than when I found out I would be sitting right behind Gina. The clarinet section was right in front of the horns. We got to talk to each other a little bit, and I told her I would see if it was ok with my mom if we went for a bike ride that weekend. She said she'd ask her mom, too.

You know, I had been disappointed about not getting a guitar, but sometimes things have a way of turning out better than you could have guessed. At least three days of the week were turning out to be pretty good, even for *school* days. That's just how funny life is sometimes.

21 THE BABY SISTER AND THE BIG CHANGE

This particular tale won't take long because everything happened so fast.

On September 30, 1963, my mom was working around the house like her hair was on fire. She had taken a week of vacation from work because she knew the baby was going to be born pretty soon and she wanted to clean the place spic and span before the baby got here. "Babies need a clean environment," she said, and clean, she did. Criminy! I was trying to help her and Jim was trying to help (as much as he ever did, anyway), but the two of us could not keep up with Mom. She was like a wild woman and had the living room, the bathroom, her own bedroom and the porches cleaned by noon. She said she was saving the kitchen for last because it would be easy – she was always kind of cleaning the kitchen anyway, so it wouldn't require a lot.

While we were eating lunch, I noticed Mom seemed kind of uncomfortable. She kept shifting around in her chair like her back was bothering her or something, which it did a lot of the time as her tummy had gotten bigger and bigger.

"Mom, do you need a pillow for your back or anything?" I asked. She looked kind of miserable.

"No, John, but thank you. I'm not going to be sitting that long. I've got to finish up the kitchen," she smiled, but her smile was not too convincing – she really looked uncomfortable.

"Well, I can help you with the kitchen. Why don't you let me clean up the sink and stuff?" I recommended.

"You've got a deal," she answered. I was determined to do the sink and whatever else she needed.

While I was cleaning up the sink, Mom brought out a mop and a bucket. "The floor is really all I've got to do in here," she said. I retrieved the Spic 'n Span from under the sink and put some in the bucket for her. She lifted the bucket into the sink and ran some hot water into it. When she lifted the bucket to take it out of the sink, a pretty bad look came across her face, and she set the bucket down on the floor hard.

"What's wrong, Mom?" I asked.

"Nothing son, but will you go next door and ask Helen if she can come over here for a minute?"

I was a little scared to leave Mom, but I had a feeling I knew what was going on now, so I ran as fast as I could over to Helen Newcomb's house. She was a good friend of my mom and dad, so much so that we called her "Aunt Helen."

I knocked on Aunt Helen's back door but I didn't even wait for her to let me in. I just opened the screen door and went running in, calling her as I entered the house.

"Aunt Helen? Aunt Helen, can you come over to our house right away?" I called out.

Aunt Helen was out in her TV room watching her stories. That's what she called them – her stories. It was just a bunch of people always fighting or kissing or murdering someone. I couldn't stand that stuff, but mostly just old ladies liked it, so the TV people still put the "stories" on TV. Yuck. Anyway, Aunt Helen came out into her dining room to meet me.

"What's wrong, John? Is your mom getting ready to have the baby?"

She seemed to instinctively know what was going on without me having to tell her, but I answered "yes" and Aunt Helen went back to turn off her TV. She followed me over to our house.

When we walked in the back door, Mom was mopping the kitchen floor. Honest.

"Good lands, what are you doing?" Aunt Helen asked her.

"Well, I wasn't going to finish this, but my water just broke so I kind of had to," Mom said.

"Oh, good grief. Go lay down. I'll call Bob and get him home. John, do you know how to mop a floor?" Aunt Helen asked.

"Yup. I'll take care of it," I said. I didn't know what Mom meant when she said her water broke, but it couldn't be good. I started mopping while Aunt Helen went to the phone. Mom headed for the bathroom. She said she needed to get cleaned up. Yup. If you had to clean again because of it, water breaking was probably not a good thing.

Aunt Helen was back in the kitchen in a real short time. "Your dad is on the way home. Do you know if your mom has a suitcase packed?"

"Oh, yes. She's had that ready for quite a while," I told her. "I know it's ready because when she was packing it, Jim thought she was going to have the baby right then and he wanted to put one of his stuffed animals in it for the baby."

Aunt Helen laughed at that. "That Jimmy," she said. "He's a character."

Well, that was true. He was a character all right.

Aunt Helen went to see if Mom was ok. She told Mom that Dad was on his way home and she asked if she could get Mom's suitcase out for her so that when Dad got there, we could get Mom right to the hospital. We were all set, really, and it wasn't all that long before Dad got home. We heard the car pull in the driveway and heard the car door slam shut and in only about two seconds, Dad was rushing in the house.

"Where's your mom?" he asked me as he ran on by. I didn't even get a chance to answer him. I finished up what little mopping there was to do and dumped the dirty water down the sink. I wasn't sure that was what I was supposed to do with it, but that's what I did that day anyhow.

By the time I had the mop put away, Dad was leading Mom out through the kitchen. She kept saying, "I'm fine, honey," but Dad seemed pretty wound-up about the whole thing.

"I know, I know, but I just want to get you to the hospital where your doctor is," he said. I had a feeling he'd be driving like he drove when we went to North Carolina. I thought I better pray for Mom because when he drives like that...yikes!

Aunt Helen came out of the bedroom with the suitcase. I got Jim out of his bedroom (which he still hadn't finished cleaning, by the way) and we started for the car.

"Hey, you guys aren't going," Dad said as he helped Mom into the front seat. "Aunt Helen is going to stay with you till I get back home."

I was kind of disappointed. I wanted to see how they got the baby out of Mom's stomach. I really still wasn't all that anxious for another kid in the house, but I thought it would be interesting to see the baby being born.

"Tell the baby about the big brothers," Jim said.

"Listen brainless," I said. "Babies don't know English."

"Boys, come give me a hug real quick," Mom said. Dad was already gunning the engine. We gave Mom a hug and I snuck in a kiss on her cheek before Dad peeled out of the driveway. We stood there and waved goodbye. I felt a little bit nervous about Mom and how she was going to get along.

"Dad burned plastic," Jim said.

"What?" I asked him, breaking out of my nervous thoughts.

"Dad burned plastic," he repeated.

"You big nerd. He burned *rubber*." Criminy that kid was dopey sometimes.

"Boys, we'll just stay at your house till your Uncle Jim gets home," Aunt Helen decided. "All your toys are here and so forth. You'd be bored at my house."

Well, that wasn't exactly correct because Aunt Helen had a collection of salt and pepper shakers that came from all over the country, and even some from Canada. I don't know how many salt and pepper shakers she had, but I loved looking at them and seeing all the places they were from. Aunt Helen and Uncle Jim had traveled all over the United States and they got a pair of salt and pepper shakers wherever they went. I resigned myself to seeing them again some other time.

Afternoon turned into evening. Uncle Jim got home from work and he came over to our house, too. My brother Jim had been named after Uncle Jim - that's how much my mom and dad thought of Uncle Jim. He was a real good man. I liked talking to him about his work. He always wore these green coveralls to his job, and he wore a little red cap with the company's name on it in big letters. CENTREX, it said. His company had just changed names not too long ago, so they gave all their workers hats with the new name on them. I guess it was just in case the workers forgot the company's new name or something.

"So you're going to be a big brother again," Uncle Jim said as we all sat down to eat a sandwich. "Are you ready for that?"

"I don't guess I have much choice," I said. "I just hope it's a brother so we can teach him to play baseball and stuff."

"You have a fifty-fifty chance on that," Uncle Jim laughed at his own joke.

"I know. That's what makes me nervous," I said.

"I don't care if it's a boy *or* a girl," Jim butted in.

"Who asked you?" I said. Gees, he was annoying today.

"Well, I don't care," Jim said. "I'm going to have a baby brother or sister and I'll be the boss of it."

He still didn't get it. Disgusted, I got up from the table and started taking dishes to the sink. "Thank you, John," Aunt Helen called after me.

The evening passed. Uncle Jim went home to mow his lawn and take a shower, but the rest of us just stayed at the house and watched TV. We still hadn't heard anything from Dad, and I was starting to get worried. It was getting kind of late, and Uncle Jim stopped back over to check on us. Aunt Helen had to report that we didn't know a thing yet. Uncle Jim said he was going to go home and go to bed since he had to get up early for work the next day. Since it was a Tuesday, that meant Jim and I had school the next day, too.

"Why don't you boys get your baths and hit the sack?" Aunt Helen asked us. "It could be a while before we hear from your Mom and Dad, and you have to get a good night's sleep for school tomorrow."

Jim went first, and then I took my bath. We were brushing our teeth, with all the usual elbowing back and forth for room at the sink. I almost spit my toothpaste out on Jim's hand because he was being such a doofus.

Then we heard it…the phone rang. I put my toothbrush away and went right out to the living room. Aunt Helen had already picked up the receiver and was nodding her head and saying, "Uh-huh," and "Oh my heavens!" and stuff like that. Finally she said,

"Well, I'm sure glad to hear that everything is all right. Ok, I'll see you in a little while." Then she hung up and turned to us.

"Boys, your dad was just on the phone. Your mom is all right, but she had to have a caesarian section to have the baby, and that's why it took so long," she told us.

"A what?" I asked her. "What happened?"

"Your mom had to have a caesarian section. Have you ever heard of that?" Aunt Helen questioned. We both shook our heads 'no'. "That's where the doctor has to do a kind of surgery to get the baby out. Your mom will have a pretty sore belly for a while."

"Well, how else would the baby come out of her anyway?" I asked.

Aunt Helen smiled. "John, that's a very good conversation for you and your dad at some future date." Oh great. Another mystery to solve.

"You boys may as well go on to bed. Your dad will be home late, and you still have to go to school tomorrow."

"What about the baby? Is it a boy or a girl?" I asked.

"Good grief. Your dad didn't say, and I forgot to ask!" Aunt Helen was clearly mad at herself.

"Well, we'll find out when Dad gets home," I said.

"You'll probably be asleep when he gets here," she said, but I doubted that highly.

I was wrong. I did fall asleep, and it wasn't till the next morning when I woke up that I realized I had missed Dad's arrival home. I got up and immediately went to his and Mom's bedroom, but he wasn't there. I found him in the kitchen already, having a cup of coffee.

"Dad, how's Mom? How's the new baby? Is it a boy or a girl?"

Dad took a sip of his coffee and made me wait for a minute. He was stringing this out just to tease me. When he finally decided to speak, it was almost like the words were in slow motion. "Yooou haaave a baaaby siiisterrr…….."

Oh no. The worst possible news. A girl.

Jim came around the corner. He was already up and dressed for school and had been first to hear the news. "I'm a big brother of a baby sister!" he said, all smiles and kind of wiggling around like a jumping bean or something. "And guess what, John? Mom had to have her independence out, too!"

My dad choked on his coffee and started cracking up. "No, Jim, I can assure you that she did not have her independence out, and I'm fairly certain she *never* will have her independence out. She will keep her independence until the day she meets her maker. She had her *appendix* out." He laughed until tears came out of his eyes. Jim just stood there with that dumb smile still on his face. He didn't really care about the independence or the appendix or whatever it was. He was just thinking about being the baby's boss.

"Aunt Helen told us Mom had to have a surgery to get the baby out. What does that mean?" I asked.

"John, for some reason no one really knows, Mom couldn't have the baby the normal way, and the doctor finally said he had to take her into surgery and get the baby out that way. He had to make a pretty big cut right in her belly and get the baby out. That's when he took her appendix out, too," Dad said. "Mom's belly will be sore, but she's completely fine and this just happens sometimes."

I wanted to ask about the 'normal way' that Dad had referenced, but Aunt Helen told me that was a conversation for the future, so I decided to just leave it at that. This was a big enough conversation for this particular day anyhow.

"When will Mom be home?" I asked.

"She and the baby will be home in four or five days," Dad answered. "In the meantime, we have to keep this house picked up so she doesn't feel like she has to start working as soon as she gets home. Can you guys help me do that?"

I shook my head 'yes' and Jim managed to disappear. Big surprise.

We men got along all right before Mom got home. I thought about Shiloh Stevens and his dad and how they had to learn how to manage without the mom being around anymore. I guess I kind of knew what he meant about cooking and doing laundry, but Dad was actually not bad at all of that and I helped him with whatever work I could do. Sometimes he would go up to visit Mom and Aunt Helen would come over to stay with us. I wondered why kids couldn't go see their mom and the new baby, not that I was all that interested in the baby. I mostly just wanted to see what it was we were going to have to contend with.

On the day Mom finally got to come home, we had the house in good shape, and Aunt Helen had made some of her homemade chicken and noodles to bring over for Mom's first meal. We were all set. The baby bassinette was in Mom and Dad's room, and there just was nothing to do but wait. It was a Saturday, four days after she had left to go to the hospital. I really missed Mom, to be honest. I was glad she was coming home, but I dreaded all this baby stuff.

The car pulled in the driveway, and Jim jumped off the couch and ran out the front door before I could even get myself together to join him. When I got out the front door, Dad was getting Mom and the baby out of the car. The baby was wrapped up in a blanket, so I couldn't see anything right away. I told Dad I would get Mom's suitcase out of the back of the car. It was just a little suitcase, so I knew I could carry it. He threw me the car keys and said, "Thanks – I'll get your Mom and the precious bundle in the house." Precious bundle. Right.

I put the suitcase in Mom's bedroom and looked around. This was the last time there would be any moment of peace in this bedroom, I thought to myself.

Mom was sitting on the couch in the living room with Jim parked right by her side. He was grinning like a goofball asking, "Can I hold her? Can I hold her?"

I walked over to Mom and she said, "Would you like to see your new sister, John?"

"I guess so."

She pulled back the baby blanket a little bit, and I saw a tiny little face with pink cheeks. She didn't have too much hair, that's for sure. A bald girl. Sheesh. The baby had her eyes mostly closed, but kind of squinching like she was trying to open them up. Mom opened the blanket a little more and the baby started waving her arms around. She had real little hands and they were balled up in fists. She started moving her legs around, too, but they were still wrapped up in the blanket and I couldn't see them.

"You can give her a little kiss if you want to," Mom said.

What? Give her a kiss? That was about the last thing I wanted to do. I didn't want to hurt Mom's feelings, though, so I put my head down close to the baby's forehead and just gave her the littlest kiss I could.

She opened her eyes and looked up, startling me. The baby looked right at me with her blue-gray eyes. I think she might have smiled, too. Something inside me kind of melted a little bit. That's the only way I can describe it. I instantly fell in love with her.

"What do you think we should name her?" Mom asked. I told her I had no idea, but it should be a pretty name at least.

"What do you think of Emma, after your grandma?" Mom asked. I thought that was a good suggestion and told her so. Jim started bouncing up and down on the couch.

"Emma, Emma, Emma," he kept saying.

"Stop it you nerd," I told him. "You'll hurt the baby."

Mom smiled and said, "Don't worry. She's a pretty tough little girl. She didn't even want to come out and fought me tooth and nail."

That was kind of reassuring. Emma was a tough one. Maybe that meant she wouldn't be all prissy like some of the girls at school, Debbie Carruthers for example.

"Would you like to hold her, John?" Mom asked.

"Well, Jim wanted to go first," I said, a little hesitant.

"You're the oldest, so I'm going to let you go first," Mom said. Jim looked at me and stuck out his tongue, his usual reaction to anything that made him mad.

I sat down on the couch by Mom, and she carefully handed baby Emma to me. She didn't cry or anything. She just kind of wiggled around a little and looked up at me. I have a feeling she knew I was her brother and she probably felt pretty safe with someone like me around. I held her for a little bit and then Jim got his turn. He was really happy. He just about never quit smiling except for that one minute when he stuck his tongue out. He sure was proud of being a big brother.

Well, that's about all there is to tell you about the whole baby situation. She was finally here, and I knew life would be different, but there are some things you just can't fight. Change is one of those things, I guess. You can try to fight it, but you'll lose because things are always going to change. When things change, I think the best you can hope for is to find something good in it. That's just the way it is if you want to get along ok in life.

22 THE WORST THING I EVER SAW

It started out like an ordinary day. It was just like any other Saturday you could name, you know? On Saturdays, Mom usually made us some kind of special breakfast. Today, it was bacon, eggs, and pancakes. You couldn't ask for anything better.

I offered to help Mom with the dishes - that's how grateful I was for that delicious breakfast. She said, "No, John. Not this morning. I think your dad wants to do something special with you and I'm going to take Jim and the baby to the library for children's story hour. You go see about your Dad and I'll work on this stuff. I'm glad you offered, though. That shows me what a responsible young man you are turning into. Before I know it, you'll be all grown up!" She smiled that great mom smile that makes you know that no matter what ever happens, you'll be ok.

I found Dad in the den. That's where his gun cabinet was. He always kept the gun cabinet locked, but on this morning he had it open, and he was pulling out a rifle.

"How'd you like to go hunting for a little while?" Dad asked.

I don't know if I showed it, but I was so excited I almost jumped up and down. Maybe my mom was right – maybe I was growing up fast.

"I'd like that, Dad." We had been to the woods together many times, but I'd never been hunting with Dad before. "Is Grandpa or anyone else coming?"

"No, John. This will just be you and me. I'd like to start teaching you some things about use of a gun and the sport of hunting. There are a lot of lessons to be learned, and it's best to do that with fewer people around."

A day with just me and Dad! Things couldn't get much better. First, I'm becoming a man, and now I would get to hang around with the best man I knew. This day was getting off to a great start.

"Go brush your teeth, wash up, and get dressed. Wear some heavy overalls and your boots, and bring a sweatshirt...it might be kind of cool in the woods."

I probably got ready faster that day than any day in my life with the possible exception of Christmas. I had to dig around to find my boots because all my other summer shoes were still in the way. I had two pairs of tennis shoes, one pair of Red Ball Jets and one pair of PF Flyers. I exchanged them depending on what I was doing that day. Red Ball Jets were for just running around with the guys, but PF Flyers were for baseball or running races. When I put on my boots, I noticed they were kind of tight. It made me think again about what Mom had said...I might be growing up faster now that I was ten. Since my birthday is in March, I was really ten and a half, after all.

Dad was still in the den, getting his bullets and the bag he would carry game home in. It was October – squirrel season. My mom could cook up a mean squirrel, so I know that even though Dad was hoping to teach me about hunting, we really were on a mission for dinner, too.

When we were in the truck, Dad started talking to me about hunting safety.

"John, the first thing you have to know is that when you are hunting, you should not be in a hurry. Hurrying leads to errors and errors lead to lost opportunities for food, or even worse, to accidents. I've actually been around guys who were not careful enough with their guns and they almost shot their own heads off. You must always keep the gun's safety on until you're actually ready to shoot, and you should usually carry your gun pointing down towards the ground. Not always - I'll show you some different ways to safely carry your gun when we get to the woods. Just remember this...you should always handle a gun like it's loaded, even when you know it's not. And *never*, under any circumstances, hand any other person a loaded gun. Oh, another thing - you should always wear some kind of bright jacket or hat or something so other hunters don't think you're a deer and shoot you by accident. It's easy to make those kinds of mistakes when you're in the woods. Your vision is obscured by the trees and any brush – it makes it very easy to mistake a man for a deer."

I was listening very hard and trying to absorb everything my dad said. He was a hunter ever since he was a little kid, so he knew a lot about this. "Dad, I've never really held a gun. Will you show me all the stuff like the safety and everything?"

"Of course. In fact, you won't really be handling the gun too much today, John…I will…but I will sit down with you and we'll talk through the different parts of the gun and I'll teach you about ammunition and how to be a good sportsman."

Suddenly it occurred to me…I didn't have anything bright to wear! "Dad! I don't have anything bright to wear!" I think I nearly shouted this information at Dad.

Dad just smiled, reached into his breast pocket and pulled out a bright red handkerchief, the kind with black and white paisley designs on it. "We'll put this around your neck when we get to the woods." Man, was I relieved. I did *not* want to be mistaken for a deer.

We pulled up to a thickly wooded piece of land and parked the truck along the berm of the road. "John, do you know who owns this land?" Dad asked.

"No, not really. Who does it belo9ng to?" I replied.

"Ted McCullough owns this property. Another very important thing you should know about hunting is that you should never go on someone else's land without asking their permission. If you do, it's considered trespassing, and that's against the law. The person who owns the land could have you arrested. Ted and I have had an agreement about me hunting here for many years. In fact, sometimes when the groundhogs get into his beans too much, he asks me to come get rid of some of them for him."

Since I thought groundhogs were kind of cute little animals, I said that I wasn't too sure I thought shooting groundhogs was all that great an idea.

"Son, I understand how you feel, but you have to look at it from the farmer's standpoint…groundhogs can be really destructive to crops, and they're hard to get rid of without just plain killing them.

They can do a lot of damage. That's why Ted asks me to help control them."

I guess I could understand that explanation, but it still didn't make me feel all that great. Have you ever seen a groundhog just standing up by the side of the road? They are funny little animals. They always stand real still like a statue or something when cars go by, like they think if they stand still, no one can see them.

We got Dad's rifle out of the back of the truck. Dad kept it in a safe, hard-shell case while we were driving, and now he took it out of the case. We walked back away from the road into the woods. I was glad I had my sweatshirt because when we got into the woods, it was mostly shade so it was kind of cool back in there. Cool and quiet, except for us crunching stuff under our feet. I was trying not to be too loud because my dad had taught me to walk quietly so you don't scare the animals. We walked quite a ways until Dad saw a big log – it was an old tree that had fallen – and we went over to sit down on it.

Dad reached into his pocket and gave me a piece of horehound candy. That was one of the best things about going to the woods with Dad. He always wore his hunting jacket and he always had horehound candies in the pocket of that jacket. I loved those things.

"Ok, let's talk about this gun a little bit. You already know where the trigger is, right?" I shook my head. That was one thing I did know. "The metal around the trigger is called the trigger guard. The people who make guns put that on there so that you don't accidentally pull the trigger when you didn't mean to."

Dad continued. "This is considered a bolt-action rifle. Here is where the bolt handle is. You use this to open the chamber where you put the bullets. Before you ever do any of that, what should you do first?"

I had been listening in the truck, and I knew this answer. "Make sure the safety is on."

"That's absolutely right. Good, son. Now. Here is the safety. You see the position it is in? That means it's on. Here's how you take the safety off. It's easy to do. That means it's easy to forget, too, so this is the number one thing you should remember about handling a gun. Make sure that safety is on until you are ready to shoot." Dad was stressing safety a lot, and I guess if you've seen someone just about shoot their own head off, you kind of make sure to put a lot of emphasis on safety.

"This heavy wood part is the stock, but you probably already know that, don't you? All of the wood at the back of the gun and under the barrel is considered to be the stock. Here's the chamber where the bullets go, and here's the magazine. This metal part, of course, is the barrel, and that's where the bullets come flying out of. That's about it as far as the parts of the gun go."

I watched Dad's face as he talked about the gun. Of course, I looked at the parts he was pointing out, but I was mesmerized by his face. It was like he was in another world or something, he was so focused. Like I said, hunting had been a big part of his life ever since he was a little kid. In fact, he was younger than I was when he started hunting. He had once told me that Grandpa got him his first BB gun when he was seven. They spent a lot of time together in the woods, and now, I got to do that same thing with my dad. He was bringing me into a kind of club, a brotherhood of men who loved the outdoors and who knew how to find food for their families if it was necessary. Not everyone could be invited into this club, and I felt special somehow. I sat up tall so maybe Dad would notice how fast I was growing and I could show him I was ready to be in this club.

"Alright, Johnny boy, let's stand up and let you practice walking with this thing."

I jumped to my feet. Dad held out the rifle to me. "What's the first thing you do?"

"Check the safety." Dad nodded his approval. I looked, and the safety was on. I took the rifle from Dad and immediately found out just how heavy a rifle is.

"What's the next important thing I told you about while we were driving over here?"

"Make sure to point the gun DOWN, not at anyone's head," I said.

Dad laughed. "Yes, definitely never point it at anyone's head! John, I should tell you that there are several safe ways to carry a gun, depending on if people are in front of you or in back of you. The important thing to remember is to always keep that barrel pointed away from other people. Keep it pointed in the safest direction and keep the barrel under control. What I mean is that you don't want it getting stuck down into the ground, and you don't want it just swinging around in the air. Another really important thing is to keep your finger outside that trigger guard. That's how you avoid pulling the trigger by accident."

This all seemed like a heck of a lot to remember. I wasn't sure I was ready for all this safety, but I didn't want my Dad to think I was still just a little kid. Dad must have thought I looked a little overwhelmed.

"Let me show you a couple of things," Dad said. He took the rifle and proceeded to show me the proper way to carry a rifle depending on if a guy was walking in front of you or behind you or even beside you. "Now you try."

I took the rifle back and walked around a little bit in the clearing. Dad watched me and gave me tips about what I was doing. Then we sat down on the log again.

"Now practice taking the safety off and putting it back on," he said to me. I did that a few times, and apparently he felt satisfied with my work.

"Do you want to practice putting a bullet in the chamber?"

A little bit of a shiver went up my spine. I wasn't sure if it was nervousness or if it was just being in the coolness of the woods.

"Sure. I'll try it." I looked to make sure the safety was on again. It was. I opened the chamber the way Dad had showed me. He gave me a bullet, and I put it in. I closed the chamber and looked one more time at the safety – still on. I don't know if I thought the safety could just magically come off. All I know is that I was relieved that it was still on.

"Ok, stand up and show me how you would carry the gun."

I put the gun down on the ground and stood up. Then I reached down, picked up the rifle with two hands, checked the safety with a quick glance, and pointed the barrel away from Dad. I took some steps like I was going deeper into the woods. I was probably about thirty feet away from Dad when he said, "That's good, Johnny boy…that's enough for this lesson."

I turned around and walked back towards Dad. He was smiling, so I knew I had done all right.

Guns were still a little scary to me, even though I had known about them ever since I was born, practically. I was trying to make sure I did everything right. When I was next to Dad, I looked at the

215

safety one more time, opened the rifle chamber, took out the bullet, and handed it to Dad.

"You did really well, John. This was your first time handling a rifle. I want you to understand something. You are not allowed to mess around with my guns without me being right with you. It's simply too dangerous when you're still inexperienced, and you're really just a kid, even though you are growing fast. You'll be a good hunter someday, but I want you to understand you are never to get out any of my guns without me, ok?"

That wasn't going to be a problem because I still felt a little nervous, but I was kind of excited at the same time. Dad and Grandpa went hunting with my uncles a lot, and I hoped they'd take me with them one day.

"C'mon...let's go walk for a while," Dad said.

We started deeper into the woods. It was so peaceful. Rays of sunlight we shooting down through the trees, some of which were starting to lose their leaves. A lot of the ground was covered in red and yellow and orange. I was noticing how Dad carried the rifle and thinking about how I would try to do it just like he did when we heard the weirdest sound I ever heard.

Dad stopped in his tracks. He looked around and didn't say anything. He took a couple of steps forward, and we heard the sound again.

"That's a deer screaming. I didn't think there were any deer around here...." Dad was not really talking to me, but he was talking out loud, turning his head to look in different directions.

"John, that deer doesn't sound right...let's see if we can find him."

Something in my dad's voice gave me a creepy feeling. His voice sounded kind of sad, but at the same time, determined to find the deer. I had only seen deer in pictures and I thought they were beautiful. I had never seen one in real life.

We had to go quite a bit farther into the woods; at least it seemed like a long way. The sound of the deer was getting louder, so I knew we were getting closer. It did sound like it was screaming. I wondered what would make a deer sound like that when off to our right, we saw movement. We took about ten more steps in the direction of the sound when I saw what it was that would make a deer scream like that.

It was a buck, and he was lying on his side on the ground. Blood was all over the place on its stomach and he looked all torn up. You could see a little trail of blood from where he had been walking before he laid down. He was kicking his legs around a little bit, like maybe he was still trying to get up but couldn't. I thought I was going to throw up.

"Gosh darn it! Some idiot shot this buck in the gut."

I could tell my dad was angry. He just stood there for a couple of minutes. He put his head down, lifted his hand up and rubbed his forehead. "It's not even deer season yet. Somebody has been out here and gut-shot this deer, John. We have to put him out of his misery or he's going to die a terrible death."

Dad looked at me. "You're not going to want to see this John." I didn't want to see what we had already seen, so I just turned and started walking back in the direction we had come from. When I had gone about six steps in, I heard a loud BANG! It made me jump, but I didn't look back and just kept on walking. I really felt sick.

I was ahead of Dad by quite a bit, and I found another old tree and sat down on it. I put my hand on the log and felt the moss that was growing there. It was soft, kind of what I thought deer skin might feel like. Right then I started to cry a little bit. I don't really know why. It had just been a jangled day; first, being all excited about hanging around with Dad, learning about some man stuff, getting to actually handle a rifle, feeling like I was older. Then to see that deer...I'll never forget it. It was horrible.

Dad caught up with me and sat down. "John, what you have just seen is what happens when people are irresponsible in their hunting. Someone shot that buck and the buck took off and they didn't bother to track him down and see if he was still alive. It's a terrible thing. I'm sorry you had to see it. There aren't that many deer around. For a long time, you couldn't even hunt deer because they were almost extinct in Ohio."

Dad's words were coming at me but I could barely process any of it. I kept thinking about that buck, lying in his own blood, kicking his legs around. He must have been in a lot of pain.

Dad put his arm around my shoulder. "Johnny, you have learned a lot today, and now you've learned some of the bad parts of hunting, too. First of all, you don't hunt any animal that's not in season. Deer season starts later in the year. No one should be out shooting at any deer right now. Secondly, you don't just shoot animals and then not try to make sure you find them. You don't want animals to suffer like that. The whole point is to always get a clean shot so that you kill them with the *first* shot."

I wasn't sure I cared to shoot any animals at that point, and I told Dad so.

"Son, human beings have hunted animals for a long time. They provide food for us. Have you ever known of me or Grandpa to just go shoot animals for the heck of it? No. We hunt animals so we can put meat on the table. It helps feed our families. Now, I like the sport of it, too. It's a challenge to be a good enough shot that you do kill that animal on the first try, but the whole point for me is to help provide food for our family. Men have been doing it almost since time began. Unfortunately, there's always some knucklehead who doesn't have the proper respect for hunting or the animals we hunt. That's what we witnessed today."

Dad paused and clenched his jaw. I could see he was really upset about the whole thing, too.

"You know, this happens to guys sometimes during deer season. Remember how I said you should not rush and make sure you get a good shot? Sometimes guys get all riled up when they see a deer and don't get a good shot. We call it 'deer fever.' But that's during deer season, which it is *not*. We'll report this to the rangers at the Department of Natural Resources. If these guys poached deer once, they might try it again. I'm going to let Ted know about this, too. He might know who's been around on his property."

"Dad, did you kill that deer?" I was pretty sure he had, but I just had to ask.

"Yes, son. It was the merciful thing to do. When a deer gets shot in the gut like that, if it doesn't kill them right away, they are in a lot of pain and they get a bad infection and they die a miserable death. You wouldn't want that."

I shook my head 'no' because he was right...I wouldn't want that. "But now what happens to him?" I asked.

"Well, truthfully, some coyotes might find him and have a meal, and after that, the buzzards will probably find him and have a meal, too. Then his body will begin to decay." Dad sounded pretty sure of all this.

I wasn't crying anymore, but I sure did feel lousy. And I started to feel mad that someone had done this.

"Sometimes I don't know if I want to be a grown up," I blurted out. I knew that didn't make any sense, but it was just what came out of me.

"Sometimes I don't want to be a grown up either, son."

We walked back to the truck. The sun was starting to set, and I shivered again. The back of the truck seat was warm, and I tried to push my back into it as hard as I could. At least I didn't feel like I was going to throw up anymore.

"Dad, thank you for teaching me all this stuff," I said.

"John, I am glad we had the time to do this today. I'm sorry for the way it turned out in one way, but in another way I'm glad. Do you know why?"

I shook my head because I had no idea why he would be glad.

"Because you are getting bigger, and while the world is a wonderful place, you also have to know that not everyone in the world is always kind. Moms and dads try to put off letting their kids know that for as long as they can, but little by little, kids start to learn about meanness in the world. You've seen some meanness already, haven't you?"

I thought about Peaches and Mr. Rader's egg house. Yes, I had seen some meanness.

"It's part of growing up, part of being in this world. There's good and there's bad. Just try to stay away from the bad, ok?"

"Ok, dad."

Dad started the truck and we drove home. I didn't feel too hungry that evening and excused myself from supper after I ate only a couple of bites.

"John, are you feeling all right?" Mom asked.

"Go on, son...I'll explain to your Mom," Dad said.

I went to my room and lay down on the bed. I could see out my window. The daylight was all but gone and the stars were starting to show up. The sky got darker, the moon came out, I closed my eyes and as dumb as you might think it is, I said a prayer for that deer.

23 HALLOWEEN

My favorite holiday besides Christmas is Halloween. I love the spooky decorations, going to haunted houses, going on hayrides and trick-or-treating. I love playing pranks, but we never play any mean pranks on anyone. We just do things to kind of scare them. For instance, last Halloween, Rusty and I went over to Miss Ruth's house and moved this little wooden wheelbarrow that she had in her front yard. She had it filled with mums, kind of like a big flower pot. We just moved it from one side of the yard to the other, but I would have loved to have seen her face when she saw it had been moved. I'm pretty sure she doesn't believe in ghosts or goblins, but it was just a little trick we did for fun. She never moved the wheelbarrow back – she just left it where we had moved it.

Since our town now had a little bit of a swell park going (thanks to having the smorgasbord), the town council decided that we would hold a big Halloween party in 1963. I was very excited for that party because it would be the first time we had anything like this in our new park. The whole town was invited, and there was a committee to plan all the stuff that would be at the party, but my mom and dad didn't really have to help with that like they did for the smorgasbord. For one thing, Mom had just had my baby sister and was busy as all get-out all the time anyway. Dad was working night shift and he just couldn't help with a town party. Since no one in our family was helping with the planning, I didn't know any details, and that made it all the more exciting to think about.

Halloween fell on a Thursday, but the party was going to be held on the Saturday following Halloween. First of all, we all had to go trick-or-treating on Halloween, of course. On Friday night, everyone would be at the football game at the high school, so Friday was no good. That left Saturday. The only thing about a party on Saturday night is that you have to get up and go to church the next morning, come rain or shine. There was no escape from church at my house unless you were about half dead. If I stayed up too late on Saturday for the party and then the next day fell asleep in church…well, it wouldn't be the first time.

I didn't know what I wanted to dress up like for Halloween, but whatever it was it had to be good because early-on we found out that there would be a costume contest at the town party. I wanted something easy so that if there were any other kinds of contests, my costume wouldn't keep me from participating in them. I figured I'd end up going as some kind of cowboy, like Marshall Matt Dillon from "Gunsmoke" or maybe Cooper Smith from "Wagon Train." Both of those guys were heroes, and I didn't want to have any sissy costume in case Gina Vanelli came to the party. I already had a cowboy hat and a holster and play six-shooter, so it would be easy to put that costume together and it would just be like wearing regular clothes. Jim wanted to go as Bozo the Clown. I thought he should go as Dennis the Menace. That would have been more fitting.

Mom wasn't back to work yet after having the baby, so she was around to help me pick out stuff to make my costume more realistic. We got a western-looking plaid shirt out, a neckerchief made out of one of dad's handkerchiefs, and jeans. I had a belt with a big cowboy-ish buckle already, too. My grandpa had given the buckle to me when I was pretty little. It was silver with inlaid turquoise. The only thing we couldn't figure out was how to come up with cowboy boots. I wanted to buy some, but Mom said that for the money they cost we could send me to summer camp so we'd have to figure out something else. She was smart – I knew she'd come up with a plan. I was basically ready.

Jim was having a harder time of it because we didn't have clown clothes just laying around and we definitely didn't have any Bozo the Clown hair. Again, Mom came to the rescue. She said she could make Jim a clown costume pretty easy. She got a pattern and some material at the fabric store and whipped out a clown costume in just a few days' time. It was really good, too. Mom had an idea for how to fix Jim's hair but she didn't share that idea with us. I have a feeling she was afraid we'd try it without her there to direct the work.

What I didn't know that was when Mom was at the fabric store, she had also picked up some material that looked kind of like brown leather. She surprised me just a few days before Halloween. She came down the stairs with homemade boots in her hand.

"What do you think, John?" she had asked, holding up the things she had just made. I didn't even know what they were at first. I must have looked kind of puzzled.

"They're cowboy boot replacements!" She smiled like she was pretty proud of herself. I took the replacement boots from her and looked them over.

The material was brown and kind of shiny. It reminded me of the material that is on car seats. It wasn't real leather, but it was close enough. She had made fake boots for me. I had to pull them on over my feet like knee socks, only with no foot part in them, and they had a little strap on the bottom to hold them in place. The only drawback I could see was that I had to wear them with my church shoes in order for them to look like cowboy boots. I couldn't wear them with my sneakers, so church shoes it was. And you know what? I was fine with that idea because it was as close as I was going to get to having a pair of actual cowboy boots.

"Thanks, Mom. You're the best," I said. "This will work out fine."

"Yes, John. I think it will. Your jeans will be hanging over most of the material, but just in case your pant leg gets caught up, it still looks like a boot under there. I think it will be good enough for Halloween, don't you?" I could tell Mom really wanted me to be enthusiastic about her work.

How could I ever hurt her feelings? "They'll be great, Mom," I said. I would never, ever tell her that at that moment I still wished for real cowboy boots. She had done a lot of work making Jim's costume and making these for me, just for Halloween. It's not like we had a school assignment or something. She just did it because she loved us.

It was finally Halloween. Rusty and I had some good stunts planned. Scotty and Dave were coming trick-or-treating with us, so I got ready extra early. I planned on taking a pillow case to collect all my treats.

I got ready and went to the kitchen where Mom was putting the finishing touches on Jim's hair. Jim's hair was a little longer than mine, but not much. Mom had somehow gotten his hair dyed red as a fire engine, and it was sticking out all around his head like a crazy crown.

"What in the heck did you do to Jim's hair?" I asked her.

Mom acted like it was nothing. "What do you mean, John?" She smiled a little smile and kept right on working.

"Ouch!" Jim complained.

"Do you want to be Bozo or not?" Mom asked him.

"Yes, but it hurts. I didn't know it would hurt to be Bozo," Jim whined.

Jim already had his makeup on and now with this crazy hair, he looked more like the Joker to me. "How did you get Jim's hair so red?" I asked.

"Cherry Kool-Aid. Oh, and I threw in some Niagara starch to make it stick out," Mom answered. "It will wash right out after trick-or-treat."

"You mean I have to take a bath after trick-or-treat?" Jim wailed.

"You most certainly do. I don't want this stuff ruining my pillowcases!" Mom said.

"That reminds me – I have to get a pillowcase for my candy," I said.

"You're not taking pillowcases for candy. It looks greedy and ungrateful." Mom seemed pretty adamant. I could tell there would be no arguing with her.

"What in the heck can we use?" I asked.

"I have a little something for both of you," she said, and she sounded pretty proud of herself. She finished fiddling around with Jim's hair, and he ran off to the bathroom to look at himself in the mirror.

"Wow!" I heard Jim say as Mom came back from the pantry into the kitchen with two orange plastic pumpkins with handles.

"You can collect treats in these." She smiled at me.

A plastic pumpkin? First of all, they weren't very big. I had plans to start a candy collection that would last till Christmas at least. Second, they looked like something a little kid would carry. Bozo the Clown might carry one, but Cooper Smith would never touch one of those things.

"Mom, I appreciate the pumpkin, but that just looks too much like a little kid for me. I don't mean to hurt your feelings. You've been so great helping us get ready for Halloween...." I didn't know what else to say, but I knew I couldn't carry a pumpkin around.

Mom looked at the pumpkins, one in each of her hands. "Of course, you're right, John. I think Bozo in there can use one, but you're getting too big for these kinds of things. I really don't want you using a pillowcase, though. Let's see what else we can come up with."

After rooting around for a bag, she found one from the grocery store. It was a nice-sized paper bag with handles. It would be fine. It actually looked better with my costume than a pillowcase.

I had promised to take Jim along because he was too little to go by himself and his friends were too little to even go as a group. They had to have someone older with them. Jim and I went up to the church where we met the guys. Church always was our main meeting place.

"Where are we going first?" Dave asked.

"Miss Ruth's!" Rusty, Scotty and I all yelled at the same time. We took off running. Jim couldn't run as fast as us and sometimes I had to stop and wait up for him for a minute.

"Come on, Jim! We'll miss the popcorn balls!" I knew we'd make it in time, but I wanted Jim to understand the urgency so he would get moving a little faster.

"I can't run too fast in Dad's shoes," Jim said. He had some of Dad's shoes on to look like big clown feet. Mom had stuffed the ends of the shoes with newspaper. I was glad I was a cowboy and not dealing with all that.

We got to Miss Ruth's a minute or two after the other guys had gotten there. They were first in line on the porch when Jim and I finally arrived. There were about twenty kids in line. I wasn't worried though – Miss Ruth always made a lot of popcorn balls. The thing is, once they were gone, they were gone and that was that.

The guys waited by Miss Ruth's door till Jim and I got up there. Miss Ruth dropped a popcorn ball into our bags and said, "Happy Halloween!"

As we were all stepping down off the porch, Miss Ruth called out, "If you guys decide to move anything this year, could you maybe move my little wheelbarrow back to where it was last year?" She started laughing.

We all just looked at each other for a minute. How could she have known?

"Just kidding!" she said, closing her door. We all stood there and watched her through the beveled glass of the door, walking back into the depths of her big old house. How could she ever have known?

We turned our attention back to the task at hand; collecting as much candy as possible. We ran all over town that night, and I'm not kidding when I say that we ran...even Jim got into the spirit of Halloween and tried to keep up with us. He finally figured out that the more territory we covered, the more candy we would have at the end of the night.

When trick-or-treat was over, Jim and I headed for home. His pumpkin was full almost up to the brim, and my bag was about half full. We had gotten quite a haul. At home, we dumped all the candy out on the living room floor to examine our take.

"Bit o' Honey, Clark bar, Tootsie Roll pops, Milky Way," Jim said. "Oh! And Double Bubble!"

My inventory was pretty good, too. "Butterfinger, Snickers, Mars bar, Sugar Daddy," I announced.

We had both gotten a couple of apples but we saved those for Mom and Dad because, you know - we had been taught to share.

Just a couple of days later, it was time to get ready for the town Halloween party. Mom had to spend most of her time on Jim, of course, because Bozo the Clown had to get his hair dyed again and get it all glued up in the crazy hairdo he had for trick-or-treat. I got myself ready because a cowboy costume was simple for a guy like me. When I got downstairs where our whole family was gathering, I saw that Mom had my baby sister all wrapped up in a brown fuzzy blanket, or so I thought till I got closer.

"John, can you hold Emma? I need to just grab my jacket." Mom held Emma out to me.

"Sure." I took the baby and noticed that her brown fuzzy blanket had ears. She was dressed up like a little teddy bear. She looked so cute. My mom had even made the baby a costume.

I looked up at Mom as she put her jacket on. "The tradition of Halloween in this family will also extend to the GIRLS." She put a lot of emphasis on the word "girls."

"She looks cute, Mom." I meant it.

Dad came in and said, "Let's go. I want to be there in time for the pumpkin pie eating contest," he said.

My dad loved pumpkin pie almost as much as he loved ice cream. I knew he could beat everyone in town when it came to eating the most pumpkin pie.

When we got up to the park, it was already pretty dark. We had walked up there, and a lot of other people had, too. It had turned out to be an unusually warm and dry October for us in Ohio, and we hadn't even had to wear coats over our costumes for a change.

The men in our town had built a little community building in the park, and that's where the party was being held. The building was decorated with fake spider webs and bales of hay to sit on. There were pumpkins of different sizes all over. There was a table where you could get apple cider to drink. I saw another table where there were lots of pumpkin pies and powdered donuts. There were bowls of candy corn and popcorn, too.

Right away I saw Gina Vanelli, and she looked beautiful. She had on a princess dress of some kind, but she looked like she really was a princess. I walked right over to talk to her.

"Hi, John," Gina greeted me first. "Who are you supposed to be?"

"I'm Cooper Smith. You know, from 'Wagon Train'," I replied.

"Oh, yes, we watch it every week. Cooper Smith is very handsome." Gina smiled.

My cheeks got really hot. It seemed like that was always happening around Gina. "He's one of the good guys," I said.

"I know, and so are you," Gina replied. She was still smiling at me, but I had to just look down at my feet for a minute.

When I finally got myself composed, I looked up and said, "Let's go get some cider."

We walked over to the cider table and each took a glass of cider that had been pressed over at the Beucler's farm. They made the best cider of any I had ever tried anywhere else. It was fresh and cold, sweet, but with just a little tanginess. It was perfect. We each took a couple of swallows and sat down with our glasses on one of the bales of hay.

"Are you going to be in the costume contest?" I asked her.

"No, I'm going to just let the little kids be in the contest," Gina replied. "Mom said the town doesn't really have a lot of money so they could only afford a couple of prizes. I'd rather see some of the littler kids get the prizes. It's really more for them." Gina's mom had been in on the planning, so Gina knew what she was talking about.

"I'm not entering, either." I turned my head away for a minute so Gina didn't see my true and honest feeling, which was disappointment. I had wanted to be in that contest so bad, but I wasn't going to do it if Gina thought it was for little kids.

"Hayrides, everyone – hayrides are starting in the back of the building!" The mayor had stood up at the front of the room and was trying to yell this information over the noise of the party.

"Want to go on the hayride?" Gina asked me.

"Heck yes. I better let my parents know where I am, though," I answered.

"Me too. I'll meet you around back in five minutes." Gina took off to find her mom and I quickly scanned the crowd to see if I could find mine.

I spotted Dad over in a corner talking to Wade Benjamin. I got over to them in time to hear them ending a discussion of how well Mr. Benjamin's corn had done this year.

"Dad, is it ok if I go on the hayride?" I butted in.

"Sure. Just be careful and listen to whatever adults are on the hayride with you, ok?"

"I will. I promise," and I headed for the hayride loading area.

Gina was waiting for me. "This is going to be so much fun. Have you ever been on a hayride before?" she asked.

"Oh sure, over at my Uncle Clyde's house. He has a huge farm and he has taken us on hayrides a million times with my cousins." It hadn't been a million times, of course, but I wanted to let Gina know I was experienced at hayrides.

"Well, this is my first. You know we lived in Pittsburgh before this so I never went on a hayride." Gina's eyes were all sparkly and

I knew she was pretty happy about getting to experience something new. It was probably like going to a foreign country, moving here from Pittsburgh.

Mr. Rader was the driver for our hayride. The hay wagon was attached to his tractor - the one I had ridden on. He stood at the back of the hay wagon and helped everyone up. There were young people, old people, kids, Miss Ruth, all sitting on bales of hay. Some of the hay was already coming loose from the bales, lying in little piles on the floor of the wagon. Gina and I sat on one of those piles.

Mr. Rader started the tractor up and hollered back over his shoulder. "Here we go, folks! Everyone stay seated, please." And with that, we were off. First we went around all the land that had been purchased for the park. Then Mr. Rader started driving us through town out towards Lieb's farm. The farther we got away from town, the brighter the stars looked. Gina and I looked up at them and talked about stuff we were learning about the planets in science class. It was a beautiful night.

All of a sudden, Gina leaned over and gave me just the littlest kiss on the cheek. I looked at her in complete shock. I had never been kissed by any girl other than my mom.

"Golly, what was that for?" I asked her.

"Just because you're such a nice boy," she said. "I like being around you. You are a good friend to everyone. I like people like you who try to be kind to others and never hurt anyone's feelings or try to show off in sports or act like you're the smartest person in class. And I just felt like giving you a kiss." She turned away then, seeming a little embarrassed.

I didn't want her to think I didn't appreciate the gesture, so I said, "Well, I think all the same stuff about you. Would it be ok if I gave you a kiss, too?"

"Sure," she said.

I leaned over and kissed her on the cheek, too. Her cheek was really soft and her skin felt warm to my lips.

We just sat quietly for a while and didn't say anything. I turned to look at her and she turned to look at me. We just smiled and didn't say anything, but when I looked at the sky again, it seemed like the stars had gotten brighter.

Before long, we were back at the park and there was a lot of activity going on. The costume contest was already over. The Harris twins had won for their Raggedy Ann and Andy costumes. Their prizes were new two-wheelers. I didn't need that anyway since I had my Schwinn. Some little kids were bobbing for apples. Half of Jim's Bozo makeup had washed off and he looked like some deranged clown now instead of a beloved children's television star. Some kids were digging around in a big sandbox full of sawdust, looking for coins that the adults had put in there. Someone said there was an actual dollar bill in the sawdust somewhere, but I never saw anyone dig it out. I knew my little brother probably would jump in there next, trying to find that dollar bill.

I heard some loud laughter at a table along one wall of the community building. I looked to see what was going on and saw my dad and a bunch of other men over there getting ready to dig into some pumpkin pie.

"Hey, Gina," I said. "Let's go over to the pie eating contest. I bet my dad can beat all those other guys with his hands tied behind his back."

We walked over to the contest area where a bigger crowd was gathering. Rusty, Dave, and Scotty were already there. "Your dad has these guys beat all to heck," Rusty proclaimed. Gina and I kind of pushed our way to the front a little bit because I wanted a good view of my dad. Mom was standing off to one side with Jim and Emma. I gave her a little wave, and she winked at me. She knew dad could win this one, too.

The Halloween committee chairman, Mrs. Knepper, stepped to the front of the table and called out in a loud voice that I had heard her use before on her kids.

"Ladies and gentlemen, the pie eating contest is about to begin. Before you, you see eight hungry men and eight delectable pumpkin pies with lots and lots of whipped cream. These eight men will compete to see who can finish off a pumpkin pie in the fastest time."

Everyone started cheering and calling out their favorite man's name. Mom was kind of laughing and bouncing Emma in her arms, rocking back and forth a little bit. I was yelling, "Come on Dad! You can do it Dad!"

Mrs. Knepper continued. "There's only one catch…." The crowd got quiet. "Each man must eat the pie without using his hands."

The men in the contest started looking at each other, astounded by this development. The entire crowd started laughing like crazy…they knew what was about to happen. Some other ladies came up behind the men and started tying their hands together with scarves. Dad was going to win with his hands literally tied behind his back.

"On three, dig in!" Mrs. Knepper announced to the contestants, once they were securely bound. "One…two… THREE!"

Each of the men bent over at the waist and just plowed their faces into those pumpkin pies. I never heard so much laughing and shouting in my entire life as I did that night. The whole crowd was having the time of their lives watching those guys smashing their faces and rooting around in pumpkin pies like pigs in mud. But guess what? My dad won. I knew he would. He pulled his face up out of that pie and grinned at the room – he had pie and whipped cream in his hair, in his eyebrows, up his nose, and just all over his face. He was a mess. But he didn't care. He had won.

Mrs. Knepper came back to the table. She had backed off in case there was any flying pie, I guess. "We have a winner," she announced, raising my dad's arm high in the air. She called for one of the other adults. "Will someone please bring me some towels and the grand prize?" she asked.

Grand prize! I wondered what it could be. Maybe a new fishing pole or something….

Mrs. Higgins came to the table with a box in her hand. Well, so the prize wasn't very big. That was ok…it was still the grand prize.

"Bob Reed, you are our grand prize winner. It is my pleasure to present you with this reward for your speed, your sportsmanship, and your courage." Mrs. Knepper always kind of exaggerated things.

My dad wiped a little whipped cream from around his eyes and looked around the room with a big smile on his face. Then he opened the box and started laughing a big, hearty laugh that made everyone get quiet.

"It's a pumpkin pie!" he announced.

The room broke into laughter and cheers again. The other men up at the table shook Dad's hand and patted him on the back. I went up and shook his hand, too.

"Gees, Dad. Do you think you even want another pumpkin pie?" I asked.

"Not tonight, buddy. Not tonight." Dad showed his prize pie to Mom. "We can maybe save this for a couple of days?" he asked.

"Oh sure, honey. I'll just put it in the frig. In fact, I'm going to head for home. The baby is getting tired, I'm getting tired…it's been a long Halloween this year. How about cleaning up a little before you walk in my house, Mr. Pie Eating Contest Winner?" She turned to me. "John, I'm taking Jim with me, and you should say your goodbyes, too."

"I'll be right there, Mom." Mom headed off to find Jim, who had returned to the sawdust pile as I predicted. I turned to Gina.

"This sure has been a swell night," I said.

"I think so, too, John. Thanks for taking me on the hayride with you," she answered.

"We'll do it again next Halloween, ok?" I said, and I meant it.

"That will be great." Gina turned to walk away.

"I'll never forget tonight," I said and was immediately embarrassed by my own declaration.

Gina just looked over her shoulder at me and smiled. I knew she felt the same way.

Even when you're a kid, you can have strong feelings about people and places and things. You might not know all the right things to say and the right things to do, but you know how you feel inside about those people, places and things. I walked home with Mom, Jim, and Emma, listening to them talk about the Halloween party, but I stayed quiet. There are times when a guy just needs to keep his thoughts to himself.

24 CORTEGE

There were four days in November that will probably stay in my mind for the rest of my life. I have to tell you about it even though it's sad. It's the only thing I can remember about November, 1963. Everything else about that time became a blur after the 22nd day of the month. I don't remember our Thanksgiving or Christmas decorating, or any of it, really. All I remember is everyone being sad for a long time.

On Friday, November 22, we were in music class, which was always right after lunch. Miss Windom was making us practice scales, which I didn't like, but it was just one of the things she told us would help us get better at playing our instruments. Someone was playing a lot of sour notes, which was distracting, and we were playing so loud that none of us heard a knock on the music room door. Miss Windom put down her baton and walked over to the door though, so we quit playing. Mr. Howard was at the door, which was kind of weird. He asked Miss Windom to step outside. She did and closed the door. Of course, the whole class started goofing around and talking and so forth. Gina and I were talking about her and her folks going back to Pittsburgh for Thanksgiving when the music room door opened back up. Miss Windom entered, dabbing at her eyes. She was real pale, like she was sick or something.

"Children, please put your instruments away – for you brass players, don't forget to clean out your valves. Let's get this done as quickly and quietly as possible. School is being dismissed early." Miss Windom didn't look happy about it, so we knew something was wrong. "When you're ready to go, I'll walk with you back to your homeroom so you can get your coats and other belongings."

We did as we were told. I had never seen a teacher cry. Glancing around uneasily at each other, sensing that something wasn't right, we stayed on our best behavior.

When we got back to our classroom, Mrs. Barker was sitting in her desk chair, looking out the window. I don't think she even noticed us at first, and you could tell she had been crying, too. Miss Windom walked over and put her hand on Mrs. Barker's shoulder. They looked at each other with real sad faces. Miss Windom stayed right by Mrs. Barker as she stood up and said, "Class, I have the worst news I can possibly think of to tell you right now. As you know, you are being dismissed early, but what you don't know is why you are going home. Just about an hour or two ago, someone shot and killed President Kennedy."

I remember hearing a gasp somewhere in the room, and a few kids started crying. I was in shock, and so were most of the other kids. We just sat silently, looking around. We didn't know what to do.

"This is a terrible day for our entire country. It's very hard to understand or to even believe," Mrs. Barker continued, "but it's all true. Right now, I want you to just collect your things and get ready to board your busses. They are being pulled up in front of the school in just a few minutes."

We set about getting our coats and any other stuff we were going to take home for the weekend. Some of the kids continued crying, but mostly everyone was completely silent. It was a creepy feeling. I had never known of anyone famous to be murdered like that. Why would anyone shoot the President? It didn't make any sense to me. I noticed Miss Windom and Mrs. Barker give each other a little hug before Miss Windom left to go back to the music room. It was easy to see that even the adults were shocked and sad. We got in line to go out to the busses. I gave Gina a little wave.

Rusty and I sat together on the bus. "What in the heck do you make of this?" Rusty mused. I don't think he really expected an answer and I sure didn't have one. The older kids were in the back of the bus as usual, and I saw more than one high school girl crying. I turned and looked out the window. I didn't really feel like talking. Jim was up in one of the front seats of the bus, and I don't know if he knew what was going on at that point. He was looking around at all the other kids, appearing confused and kind of lost. It was an eerie ride home.

We got off the bus at Calvary Church as we always did. Pastor Miller was standing out in front of the church waiting for us on this day. "Hi, kids," he said as we dismounted. "How are all of you doing?"

At those very words, Gladys Martin, a girl in high school, started crying really loud. She walked over to the Pastor and said, "Why? Why would anyone kill the President?"

Pastor Miller looked sad and put his hand on Gladys' shoulder. "Gladys, I do not have an answer for you. I don't have an answer for this terrible thing at all. I only know this…God is watching out for our country. He can get us through this, and He will. Our whole country will stick together and prevail against this evil." Somehow that answer didn't seem like enough.

Not wanting to hear anything more about the killing right at that minute, I said to Jim, "Come on. Let's go home."

I felt suddenly tired and we walked kind of slow. No one was home from work yet, so we let ourselves in. I got some chocolate chip cookies for us and got a couple of glasses of milk out of the refrigerator. Jim and I sat at the kitchen table and ate our treats in silence. Chewing and sipping was the only noise in the house.

Jim was first to break the silence. "Do you think it's true? Do you think someone really shot the President?"

"I guess it must be true. The only time they ever send us home from school early is when there's a big snowstorm coming, so it must be true," I reasoned.

"Did the killer use a big rifle?" Jim asked, as if I had all the answers.

"Jim, I don't know what kind of gun he used. All I know is that it was big enough to kill the President, and that's a terrible thing," I answered.

"Maybe Dad will know," Jim said.

"Yeah, maybe Dad will know." I hoped Jim would quit asking questions. This was definitely a time we needed the adults to answer the questions, but would they know? Pastor Miller didn't know, and he knew a lot of stuff. I sure didn't have any answers for Jim at all.

Mom got home at her usual time, and Dad got home just a minute after. They both had grim looks on their faces. They hugged and kissed, then hugged us. They went directly to the television and turned it on. Mom was still carrying Emma, who she had picked up from the babysitter's before she got home. She didn't even take her coat off or unwrap Emma's blanket.

On the television, all three channels were giving the news about President Kennedy. All the reporters looked as grim as Mom and Dad. There was no friendly banter, no discussion of the weather or anything else but President Kennedy's murder. We found out that the killer did use some kind of rifle and that he had been hiding in a building in Dallas, where President Kennedy had gone with his wife. His poor wife! She was right with him when he got shot. It couldn't be more awful.

By now a guy from Texas, Lyndon B. Johnson had been sworn in as President. We saw pictures of him with his wife and President Kennedy's wife standing right by him. They were on an airplane with the President's dead body when he took the oath of office and became President. There were reports, also, that a man had been arrested. His name was Lee Harvey Oswald. The police thought he had killed the President, and they knew he had killed one of their officers that same day.

My dad stood up, walked over and turned off the television. "That's enough of that for now. I'm sure we'll be hearing the news about this all weekend. I want to talk to you boys. Do you understand what has happened?"

I shook my head 'yes' but Jim just sat there.

"The job of the President is a very important one, and it's not one that a lot of people can do or even want to do. Our country elects the President by voting. John, you already knew that, correct?" I nodded again as Dad continued. "We're one of the few countries in the world to have a peaceful process for choosing our leaders. It's one of the reasons we love our country. We all work together, even when we don't agree on things. We figure it out. Just like electing a President. Your mom voted for President Kennedy, but I voted for Richard Nixon. We have different opinions about things, but we still work together to make our country strong. We certainly don't go around killing each other, and we don't murder our Presidents. Most of the people in the country wanted John F. Kennedy to be President, and the majority wins, right?"

We both shook our heads. I think Dad should have been a social studies teacher.

"So now, with President Kennedy gone, someone has to be the President, and that's why the Vice President has to step up and take the job. President Kennedy is gone. Now we have President Johnson." Dad turned to Mom. "I'll bet old LBJ never thought he'd have the job this way," Dad said to her.

"No, I'm sure he didn't," Mom said, standing up, too. "I've got to change Emma's diaper and feed her. Then I'll get some dinner around."

"No hurry," Dad said. "I don't feel like eating too terribly much right now, myself."

"Me either," Mom answered.

We all kind of felt that way. We turned the TV back on and listened to the news. The reporters said a lot of the same things over and over, but for some reason, I couldn't tear myself away. Eventually Jim got up and left for his room, but I was glued to the TV. I just couldn't miss one minute of what was going on.

On Saturday, there was more of the same on television, except that now the reporters were talking to people who lived in Dallas. They had been at the parade President Kennedy was riding in when he got killed. People were talking about what they saw and how they felt. A lot of them were crying, even the men. It was one of the saddest things I ever saw. The President's coffin was moved into the White House. There was an honor guard staying with the President's body. I had never seen an honor guard before, and I wondered how they could stand so still all the time. I was amazed by that. I tried it myself…it's not easy. I went outside for a while, just to get away from the sadness, but it was kind of a gray day all the way around. A usual and unusual November day – that's what it was.

That afternoon, Mom told us there wouldn't be any school on Monday. Normally that would have been cause for celebration.

"All the schools are closed and the government offices are closed…there won't be any mail. A lot of businesses are closing, too, out of respect for President Kennedy," Mom said. "His funeral is going to be that day. They are going to show it on television, John. Dad's business is closed that day and he'll be home with you so you guys can watch it, but I have to work. You'll have to help Dad with Emma and Jim, ok?"

"Sure Mom. How come your business isn't closed?" I replied.

She smiled a little smile. "Buddy, hospitals can never close. Someone's got to be there to take care of the sick people and if you're not taking care of the sick people yourself, you have to be helping those who are," she said. That made sense, I guess.

That Sunday, we went to church. Everyone there was quiet, sad, and looking worried. There was not the same cheerfulness and gusto in singing hymns, and I saw people with their heads bowed and praying a lot of times, even during Pastor Miller's sermon, which was mostly about how we have to rely on God in bad times like this, that there have always been bad people in the world and that there always would be, that we have to hold on to the good, that we have promises of a better life in Heaven – all that kind of stuff. I don't know if it made anyone feel any better to tell you the truth.

My dad was just like me when it came to watching everything on TV about the assassination. I don't know why we were that way. I think it was because it was just so shocking and hard to believe that seeing all the sad news on television somehow made us know that yes, it really had happened. When we got home from church that day, the first thing Dad did was turn on the TV, and then came our next shock. On every single channel they were showing a man get shot right on TV. That man was the guy they thought shot the President. Over and over again we watched him being brought by the Dallas police through a big crowd of reporters, and then out of the blue, a guy steps out of the crowd and just shoots Lee Harvey Oswald right in the stomach.

Dad got up and turned the TV off. "John," he said, "we're not watching one more minute of this today. We will watch the news this evening, and we will watch the funeral tomorrow, but that's enough. You don't need to have these images in your mind. This is terrible. It's like the wild west out there."

"What do you mean, Dad?" I didn't see any cowboys or anything, so I didn't know what he meant by the wild west.

"I mean the unbelievable degree of lawlessness…allowing someone to just walk up and shoot a suspect right in the very middle of the doggone police department…unbelievable. This whole mess is unbelievable," Dad said.

"Well, Dad, if this fellow killed the President…" I started to say, but Dad interrupted.

"Son, in this country, the accused person has a right to a fair trial. This man certainly was highly suspected of killing the President, and he probably did, but until all the facts are presented in a trial, he was considered innocent. That's the way our country works. It's part of the Constitution. You know about the Constitution, right?"

"Sure. We learned about it in social studies class," I told him.

"Well, this is another terrible event. If he had gone through a trial, he might have gotten the death penalty anyway, but now…well, now we will never know all the facts behind the assassination. He might have talked to the police about whether or not anyone else was involved or if it was just him acting alone or all kinds of information that would help the American people understand this crime. Now all we have is a dead President, a dead suspect, and another murderer. This is not a good thing, John."

I decided to see if any of my buddies could play football. I needed something to do. I called Rusty first.

"Hey, do you want to do something?" I asked him over the phone.

"Heck yeah. Everyone's so depressed around here," he replied.

"Football?" I asked. I couldn't really think of anything else right then.

"What about a ride around the three-mile square?" Rusty said.

The day was cool and cloudy, but it wasn't raining or snowing. I thought a bike ride sounded like a good idea.

"Yeah, let's do that. Listen, you call Scotty and I'll call Dave. Let's get the gang together for a bike ride. We probably won't have too many more chances to do that since it's going to be winter pretty soon," I said.

Mom and Dad gave me permission to go and our whole gang got together for a good ride around the three-mile square. At first, everyone was kind of quiet. Then Scotty spoke up.

"Did you guys see Oswald get shot on TV?" he asked.

"Sure did. It was real. It was a guy really getting shot, right on TV. Not like a Western or army show with fake blood. It was a guy really getting shot right on TV," Rusty said.

"I've heard enough about people getting shot for one weekend," Dave said. "Can't we talk about something else?"

"Dave, you dork!" Rusty said, stopping his bike. "Gosh you're dumb sometimes. Don't you get it? This is real. This is what the world is like. Guys are getting killed in Viet Nam every day, but we just don't see it. Heck, there are people getting murdered all over the place, but we just don't see it. Now, because the President is famous and because Oswald is famous in a bad way, we see it on TV every minute. There's so much more murder going on in the world. This world is a crazy place, and you better wake up to it!" Rusty was pretty agitated. "When I grow up, I'm going to be a reporter, and I'm going to get the true stories out there so people know what they're up against."

"You don't have to be a jerk about it," Dave countered. "I know what's going on in the world. I just don't want to think about it every minute of every day."

"Well, you better get used to it." Rusty got back on his bike and started pedaling.

We rode in edgy silence for a while till suddenly, Rusty stopped his bike again.

"I'm sorry Dave. I really am. I didn't mean to act like such a jerk," Rusty said.

"Yeah, it's ok," Dave answered. "It's been kind of a crummy weekend anyway. You guys, let's go to Janie's and get some cocoa."

That was an idea we could all get behind. We sped up a little and hoped out loud that Janie's would be open. When we got there, Janie was just turning over the sign from OPEN to CLOSED in the front window. Rusty rode his bike right over to the window and waved his arms at her. She left the sign on the OPEN side and came to the door to unlock and open it.

"Hi, boys. What can I do for you today?" she said with a smile. Gosh, it was nice to see somebody smile for a change.

"Were you closing?" I asked. I didn't really want us to butt in if she was trying to close.

"Well, yes, I was going to because I don't have much business coming in the door today. I imagine everyone is home watching the TV about President Kennedy, but I'm happy to stay open if you guys need something to eat." Janie was such a nice person. It was good to be around her.

"We just wanted to have some cocoa," Dave said.

"No problem. Grab a seat. I'll be right back with it," Janie answered.

We all sat at the counter where Janie had those stools that spin around. I was kind of spinning mine when she came back in with the cocoa.

"Here you go. This sure isn't a very nice day for a bike ride," she said.

"Well, it was better than hanging around in the house where everyone is all down in the dumps," Rusty said. "My mom and dad are kind of grouchy, and they're making me feel grouchy, too." Rusty glanced over at Dave when he said that. I think that in a way, he was trying to explain why he had sniped at Dave the way he did. "I had to get out of there for a while."

"This has been a tough weekend, that's for sure," Janie said. "You have to understand, boys - it's a real rough time for our whole country - all the adults feel it, you guys feel it, but can you imagine how Mrs. Kennedy feels? And what about her kids? Just think about those kids who lost their dad. It's pretty terrible."

She was right. If this was hard for kids our age to understand, if it was hard for us to deal with grouchy parents or sad parents, think about what President Kennedy's kids must be going through.

We drank our hot chocolate and Janie changed the subject to Ohio State football and what we wanted for Christmas this year, and just about anything she could think of to keep us from thinking about President Kennedy, I guess. All I know is that when we were ready to leave, I felt better. I think all the guys did. That was one thing about Janie. No matter how you felt when you walked into her place, you always felt better when you walked out.

That evening, we watched the President's casket get put on a wagon that was pulled by some horses. My dad told me this was a cortege. He pointed out that there was a horse with no rider. It was a black horse. I guess they picked black because of the sadness. Everyone always wears black at funerals, so it made sense that they picked a black horse. I was glad Dad explained about the cortege because I had never heard that word before. The cortege took the President to the capitol building and they showed about a million people on TV filing around his casket just to show how much they respected him.

The next day was President Kennedy's funeral. Mom went to work, and I helped Dad take care of Jim and Emma. Dad had to take care of Emma mostly, but I could do more with Jim, like getting him some Rice Krispies for breakfast and keeping him occupied while Dad took care of the baby. When it was time for the funeral to start, Emma had fallen back to sleep. Dad told Jim and I that it was time to watch the funeral and pay our respects in the only way we could. I think even Jim got that this was serious business. Dad got some TV trays and we had our lunch right in front of the TV. Somehow, it seemed even more gloomy because all the pictures were in black, white, and different shades of gray. The TV would get full of static sometimes, so Dad would jump up and move the rabbit ears around a little bit. Then the picture would get better, but it was still kind of grainy, as Dad called it. It just made everything and everyone seem more miserable.

The funeral was in a real big church. I had never seen such a big church. Dad called it a cathedral. There was a heck of a lot of people there. Some people in the crowd were crying, but Mrs. Kennedy never cried one time. Of course, she had a black veil over her face, so I couldn't tell for sure, but she didn't look like she cried at all. I thought that was amazing. After church, there was a big procession to go to the cemetery.

"The President's coffin will be carried on caisson," Dad said. "That's a type of wagon that usually carries some kind of ammunition, but today, it will carry our President." I thought it seemed kind of strange to have the President riding on an ammunition wagon after he had been shot with ammunition, but I guess it was so everyone could see his coffin one more time.

The President was going to be buried in Arlington Cemetery, which is where all the soldiers and sailors can be buried, my dad told me. In fact, since he was in the Navy, my dad said even he could be buried in Arlington cemetery. I thought that was pretty cool, really. I didn't want my dad to die *ever*, but if he did, he could be right in the same cemetery as the President.

The TV cameras were focused on Mrs. Kennedy and her children, and then another thing happened that I will never forget as long as I live. President Kennedy's little boy John John stepped away from his mom and saluted. He saluted his dad's coffin just like a little soldier. It was probably the saddest thing I had ever seen, and probably the bravest thing I had ever seen a little kid do. The reporters were saying that the very next day was going to be John John's birthday. That was pretty crummy...his dad's funeral the day before his birthday. He wasn't going to have much of a fun birthday, that's for sure.

In Arlington Cemetery, the President's wife and brothers lit a little fire that the reporters said would never, ever go out. I never had heard of such a thing, but it was supposed to symbolize how the President's spirit would always be remembered, or something like that.

Well, that's really all I want to tell about November. Like I said, I don't remember much else about the month anyhow, but I can tell you this...I'll sure never forget those four days. People talked about it for quite a few days after it all happened. I guess no one will ever forget it, so I wasn't alone. I was right there with everyone in the whole country, and believe me, it wasn't the best place to be. It was a good thing Christmas was coming.

25 CHRISTMAS FRUITCAKE

Everyone has had fruitcake. My family had one every Christmas. Mom knew how to make a really good fruitcake because Mammy had taught her how to make it. It wasn't like those awful fruitcakes you get at the store or that people send you in the mail as a gift from some dumb fruitcake company. This was *real* fruitcake.

The first thing you had to do was to use Miss Rosalie Griffin's pound cake recipe, Mom told us. That was the key to the cake. The other key was to not use any of that weird dried out fruit that comes in little clear containers from the grocery store. Mom used red and green cherries, golden raisins and regular raisins. The other thing that made her fruitcake really good was pecans, my favorite nut. She put lots of pecans and coconut in her fruitcake. I guess you can see just from this that her fruitcake was already miles ahead. And believe me, my mom knew something about making cakes. She told me that down south, people made lots of cakes at Christmas and that when she moved to Ohio, she had to learn a new tradition – making cookies, which was more what people did in the north.

For Christmas 1963, Mom was in full fruitcake-making-operations planning by the first of December. She was like an Army general, setting strategies for the Battle of the Fruitcakes. Her objective was to make ten fruitcakes to give away as gifts. She would have to make them ahead of time and store them until closer to Christmas. Of course, this was no small feat since we now had a baby sister to deal with. It seemed like every time Mom turned around she was having to feed or change that baby. She didn't get much rest. On top of that, we had all kinds of school and church Christmas pageants, which meant after-school and extra Saturday practices. Jim and I offered to not be in any this year, but she would have none of that.

On the very first December Saturday, we went to the grocery store to pick up everything Mom still needed so she could produce the delectable treats which had been a tradition in her family. Thank heavens she had left the baby at home with my Aunt Emily. Inevitably, when we took her to the store, she started bawling as loud as anything. The baby – not Aunt Emily. Anyway, it was better to just have Mom and me doing the shopping. When we got up to the cashier, and we found out the price of all that fruitcake stuff she was buying, Mom about had a cow.

"These prices are making it hard for me to continue this tradition," she said once we were in the car. "I love doing this, but I doubt I will be able to make as many next year."

I had a suspicion that my baby sister probably cost too much and it was making Mom and Dad run out of money faster, but I didn't say anything because Mom loved that baby.

When we got home, I helped Mom carry in the precious cargo. Eggs, butter, raisins, cherries, pecans…these were like gold now.

"John, can you please see to it that the eggs, butter, and fruit get to a safe place in the frig?" Mom asked me as she pulled off her coat and threw it over the back of a chair. "I've got to tend to your sister."

Of course she did. That's mostly what she did these days. I mean, my baby sister was cute and alright, I guess, but she took a lot of Mom's time.

I put away all the refrigerator stuff, and then I unloaded the rest of the bags for Mom. I thought it was the least I could do, and with Christmas coming, I thought it might earn me some brownie points, too. I didn't know exactly where she kept some of the stuff, but I lined it up on the counter all neat and everything, so it was easy for her to organize in the cupboards the way she wanted it. I folded up the paper bags and put them in the pantry where we saved them to use for trash can liners.

I went to find Jim to see what he was up to. Of course, he was right by Mom's side, rubbing our sister's head. He loved Emma so much. He was pretty proud of being somebody's big brother, finally.

"Mom, I put the stuff in the frig that you told me to, and I put all the other stuff on the counter so you could just grab it and put it away easy," I said. "I folded up the grocery bags and put them in the pantry. You're all set."

"Thanks, John. That will help me a lot. You're a good son for helping me like that," she smiled with tired eyes drooping.

"Well, I just know how busy you are," I told her. "You work so hard and are the best mom of anybody's moms!" I was really racking up the points towards Christmas today.

Mom looked at me, a little suspicious, and I thought I better not press my luck anymore. "Thanks, buddy. Now why don't you and Jim go play or watch TV for a little bit. Oh, first make sure your rooms are cleaned up, ok?"

Jim and I trudged off to our room cleaning duties. I would rather do just about anything than clean my room, but I did have a sort of order to how I got it accomplished. After ten years of cleaning my room, I had developed a system and it kept it from being a prolonged process. Jim, on the other hand, was still kind of disorganized and unfocused. He usually wound up on the floor playing with some old toys he had found under his bed or in the bottom of his closet. Today was no exception. I went out to watch cartoons.

After "The Jetsons" was over, I watched a "Sky King" rerun. Still no Jim and no Mom, so I watched a "Roy Rogers" rerun, too. My aunt had left a long time ago and I wondered what in the heck everyone was up to.

I went to find Mom first. She had fallen asleep on her bed with the baby lying right beside her, also asleep. I tiptoed back out of the room.

I went down the hall to Jim's room. He was asleep, too, but on the floor, surrounded by little green soldiers and a couple of marbles, some baseball cards, and a pack of gum that looked old and crummy. It had dust bunnies on it, so I knew he must have pulled that out from some corner of his closet. The baseball cards looked pretty ratty, too, so they were probably all in there together.

I went back downstairs, restless. Dad had to work that day, so he wasn't even around to bother. Then I got to thinking. If Mom was busy and tired a lot, and if I wanted to achieve some additional Christmas brownie points, maybe I could go the extra mile and make the fruitcakes. How hard could it be? I knew how to follow a recipe. Mom had showed me lots of times and I had helped her make cookies on more than one occasion.

I pulled out her recipe box and started looking for Rosalie Griffin's cake recipe. Mom tried to organize her recipe box by main topics: cakes; cookies; desserts; ice cream; pies. She didn't need recipes for anything else she made. She just started throwing stuff together, and somehow it always came out delicious. "A little of this, a little of that," she would sometimes say. She was like an artist in the kitchen, but for some things, she said she needed the recipes.

I rifled through the cards, looking for Miss Rosalie's cake recipe, and in short order, I found it. It was named exactly what it was: Miss Rosalie Griffin's Pound Cake. I pulled the card from the box and set it on the counter so I could read the ingredients, all in Mom's neat handwriting. Then I remembered another thing – Mom wanted to make ten cakes. I knew enough about this that I knew I'd have to multiply each ingredient times ten in order to make the number of cakes Mom wanted.

I got out Mom's biggest bowl and the mixer. Then I started down the list. This was going to be an undertaking.

Three sticks of butter. Times ten.

Three cups of sugar. Times ten.

Five eggs. Times ten.

I didn't think Mom even had that much stuff from the grocery store, so I started thinking maybe I better just make three cakes. It was still going to be a lot to mix up together.

First I had to find our footstool to stand on. I was tall enough, but with the big bowl on the counter, I knew that I would need to be taller to mix up all the ingredients. I got the butter out of the papers. Nine sticks. Then I put in nine cups of sugar. I knew Mom usually beat that stuff up together first. Like I say, I had helped her with a lot of cookies. I turned on the mixer and tried to start getting the sugar worked into the butter, but the butter was still hard, and it was just getting kind of lumpy. Some of the mixture was flying out of the bowl and getting on the counter. I turned the mixer back off and decided to wait until the butter got a little bit softer.

After about half of a "My Friend Flicka" show, I went back into the kitchen. The butter was definitely softer now, so I began mixing again. Wow, this was a lot of batter so far and I still had stuff to put in there. Next came eggs. The recipe called for five, so I needed fifteen. I pulled the eggs out of the refrigerator and started cracking. I thought I was never going to get all those eggs cracked. What a mess they are, egg white dripping down on the counter and all.

Next came vanilla, baking powder, flour (nine cups of that, too!). The mixer wouldn't even mix it up now. It kept making a real low grinding noise, and the beaters were hardly turning. I knew I had a problem.

I pulled the beaters out of the cake batter and set the mixer on the counter with the beaters hanging over the bowl, like Mom had showed me. Big globs of batter dropped off the beaters into the bowl. How in the heck was I going to mix all this stuff up?

Then I remembered something very important – sometimes when Mom was mixing up a big bunch of dough, she would wash her hands really good and use them to mix up the dough. I could do that.

Before I washed my hands, I looked to see what else I needed in the recipe. I was going to need three cans of crushed pineapple and three jars of peach jam. I wasn't even completely sure where Mom kept that stuff, so I went on a manhunt. Or, I joked to myself, more of a jam hunt. I found the pineapple and peach jam in the pantry, and I was glad it was on a shelf low enough that I could reach it without a problem. I pulled it out and made a couple of trips back into the main kitchen to set the stuff on the counter.

I always have trouble opening cans, and the pineapple cans were no exception. I have tried and tried to help Mom with this in the past, and I never seemed to get the can opener positioned on the can in a way that it would be easy to peel back that lid. It took me several attempts on each can to get this job accomplished. I was determined, though, because I didn't want to leave my cake-making job half finished. After that, I still had the peach jam jar lids to deal with. I always had trouble with that, too, and it was particularly vexing because Jim and I always had a clash about who was going to get to stick the knife in the smooth top of the jam first. If I could open the lid on the new jar, I won that battle, but if Mom or Dad had to open it, it was a fifty-fifty split as to who would have the privilege. I used all my jar-opening tricks on these three jars of peach jam. I ran them under hot water. I tapped them lightly on the counter. One of the jars was tough, but I got the other ones without too much trouble. I was pretty proud of myself, and best of all, I got to put the knife in the smooth jam surface three times in a row, a very satisfactory process indeed.

I still had to add milk, too. This was going to be tricky because the batter bowl was now filled almost exactly to the top. I got the milk out of the refrigerator and started measuring out three cups…I put the first cup in and tried to mix up the batter a little bit with one of Mom's big spoons. I added the next cup and used the spoon again, stirring slowly and carefully so as not to make a bigger mess than I already had. By the time I got to the third cup, I knew I was getting ready for a disaster. There would be no avoiding it.

I carefully added the third cup and rolled up my sleeves as high as they would go. I took a deep breath and pushed my hands down into the bottom of the bowl. The cold, gooey batter was almost up to my elbows. I knew I had to be careful, so I just slowly moved my hands and arms around, back and forth, sometimes making little circles, trying to make my arms be like the beaters of a mixer.

It seemed to work. The batter was getting mixed up and smoother-looking. I was already starting to think of what I would put on my Christmas list for getting this job done when I heard the baby cry. Drat! That meant Mom would be waking up before I could do a grand presentation of my work.

I started stirring my arms around a little faster. I still hadn't added any fruit or nuts to this conglomeration. Pretty soon, the batter looked like there wasn't anything more I could do with it, so I took my arms out of the mess and started trying to clean them off, returning as much arm batter to the bowl as I could.

I held my arms up like the surgeons I saw on "Ben Casey" and headed for the sink to wash them.

"What in the world…." I heard behind me.

I turned to face Mom, standing in the doorway, one hand holding baby Emma on her hip and the other hand over her mouth.

Her eyes were open wide, like she had just seen a ghost or something.

"John, what in the world are you up to? What are you doing?" She started walking into the kitchen slowly, looking around. It did look a little bit like a bomb had gone off in there.

"It looks like a tornado has been through here." I knew she would say something about that first.

"Don't worry, Mom. I'll clean it all up, I promise. I started mixing up the fruit cakes for you."

Mom just sat down on a kitchen chair and looked around the kitchen, kind of like she was confused or like someone had bonked her on the head real hard. Then she started laughing. And crying. She kind of went back and forth between laughing and crying.

"Ok, John, you've got to tell me what you've done here. It looks like kind of a disaster, so you've got to explain to me exactly what you've done."

I was still standing there with my arms up in the air like a surgeon. The batter was starting to dry up on my arms and it felt weird. I went over to the sink to go ahead and wash them, which I did as fast as I could. "I started working on your fruitcakes so you wouldn't have so much work to do. Wait a minute and I'll show you."

I finished up washing my arms and hands as fast as I could, then I grabbed Miss Rosalie's recipe and took it over to Mom. She was looking kind of grim by that time.

"Look, it's all ok, Mom. I just followed the recipe. I got everything done except putting the fruit and nuts in. It's all set to go. That's all we have to do now. Well, that and clean up."

"John, there is a lot of batter in that bowl. The counter is a mess. How much of everything did you put in there?" Mom closed her eyes like she didn't want to look at the messy kitchen anymore or like if she didn't have her eyes open, maybe the mess would go away.

"I made three batches." I explained to Mom how I knew she wanted to make ten cakes, but that I knew that would be too much to try to mix up at one time so how I figured out how to make three batches.

"Tell me everything you put in the cake batter. Please...in detail...tell me how much of everything you put in the cake batter," Mom said tiredly.

I went through the recipe, and with each ingredient, I told Mom exactly how I figured out how much I would need and how much I added. With each ingredient, she looked a little less worried. When I got to the bottom of the recipe, she was actually smiling a little.

"Well, it sounds like you've done a very good job, son. Now tell me, how many cakes do you think we can make with this amount of batter?"

"Three," I answered. "I timesed each ingredient by three so three cakes it is."

"Turn the card over, John," Mom said.

"Each batch makes one tube cake pan and one loaf pan," I read out loud.

"Two cakes times three batches is how many cakes?" Mom asked me.

I knew my times tables very well. That's how I knew how to mix up the cake batter.

"Six. Six cakes," I said.

"That's a lot of cakes to bake in one day," Mom answered, "but we can do it, and I have you to thank for it."

I wasn't sure if she meant that in a good way or a bad way, but I held true to my promise to start cleaning up the kitchen. Mom took the baby over and put her in her play pen, where she lay just kicking her legs around and making baby sounds. Mom pulled out the fruit and nuts for the fruitcakes and went to work. It really wasn't long for her to get all that stuff ready, but then we had to figure out how to mix all that stuff into a bowl where the batter was already just about flowing over the sides. Mom is smart about this stuff though. She just pulled out another big bowl, put some of the batter in it, and then started mixing all the fruit and nuts into both bowls of batter. She figured it out and got it done in a jiffy. I wasn't even done with the dishes yet when she told me she was ready for some cake pans. "Get me the tube pan and two loaf pans," she said.

I pulled the pans out of the cupboard and took them to her. She greased and floured them and started pouring batter in them. Then she set them on the counter.

"Ok, John. One more time. Tell me exactly everything you put in this batter."

I went through the recipe again with her. I'm pretty sure I heard her sigh in relief before putting the pans in the oven. I went back to my clean-up, as I had promised. I couldn't let Mom down now.

The house smelled wonderful within the hour. I had moved on to other activities and Jim was preoccupied with the baby when Mom called out, "Come see what you've done, John."

I ran into the kitchen and saw the first three fruitcakes sitting on wire racks on the kitchen counter. They were golden and beautiful. I was so proud that I had been able to help Mom with her work. She was cleaning up the pans the cakes had baked in so that she could refill them with the batter that was left.

"Because of your help, I will be able to get done with my work so much faster, John. You really showed a lot of maturity today. Here's something I want you to remember, now. There is no reason that only women should work in the kitchen. What you have done today shows me that someday, you'll be a good husband to some lucky girl."

I wasn't planning on being a husband to some lucky girl right at that point. I figured I'd be playing in the big leagues or the NFL and would be way too busy for girls. I still felt good about helping my mom, though.

Mom finished getting the fruitcakes baked to send to her relatives and friends that lived far away, and in every package, she included a note about how I had helped her. She even asked me to sign the notes with her, like it was a present from both of us. She was busy with the baby, so Dad and I went up to the post office to mail the packages together.

There were lots of people there that day, mailing their Christmas packages all over the country. "John, I sure am proud of you for helping your mom so much. You don't know how much that means to her, and to me, too. I'm working all the time so I can't help her as much as I'd like to. You really stood up like a man to help your mom. You are such a good son," Dad told me as we waited in line.

Suddenly I didn't care that much about getting extra Christmas brownie points. My mom and dad both told me they thought I was acting like a man, that I was a good son, and it occurred to me that their words were better than any Christmas present I could have gotten.

"Thanks, Dad. I like helping people, especially you and Mom."

"Well, we appreciate it, and we love you, you know." Dad didn't really tell me he loved me that much...it was kind of an unsaid thing between us guys...but it was nice to hear and I stood up a little taller that day. I could do some things. I wasn't just a helpless little kid. I could do some things that helped other people. Cool, I thought...cool.

26 PLAIN DAYS

1963 was coming to a close, and I started hearing people on television talking about the events of the year. You know, they would talk about famous people who died or what happened in Viet Nam or about President Kennedy's assassination and other things that happened over the whole year. After I watched one of these shows, I started thinking about all the stuff that had happened to me and my family, to people at my church, to people in my town. It really was a year that was full of amazing discoveries and surprises, but it was also a year of regular old days where nothing big happened. Life just kept going on. There were a lot of plain days.

First I started thinking about all the great times we had playing up at the gravel pit – we didn't just go sledding up there. Sometimes we played 'war' or 'gold miners' and stuff like that. We could always dream up some kind of game to play. And better yet, the land around the gravel pit was now becoming our new park. By spring of next year, we were supposed to be getting swings and monkey bars and lots of equipment like that to play on. It was going to be a wonderful place for everyone in our town, and of course, we could have more town parties there. Even if there wasn't a pool, it was going to be a great park.

I thought about the three-mile square and how many bike rides we had been on from spring through summer and fall. I saw my first killdeer of the spring when I was on a bike ride, and I saw a pheasant in the fall. I loved watching the wheat and corn grow in the fields around the three-mile square. It gave the air a real clean smell, almost as good as right after we mowed our grass.

There were a lot of baseball games, football games, snowball fights. We went ice skating on the creek and then had a bonfire with hotdogs and toasted marshmallows. In the summer time, we played freeze tag. Why did we play freeze tag in the summer? Maybe on the hot evenings it made us think of cooler weather. We caught about a million lightning bugs on those hot evenings, too. That was one of our favorite things to do. It was fun to watch the little bug light go on and off, fun to pretend the tail was a diamond ring, fun to put them in jars with holes in the lid. One time Miss Ruth even painted a picture about us outside catching lightning bugs, and it was really good. Jim looked just like Jim, Rusty looked just like Rusty, and I looked just like me. In the painting, it looked like real light coming out of the Mason jars we caught the lightning bugs in. I never will figure out how she does that.

Then I started thinking about the normal stuff that every family does. I tried to help Mom and Dad with stuff like pulling the weeds in the flower beds and in the garden. That doesn't count getting in dirt clod fights with Jim because I'm pretty sure Mom would say that was not particularly helpful. I was good about cleaning my room. About every kid I know had to help with that kind of stuff. And of course, I learned a little bit about how to take care of babies. Mom did most of that, but I helped a little bit. I think the biggest way I could help her was by keeping Jim out of her hair. I also helped by taking care of Button before he died. That was one rascally dog, I don't mind telling you. He was a handful all by himself.

Of course, there were different little arguments we got in with Mom and Dad. I remember Mom making me eat collard greens one night for supper. I hated them, but she reminded me that there were "starving children in China" and I had to sit at the table until they were gone. By the time I got close to the end, they were cold and I thought I was going to puke. After one argument (I forget about what) I lost my bike privileges for a week, and one time I even lost my TV privileges for "My Favorite Martian" for *two* weeks. That one was bad. I remember my mom always getting after us for trying to watch thunderstorms from the porch. After having been through a couple of tornados in my life, I was especially fascinated by the weather and wanted to learn as much about it as I could. I can still hear Mom yelling at us to get in off the porch, but then we'd stand at the aluminum screen door watching the lightning and we'd hear her holler, "You kids get away from that aluminum screen door before you get electrocuted!" That admonition usually got Jim moving, but I would only back off about a step because I didn't want to miss a thing.

Our family had lots of good times that were just regular, plain days, too, like going for picnics at Riverside Park or going fishing at Aunt Peewee and Uncle Clyde's house. We had a family reunion there in the summer, and it was loads of fun running around with all my cousins, jumping out of the haymow in Uncle Clyde's barn, swimming in the pond and so forth. My grandma and grandpa were there and I think they couldn't believe all the little grandchildren they had now. There were a bunch of us.

My dad taught me how to use a hammer and a saw, and we built a birdhouse together in 1963. He taught me about hunting in 1963. He got me my own tackle box in 1963. It was a good year for learning new things.

Sometimes on Sunday nights when we were watching Walt Disney, we'd just have popcorn or an ice cream sundae for supper. That was the life. Usually it was only when Mom had made a big Sunday lunch, though. I remember coming home from church sometimes to the smell of meatloaf and baked beans in the oven. She'd fix mashed potatoes and we'd be in tall cotton with a meal like that. That's what my dad would say anyway, "John, we're in tall cotton today!" We'd be so full after such a meal that the only thing we could even fathom for supper would be some popcorn or a bowl of ice cream.

On my mom's birthday, Dad sang Mom a Tony Bennett song called "Because of You" and danced around with her in the living room. I had never seen them dance before and it gave us a fit of giggles because it was kind of mushy. For her birthday present, Jim and I got her a hummingbird wind chime at DeHaven's. She hung it in the plum tree, where it rang a lot because there was always a breeze out there. I remember that after Emma was born, Mom took her out walking around in the yard. She stopped at the plum tree and was telling Emma all about hummingbirds (which

Mom loved) and about wind chimes (which Mom also loved) as if Emma could understand it all. The whole scene was so sweet and beautiful. My mom and her new little baby…it was one of those times when you feel so much love for your mom that you think your heart could burst wide open.

There were a lot of other people who made the year special, even on the plain days; people who came and people who went. There were friends like my buddies and Peaches and Shiloh Stevens and Gina. They made even ordinary days interesting and fun. Of course, Peaches and Shiloh Stevens left, but Gina stayed. There was Jack Michaels, the Viet Nam veteran. He made a plain day interesting not just for me, but for everyone in our town.

Our town…that's another thing I learned more about in 1963. I wanted to really find out all I could about all the people and groups of people in our town, especially after what happened with Jack. I wanted to walk or ride my bike down every single street, and I think I did. I don't know how many miles I put on my bike. Sometimes I went by myself or sometimes I went with one of my buddies. Sometimes I took Jim because he almost always wanted to tag along with me. Anyway, I always found someone interesting to talk to or something interesting to see and learn about.

One thing I found out that I had never known before was that our town had a ladies' gardening group. I discovered them by accident because they were walking around in Mrs. Davis' garden one morning when I was out riding my bike. Of course, they all knew me from church and waved me over when they saw me. They told me they would get together every week in the summer and walk around to each other's houses and check out their gardens. They had flower gardens and vegetable gardens. Not being a huge fan of working in gardens, at first I didn't see why it was such a big deal, but I think a lot of it was about them being friends and staying linked together. I think older people like that – checking in on each other and appreciating their friends because once old people start to die off, they don't have as many friends left to hang on to.

There were other groups, too…the town council, the Boy Scouts, the 4-H kids, the Shriners. Lots of people wanted to be part of something that was bigger than just them, I think. No one wants to be lonely. And that made me think of Jonas Henderson. He was a guy who wasn't connected to anyone at all, really. In a town where people are mostly kind and have concern for each other, where people like being connected, he was all alone.

I watched how our town changed from day to night. I watched how shafts of sunlight hit different houses or buildings like the church and the hardware store. There were times of the day you couldn't see in the big window at Janie's because of how bright the sunlight was on the plate glass. I remember the Coke machine outside the gas station and how hot the metal felt around noontime on a summer's day. I always wondered how the pop could stay cold when the machine felt so hot. I also remember the coolness of the shade in front of Connally's. Sometimes people would just sit on a little bench that was right out in front of the store and visit with each other right there because it seemed like the coolest place in town on really hot days.

The new park was a great place to go to hear all kinds of different birds. Because it was still basically an open field, you could see goldfinches lit on thistle that grew there. There were cardinals and grosbeaks and plain old sparrows and crows, too. They all made their own song for the whole town to hear. To me, that was the sound of God at work. I also appreciated the sound of lawnmowers on nearby lawns and tractors in the fields around us – that was the sound of people at work.

I liked following shadows all around our town. It would start about one o'clock in the afternoon, the change in the town. Shadows would start to grow longer and envelop each house as the sun dropped lower on the western horizon. Our house was one that was always in shadow early because of where we lived, and that helped us cool down faster on the summer evenings. It made things a little spookier in autumn, though, when the days started getting shorter. I remember a few times that I was walking home when it was really getting dark. I sometimes thought I heard someone walking behind me and would turn around to see who was there. There never was anyone there. I figure it must have just been the echo of my own footsteps, so then I would sing a song just for some other noise besides the crickets and my footsteps. We had some streetlights, of course, but not like in a big city. It could be a little unnerving to be out there in the near-dark, alone. You know something, though? I also remember being in the car on nights when we had been out with Mom and Dad somewhere, seeing all the streetlights and the warm yellow glow from the windows of people's houses as we rounded the final curve in the road that took us into our village. Our little town looked peaceful, quiet, and safe. This was especially true around Christmas, when people would put colored lights out on their trees and hedges, making the town look like some magical place you might read about in a book. Even the farms that were more on the outskirts of town would decorate their houses and sometimes their barns with colored lights. It was beautiful.

Each of the four seasons was special in its own way. In the winter, everyone would enjoy Christmas and New Year's, and then the adults would hunker down while us kids built snow forts and poorly-designed igloos. In spring, everyone would emerge and start planting gardens and discussing how to get a bumper crop of green beans this year. In summer, mothers would take their babies out in buggies for a stroll and to visit their friends, while neighbors hung over back fences sharing the latest gossip. In the fall, we watched the last of the leaves lose their color and drop off the trees, only to be raked into big piles and burned, the smoke curling up into the crisp autumn air. These were the rituals of each year, and 1963 was no different in its consistency.

I guess when you think about it, the plain days made 1963 just as good as the exceptional days did. On the plain days, I had learned about what jerks people can be, but I also learned about how very kind people can be. I had learned about hard work and how it then made you appreciate having a heck of a lot of fun. I had learned that not everything is what it first seems; that sometimes love stops when you least expect it but that sometimes love holds on forever. I learned that people in my town shared a lot of the same values, were generous, and cared about each other. I learned that no matter what, I would always be able to rely on Mom and Dad. Even in the comfort of that thought, I guess I also learned that I could think for myself.

Clear back in January I had known it was going to be an extraordinary year.

It really was.

ABOUT THE AUTHOR

Theresa Konwinski is a wife, mom, and retired registered nurse living in Holland, Ohio. She spends her free time in a variety of activities which include writing, with a second novel currently in development.

Made in the USA
San Bernardino, CA
15 January 2017